Advance Praise for
Smoke in the Cypress

"When Owen Pataki's protagonist, the one-armed mercenary Marcel Moreau, finally takes his own advice that to be a really good soldier a man must do what he knows to be the right thing in the moment, regardless of his superior's orders, he comes into his own as a hero and finds the missing pieces of his wounded soul. Pataki's talent for creating atmosphere that is as dynamic, intriguing, and treacherous as his characters, sweeps readers into the violent secret world of Louisiana's bayous during the run-up to the Battle of New Orleans."

— Juliet Grey, Author of the acclaimed Marie Antoinette trilogy

"An absolutely thrilling foray into one of the most fascinating times in American history. If you're a fan of Bernard Cornwell, Patrick O'Brian and even Alexandre Dumas, you will love Owen Pataki and this new, electrifying tale of war, honor, and survival set against the lush backdrop of Louisiana during the War of 1812. This is a special book!"

— Michelle Moran, International Bestselling Author

Advance Praise for
Searchers in Winter

"Owen Pataki's second novel emerges from the rubble of the French Revolution into the legendary conquests of Napoleon. Readers will love the richly drawn characters and evocative settings in this story that pits the values of humanity against those lusting after power and greed."

— Steven Pressfield, bestselling author of *Gates of Fire*

"Armchair time travelers who've wondered what it's like to be embedded in Napoleon's Grande Armée will devour Owen Pataki's *Searchers in Winter*."

— Juliet Grey: Author of the Marie Antoinette trilogy

"From the very first page of *Searchers in Winter*, you know you're in the hands of a master storyteller. Owen Pataki brings Napoleon's era to such vivid life you will think you spent time with the people themselves. An utterly absorbing and completely fantastic read!"

— Michelle Moran, international bestselling author of *Madame Tussaud*

"Pataki's keen attention to historical detail and devotion to his subject matter bring readers directly into the heart and grit of the Napoleonic wars. *Searchers in Winter* boldly plants two feet in the past and never flinches."

— Sarah McCoy, *New York Times* and international bestselling author of *The Baker's Daughter*

Advance Praise for
Where the Light Falls

"Compulsively readable . . . a compelling tale of love, betrayal, sacrifice, and bravery . . . a sweeping romantic novel that takes readers to the heart of Paris and to the center of all the action of the French Revolution."

— *Bustle*

"Succeeds in forcefully illustrating the lessons of the French Revolution for today's democratic movements."

— *Kirkus Reviews*

"Devotees of Alexandre Dumas and Victor Hugo will devour this tale of heroism, treachery, and adventure."

— *Library Journal*

"This is a story of the French Revolution that begins with your head in the slot watching how fast the blade of the guillotine is heading for your neck—and that's nothing compared to the pace and the drama of what follows."

— Tom Wolfe

"A beautiful novel that captures the spirit of the French Revolution and the timeless themes of love and truth."

— Steven Pressfield

"While not stinting on gorgeous detail, Allison and Owen Pataki know exactly how to write a gripping historical novel: Concentrate on the intimate stories playing out against the epic background, in this case, the French Revolution. And so *Where The Light Falls* is exactly that; a gripping historical novel of both intimacy and scope."

— Melanie Benjamin, *New York Times* bestselling author of *The Swans of Fifth Avenue* and *The Aviator's Wife*

"Told from the points of view of four extraordinary characters… *Where the Light Falls* delivers everything a reader hopes for in a great book: passion, intrigue, insights, and above all, a story you won't soon forget. I really cannot recommend this highly enough!"

— Michelle Moran, bestselling author of *Mata Hari's Last Dance* and *Rebel Queen*

"For all those who didn't want Les Miserables to end, Allison and Owen Pataki have answered your call. Replete with historical grounding and eminent characters, the Patakis take us past the pristine archives to the blood and bone of the French Revolution, commanding our attentions and winning our hearts."

— Sarah McCoy, *New York Times* bestselling author of *The Mapmaker's Children*

"Passionate, intense, and rich in atmospheric detail, the Patakis' luminous tale of love and betrayal in a world gone mad is as timely as it is timeless."

— Juliet Grey, author of the *Marie Antoinette* trilogy

Also by Owen Pataki

Where the Light Falls: A Novel of the French Revolution
Searchers in Winter: A Novel of Napoleon's Empire

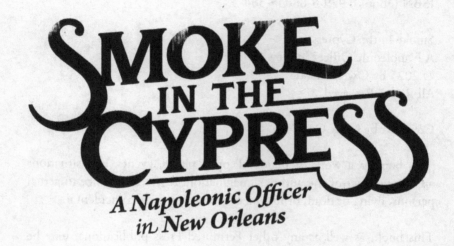

SMOKE IN THE CYPRESS

A Napoleonic Officer in New Orleans

OWEN PATAKI

author of *Where the Light Falls* and *Searchers in Winter*

A PERMUTED PRESS BOOK
ISBN: 979-8-88845-583-8
ISBN (eBook): 979-8-88845-584-5

Smoke in the Cypress:
A Napoleonic Officer in New Orleans
© 2025 by Owen Pataki
All Rights Reserved

Cover art by Cody Corcoran

This book is a work of fiction. People, places, events, and situations are the product of the author's imagination. Any resemblance to actual persons, living or dead, or historical events, is purely coincidental.

This book, as well as any other Permuted Press publications, may be purchased in bulk quantities at a special discounted rate. Contact orders@permutedpress.com for more information.

No part of this book may be reproduced, stored in a retrieval system, or transmitted by any means without the written permission of the author and publisher.

Permuted Press
New York • Nashville
permutedpress.com

Published in the United States of America
1 2 3 4 5 6 7 8 9 10

This book is dedicated to those fighting to defend Liberty and Democracy around the world.

Gaze where some distant sail a speck supplies
With all the 'thirsting eve of Enterprise:
Tell o'er the tales of many a night of toil,
And marvel where they next shall seize a spoil:
No matter where—their chief's allotment this;
Theirs, to believe no prey nor plan amiss.
—"The Corsair Poem," Byron

I expect at this moment that most of the large seaport towns of America are laid in ashes, that we are in possession of New Orleans, and have command of all the rivers of the Mississippi Valley and the lakes, and that the Americans are now little better than prisoners in their own country.
—Lord Castlereagh,
British Foreign Secretary, Autumn 1814

CHAPTER 1

Gulf Waters, Louisiana
November 27, 1814

The sound of wreckage bumping against the hull of *La Panthère* had carried on steadily for perhaps a quarter of an hour, causing some of the sailors to murmur quietly as they gazed out over the dark-blue waters of the Gulf of Mexico. One claimed it was debris from an American trading vessel, another that it must have been a British warship. It was the barrelman's cry from the foretop that finally brought the sailors' attention back to their duty. "Man overboard!" he shouted in his native French. "Hard turn to starboard!"

Within seconds the men of the crew had sprung into action, some darting to tug on sheets while others scurried like squirrels up into the rigging. The few passengers on deck stood frozen in place, hoping to avoid a collision with the scuttling crewmen. A plump older man in a claret-colored dinner jacket sucked in his belly to take up less space, but was jostled to the deck by a fast-moving deckhand as he tied off the halyard to a cleat at the foot of the mainmast. As the heavyset man lay sprawled on the deck like an overturned beetle, the sailor paid him no notice and slid off to his next task. Once the commotion had slowed, a few of the onlookers made their way starboard to catch a glimpse of the unfortunate who had fallen into the water. "Not one of ours," a sharp-eyed sailor called out, raising a hand to shield his eyes. "He's in with the debris."

While additional orders were shouted and the rest of the crew hurried about their tasks, one man stood beside the mainmast, seemingly oblivious to the hectic scene carrying on around him. The commotion had interrupted a game of quoits he'd been playing with some of the crew, and a slight frown indicated his irritation. His left arm was missing below the elbow, his coat sleeve folded and sewn up where his forearm should have been. Eventually he breathed a disappointed sigh and walked slowly over to where a small wooden peg was fastened to the deck. With a gentle motion he tossed a rope at the peg; it spun several times before settling on the deck with a soft *thud*. He scooped up his large black bicorne hat from the deck and made his way starboard to see what had caused the commotion.

The sailors clustered along the gunwale were jostled back by the first mate, who tugged shoulders aside as he shouted for room. The cleared space offered a view of the man overboard as he was hoisted over the gunwale by a length of rope looped underneath his arms. Briny water splashed the nearby sailors' feet as he thumped onto the deck, coughing up seawater as he wheezed for breath. "Inform the captain," the first mate told the sailor beside him, "we've taken on a passenger."

When his fit of coughing had subsided, the rescued wretch looked up at the men looming over him. Partially obscured by their shadows, it soon became evident this was not a man but rather a frightened boy of perhaps twelve or thirteen. His breath slowed to steadier, less desperate gasps, but his darting eyes betrayed his confusion and fear.

The quartermaster removed his cap and put a pipe in his mouth. "This one's a Baratarian."

"A what?" another asked.

"A *pirate*," the quartermaster replied. "They ship out of Barataria, Jean Lafitte's territory, in the swamps out of reach of the Americans." He poked a shoe at the boy's wrist, where a small tattoo of an anchor beneath a heron had been inscribed in black ink. The quartermaster spoke in a low voice, "*His corse may boast its urn and narrow cave, And they who loath'd his life may gild his grave:*

Ours are the tears, though few, sincerely shed, when Ocean shrouds and sepulchres our dead."

Silence hung in the air, and some leaned in for a closer look at the tattoo. The first mate motioned for the men to back up. "What should we do with him?" one of the younger sailors asked.

"We deposit him when we reach the city," the first mate replied, as though the answer were obvious. "I'd sooner see the young rascal go free than be put in a cell, but we can't alter our course; some of our passengers are already...*keen* to see us arrive in the city."

A muffled murmur of agreement passed among the sailors. Several looked back at the passenger standing a few paces behind the crowd.

"But who could have done this to a privateer ship?" another sailor demanded. "They're supposed to know these waters better than anyone."

"The Royal Navy," the first mate answered. "The English patrols did not cease when we reached Gulf waters. We're lucky they have not found us."

"But the Royal Navy is at war with the Americans; why would they attack a corsair ship?" A nervous silence followed.

"In these waters anyone may be attacked," a voice said from behind them. "It is none of our business."

The crew turned their attention to the man who'd spoken—his hair was black and he wore white breeches and a dark-blue coat, tailored for his missing arm, marking him as one of the civilian passengers. The fingers of his remaining hand gently drummed the bicorne hat tucked beneath his elbow. The first mate turned and squinted down at the half-drowned boy. "And that is what you make of this then, Major?"

"I make nothing of it." Marcel Moreau took a few steps forward, and the sailors parted to give him space, a courtesy they would have afforded few of the other civilians. He looked down at the shipwrecked pirate with a cold frown. "Two ships engaged, one was sunk. If the sea had wanted this one, it would have taken him."

The quartermaster rubbed his scalp as he looked at the boy. "That may be, but the question remains of what to do with this fellow."

"As your first mate said," Moreau replied, "we continue on to New Orleans. We can deposit him there."

Two crewmen lifted the boy by the arms and proceeded to drag him across the deck and below to the first mate's cabin, dissipating the excitement caused by his rescue.

As the day wore on, the ship left the heaving swells of open water behind and came within sight of the archipelagos of the Louisiana shoreline. The cry of "Land ahead!" from the foretop caused a new ripple of anticipation, and this first glimpse of land brought all of the civilian passengers and unoccupied sailors up on deck. The sails caught a northeasterly wind, and the order was given to tighten the sheets; meanwhile, every pair of eyes on deck turned to the green labyrinth that seemed to reach across the horizon with no beginning or end. As the ship approached the shore, the sprawling vegetation came into clearer view: stalks of smooth cordgrass beneath shrubby dwarf oaks and bald cypress trees, their branches draped in Spanish moss and their gnarled trunks jutting out from the water like crooked knees. This rich tropical canopy was broken only by an occasional bayou filled with brackish water, or a solitary island lined with reeds reaching as high as a man's chest. As the ship made its way into one of the larger water passages—the mouth of the Mississippi—the onlookers sporadically caught sight of the white lateen sail of an oyster or crab fisherman or a trading sloop, drawing curious stares from the faces peering back from these smaller vessels.

A day's journey up the Mississippi followed, the ship helped in its progress upriver by a cool late-autumn breeze that swayed the branches of the cypress trees along the shore. For most of the passengers, and even some of the sailors, the excitement of sighting land after nearly two months at sea soon grew into a nagging claustrophobia, as the tangled wilderness seemed to be slowly enveloping *La Panthère* as it struggled against the strong downriver currents. Now and then the austere wilderness was broken by the sight of a solitary traveler rowing a narrow blunt-bowed pirogue downriver. The occasional sight of a heron bursting through the weeds or the strange wailing of a sheep frog always brought a murmur of amusement from the passengers; one of the sailors even claimed to have seen an alligator lurking among the weeds, but the other crewmen dismissed his claim outright.

As the cypress swamps gave way to sumptuous plantations along the riverbanks, sightings of elegant two- and three-story houses surrounded by stumps of recently cut sugarcane became more frequent. An ever-increasing flow of carts, wagons, and carriages moved along a road paralleling the river's north bank— called the 'left' bank—and behind it rose a levee: an elevated ridge of earth perhaps ten feet high meant to hold back the inevitable flooding that followed heavy rain and tropical storms. The morning of the second day of their journey upriver brought the ship within sight of the spires and gables of New Orleans' churches and taller buildings.

Weaving between the heavy traffic of ships and fishing boats, *La Panthère* reached one of the city's wharfs as the sun rose in the eastern sky. Once the moorings were tied off and the gangplank laid, the first of the passengers descended to take their first steps on dry land in weeks. One of the crew pointed Moreau—now dubbed "the lucky passenger" owing to the small fortune he'd accrued from his success at card games—toward the city's customs houses. Moreau had not taken three steps along the wharf before his legs began to wobble and he was forced to halt for a moment to regain his balance. He had not vomited over the ship's rail for several weeks, but the abrupt change brought back the lurching feeling that always preceded seasickness, and he took several slow breaths to settle himself.

Behind him loomed a matted forest of ships' masts and rigging, sails reefed tightly or wafting loosely in the morning breeze; before him, beyond the stacked crates of produce and bales of cotton, he saw a city teeming with urban dwellers bustling through the streets. He couldn't be sure which direction he wished to avoid more.

The briny gusts off the river receded as he left the wharf and stepped onto the cobblestones of the street. Despite his unsteady legs, he could not deny the relief he felt standing on dry land after such a long sea journey. He took another deep breath, and his nostrils were assailed by the familiar odors of a port city: fresh fish, salty breezes, and a mingling of human sweat and horse manure. The bustling groups of sailors and merchants along the docks seemed small in comparison to the swarming crowds visible ahead among the markets and narrow streets leading deeper into the city. Setting off along St. Ann Street, Moreau soon passed a large square on his left, *La Place d'Armes*, bulwarked by the lofty Basilica St. Louis, a Spanish cathedral with two prominent cupolas that marked the highest point in the city. He skirted the edge of the square without so much as a second look at the church, which, in his view, would hardly have been considered more than an average-sized chapel in France.

Pockets of vegetation seemed to abound on every street, punctuated by tall, thin groves of coconut-bearing palm trees visible from blocks away, and despite the chill of oncoming winter, a smell of flowers and citrus seemed to pervade the city. Stalls beneath awnings of red, blue, and green canvas overflowed with jugs of rum, tobacco, sugar, and brightly colored spices, while others were stacked with crates and boxes offering fish, shellfish of various sizes, and chickens and other fowl. A few vendors even cried out their select frog and alligator meat. A loud, steady *pang* of metal on metal echoed from a blacksmith's forge, and the heat from its furnace wafted out onto the crowded street. As he ambled along this strange and colorful promenade, Moreau's nostrils were once again filled with the heady blend of odors that had thus far distinguished New Orleans from any other city he had ever visited.

At first glance this did not look like a city readying itself for war, but he knew outward appearances could be deceiving. Everywhere a buzz of voices hummed through the air; more often than not the speakers were French, which reassured him that his task might not be as difficult as he'd imagined. No stranger to people of foreign tongues and cultures, Moreau nonetheless wondered at the strange and exotic appearance of those passing by. Men, women, and children with white, black, and bronze faces, dressed in all manner of clothing, scurried down the streets, some balancing baskets or small crates on their heads. His service with the army had habituated him to marching alongside men from of all stations, but he had never seen so diverse a group of people in one place.

Passing onto a wider street leading to his right he noticed a group of men with dark skin and even darker hair, dressed in tan wool pantaloons and thin white smocks, standing one behind the other. From their organized line, he at first thought they might be some military group, but noticing the shackles around their ankles and the way they stood—alert and agile but with necks uniformly bowed, none looking up even for a moment to reveal a face—he quickly recognized them as slaves. He supposed a large number of these poor wretches would fetch a small fortune for their sellers. The sight kindled a feeling of revulsion, and he turned his gaze to the other end of the street to put them out of mind.

As he crossed another street, he walked past a formation of soldiers, who marched past by twos, carrying muskets on their shoulders. Their uniforms were simple grey trousers and black coats beneath tall black shakos not unlike those he'd seen on the Continent. Their officer held a long saber at his shoulder as he called their cadence. Their pacing was satisfactory and they carried themselves with confidence. Still, Moreau suspected few had ever fired a weapon anywhere more dangerous than a parade ground.

For another block or so, the steady clanging of a blacksmith's hammer resounded through the droning hum of the crowd. A short walk down Dumain Street, and the promenades and colorful market stalls gave way to one-and-a-half-story Creole cottages with brightly hued shutters, stuccoed facades, and low, steep roofs covered with shingles or tiles. Opposite the cottages were rows of larger two-story town houses whose wrought-iron balustrades overlooked the street. Some of the larger houses had passageways leading to inner courtyards, or high, arched porticos along the ground floor, often loaded with sacks or barrels watched over by a merchant or shopkeeper.

Moreau halted in front of his destination, a nondescript grey town house with chipped paint on its facing and a short flight of stone steps leading to the first-floor entryway, above which hung a sign for the customs house. Taking a look down the street, he admitted a strange feeling at what he had seen of the city so far; it was certainly unlike any European city he had ever encountered. Perhaps he hadn't expected Paris or even Le Havre—but thus far, to his mind, New Orleans hardly seemed a city worth sending an armada of warships to conquer.

He ascended the steps and entered the house, relieved to see only one client in front of him. After a few minutes he was called forward, and he set his two bags down and slid his travel papers across the counter.

"In French?" the mustached clerk asked. Moreau nodded in reply. After a minute of scanning his travel documents the clerk set down his spectacles and looked up. "*La Panthère*," he drawled in a strange accent, "arrived direct from Le Havre. One stop in Pensacola, which must mean the city hasn't fallen to the enemy yet." He straightened the stack of papers and snatched up several dollar and half-dollar coins converted from francs, sliding them across the counter to Moreau.

"Your documents are in order," the clerk continued, "but I'd hold your money close; banks are hoarding specie, and you'll find few willing to lend anything out. Furthermore, I hope you're aware of the temperament of the city you've just arrived in."

"Your countrymen are still at war with England."

"That's right. And though it may be impertinent for me to disclose, it may come as your only warning: Three days ago, a foreign man was snatched up outside this very house in which you stand. Taken for a spy. Were he a spy? Don't know—it hardly matters. Any man—foreign, Creole, or simple drunk—might be snatched up and thrown in the calaboose for…*public safety*. That's the mood of the city."

Moreau said nothing.

"And the purpose of your travel?"

Moreau slowly turned his hat in his right hand. "I've come to retrieve a young woman, the daughter of a very wealthy man in France. She boarded *El Mendigo* in Saint-Domingue—or the Haiti Republic, whatever it is called now—in the first week of October, bound for New Orleans. She is believed to be somewhere in the city."

The clerk offered him what looked like a skeptical expression.

"Her parents wish her to return home," Moreau went on, "but she has expressed no willingness to do so. So, I am called to... *persuade* her."

"And the young woman's name?"

"Celeste de Beaumais," Moreau uttered in a low voice. "She is believed to be traveling with a female servant. It is imperative I find her before the year is out."

The clerk glanced at a pair of travelers who had entered and put his spectacles back on. "Well, monsieur, you are free to be about your business then."

Moreau thanked the clerk as he picked up his suitcases. "If you wish to collect this woman," the clerk said in a quiet voice, "and be on a ship before the Royal Navy blockades the river, you best be quick about it. Half the folk in this city are scared senseless; the other half are in denial. So, tread carefully."

Moreau nodded, recognizing the genuine chill in the man's voice, and left the customs house.

As the sun reached its zenith over the city, the pace of foot traffic seemed to slow the farther Moreau got from the markets by the docks. He visited several other customs houses, but inquiries about a young French noblewoman yielded no more answers than the first. One clerk mentioned the likelihood of martial law soon coming into effect, another claimed that it already had, but none had anything to offer on Moreau's target. He was once again warned that foreigners of all backgrounds were advised to avoid arousing suspicion given the impending "clouds of war," or else they would have to volunteer their service to the city's militia. The remainder had fled the city.

As he considered these warnings, Moreau came to the conclusion that the threats were being exaggerated. Nervous populations always reacted to the threat of invasion with panic and excessive precautions; in all likelihood the English would arrive in their ships by the thousands and march into the city unopposed. Ideally Moreau would be long gone if it came to that; on the other hand, an occupation might actually help his cause by flushing out this foolish noblewoman and making her an easy mark.

After purchasing a crunchy baguette from a street vendor, he checked in at an inn on Dauphine Street. The squat old building sat wedged between two shops, a flimsy wooden plank the sole partition separating his room from the noisy grocer's shop on the other side. His inquiries found no luck with the matron, who spoke with the same curious Louisiana accent. "You not likely to find aristos from France on this street, messieur," she said as she poured out a glass of wine. "People here ain't 'xactly cut from that cloth. And your lady ain't likely over in the American quarter."

"Are we not in America, madame?"

The woman gave him a wry look as she set down the bottle. "Yes, *American*, across the neutral ground along Canal Street where they speak English. Where you at now—*French Quarter*—folk speak French like you and me—they's Creoles. Anyhow, if you lookin' for them, try Maspero's Tavern down on Burgundy Street."

Moreau, if still a bit confused, thanked the woman and set out for the tavern. As he stepped outside, he felt an unexpected chill in the early evening air. For all the crew of *La Panthère* talked of Louisiana's semi-tropical climate and exotic wildlife, the cool breeze took him aback and he fastened the top buttons on his coat. The sailors had also spoken of New Orleans after dark, how the city took on an air of mischief and mystery and a strange magic called voodoo. Moreau had soldiered enough to know that men confined in tight spaces for long periods often lent their imaginations to flights of fancy, whether from nerves or simple boredom. Setting his bicorne hat on his head, he set off into the streets to find the tavern and, hopefully, the woman he was looking for.

Along the way he caught mutterings of French from a merchant shuttering his stall for the evening, so he presumed to still be in the French Quarter. A few minutes later he halted before a rectangular house in the colonial style much like the others on the street, above which hung a sign for "Maspero's." A group of men dressed in slightly ragged clothes stood outside the door, and the raucous sounds coming from within confirmed it as an establishment where strong drink could be found. Two men leaned on the cast-iron railing of the small balcony cantilevered over the street, gazing down at him as they talked quietly. Their conversation ceased when Moreau passed beneath, their wary gazes following him until he had stepped through the door.

Inside, the candlelight from several hanging lanterns cast flickering shadows across a large common room. A layer of dirt and straw covered the floorboards, and plumes of smoke wafted up into the rafters. The room was crowded, and the tavern's patrons, seemingly all men, sat along wooden tables or around old wine barrels playing cards and rolling dice in the midst of the bustling ruckus. In one corner a man beat a drum tucked under his arm, while another tapped a foot as he played a quick tune on a fiddle. One group clustered around a table were playing a game involving a ring attached to a piece of string that a man was trying to catch with a short stick. Moreau didn't recognize any of these as games played by the sailors on his ship; nevertheless, the sight sparked in him an instinctive urge to reach into his pocket and wager a bit of money. With an effort he pulled his eyes away, reminding himself to stay focused on his business.

Strolling over to the counter, he heard a mingling of loud, coarse speech, most of it in his own language, though some was in English and perhaps an equal amount in Spanish. He guessed there to be at least thirty patrons, almost all with the sun-darkened skin and robust physique of laboring men. Doubting any had spent much time in the company of an aristocratic French woman, he nevertheless ordered a glass of wine and struck up a conversation with the innkeeper, who named himself as Maspero.

"Business is well, as one might hope in war time, monsieur," the thin, mustached man drawled in Creole French. "For now, the slower ship traffic from the Gulf seem about offset by the presence of the army, who certainly drink they fill when allowed."

Moreau nodded as the innkeeper handed him a cup of soupy-looking wine and took another glance around the room, scrutinizing the different groups clustered around the tables and barrels. Most seemed absorbed in their dice games or their supper, dabbing bread into soup as they splashed wine and ale over the tables. In one corner a dog drooled onto the floor as it stared up hungrily at a man eating a chicken leg, his left eye covered with a black patch. Beside him an individual appeared to be asleep sitting upright on a bench.

"Not many patrons of the fairer sex then?" Moreau asked.

The innkeeper shook with a chuckle but didn't look up from the slice of bread he was cutting. "Y'ain't likely to see no society ladies here, monsieur. Tho th' harlots gon' be about in an hour o' so—if you interested." He gazed up briefly with another chuckle.

"These men here," Moreau said, nodding at a group of men playing cards at a nearby table. "I take them for sailors—the English blockades must affect their livelihoods, no?"

"Of course," Maspero replied. "By now most of them preparin' for the possibility they will be...*volunteering* to serve in the American navy. If they ain't, Old Hickory is like to see they skills put to some other use when he arrive."

"Ol' 'eeckory?" Moreau asked in a strong accent.

Maspero coughed. "General Jackson. You ain't heard o' Andrew Jackson?"

Moreau shrugged.

"Heh, thought it wasn't a man within a hundred miles of this city who don't know Old Hickory. Where you say you from again?"

"I didn't say," Moreau replied. "But if you're asking—Port-au-Prince. I'd hoped to return when the island was recaptured, but that no longer looks possible."

The innkeeper gave him an appraising look and set to work cleaning a pewter mug. "Fine. Well, they's plenty of island folk in this city, some right here in this establishment sure enough."

Moreau looked down at his cup and considered taking another small sip, then looked up to notice a man descending the narrow stairs along the opposite wall. When he reached the ground floor and stepped into the light, Moreau recognized him as one of the men he'd seen on the balcony. His gait was slow, with an agile assuredness, and a short cutlass dangled from his left hip. Silky black hair darker than Moreau's flowed down to his shoulders, matching a thick mustache and dark, deep-set eyes. The light-blue frock coat he wore over a crimson undershirt gave him the flamboyant look of a seafaring man, possibly a privateer. His gaze passed over Moreau as he settled alongside him at the counter.

"*Otra jarra de ron, Pierre*," the man said, tapping the counter with his knuckles. He shifted his feet and took a long glance at Moreau. "And who are you?" he finally asked in French tinged with a Spanish accent. "A priest?"

Moreau held the man's gaze for a moment before tilting his shoulder to reveal his missing arm. "My hands have not joined in prayer for some time."

The man studied Moreau with a frown, ignoring the comment. "To me, you have the look of a priest. But if you don't care to give me your name," he raised his cup in salutation, "then I say good health, father." With a wink to the innkeeper, he turned and walked over to join a group of men rolling dice at a nearby table. Their game continued, but they seemed to give most of their attention to the dark-haired man hovering over them. A few words were exchanged, with one or two glances back at Moreau, and a moment later the man walked back across the room and up the stairs, disappearing from sight. Setting his cup down, Moreau pulled a thin cigar from the breast pocket of his coat and held it over a nearby candle for a moment before taking several puffs, exhaling puffs of smoke as he gazed across the room. He licked his lips as he looked back at the stairs. "Who was that?"

The bartender finished cleaning a wine glass and set it on a shelf behind him. "Captain Tadeo Araza. One of the best-known privateer captains from here to Guadeloupe."

Since the visit by the man known as Araza, much of the conversation at the nearby tables had ceased, though the drummer still beat a steady rhythm. From the way one of the men at a nearby table stared at Moreau, they seemed to have heard the name mentioned. The others sitting with him turned slowly and peered at Moreau, who raised his cup to them before taking another sip.

The innkeeper leaned closer to Moreau. "Those ones won't cause any trouble—at least not without leave from the captain. All the same, I'd caution against any...untoward remarks, given the mood in this city. Fear of spies and provocateurs has folk settling old scores, denouncing neighbors with no evidence, and so forth."

One of the men at the table turned toward Moreau, calling out in accented French. "Do you have business with our friend?" The hard look on his face made his disquiet plain. Four or five rings studded his left ear, and his bald head glimmered beneath a filmy layer of sweat.

"That remains to be seen," Moreau replied.

"Come," the man said with a gesture, "join me and my fellows for a drink. I insist."

Snatching his cigar from the counter, Moreau slowly made his way to the table, sidestepping a drunk who almost stumbled into him on his way to the bar. The bald man who had called Moreau over motioned for one of his companions to fetch a stool, which was brought over, and Moreau took a seat. He noticed their fanciful clothes matched the style of the man known as Araza: shirts lined with red or black stripes, trousers wide and baggy. They scrutinized Moreau with half-interested expressions, or ignored him entirely, as they continued their card game.

"Your accent is not Creole," the bald man said finally, his own accent a singsong rhythm, perhaps Italian. "What is your name?"

"I am called Lenoir."

"Well, you are no sailor of these waters—I know all of the one-armed privateers."

"I've been told it is wise," Moreau said carefully, "for visitors in this city to hold their business close."

"In this city it is wise for *any* man to hold his business close. Isn't that right, lads?" The man slapped one of his companions on the back, then stretched his hand to Moreau. "I am called Gambio. And this is my first mate, Rimbaud."

The man called Rimbaud looked up as he shuffled a deck of cards. He had dark eyes and long black hair and wore an open-collared smock that left most of his hairy chest bare. The man beside him had dark skin, almost black, and ignored Moreau as he studied his cards.

"So," Gambio continued, "what does the visitor make of our city, then?"

Moreau exhaled a puff of smoke. "Thus far, the greatest impressions left on me have come from the mosquitos."

"If you have aversions to mosquitos," Rimbaud said slyly, "I say you have come to the wrong place. In this city, if all your blood isn't sucked by a mosquito, the women will take the rest."

Gambio nodded. "Some say they spread disease, and that is why Napoleon's soldiers were chased from Saint-Domingue."

"The mosquitos or the women?" Rimbaud asked, bringing a hearty laugh from the others. Moreau pulled his gaze away from a pair of dice rolling on a nearby table, the fingers on his remaining hand twitching slightly.

The fiddler and drummer were now belting out a steady rhythm as Moreau set down his cigar and gestured with his arm around the room. "You are lucky men, if this is the life of a sailor calling from New Orleans. In Port-au-Prince it is no longer safe for one to enjoy such…leisure."

"Is that where come you from, monsieur?" the youngest-looking member of the group asked.

"Don't be meddlesome," Rimbaud admonished him. "From where he comes is none of our business. Like our blacksmith, surely to some he comes from France, to others from Saint-Domingue, or else he is born of Louisiana."

"Your blacksmith?" Moreau asked. A brief silence passed over the table, until at last Rimbaud laid down a card and picked up another. "The blacksmith of St. Philip Street," he said. "Monsieur Jean Lafitte."

The others remained silent, holding their eyes on their cards or darting quick glances at Gambio, who took a long sip of his drink and then lowered his cup with a belch. "You have heard of him?" he asked.

"Lafitte, the pirate of Barataria," Moreau answered. "Yes, I have heard of him." All eyes at the table, and some from those sitting nearby, turned to him now. The sudden quiet in the room was broken only by the creak of weight shifting on a nearby chair; even the drums seemed to be beating low and soft. "And by the looks on all your faces, I think you expect to hear that I have some dispute or quarrel with him. Alas, I hate to disappoint, but whatever I know of the man comes from the trifling gossip of French sailors, nothing more."

A collective exhale passed over the table, and those sitting nearby who had craned their necks now eased back in their seats or returned to their own conversations. Moreau's lips spread in a humorless smile. "And you lot dress, drink, and speak like privateers…privateers who sail with Monsieur Lafitte?"

The dark-skinned man let out a laugh. "What gave it away?" A moment later he smacked his cards down in frustration, and Rimbaud collected the small pile of coins from the center of the table.

"And that man who just visited you," Moreau continued, "called Araza. Might that be an alias for the blacksmith of St. Philip Street?"

The young privateer let out a laugh now. "That's not Lafitte. Araza is one of his captains—some say the best." He flashed a smirk at Gambio, who pursed his lips.

"He is *a* captain," Gambio drawled, "as am I. But not *the* captain. That is the blacksmith."

"Even so," the younger corsair blurted, "Araza is our finest swordsman and can best any man in this flea-ridden town. His ship is docked, and we all know what that means."

"The little folk of the city say," Gambio explained, "that when *El Mendigo* is docked in the city, New Orleans plays host to its greatest swordsman."

At the name *El Mendigo*, Moreau's pulse quickened, and he attempted to disguise his eagerness with an impressed nod. "I see," he said at length. "I speak only a little Spanish, but does *Mendigo* not mean 'beggar'? Strange name for the ship of a feared corsair."

Gambio chortled. "He's a funny one, Araza, with a long memory too. He grew up an orphan, had a hard time of it, begging for charity with the other urchins on the streets of Caracas, until he learned how to pick a pocket. He developed quite a taste for it, so they say, until his successes caught up to him and chased him to a life on the sea, where he learned how to pick more than pockets. Now, he's one of Lafitte's best captains. I suppose he likes to remind others of his humble origins."

Rimbaud smirked. "Not so humble now, then, is he?"

"Nor poor," the Black man added. "But the more loot he finds, the harder he drives us—and himself. His riches have not softened him. If anything, they only seem to kindle his desire for more."

Moreau gazed down at the cards as they were shuffled, no longer distracted by the game. His mind was turning over the likelihood that he might have just caught the scent of his prey with surprising ease. Nevertheless, years of soldiering had taught him to trust his instincts, and something told him his task would not be completed quite so easily. He took another puff and blew out a large ring, watching it as it drifted up to the dusty rafters above. "So what keeps this fearsome captain upstairs, away from his men? Does he prefer a quiet drink alone? A woman perhaps?"

The men around the table carried on with their game or continued drinking. "Business, pleasure, and drink," Rimbaud answered flatly, "are hardly distinguishable for a Baratarian, monsieur." Moreau's face twisted in a crooked smile.

Gambio grinned, though Moreau sensed the vague hint of a warning in the look. "Of course, normally we would never give so much information to a stranger; we've only shared this with you because of the truce monsieur has recently offered."

Moreau squinted. "Truce. With whom?"

Gambio's smile faded. "With those fellows right there."

The sound of boots and shuffling chairs on the wood floor replaced the drum and fiddle, which had ceased abruptly, and all eyes turned toward the entrance. Seizing on this momentary distraction, Moreau took another hasty glance around the room, wondering if there might be a stairway back by the kitchen. Given whatever had caused this momentary disturbance, he considered if he might be able to just sneak up the stairs unnoticed, but as he turned back to the entrance, he quickly abandoned the idea, as he saw, shuffling through the doorway, perhaps a dozen men in dark uniforms.

CHAPTER 2

French Quarter, New Orleans
November 29, 1814

The soldiers entered the tavern without a word, ducking their heads to keep their shakos from bumping the ceiling as they shuffled inside. Once they had all gathered inside, they began forming up along the wall on either side of the entrance, their drab uniforms of grey and dark blue contrasting starkly with the colorful dress of the sailors and privateers, who glanced at them with somber expressions. At a gesture from their sergeant, the soldiers lowered their muskets to the floor in one motion. Their commanding officer was young, perhaps a little over twenty, with light-brown hair and active eyes that darted around the room. He was of average height and, although well-built, carried himself with the rigid posture that Moreau recognized in junior officers who had yet to earn their soldiers' respect. Tucking his shako beneath an arm and resting the other hand on the sword at his hip, the young captain cleared his throat and faced the crowded room.

"Attention, citizens," he called out, his voice quavering slightly. "Effective nine o'clock this evening, the stables, tannery, and blacksmith forge across from this establishment are hereby requisitioned for the Seventh US Infantry Regiment."

Moreau's understanding of English was tenuous and his speech far from fluent, but he had spent much of the Atlantic crossing practicing with the English speakers aboard, adding to the little he had learned while serving on the Iberian Peninsula. After a quick glance at the others beside him, he turned back to the officer and his men, tilting his head as he strained to hear what was being said.

"Any who conduct business in these locations," the American officer continued, "may report to the headquarters of Colonel Winfield on Canal Street for compensation. All horses are to be removed from the stables by first light tomorrow, or else they will be confiscated."

A hush settled over the room as the men seated at the tables exchanged glances. Moreau caught sight of two figures descending the stairs at the back of the room: the corsair captain Araza and the other man Moreau had seen on the balcony. He watched as they took up positions at the bottom of the stairway, apparently unruffled by the sight of a dozen soldiers. Moreau's gaze lingered on the corsair captain a moment before he turned back to see one of the soldiers pass a piece of parchment to the young officer, who yanked his hand from his sword's pommel and took it. Despite, or perhaps unaware of, the paper shaking in his hand, the captain held it up for the crowded room to see.

"The state militia," he exclaimed, his voice growing somewhat steadier, "under command of Major General Jacques Villeré, has called the New Orleans Battalion to arms. Any who have not volunteered for service may expect an order of conscription in the coming days."

At this proclamation, the group of privateers—who until now had listened quietly—let out a collective groan. Some even chuckled aloud, muttering to each other and gesturing dismissively. "In accordance with the amnesty granted," the captain continued, raising his voice over the growing clamor, "to all privateers under sail with Pierre and Jean Lafitte, no ship captain holding a government-issued letter of marque is to be waylaid or his property confiscated without due cause." At the mention of Lafitte, the room grew quiet once again. "Furthermore, no privateer who swears allegiance to the flag of the United States, and agrees to serve willingly in such capacity until the current crisis has passed, is to be unlawfully detained or hindered in his private affairs. However, should any free citizen of New Orleans be found in communication with the enemy, or suspected in acts of espionage or incitement of slaves or

Indians to rebellion, he shall be detained and held without trial. In accordance with the sound righteousness of our cause, Louisiana Governor William C. Claiborne calls for the people of this state to form one body, one soul, and to defend to the last extremity their sovereignty and their property."

A weighty silence followed as heads turned to gaze at one another, and then the room erupted in a fit of mocking laughter. Men standing keeled over, while those seated clasped one another's shoulders and rocked back and forth. Even Araza and the man beside him wore amused expressions. Moreau was not smiling; his eyes remained focused on the soldiers standing at the entrance. At this outburst of scornful laughter, their nervous looks hardened into angry frowns, and the sergeant, seemingly more experienced than the young captain, glared at the group of privateers with a face that showed a sincere readiness to do violence. The captain raised a hand in a vain attempt to quell the uproar. "A bonus for enlistment of ten dollars will be issued to any who join one of the state's militia battalions, or agree to serve with the United States Navy."

A voice in French from the back of the room cut through the noise. "You hear that, boys? An enlistment bonus of up to ten dollars!" Moreau turned and saw that it was Araza who had spoken. He was looking out over the room with a sardonic grin and spoke again, in English. "Surely to be paid *after* victory is claimed—if it is claimed at all. Any man to pass up such an offer would be a fool... that is, unless he's killed in the fighting. Or the English win out and take the city."

Taken aback, the captain moved his mouth to speak but was preempted by several drunk-looking privateers. "Capitaine, does Old Hickory pay in Indian scalps?"

"What is your general's policy on practicing voodoo in camp?"

"Are volunteers issued rum?"

"Are volunteers issued *whores*?"

More raucous laughter followed the barrage of mocking questions, and the captain sputtered a few words for quiet, but the shouting only grew louder. Across the table from Moreau, Gambio and

Rimbaud hurled their own insults at the soldiers. "To hell with Claiborne! Throw Jackson to the sharks!" "Long live Barataria! Long live Jean Lafitte!"

Glancing at the entrance, Moreau thought perhaps the young captain would turn and run from the scene. He had seen enough to know when a quarrel threatened to escalate to a full brawl, and now seemed as likely a time as ever. A cup hurled from one of the tables flew across the room and crashed at the feet of one of the soldiers, splashing his boots with wine. Another corsair wearing a red bandana stood up, a large vein bulging in his neck, and bellowed, "Your navy ships blasted our homes to bits on Grande-Terre! Take your pay and false promises straight to hell!"

The captain took a deep breath, ignoring the sergeant as he tried to say something in his ear, and strode forward with a grimace on his face. With a fluid motion, he reached down and unsheathed the saber at his hip. Those nearby who noticed the action froze when they saw him swing the pommel of the sword and smash it into a mug perched on the edge of the closest table, shattering the vessel and splashing ale against the wall.

One of Moreau's eyebrows arched slightly, and he almost chuckled seeing the stunned faces all around him. In the ensuing silence, the captain's expression showed nearly as much shock as those of the privateers, and he lowered his saber with an audible exhale. For a moment, words seemed to fail him, but eventually he lifted his chin and spoke in a clear voice. "Disrespect toward the soldiers sent to defend this city will not be tolerated."

Moreau took a puff on his cigar as he stared at the dazed-looking officer, and then stole a glance at the mess behind the counter. Shards from the smashed mug had broken several wine glasses and cracked a mirror, and filmy streaks of ale were sliding down the plastered wall. The innkeeper was nowhere to be seen.

Overcoming their initial shock, the privateers' grumbling soon took up again, and they challenged the captain's defiant expression with savage glares. The soldiers, for their part took their commander's action as a signal and had raised their muskets up from the floor.

Across from Moreau, Rimbaud and Gambio exchanged a look and then slowly rose to their feet. Around the other tables, the rest of the privateers began standing as well. Moreau thought the captain surely would choose this time to make a hasty retreat, but despite his uneasy expression, he and his soldiers showed no sign of yielding.

Moreau took another puff, wondering how many of the soldiers would die before they realized that escape was their best hope. He then noticed the two figures making their way across the room to the front. They approached the soldiers at an easy pace, Araza following behind the other man, who looked to be about thirty years of age and likely not a corsair himself, given his fine-cut clothes and well-groomed appearance. The sergeant drummed his fingers along the barrel of his musket, but the privateer captain extended his palms as he halted in front of the soldiers. "Señores, allow me a few words before this unfortunate misunderstanding turns into something warmer."

"Who are you?" the captain asked warily.

The man beside Araza brushed back his coat, resting his hands on his hips. "'e is not your first concern, capitaine," he replied. "*I* am Major Jean Baptiste Plauché, commander of the Battalion d'New Orleans militia. And before either of us are interrogated any more, I would 'ave *your* name."

The captain glanced at his sergeant before turning back to the man called Plauché. "I am Captain Hubbard, of the Third Battalion of the Seventh US Infan—"

"Oui, yes," Plauché cut him off. "I know what battalion 'as arrive tonight. I want your name." At that Hubbard blanched, swallowing hard.

Araza took a step closer. "These men you see here, Capitán Hubbard, are not accustomed to being spoken to by strangers so...indelicately. Even so," he turned back to the privateers with a sharp look, "my men know the consequence of shedding blood without a capitán's permission." The corsairs exchanged glances and eventually settled back into their seats, muttering curses at the soldiers and offering a few crude gestures. Araza turned his attention back to Captain Hubbard but seemed to address the sergeant more than his commander. "Capitán Lafitte would not like to hear of unsanctioned mischief—not after he has so long negotiated with Governor Claiborne's government."

"And to that point, monsieur," Major Plauché added in a hard tone, "it would be unfortunate were American soldiers to make unnecessary enemy of those likely to join them in the coming struggle as *allies*."

A murmur passed over the room, and the captain blinked, looking around the room as if seeing it for the first time. "Yes, of course. It was not our intention to cause a disturbance. I apologize for the broken mu—"

"There is no need for apologies, señor," Araza cut in. "You were simply doing your duty." He turned to his men and spoke in French. "The boy is raw, and doesn't know our ways. He will learn...or we will feed him to the *rougarou*." At that the corsairs burst out in another fit of laughter, eyeing the young captain like hungry wolves would a buffalo calf. "And now that it has been seen to," Araza went on, placing an arm on the captain's shoulder and gently guiding him back toward the door, "I will see that your decrees are passed along to Barataria." He smiled at the sergeant as they passed. "But now it grows late, and I must begin clearing out these ruffians. Please give Monsieur Lafitte's respects to General Jackson." He removed his hand and nodded his thanks to Captain Hubbard, who by now was standing halfway through the door. The other soldiers shouldered their muskets and began making their way outside, glancing back at the privateers over their shoulders as they went.

Moreau watched their departure from his seat, snuffing out what remained of his cigar. The wound-up privateers gulped their drinks or toyed with freshly drawn knives, and Moreau turned to look at Araza, who stood aside with Major Plauché. The two were immersed in conversation, as if the soldiers had been gone for hours. A moment later they concluded their discussion with a handshake and separated, Major Plauché exiting through the door while Araza turned back to the room of privateers. One of them saw the captain's expression and hushed the rest to silence.

"Well," Araza called out, "did you not hear me? I said it's time to get the fuck out of here. *Vayan, tontos*! You nearly caused me great trouble tonight. Now go!"

Moreau considered the man's own role in inciting the group's anger and scorn, and wondered if his show of temper was genuine or simply the theatrics required of a corsair captain who wished to keep his authority. At any rate, the rest of the privateers quickly complied with the command, shuffling out of the tavern in a single drunken murmur.

Araza watched the last of his men depart and stood in the doorway for a few seconds, peering out into the street. Only a few patrons remained in the common room, the lingering silence contrasting sharply with the dramatic scene that had just played out. With a roll of his shoulders, Araza stepped forward and stalked out into the night. Moreau watched him leave, unsure if the man wished to simply take some air or had indeed left for the night.

In any event, Moreau rose to pursue him when a movement near the entrance caught his attention. A figure concealed beneath a hooded green riding cloak walked briskly past him and headed toward the stairs. Moreau could not see much beneath the hood, but judging by the contrast in height with the privateers and a quick glimpse of facial features as the newcomer shuffled past, he figured it was a woman. She made her way across the room at a deliberate but unhurried pace, as if she knew where she was and where she was going. Moreau realized he had stood frozen in place since first spotting her, and he moved quickly to follow. As she gained the first steps, he called out for her to wait, but the woman only paused briefly and gave a slight turn of her head before she lifted her cloak and climbed the remaining steps, disappearing from sight. Moreau reached the bottom of the stairs and took the first step when a firm hand grasped his shoulder and pulled him back down to ground level.

"*Perdón, amigo,*" a cold voice said, "where is it you think you are going?"

Moreau slipped his shoulder free as he turned around, and the two men stood face-to-face. Araza's dark eyes probed with an expression that fell somewhere between suspicion and warning, and it took several seconds for him to recognize Moreau. When he did his features hardly softened. "Ah, it is you, priest," Araza said in French, his gaze lingering a moment on Moreau's missing left arm. "What do you want?"

Moreau resisted the urge to turn and look back upstairs for the woman who had so quickly come and gone, instead taking his turn to examine Araza. He met the man's gaze before peering down at his clothes, and suddenly the sight of the bright-blue coat, crimson vest, and saggy white pantaloons—seemingly out of some long-lost tale of buried treasure—seemed rather ridiculous. Moreau fought back a fit of scornful laughter, and the sound of a door closing upstairs broke the silence.

"Well?" Araza demanded sharply. "You see this establishment is now closed for the evening."

In that moment Moreau felt an overwhelming sensation come over him, a desire to indulge an old habit that he had managed to quell some years ago—at a considerable expense of willpower and blood. During his time as an officer in Napoleon's *Grande Armée* he had fought nearly a dozen duels in a span of six years. The first challenge had, in fact, not come from him, but from another officer who had taken offense at some offhanded comment. But following that first mortal contest, when the knot of fear in his stomach had transformed into a feeling of invincible wrath, and his skill with a sword had turned his enemy's arrogant smile into a grimace of terror, Moreau had engaged in the practice with less and less hesitation, until it became something of a compulsion. At the slightest insult or rude gesture, he would challenge the other man, resorting to ridicule if a simple challenge failed to goad him, impugning a man's honor and manhood in front of his comrades if he was particularly reticent. The intervention of his commanding officer, and future friend, Andre Valière, had served as the harsh but necessary rebuke that likely saved him from death. Since then, the habit had diminished to a faded stain on the canvas of his memory, and gambling, sporting, or hunting were usually enough to expiate the impulse.

He closed his eyes and exhaled, hoping his inner turmoil would not be mistaken as a sign of fear. Thankfully, when he opened them again, he saw no evident scorn or aggression from Araza, and in the hanging silence Moreau allowed the urge to pass. He collected himself and offered a sheepish shrug, turning so that he no longer blocked the stairs. "You've caught me, monsieur," he said in a friendly tone. "If you only knew me a little better, you'd know I am certainly no priest, as my weakness of the flesh often seems to get the better of me."

Araza's reaction told little, save a pervasive half squint and slight pursing of his lips. "I thought I saw," Moreau continued, "a young woman pass by on her way up these stairs. After a long sea voyage with only sailors and stars for evening company, I confess I've grown hungry for more *satisfying* companionship. Your men led me to believe that once the sun had gone down one might find as much."

It was Araza's turn to suppress a derisive grin, and he held Moreau's eye without saying a word for some time. It quickly became clear to Moreau that this one was no half-crazed, uncivilized barbarian; he seemed to hold a mastery of himself and his senses, and seemed to do it with ease. Although equally comfortable in silence, Moreau felt a nagging impatience now that he had caught a possible glimpse of the woman responsible for his coming all the way to this godforsaken city. "That one is not for sale," Araza said finally, his expression hardening as he spoke.

"Come now," Moreau rejoined, "you wouldn't begrudge a man his willingness to barter for a woman's touch."

Araza gazed up the stairs before turning back to look at Moreau. "I do not barter for a woman's touch, señor. I pay for her to depart when I'm finished with her." The corsair turned and glanced over his shoulder into the empty tavern. Satisfied that no one remained, he moved his lips to speak when a soft voice rang down the stairs.

"Deo, will you keep me waiting all night?"

Moreau's heart leaped in his chest, but he quickly cast off his eager stare and assumed a knowing grin when Araza turned back to him. If the corsair felt any impatience, he did not show it. He stood perfectly still, as if challenging Moreau to say or do something to reveal more of himself. For his part, Moreau felt the instinctive pull of violence once again, and for a moment his face darkened. His stare wasn't angry, but his eyes were cold and hard as stone as he looked at the corsair. Deciding that a fight with the man—however tempting it might seem in the moment—would do his purpose more harm than good, he managed to bring his expression back to neutral.

"Wait in silence," Araza barked up at the woman, then turned back to Moreau. "If you are an agent with the government, American or British, you must take up your solicitations with Lafitte himself. I have no authority to make decisions or sign treaties."

"I speak for no government," Moreau answered, amused by the insinuation. "And I offer no solicitations."

Araza nodded slowly. "Well then, if you offer me nothing… get out of my tavern." He moved past Moreau and took two or three steps up the stairs before turning and looking back down. "Tomorrow, I will find out who you are and what you are doing here."

Although only separated from the woman he presumed to be his objective by a narrow staircase, Moreau concluded that he would simply have to wait until tomorrow.

CHAPTER 3

French Quarter, New Orleans
November 30, 1814

The following morning Moreau rose early and set off for Bourbon Street in the direction of Maspero's, stepping into the fresh morning air and a stinging chill. As he walked, he blew into his fist for warmth, recalling the curious events of the evening prior: the corsairs with their flamboyant garments, the soldiers, and their nearly disastrous dustup. His stroke of luck in stumbling upon the captain of *El Mendigo*—and a woman who seemed to match the description of his quarry—tempted him to return straight to the tavern, but simply waltzing in or loitering outside in hopes of catching a glimpse of her seemed the surest way to draw suspicion. In a city of frayed nerves and factional rivalries, the last thing Moreau needed was to draw undue attention to himself and end up on the wrong side of prison bars.

He also considered Tadeo Araza and how he had seen through Moreau's halfhearted attempts at discretion. The privateer captain clearly possessed the temperament of a commander, holding sway over his men with an iron grip, and no doubt the ambition of a ship captain, so the idea that he could have seduced a Frenchwoman of noble birth did not seem far-fetched. How she came to be entangled with the leader of a gang of pirates was a question for later. For now, Moreau needed to find a way to arrange another rendezvous with the woman from the night before, to confirm that it was she. He considered it possible that she was merely a local paramour, but he had heard her speak, and he felt sure it had been an accent from Normandy.

As he traversed the French Quarter, he heard mostly French spoken, albeit with that peculiar Creole accent, the small talk and haggling of buyers and sellers. At this early hour the city still felt close to brimming, foot traffic and horse-drawn carts clogging the streets, while the houses and shops flaunted a cornucopia of brightly colored flowers and plants. Hawkers sold or displayed exotic-looking birds and animals on the corners, while chickens pecked at crumbs and seeds along the ground and pigeons warbled from windowsills and rooftops. A woman holding a number of small, scaly alligators with bulging eyes cried out, "Soup! Perfect for soup!"

A squad of soldiers marching down St. Louis Street brought Moreau's thoughts back to the present. Their dark uniforms and crisp movements served as a visible reminder that beneath the humdrum of daily life, the threat of war still loomed, coming closer each day.

A few minutes later he arrived on Chartres Street and halted outside a small shop within sight of Maspero's. The sign above read *Banquette Lachappelle.* He cast a quick look around and saw no sign of the woman, or Araza and his corsairs, and decided this was as good a place as any to keep watch on the tavern. Thinking there likely to be some time before the drinking crowds arrived, he ducked into the banquette.

Upon entering, he tipped his cap to the elderly couple, presumably the owners, standing behind a counter in the back of the shop. He strolled past a vast and varied inventory of items: coat racks with assorted formal wear, heaps of linens and fine silks, rugs, porcelain figurines, lamps, and ornately carved chairs, tables, and bedframes. A woman in a light-blue dress with her back to Moreau stood examining a collection of china and silver flatware in the opposite corner. From what Moreau could see of her neck and arms, her skin appeared darker than a French woman's. In any case, his gaze didn't linger, and he made his way over to the elderly couple standing behind a counter topped by a slab of polished marble. He feigned interest in a satchel of fine hazelnut leather, running a hand along its smooth surface for a moment before turning back to the proprietors. The man greeted him with "*Bonjour,*" to which Moreau responded in his own tongue.

"Monsieur Lachappelle, I presume?" The man nodded with a tight-lipped smile, while the woman beside him gave Moreau a quick look before turning back to her ledger. "I was hoping to find the proper attire for a walk among the cane fields."

Lachappelle smiled and his eyebrows rose slightly, while his partner kept her nose buried in her scribblings. "I am new to the city and seek to procure property for planting sugarcane," Moreau said, "but I confess my clothing is more suited to France."

The man peered aside at his partner, whose lined face showed no indication of an answer.

"Perhaps," Moreau persisted, "we might start with a pair of boots you'd recommend."

A moment later the older man brought to the counter a pair of knee-high black boots, describing their Cuban leather as finer than anything the tanneries in New Orleans could produce. His explanation quickly turned into an apology that he had no other boots fit for the cane fields, as the English blockade amounted to an embargo on goods imported from the Caribbean. Moreau seized on this idle chatter to open a broader conversation. "The damned blockade," he said with emphasis. "My ship was lucky to have made it through. If it wasn't the English—or Spanish—we half expected to be set upon by pirates. I've heard the city is teeming with them now that there's a war on."

The woman paused in her writing but said nothing, and her partner gave no response either. Moreau kept his gaze on the boots as if carefully weighing whether or not to make the purchase. "I suppose I shouldn't disparage privateers; the gentleman I happened upon last night was one. His dress was a bit eccentric, but he had the knack for spinning a tale. What was his name... Amaza? Aruza?"

"Araza," Lachappelle answered in a husky voice. "Tadeo Araza."

"Araza." Moreau said, setting the boots on the counter. "That's him. Well, pirate or not, he seemed a decent fellow. And how could

I forget? He enjoyed the company of quite a fine lady. She spoke little, but I'd say she had the air of a Frenchwoman. I can only presume her to be the señor's wife."

The couple exchanged a quick glance, but apart from a slight smirk from the woman, neither showed any interest in continuing the conversation. "To that I can't say," the man answered. "Baratarians have their own ways."

"Indeed. I've heard it is a perilous life, and surely the clouds of war have darkened their prospects."

"They've darkened the prospects of the entire city," the woman replied without lifting her eyes from her ledger.

"War closes more doors than it opens," the man said ruefully.

Moreau offered a knowing look, though it seemed to him that the inventory of the store seemed full enough. Perhaps his talk of privateers had touched a bit too close to home, as he'd heard that smuggling operations were more than common, and it was no mystery who benefitted from the "customs-free" importation of goods into the city. Not wishing to lose the slight nibble on his line, however, he decided to change tact. "I expect my own prospects to be somewhat muddled, among so many English speakers. Are there any hospitable French homes where I might go for a glass of decent wine and friendly conversation before the damned English arrive? One of the established planters, perhaps?"

The man glanced down at the boots once again, like a dog eyeing a bone placed just out of reach, and his partner's expression hardly revealed any more. Moreau held back a frustrated sigh and looked down at the boots on his feet. Although not exactly in poor condition, they were rather old and worn and barely reached above his ankles. He shifted his feet, gauging the fit, and when he looked up, he was startled to see the young woman he'd noticed earlier standing a few steps to his left. Her skin was caramel-colored, her deep-set eyes light brown, and she wore a long, blue cotton dress and a matching bonnet. She gazed at him for a moment, and then cocked her head.

"Pardon, monsieur," she said in slightly accented French. "I wish to pay."

Without waiting for Moreau to move, she stepped to the counter and gently set down a four-piece china tea set on the marble countertop. Moreau took a step back and studied her profile. Although fairly young, perhaps a little over twenty, she was rather tall and stood with an erect posture that indicated some schooling in manners and proper etiquette. Her long black hair was braided and hung in two strands down to her waist, and from what Moreau could tell, she seemed to have African, or partly African, features as well. He turned back to the elderly couple, who smiled at their more decisive customer and made small talk as she pulled coins from a pouch and placed them on the counter.

"Will there be anything else, mademoiselle?" the old man asked as he began wrapping the china pieces with paper and placing them in a crate.

"Nothing more, thank you."

"Are these for your own collection—or someone special?" the older woman asked with a wry grin.

"For my mother and father," the young woman replied, grinning sheepishly. "I've got to leave these at their house before making my way to *Le Mouton* tomorrow."

The older man nodded his tight-lipped smile as he finished wrapping the last piece. "Well, we wouldn't want to delay you if you're going all the way out there."

"Oh, it isn't a difficult journey," the woman replied, taking the crate from him. Moreau ran his hand along the stitching of one of the boots, silently willing her to hurry up and leave.

"You know, monsieur," she said, turning to Moreau, "if you are seeking a planter who speaks French and is considered friendly to newcomers, you might—"

At that moment, the woman's eyes bulged and she dropped the box on the counter with a loud *clang*. With stunned looks, she and the two shop owners turned toward the entrance. Moreau turned just in time to see a figure fly past him in a blur of motion. With an instinctive leap backward, he reached toward his belt to draw his sword—and quickly remembered he had not worn one for a long time. The next reflex took hold, and he reached out and clasped the shoulder of the woman in the blue dress, tugging her back so that they were both partly shielded behind a coatrack. Ignoring the woman's startled protest, he peered out to see what had caused such confusion. The elderly couple had disappeared behind the counter, and the only sound came from the floorboards creaking beneath his feet. He saw nothing out of the ordinary.

A few seconds later the *thump* of something bumping against a cupboard brought Moreau's attention to the far corner, and he bent low and began creeping toward whoever, or whatever, had made the sound. Cursing his lack of a sword, he continued his slow crawl forward until he heard the unmistakable sound of a pistol hammer being cocked, and he froze in place. The elderly man rose slowly from behind the counter, holding a pistol that he pointed toward the cupboard. His hand was shaking slightly, and Moreau made a noise that caused the man to spin the weapon around and level it at him. Raising his hand defensively, Moreau slowly shook his head, then motioned in the direction of the cupboard. The man gaped at him for a moment, then a noise from outside drew his attention and he lowered the pistol, swiveling his head toward the front of the store.

The indistinct shouts coming from outside pulled Moreau's gaze as well, but he continued moving slowly toward the cupboard. Crouched beside the old man and brandishing a small blade was the elderly woman, who glanced at Moreau from behind the counter with an expression that looked surprisingly calm given the circumstances. Moreau crept closer to the cupboard, then stood up to his full height. "Whoever you are," he declared, "I am only a customer and wish you no harm." The shouting from out in the street seemed to be coming closer now. "You have frightened the owners of this store, but I'm sure they will excuse your trespassing if you show yourself." He edged closer to the cupboard, his fingers twitching. "If you come out—"

A crop of shaggy blond hair popped up from behind the cupboard, and a pair of wide brown eyes peered at Moreau, then darted toward the others—plainly frightened. Moreau stared with a hard expression as the face of a boy rose into full view. An audible exhalation came from behind the counter.

Moreau edged closer. "Show me your hands."

Still staring wide-eyed at Moreau, the boy slowly raised his hands. Moreau refrained from any sudden movement, wondering what could have panicked the youngster so. As their eyes met, Moreau sensed something strange and squinted as he examined the boy. Had they met before? The sound of shuffling footsteps behind him caused Moreau to glance over his shoulder, and he saw the elderly couple. They no longer held weapons, though the man's bulging eyes showed he had yet to fully recover from his start. "The damned rascal darted in so quick I thought he was an Indian," he panted.

The woman took a step forward, examining the boy with a stern expression. "The damned rascal is no Indian, Louis. He's just a boy. No more than twelve." The man called Louis let out a grunt but did not argue. His partner reached out a hand and motioned for the boy to come out. After a nervous look at the entranceway, the boy stepped around the cupboard and shuffled into view. His shirt was a dirty white smock, and his trousers were worn grey and streaked with mud. The younger woman, who until now had remained hidden, emerged from behind the coatrack with a supplicating smile.

"It's alright," she said soothingly as she approached, "no one's going to hurt you. Are you an orphan?"

The boy did not respond.

"He's no orphan," Moreau said in a harsh voice. "He's a pirate." With a riding crop he'd snatched from one of the shelves, he lifted the shirtsleeve from the boy's wrist, revealing a small tattoo of an anchor beneath a heron: the mark of the Baratarians. He now remembered the lad as the one his ship had rescued from the wreckage on the Gulf two days prior. Moreau lowered the crop, taking a step closer.

"What brings a shipwrecked Baratarian into this shop in such a hurry?"

Again, the boy held his tongue, unwilling to meet Moreau's gaze.

The tense quiet in the room was broken by more shouts approaching from the street outside. "I'd wager this one is on the run." Moreau looked at the door. "I wonder from whom."

He walked across the shop to the window and peered out, lifting his arm to shield his eyes from the midmorning sun, which shone brighter than he'd imagined. Peering down the street, he didn't see anything out of the ordinary, just a couple casually strolling and a couple of vendors sitting lazily on stools beside their wares. Then he noticed two men emerging from a building across the street. Soldiers. They stalked down the street with purpose, bayonets fixed to their muskets. Moreau sneered, half turning to look back into the store. "What have you done now? Stolen hidden treasure?"

The owners had gone back behind the counter, Louis smoothing a hand across the marble top while the woman picked up her ever-present ledger and resumed writing. The younger woman was still standing beside the cupboard, looking at Moreau with a slight frown. He smiled at her apparent nervousness, and turned as the soldiers walked in the door.

Both wore the same dark coats and grey trousers as the soldiers from the tavern the night before. The first soldier was short and stocky and held a musket with a long bayonet in front of him as he strode into the shop, his eyes scanning quickly to either side. The man behind him looked several years older, the epaulettes on his shoulders and sword at his hip marking him as an officer. As he entered, he removed his bicorne hat, its peaked brim sloped front to back like those worn by Moreau's countrymen, and tucked it under his arm in a fluid motion. He stood at above-average height, with keen, sea-grey eyes and auburn hair that fell almost to his shoulders, framing a long face with a cleft chin. His steely expression revealed little of his thoughts or temperament. Several steps into the shop, he halted and glanced back out into the street, calling out a few orders to a group of soldiers marching past. A moment later he faced the two owners, addressing them in English. "I'm sorry to inconvenience you, monsieur and madame, but I have reason to believe a fugitive has passed through this street."

The couple exchanged a glance, and the woman titled her head with a concerned expression. "Is something amiss?"

"No, ma'am," the officer replied. "We're just searching for a young man who's escaped from the calaboose. Apparently he took advantage of a dozing guard."

Without turning his head, Moreau snuck a look back to where the boy had dropped out of sight behind the cupboard. The man called Louis cleared his throat. "If I may ask, who is this prisoner?"

The officer looked at Moreau, his gaze lingering on Moreau's missing arm for a moment before turning back to the owners. "The escaped prisoner is a corsair outlaw from Barataria. His hair is blond, and he is clothed in threads of simple grey. More than that I am not at liberty to say." Moreau looked over at the younger woman, who had backed up and was standing against the wall, with the cupboard beside her. The shop owners exchanged a subtle glance, and the old man shrugged, his head bobbing slightly to either side. "We have had a few lone customers this morning, but no boy has entered here."

The officer's eyes narrowed slightly, and he pulled his eyes from the dress coat he was examining. "I said nothing about a boy, sir."

Louis opened his mouth to speak, but no words came out. His partner frowned pensively but said nothing. Moreau exchanged a look with the woman standing in the corner before turning to the officer. He spoke in his best English. "Monsieur, I 'ave been inside this shop for several minutes, and I am seeing no one enter besides those you see 'ere."

The colonel started to respond, then frowned as he turned his attention to the other soldier, who was inspecting a glazed porcelain statuette of a shapely female ballerina. The soldier jumped when his commander spoke. "Private, you're not here to lollygag. Conduct your search and be quick about it." He passed another quick look over Moreau, then spoke to the shop owners. "My apologies. Our regiment is newly arrived after a march of nearly two hundred miles from Mobile. Some of my soldiers are tired and have forgotten their discipline. Now, would you object to a brief search of your shop? Perhaps this outlaw managed to skulk in unnoticed."

Louis gestured his assent with open arms, and his partner slowly set down her ledger, nodding hers as well. The officer pointed for the soldier to search in the back corners of the room, then looked back at the others with a curt nod. Moreau took a step back to allow the soldier to pass and kept his eyes on the younger man as he stalked nervously through the piles of merchandise. Moreau wondered if he was ready to use the bayonet should he find who he was looking for.

The officer looked around the shop before turning back to Moreau, once again eyeing him and his missing arm appraisingly. For his part, Moreau shifted his gaze to the young woman beside the cupboard. She watched the soldier's painfully slow search with a taut expression, forcing a smile as he approached her.

"I am new in this city," Moreau said, breaking the silence, "but 'ave I not 'eard there is amnesty for those who are volunteering service for militia?"

The officer looked at Moreau and folded his gloved hands in front of him. "Any amnesty offered applies only to those who have enlisted. Not those who've escaped from the city prison." Moreau pursed his lips and nodded. The officer turned back to the owners, who met his look with friendly smiles, then gazed at his subordinate with a thoughtful look before turning back to Moreau. "You say you are newly arrived to the city. Have *you* declared yourself for the militia roll, sir?"

"I 'ave not."

The officer nodded. "Well, I see that your condition likely exempts you from active service, but all men are being called on to offer what they can. My superiors have given us orders to secure the loyalty of the people of this city, be they Creole, Negro, or otherwise. Those with dubious loyalty to the flag of the United States—corsairs, for instance—erode that loyalty."

The soldier conducting the search took several steps and halted in front of the cupboard in the far corner. The woman in the blue dress looked at him with the nervous smile that now seemed fixed on her face. As the soldier stepped closer, she slid forward, positioning herself between him and the cupboard and offering a half curtsy. "I am sorry to be in your way, monsieur." She then motioned to the side, away from the cupboard, to a corner where a small table stacked with boxes was pressed up against the wall. "Perhaps you wish to look in the corner?" The soldier stood in place, his gaze taking in the woman's full figure. A moment passed, and eventually he leaned over and picked up a brass oil lamp. Turning it in his hands, he muttered to himself, something about making camp in a swamp, then set it back down on a mahogany table. With a glance back at his commander, he lifted his hat and rubbed his scalp.

"There's no one here, sir."

The officer nodded to the shop owners. "Your cooperation is most appreciated." He then turned in the direction of the younger woman, resting a hand on his sword. "Once again, my pardon for the disruption. If you see anyone matching the description I've given, you may report it to my headquarters at Fort St. Charles. My name is Colonel Silas Winfield; I serve with the Seventh US Infantry."

The man named Louis bobbed his head several times in agreement, while the young woman smiled warmly. "We will be sure to do so, Colonel."

The officer bowed slightly and then turned to Moreau. "See that you give your name to the local authorities. They'll determine what duty best suits you."

Moreau nodded slowly. "I will be sure to do this."

The officer looked down once more at Moreau's missing arm before turning toward Louis. "As stated, any sign of fugitives is to be communicated directly. Good day."

With that, he put his hat back on and waved the other soldier out of the shop. Moreau turned and looked at the young woman, who seemed to be frozen in place. The elderly couple watched the two military men pass in front of the shop window before turning back to the cupboard. The young woman exhaled and moved aside, turning to look as the boy rose from where he had hidden himself between the cupboard and the wall, his expression only slightly less nervous than the woman's. Moreau took a few steps closer and fixed him with a hard stare. "Of all hiding places, you had to pick this shop. If you'd been caught, we could have all been thrown in chains."

The young woman had her hands on her hips and looked none too happy herself. The boy shook a pant leg and looked at the others in turn, plainly embarrassed, though his eyes showed a subtle hint of a thrill. "I'm sorry," he said quietly, evidently able to speak French.

"You're sorry?" The boy shrank back as Moreau moved closer, and even the young woman stepped back; something in Moreau's glare had wiped the relief from both their faces. "Why did you run in here like a damned fool?" All eyes turned to the boy, and his head drooped.

"Please, monsieur." The young woman's blue dress swished on the wood floor as she stepped between Moreau and the youngster. "You won't get an answer from him with that tone." She turned to the boy and gestured for him to come forward. "Before he's interrogated any further, I should like to know why a strange, one-armed Frenchman helped conceal him."

Moreau stared at her without speaking.

"You told the colonel you'd seen no one enter," she said, eyebrows raised. "Why did you help him?"

Moreau frowned at her. "I have my reasons, and they're none of your concern. You're the one who had him hiding him behind your skirts."

She let out an exasperated sigh, and Moreau stepped forward again, looking at the owners behind the counter and then back to the boy. "A mangy young pirate storms in here like a rabid hound, has soldiers in the streets hunting him...what *I'd* like to know is what crime this halfwit committed to draw such attention."

"Don't speak about him like that!" the young woman blurted, frowning at Moreau. "I'm sure he's frightened beyond belief right now."

"No I'm not," the boy piped.

"Shut up!" Moreau and the young woman said simultaneously.

The two glared at each other for several seconds before the sound of someone clearing their throat broke the tension. The elderly woman behind the counter looked intently at the boy, content to ignore the argument between Moreau and the young woman. As her partner took hold of the boots Moreau had placed on the counter, she held out a hand and indicated with a bony finger for the boy to come closer. He complied, ducking his head as he stepped between Moreau and the woman in blue. The older woman began conversing with him, asking him questions in a gentle voice.

Moreau exhaled, reminding himself why he'd entered the shop in the first place, thinking suddenly about the boy's possible connection to Araza and the other corsairs. Ignoring the smoldering glare of the younger lady, Moreau approached the counter, sliding aside the pair of boots he'd considered purchasing. "Madame," he said in a calmer tone, "if it's alright with you, I would have a quick word with this one."

He glanced down at the boy, who looked back at him with red cheeks. The older woman nodded, gliding back to her stool. Moreau glanced at the door to make sure no one else had entered, then turned to the boy with a stern expression. He studied him a moment, his drab clothes dirty and stained, his cheeks freckled, pale, and somewhat sallow, likely from a lack of nutrition, but his eyes held a hint of mischievous vitality that enhanced his otherwise shabby appearance. As Moreau leaned in closer, the boy wilted slightly.

"What trouble you've gotten into with those soldiers does not concern me," Moreau said in a low voice, "but I remember you. We plucked you up out of that wreck in the Gulf. By all appearances, you were the only survivor from your ship. How you managed that is also not my concern. What I would like to know is the name of the woman who has been seen consorting with Tadeo Araza—who I know is one of your captains. I will not ask you to betray your comrades or divulge anything that will get you into trouble, but I ask you this now, and you will give me an answer. Have you seen this woman?"

The boy swallowed hard and wiped his runny nose with a dirty sleeve. His eyes drooped, and for a moment his whole aspect took on a dazed appearance. Moreau stood expectantly, the only sound the ticking of a clock nestled somewhere in the crowded store. Eventually the boy looked up at Moreau and nodded. As this went on, the younger woman finished packing her items into the crate and took her change from Louis. When she reached the entrance, she turned and looked at Moreau.

"Monsieur," she said in a disdainful voice, "I was of a mind to recommend to you a friend that might be found in this city. I am traveling out to his plantation tomorrow morning and would have even offered you a ride in my carriage. But you have shown little in the way of manners and even less in the way of kindness. All that's left to say is...I hope the woman you are seeking does not have the misfortune of being your wife. Good day." She nodded politely at Louis and his wife and departed the store.

Moreau watched her leave, then brought his attention back to the boy, who was looking at the older woman with a focused expression. "Am I interrupting something?" Moreau demanded. The woman set her ledger down, meeting the boy's look for a moment before speaking in her typically quiet voice.

"I'm sorry to disappoint your friend, but if he asks—the ruby was a fake."

"Charlotte, *hush*," Louis blurted out, lifting a hand as if to cover her mouth but then, thinking better of it, dropped his fingers onto the counter and began anxiously drumming them. After a quick glance at Moreau, he turned back to the woman. "Why would you tell him that in front of *him*?"

"Ruby?" Moreau asked, his eyes narrowing. "What are you talking about?"

Charlotte gazed at him and sighed. "I believe this man when he says he's a stranger to this city. He's too confused to be a marshal or agent of the government, however confused *that* lot always seem to be." Louis sighed, lowering his gaze to the counter. Charlotte looked at Moreau for a moment before turning back to the boy. "I will give it back to him if he wishes, but I have no appraisal. It is of no value."

The boy nodded, then rolled his shoulders in something of a shrug. Moreau shook his head and glared at the woman. "I don't know what friend or ruby you are on about, but I would like—"

"I don't think," she said to Louis, ignoring Moreau, "he means the boy, or us, any harm simply for…associating with privateers."

"Associating," Moreau said flatly, glancing around the fully stocked room, his suspicions now confirmed. "I suppose one doesn't find oneself flush with such inventory during a war without finding suppliers who can break the naval blockade and circumvent customs duties."

Louis looked at Moreau, his chin lifted slightly. "It's simple survival. You'll not find a trader in the French Quarter what doesn't supplement his stores with an item or two from *Le Temple*."

Moreau's eyes swept around the room. "An item or two indeed."

Charlotte tilted her head at Moreau. "Yes, we've dealings with them—along with the rest of the city's merchants. So, monsieur, you've learned our secret…now for you. What are you doing here asking about Tadeo Araza and his romantic liaisons? What secrets are you hiding?"

Moreau looked down at the boy. "I have reason to believe that the man called Araza is romantically involved with a woman I must find. Why I must do so is my business." He turned back to the elderly couple, "But I will find her. And this one here is going to help me." The boy's shoulders sagged, but his eyes showed more confusion than fear. He exhaled and looked up at Moreau. "I know of him. I don't think he knows me."

"But you've seen the woman he consorts with?"

The boy smirked. "He consorts with lots of women."

Moreau shot forward and grabbed the boy's collar, lifting him onto his toes. "I don't have time for this. A woman from France. She sailed with him from Saint-Domingue—Haiti. Before that, Guadeloupe. Do you know her?"

The boy shook his head fearfully. "No. I don't know—I know Araza captains *El Mendigo*. I know he is one of our best swordsmen. I know he has his own house on Grande-Terre, and I've heard others say he is searching for a ruby—a ballast ruby. One was brought here to be appraised, and I was sent to learn of its value. They've just told me it has none. That's all I know, honest."

Moreau's glare hardly softened, but he released the boy's collar. "What's so important about this ruby you keep going on about?" The boy licked his lips, his confused face answer enough. Moreau looked at him thoughtfully for several seconds, then exhaled. "You know, for a pirate you scare quite easily."

The boy gave no reaction, and Moreau wiped a ball of lint from his collar. "What is your name?"

"Will Keane." Moreau nodded, then turned back to the elderly couple with a sigh. They looked at him with matching frowns. "Well, I suppose this was not how you expected your morning to go," he said. With a rueful look at Louis, he reached into his pocket and produced several coins, then slapped them on the counter.

"I'll take the damned boots."

Beloved Maman,

A mere week has passed since my first letter, but I felt a need to assure you, again, that I stand in good health. The melancholy that I spoke of seems to have lifted, and I feel a stronger constitution for it. In fact, I've begun to view my surroundings in an altogether more positive light, but for now I shall simply say that I am well.

Circumstances regarding my mission to the islands have begun to make themselves clearer, but I caution you against drawing any conclusions until matters are settled. The friend I told you I met on Guadeloupe has unfortunately thrown a complication into the retrieval of our stones, but worry not, I have the one and will soon recover the others.

Do tell me you are well and how things fare at home. I often think of Father and that wretched grisette of his—if all goes well, we'll soon have no need of either of them. He's a fool to have relegated you for that trollop, but I know you are stronger than he, and when we are reunited, we will show him the grave mistake he has made. I shall write soon, but for now please do not worry after me, I am quite well. I send you my love and affection.

Celeste

CHAPTER 4

French Quarter, New Orleans
November 30, 1814

An afternoon making inquiries at the other customs houses yielded no word on a Celeste de Beaumais, so Moreau decided to make his way back to Maspero's tavern on Chartres Street. The pale December sun dropped behind the roofs of the French Quarter as early evening came on, and once again long shadows descended over the unpaved streets. A crisp breeze blew through the air, a reminder that winter had indeed arrived, however incongruous that seemed among the tall palm trees and leafy plants lining the streets. The crowds were as numerous as they'd been that morning, and a drunken fistfight broke out as Moreau rounded the corner of Bourbon and Toulouse Streets. He sidestepped the scene with hardly a glance, his thoughts still preoccupied with the events of that morning in the Banquette Lachappelle.

A cough at his side reminded him that Will, the fugitive pirate lad, had accompanied him as he made his way across the city. Annoyed by the company at first, Moreau had nevertheless kept the boy close, in the event he had any other useful information. With a nod, he motioned for the boy to follow him into the tavern. "Come along. Keep your head down."

Once inside, they sat at a small table in a corner, Will sipping a mug of cider while Moreau, his hat set on the table in front of him, drank from a cup of red wine that he'd been told was the strongest on offer. Steadily men began entering in groups of twos and threes, and Moreau kept a wary eye out for Tadeo Araza and the woman from the night before.

"Those two," Will said, indicating a pair of men, one in a grey smock with a red bandana around his head, the other wearing a long-sleeved blouse with blue and white stripes and flowing black pantaloons. "I don't know their names, but I've seen them. They're part of our number. *Their* number." Moreau watched the two men, and for a while Will was content to sit across from him in silence, basking in the warmth of the fire and the cider on his tongue. Abruptly Moreau looked up as if waking from a reverie. "One of those fellows said something…" he muttered, his eyes regaining their intensity. "Something about…Le Temple."

Will exhaled as the music picked up again, raising his voice to be heard. "It's an open-air market, the largest trading ground they have, halfway between the city and Barataria. It's meant to be hidden—but half the city's been there one time or another. Merchants, lawyers, even ladies go there to buy duty-free goods."

Moreau nodded thoughtfully. "The old couple from the shop said something about Le Temple." He glanced aside. "And the other fellow, he said something about *Le Marais*. I've heard of that in Paris, but I don't see what it means in this city."

Will glanced sideways at him, then looked away—his turn to drift off in a faraway stare. He spoke in a quiet voice. "Le Marais is another place. It's one of the *maroon* colonies, as they're called."

"Maroon?"

Will shrugged, but it looked more like a shudder. "Slaves—runaway slaves. It's where they run away to. Lots of 'em. A colony. Only I've heard…well, I don't know if it's true, see, but some speak of it like it's the lair of the devil himself. Frightening things happen there: witchcraft, women speaking in tongues and practicing voodoo arts. The menfolk are cannibals who conduct human sacrifices. All sorts of wickedness…" His voice trailed off, and he turned to look at Moreau, who stared at him with a bemused expression.

"Cannibals," Moreau said flatly.

The boy pulled his hand from his drink. "I said I don't know if it's true."

Moreau kept his gaze on the boy a moment before flashing one of his rare grins. He reached into his breast pocket and pulled out a cigar. "Light it for me." Will complied, and a moment later Moreau puffed out a plume of smoke. "Araza said something to his men last night, said they would feed someone to the…rougarou. What does that mean?"

The boy took a sip of cider. "It's a legend. Passed down by the Creoles who've lived here in the bayous and cypress swamps for many years. Supposedly the rougarou haunts the swamps, a creature that gobbles up children who don't follow their religious vows, or something like that. A sort of werewolf, if they have those in France."

Moreau listened attentively, his smirk never fading from his features. "I've been in this city for two days, and already I've encountered pirates, slaves, soldiers, and now you're speaking to me of cannibals, voodoo witches speaking in tongues, and werewolves that stalk the swamps. God help me if I were to stay here a whole month." He looked at Will, who seemed confused by the sentiment. Moreau gave him a rough pat on the head. "Cheer up; I'm not finding humor at your expense. Even if there seems enough to go around." He took another puff of his cigar and looked at the boy, who swallowed hard, evidently still upset at something.

"It's not—" Will stammered, then cleared his throat, "it's not humor at my expense. I just…no longer have a home."

Moreau frowned as he pulled a small bit of tobacco leaf from his tongue. "You're a corsair. I thought the sea was your home."

"We're not corsairs," Will answered sharply. "We're…*they're* privateers who sail under the flag of Cartagena with letters of marque."

"Why do you say *they*?"

Will's eyes drooped and he spoke in a quiet voice. "They've banished me."

"*Banished* you?" Moreau swallowed a derisive snort behind a gulp of wine.

If the boy heard the mockery in his voice, he didn't let on. "They left me clinging to a piece of wood and sailed off without me. Even if I were to go back to Grande-Terre, they wouldn't have me."

Moreau considered this a moment, puffing a wreath of smoke up over his head to mingle with the other clouds wafting along the white plastered ceiling. "What cause had they to banish you?"

Will lowered his eyes to the table, unwilling to meet the older man's gaze. "I don't know," he mumbled. "Ask them if you like."

Moreau squinted at him. "Sulk if you wish. If it were me, I would not be so forlorn to be rid of a band of men that left me for dead in the sea. Why not move on? Find a safer trade here in the city."

"I've the mark of a Baratarian. I'm not worthy of work."

The boy spoke in a tone of such innocent guilt that Moreau felt a momentary pang of pity. A fiddler struck up a tune in the far corner, and Moreau couldn't be sure which he'd like to hear less of—the Creole fiddler or the boy's laments. "Well, if you're no longer in league with those men," he said, taking another sip of wine, "why would Araza break you out of prison?"

"He didn't break me out—I picked the lock with a blade I took from the cook on the ship. While he served the captain supper, I snatched one of his knives."

Moreau stared at him flatly.

"It's simple, really," the boy continued. "All you need is a piece of twine or any thin rope—on a ship there's more than enough—then you tie the blade to your leg or on the flat part of your foot, and there it is, if you're ever locked in a cell."

"I suppose you are a pirate," Moreau muttered. "But why would Araza send you on an errand after you'd been *banished*?"

Will's eyes showed a deep melancholy that seemed incompatible with the furtiveness with which he'd just explained his escape. "He doesn't know yet. I was lost to my ship less than a week ago. We were sailing northeast, to Pensacola, I think. Either way, he hasn't yet learned of my condition."

Moreau signaled a passing server for another cup of wine and gave the boy a hard look. "So, he sent a boy to retrieve his prized ruby. A responsible captain indeed."

Will cleared his throat and spat a gob of phlegm at his feet. "He can't conduct business without risking arrest by the authorities."

"He made no pretense of hiding himself here last night."

Will wiped his nose with his sleeve. "The Americans know Maspero's is a place only sailors and Creoles frequent, and they rarely disturb us here."

"You are no Creole," Moreau countered.

"I'm a sailor, a Barata—" he caught himself. "I *was* a Baratarian." He looked down at the tattoo on his wrist with a sigh.

Moreau took another puff of his cigar and set it down. "I think I'm starting to understand your sad story, but I'd like to know what this ruby means to Araza. Why is he so desperate for it that he'd send an outcast boy to retrieve it?"

If Moreau's last comment hurt Will, he didn't show any reaction, nor did he seem quick to offer an answer. Moreau pursed his lips and leaned closer. "If you know more than you've said, tell me now." His eyes darkened, his brow furrowed, and the scar along his temple brought a severity to his face that turned his erstwhile handsome features into a look some had called sinister.

"I don't know why he wants the ruby—I wasn't told anything more than to retrieve it from Banquette Lachappelle." Moreau glared at him, his features hardly softening, evidently unsatisfied with the answer. "If he was given a fake," Will went on, "then he'll soon learn as much, and go hunting for the real one. But I don't know where it is, or why he wants it."

With a shrug, Moreau took a final puff of his cigar before snuffing it out on the table. As he exhaled, his gaze took in the rest of the room, drifting past the growing crowd of drinking sailors and landing on a woman standing at the counter. Moreau could see only part of her profile and a head of light-brown hair half concealed by a hood, but he recognized the green riding cloak immediately. Without wasting a moment deliberating, he rose from the table and walked over to where she was standing.

Facing the counter, with her back to the rest of the room, the woman didn't notice Moreau approaching. Suddenly aware of his impetuous act, Moreau paused and took a careful look around; seeing no sign of Araza or the Baratarians, he moved several steps closer. The woman exchanged a few words with the innkeeper, who handed her a mug, and as she turned, she caught Moreau's eye. From this angle he could not see her fully, but her light-blue eyes contrasted with her flushed cheeks, and her long nose and expressive lips gave her a hawkish yet thoughtful look. Indeed, a moment later she offered Moreau a thin smile, then took a sip and turned so she was facing the rest of the common room.

"Good evening, mademoiselle. If I might have a word?"

She gave him another brief look, one of confusion, then stepped forward as if to leave. Moreau set his cup on the counter and reached his hand out, gently but securely placing it around her wrist. "Pardon the intrusion," he leaned closer, "but I would have a word with you, Mademoiselle Beaumais."

With a sharp inhale the woman stepped back, pulling her hand away from his.

"Where did you hear that name?" she blurted in a low, somewhat husky voice.

Moreau smirked and let out a slow breath. "I first heard it in Normandy, outside Rouen. From a nobleman named Andre Valière, if you must know."

"And what business is that name of yours?"

He looked her over with a half grin. "I would be more willing to answer, if I were to learn what the name means to you."

Reaching up to smooth a strand of hair over her ear, she sighed, then looked back at him with a self-possessed expression that showed she had recovered from her initial surprise. "I am not accustomed to being spoken to in such a fashion by strange, one-armed men." She pulled her cloak over her right shoulder and tightened it around her bosom. Reaching behind Moreau to grab her mug, she glided forward and walked across the common room at a brisk pace, stopping at an empty table in the far corner and seating herself without looking back toward the counter.

Moreau watched her with an unreadable expression. He then noticed Will still sitting at their table watching him, looking to Moreau like a loyal dog waiting for its master. With a sigh he looked back at the woman, who had gathered herself and was glancing around the room, conspicuously avoiding eye contact with him. Moreau snatched up his cup and strode over to where she was sitting. As he approached, she looked up at him and scoffed.

"I think you should be about your business, monsieur."

"I've been about my business all day. It has led me to you."

She took another glance around the room. He wondered if she would shout or cry out in alarm if he were to sit down. He took a half step forward, forcing a smile he did not feel. "If I tell you that I bring word to Mademoiselle Beaumais from France, perhaps you will allow me to sit?" She stared up at him for several moments without giving an answer, which he took as the absence of a refusal and slowly slid onto the bench opposite her. He took a sip of wine and set his cup on the table, exhaling comfortably. "That wasn't so bad now, was it?"

He clicked his tongue, and after a moment his eyes turned cold and he spoke in a slow, clear voice. "Celeste de Beaumais was last seen boarding a ship leaving Petit-Bourg, Guadeloupe, nearly three months ago. She has been missing ever since." The woman barely reacted to his statement, simply staring back at him with a hard expression. "Her parents have grown worried."

"I am sorry for the lady de Beaumais, and her parents. But why is this any concern of mine?"

Moreau stifled a wry chuckle, lightly drumming his fingers on the table. "Wherever *she* may happen to be, I bring a message from her parents. They have offered certain *incentives* to bring her home to them. They are, 'fretful beyond compare.'"

The woman snorted and took a sip. "And that makes you what—their valet? An errand boy tasked with crossing half the world to *bring word* to this woman?"

"If my message isn't enough," Moreau replied evenly, "to induce her to return, then I am sanctioned to use more *persuasive* means. But I was hoping the lady might be persuaded by my…generosity. And come willingly."

The woman nodded slowly as she looked at him with an expression of mock solemnity. She tapped her pointer finger to her chin several times, then tilted her head. "That sounds like noble work, and I wish you all the best in your search. The only problem, monsieur," she looked to either side, then leaned forward and spoke in a hushed voice, "I'm not Celeste de Beaumais. So I'd kindly ask you to leave this table and not bother me again, before *I'm* forced to use more…persuasive means." She took a sip from her mug and looked back at the counter expectantly.

"Listen to me, you spoiled little trollop," Moreau growled, and she swiveled her head back to him with an angry blush. "I don't care about you, your fool parents, or the pirate dandy you make love to. I *will not* fail in my task to bring you home. So, you can either come with me willingly, or I can…" his voice trailed off as he noticed her attention drawn to the front door. As if expecting what was coming, he sighed and slowly turned his head to see what had drawn her gaze.

Tadeo Araza stood near the entrance flanked by two men—Baratarians, by their dress. In contrast to their rigid stances and hard faces, Araza stood comfortably and at ease, one hip partially leaning against the doorframe. His eyes swept over the room and landed on Moreau and the woman seated across from him. A slightly raised eyebrow was his first discernable reaction, and the chuckle he let out was audible from where the two sat. He gestured to his companions, who followed him to the bar, where he flung back his coat and rested a knee on a crook in the woodwork.

Seizing this momentary lull, Moreau looked at the woman, who was staring at him with an unconcealed smirk. He hid his discomfort behind a scowl. "This perfumed fool again."

The woman laughed aloud. "A man who thinks too highly of himself, disparaging another man who thinks too highly of himself. How novel."

Moreau did not look away as he heard the boots of the three Baratarians as they approached. He glared at the woman for a moment until he felt a rough hand on his shoulder. It tugged ever so slightly, and Moreau turned to see one of Araza's men looming over him. He looked to the other side and saw the other man mirroring him. Araza stood beside the table, looking at the woman. She looked back with a flat expression, perhaps bored. His gaze lingered on her for several seconds before turning to Moreau, who took advantage of the silence to finish off his wine. Moreau peered back to where Will had been sitting and noticed that the boy was gone. Frowning irritably, he muttered a curse and set his cup down. Araza turned his gaze toward him.

"Am I interrupting something?"

He looked at each of them in turn. When neither answered, he raised his eyebrows expectantly. "This man wanted to know—" the woman began.

"Be quiet," Araza snapped, rounding on her. "I was asking the gentleman, not you." Fixing her with an angry glare for a moment, he then turned to Moreau. "Well?"

Moreau peered sidelong at the man standing behind him; he was average height, with dark eyes and black hair slicked back, both his hands now gripping Moreau's collar. Turning back to the corsair captain, Moreau said, "I was told that when *El Mendigo* is seen at the docks, the city is known to be hosting its greatest swordsman."

Araza looked at him impassively.

"I'm sure," Moreau continued, "for a city of thieves, whores, and drunkards, that must make quite an impression."

The hand on his collar twisted tightly, and Moreau winced as his breath was constricted. Araza studied him for several seconds before waving off the man gripping his neck. With a grunt the man released Moreau, shoving his head forward for good measure. Swirling the cup in his hand, Araza's eyes narrowed as he looked down. He cleared his throat and moved to speak but stopped as the woman rose quickly from her seat.

"If you two wish to act like strutting roosters, I won't waste my time." Adjusting the hood of her cloak, she stepped past Moreau. Before she got any farther, Araza whistled softly through his teeth, and she halted, half turning to look back. "Señorita," he said in a silky voice, "have I waited all day to see you, just to watch you go?"

"I came all the way here," she replied irritably, "like I've done for three nights now, against my wishes. If you wish to speak, then I will speak, but I will not waste my time with two fools vying to see who can mine more deeply for petty insults." She turned her head so her back was to the four men.

Araza smiled. "*O dio mio*," he said, clasping his hands together, "the gods are cruel to send a beauty like you my way, only to keep you from ever coming too close. Why don't you leave that awful plantation and come stay with me?"

Moreau lifted his head slowly and gazed sidelong at the woman.

"You're the reason we found ourselves there to begin with," she spat indignantly.

"Of course," the corsair captain said soothingly, "but what better way to make amends than to rescue you from that vile man? Your lady may still cling to the stifling customs of her old life in France, but you are the one with sense. And besides, this is the New World; a new life without her is within your grasp—if you would just reach for it."

Moreau forced back an eager grunt, hoping against hope that the captain would say more. When he didn't, the woman sighed. "You know what I've come for, Araza. If you are not prepared to offer it, then I will be leaving." After a barely perceptible hesitation, she stepped forward and walked across the room and out the front door.

Araza's gaze followed her out and then returned to Moreau, his expression darkening. "This is the second time I've found you advancing on that woman, señor. You might find a third opportunity difficult to come by." He motioned to one of his men, who promptly grabbed Moreau by the collar and pulled him to his feet, pushing him roughly up against the wall and tightly gripping his throat. Moreau took as deep a breath as he could, ignoring the other man's glare and pretending his foul breath didn't touch his nostrils. Resisting the urge to raise his arm in defense, he squared his shoulders and looked at Araza, noticing for the first time the knife blade pressed against his throat.

"Steady, monsieur," the man muttered icily. "Any foolishness and I'll cut 'til I reach bone."

Moreau turned to the man with an ugly sneer, his heart beating slightly faster than usual, but with an effort he managed to force his thoughts back under control. "Brave men you are," he growled, "sneaking up on a man outnumbered three to one."

"Oh, we never claimed to be brave," the man snickered. "But if you don't behave yourself, then we won't give you the dignity of a brave man's death. Men have died worse than dogs in this very room."

Araza then turned to face those left in the room and, with a sharp whistle, made it clear that it was time for the tavern to clear out, hustling the nearest man along with his boot. In a matter of seconds, half the room had emptied, mugs and unfinished dinner plates discarded on the tables, while those remaining jostled each other to squeeze through the door. Araza struck a match and held it to the bowl of a small, half-bent pipe. "Well?" he asked between puffs, "have you anything to say for yourself then?"

Moreau cleared his throat and muttered loudly enough for those still inside to hear, "You clearly have no honor, but I did not take you for a *coward*."

The quiet mumbles and shuffling feet of the fleeing patrons turned to dead silence, and for a moment not a single person stirred. Satisfied at the effect, Moreau ignored the rough hand squeezing his throat even tighter now and spoke as loudly as his constricted windpipe allowed. "You chase these people...out to... murder a one-armed...man. If you're so...deadly with a sword... face me at ten paces."

With an effort he exhaled, then wheezed sharply. The man grasping his throat adjusted his stance and changed hands for a better grip.

Araza received the words with a wry expression, his lips curling in amusement beneath his dark moustache. He took several steps toward Moreau. "Bold, this one." He laughed aloud for a moment before turning to look at the patrons lingering nervously by the door, evidently curious about what was to come next. His faced darkened as he snatched Moreau's cup and flung it at them. "*Salid, bastardos! Ahora!*"

With a collective jolt they pushed and shoved to get out the door, the last man slamming it shut behind him. Araza ran a smoothing hand through his hair and turned back to Moreau, his wry expression returning. He rested both hands on his hips and stood at ease for several seconds. "Señor," he said finally, "if you think I care about looking a fool or a coward in front of those men—well, then, you know little of me."

Moreau crooked his neck, still gasping for air beneath the gloved hand at his throat. "There's nothing about you...I'd care to know."

Araza titled his head back slightly and laughed. "Bold indeed." He waved away the man holding Moreau's throat, who reluctantly released his grip, grimacing at Moreau as he did so.

"What do you want?" Moreau asked finally. His breathing and heart rate had returned to normal, but his temper was rising steadily.

"Did I not tell you I'd learn who you are?" Araza asked, puffing gingerly at his pipe. "We're here to learn a little more about you... before we decide what to do with you."

A brief pause, then the third man, who looked to be little more than a teenager, drawled at Moreau in a harsh voice. "What are you doing in this quarter?"

Moreau turned to the younger man and tried not to answer with too much scorn. "I'm looking for someone."

"Who?"

"A woman," he rasped. "She ran away from home."

"Do you know what we do to spies and agents that come snooping in our business?"

"I'm no agent," Moreau answered, licking his lips. "I've come on private business. The girl's parents want her back."

Another silence, slightly longer this time. "I don't believe him," the teenager hissed.

No longer able to control the rage now coursing through him, Moreau leaned toward the young man with a murderous expression. "Listen to me, you little shit-stained whelp. I was killing my countrymen before your father first lied to your mother to get her out of her soiled shift. Give me a knife, boy, and make it a fair fight—unless you're scared to be cut open by a one-armed man in front of your betters."

The young man took a step forward but was quickly restrained by Araza, who put a hand on his shoulder and dismissed him with a shove. At length, Araza reached a hand beneath his coat and pulled out a pistol. He raised it and pointed it at Moreau's head, cocking the hammer. "You have five seconds to convince me you're not an agent sent to spy on Jean Lafitte. If you give no answer, I will blow your brains out."

For the first time that night, Moreau felt a chill run down his spine. In this moment, Araza, older and in more possession of himself than the other two, did not seem one for idle threats. "If I were an agent," Moreau said evenly, "would I admit that I know you attempted to have a ruby appraised at Banquette Lachappelle? And if I were an agent, would I reveal to you that it is a false ruby, and you will get nothing for it?"

Unsure where the thought had come from, he felt as much surprise as Araza's eyes showed. For a moment no one spoke, then the younger man looked to his captain, back at Moreau, and lurched to his feet as if preparing for action. Meanwhile, Moreau's fingers twitched, ready to knock away the pistol and smash Araza's head against the plastered wall.

"And why would an agent not lie about such a thing?" Araza asked, his left eye twitching slightly. "Is that not one of his tasks, to spread misinformation?"

Moreau gazed at him with a cold expression. "Three days ago, a boy was plucked from sea wreckage in the Gulf. He escaped from the city jail earlier today. If I were an agent, I would have apprehended him when I found him skulking in a shop, hiding from soldiers. I didn't."

The younger man facing Moreau shook his head. "He says he's from France—I say he looks like a damned agent."

The other standing behind Araza scoffed. "He looks half a savage to me. How do you think he lost the arm?"

"He does look a brute. Maybe an alligator took it."

"*Cállate*!" Araza barked, flashing an irritated scowl. He turned slowly to Moreau. "You say the ruby is false; what proof do you have of this?"

"As I told you," Moreau said with a shrug, "the boy was hiding from soldiers in Banquette Lachappelle. After they departed, he exchanged words with the owners, and one of them blurted out your misfortunate attempt to have a false ruby appraised." A smirk grew on his features as he spoke, and he savored the frustration evident on the other man's face.

For a moment longer, Araza held his stare then turned his back to Moreau. "Kill him."

The nearest man lifted his knife, and both took a step forward as Moreau said in a firm voice, "I've come for Celeste de Beaumais."

Araza immediately halted and raised an arm for his men to wait. Turning slowly, he approached Moreau once again. His mustache twitched, and his almost-black eyes glared without revealing any emotion. "Have you now?" He opened his arms and showed his palms, his eyelids drooping lazily. "Celeste de Beaumais is a liar and a whore. What do you want with her?"

"I've come with information," Moreau said carefully, "from France. I must speak with her."

Araza squinted at Moreau, then tilted his head back, looking at the sodden white plaster above. "What is that to me? There is nothing I want from that damned country. The real question is... why are you better to me alive than dead?"

Moreau considered the question, studying Araza in turn. "You need not believe me—but consider the cost if what I say is true and you ignore it. If she is important to you, or, more likely, she is somehow involved with your precious ruby, then you might wish for her to hear what I have to say, before she decides to depart with the ruby and without you. You may regret killing me when you could have walked away with a fortune."

Araza smirked and then let out a high-pitched laugh. "If these were normal times," he explained, "I would have had you killed for a spy already. But these are not normal times."

Moreau grinned ominously, sensing the other man's attempt to change the subject "You didn't know it was a fake. And now you don't know what happened to the real one. I suppose you're beginning to suspect your *lover*, Celeste de Beaumais, was involved in something of a swindle. You don't hide your anger well."

Araza stared at him flatly for a moment before flashing a toothy smile. "If I am angry, you know nothing of why. And if you're attempting to play on my greed, or my *hurt* at the woman's betrayal, then I say again, you know nothing of me." He rocked slowly forward with a smirk. "You look as one who may have wielded a sword in his younger days; you'd probably like to test my claim as best swordsman. But alas, I only fight men with all their parts."

The laughter from Araza's men put a frown on Moreau's face, and he glanced at the younger man with a sneer. "Send this baby-faced jester away—and we'll find out which one of us leaves with all his parts."

"I'm beginning to like this one," Araza chuckled. "Perhaps I *should* challenge him."

Moreau nodded grimly. "Perhaps. I'd be a happy man returning to France with your woman. And your ruby."

Araza glared at Moreau, his expression darkening. Before Moreau could react, the corsair captain slammed his knee into Moreau's stomach, dropping him to his knees. As he gasped for breath, Araza bent down beside him. "Here's what we shall do," he declared, his voice turning cheerful once again. "I am going to allow you to leave this tavern with your life. Why? Because I can see you have *cajónes*—if not brains."

Moreau caught his breath and stared up at him, willing himself to restraint.

"I have business that will have me out of the city for the next three days. My men shall keep an eye out here to make sure you do nothing...out of the ordinary. If I see you, hear you, or even smell you when I return, I'll have worse men than these go to work on you with their cutlasses. Alligators do not usually hunt men, but they'll not turn down easy meat handed to them...piece by piece."

He rose slowly to his feet and lifted two fingers, gesturing for Moreau to do the same. Stifling a groan, Moreau hoisted himself up. "Now," Araza said, stepping aside, "make your way from here and out of my sight. Go, before I change my mind."

Moreau stared at him, his anger only slightly exceeded by his surprise at this sudden release. Exhaling slowly, he forced himself to turn away.

"Anything more than slow and steady," the man holding the knife growled, "and you'll feel a shooting pain; that's your spine being severed. You'll then crumple to the ground, paralyzed and trembling; in less than a minute, you'll be dead. Slow and steady, then."

Moreau walked past them, stopped at the table where he'd been sitting with Will, and reached down to pick up his hat. He wiped away a patch of grime, then turned his head, addressing the man with the knife. "If we ever meet again, it will take longer than a minute for you to die." He placed the hat on his head and walked slowly across the room. When he reached the door, Araza's voice called out. "Three days, Frenchman."

~~~~~~

Moreau cursed as he limped through the doorway and made his way into the night.

Only a couple of blocks from the tavern, Moreau heard the sound of quiet steps echoing behind him. Turning, he saw a short figure *hiding* in the shadows a few paces away. He squinted, leaning forward to get a clearer view.

A brief pause and then a boy stepped into the faint light: Will Keane. Moreau stared at him with a cold expression for several moments, saying nothing. Eventually he sighed, chuckling grimly to himself. "I should have expected a banished pirate would run at the first sign of danger." He shook his head at the boy, who turned away, his eyes turning to his left and right. A moment later he turned slowly to look at Moreau, who stared at him with a scornful expression.

"I didn't mean to leave you...with them."

Moreau said nothing, and Will rubbed his scalp absently.

"I think—I thought some of the Baratarians saw me, so I slipped out the front door. A moment later Captain Araza arrived. I watched him walk in the front door, and he said something to the men with him, but it was quiet. I didn't expect him to...attack you."

With a sigh, Moreau adjusted his hat and looked the boy. "I should not have gotten you involved in my affairs. Go home."

Will rubbed a hand over his eyes. "I don't have a home."

"No," Moreau muttered, "I don't suppose you do." He uttered a curse to himself, then added, "I suppose for one night you can sleep at the foot of the bed like a hound. Come along before I think better on it."

At that Will looked up with wide eyes as Moreau turned and began walking away. For a moment he stood frozen, unsure if the man was serious. With a stunned look, he lurched forward, almost stumbling over himself as he hustled to catch up.

As they rounded the corner onto the street where Moreau's inn was located, Will stopped suddenly. "I heard Monsieur Araza say something to his fellows as he was departing."

Moreau kept walking. "Yes. That one never seems to shut up."

Will cleared his throat and stepped to catch up. "Well, he mentioned a plantation. He said, 'I should follow her back to...Le Mouton tonight and set her straight myself.'"

Moreau's eyes went cold, and a moment later he stopped in his tracks. "You heard him say that?"

"Yes, monsieur, as he was leaving. I didn't want him to see me, so I stayed hidden and didn't hear any more. But..."

Moreau waved off further explanation, turning aside with a pensive expression, wondering why that name sounded familiar. After a minute it struck him, and he recalled the pretty face of the young lady in Banquette Lachappelle; she had said something about Le Mouton. He motioned for Will to follow him, and a few moments later they arrived at the entrance of Moreau's inn. Halting and looking down at the boy, Moreau's eyes were no longer cold but keen in the faint lantern light.

"You can stay here tonight, but I leave tomorrow at dawn."

Dearest Maman,

In my first letter I said I would inform you of circumstances regarding our current living situation, and so I shall—but first I must tell you of affairs at our home on the island, and explain how I came to find myself in such a singularly peculiar corner of the new world.

With regards to our undertaking on Guadeloupe, the series of events that brought us here would be quite a long story, so I might need more than one letter to do so. While harrowing and dangerous to be sure, it was not all bad, nor without glimmers of feeling. After all, what is an adventure without risk-taking, or the thrill of a new and unexpected romance?

My "mission" to Point-à-Pitre was successful as we'd hoped, with a young mulatto helping me with the task of excavating the chest beneath the middle palm tree in back of the manor. The gardens were overgrown with weeds, while the house had been utterly ransacked during the uprising, and in the interim redecorated and furnished in such a pell-mell clutter that to describe it in detail would likely cause you a bitter nostalgia. It will suffice to say that the house still stands and looks fairly unchanged from our happy days there, and, after retrieving our stones, I returned to the city to arrange my return home—only my return did not happen; I shall now tell you why.

The city was fairly tranquil, though occasionally the name of Delgres was cursed in the streets, or an effigy of the rebel leader could be seen burning or stomped on by whites—yet another reminder that though politics are always changing, nothing seems to change because of politics. Families must look to themselves, and I must say I am ever grateful to have a mother who possesses both prudence and intrepidity. All the better, since my father is an indolent fool who thinks only of his little trollop. Do please tell me there is bad news from him on this matter; if there is not, make some up for me.

At any rate, while waiting for our ship back to France, we made for a coffee shop in the city that was rumored to be safe for a lady, though I'm not sure any fitting such a description could be found on the entire isle of Guadeloupe currently. After supper, Elyse and I had paid our compliments to the fiddler and dancers when we returned to our table to find a squatter occupying our place. A dark-haired man, looking Spanish or Italian, sat in my chair, eyeing me as he rubbed a ring between his thumb and forefinger. With a gasp, I noticed it was mine. I had removed it when I'd stood up. I told the man it was mine and that he should give it back, to which he replied he would—if I gave him one dance. As I had no pressing affairs awaiting me, and felt a heady lightness in the island clime, I reluctantly agreed.

The dance was fine. The gentleman was practiced in Fandango and Flamenco, but "took pity" on me and chose a medium-paced Bolero, to which I felt utterly ridiculous, but his guidance—if a bit rough—helped me through it. When we finished, he brought me back to my table and returned my ring. He told me he was a ship captain sailing for a powerful man. I then gave him my name, and where I'd come from (without saying why), and then he smiled, and took my hand. What a smile it was. I would have thanked him, and likely never seen him again, only he then asked if my lady would dance with his first mate. One look of the man, decidedly less handsome, and I raised my chin, telling him I could not order such a thing. He smiled again, shrugging indifferently, then held open his hand to reveal my silver bracelet! With a frown I reached out to snatch it, but he closed his palm, taking my hand in his. "My dear, your bracelet shall be returned to you—when your lady has agreed to a dance with my first mate." Blushing, I slapped him, not hard, but enough to show my displeasure.

Oh, Maman, I have never met such a man. So vexing, and yet I don't think a single part of me wished to deny him what he wished. What was I to do?

Elyse had her dance, my bracelet was returned—and two days later the two of us found ourselves aboard El Mendigo bound for Saint-Domingue, now called the Isle of Haiti. Oh, if only I knew then who and what would take the place of this breathtaking man.

With love and affection,
Your Celeste

P.S. Elyse made a humorous remark earlier today. We were walking in the garden and saw a goose with a shorter neck than the others, and it moved with a strange, limping gait. She wondered aloud if it did not remind me of father! Of course, a servant should not disrespect her master so, and I told her as much, but later, when I was alone, I laughed outright at the notion. I don't know what I'd do without her.

CHAPTER 5

French Quarter, New Orleans
December 1, 1814

The first light of dawn brought a gloomy sky of swollen grey clouds that seemed to threaten rain—or at least a drizzle—as they drifted slowly over the New Orleans rooftops. Bells chimed from the city's several churches, and Moreau stepped out into the predawn light dressed in a dark-blue frock coat and coarse white breeches. A crisp breeze nipped at his nose, and he stamped his feet several times, partly for warmth, but also to try and find a comfortable groove for his toes in his new "sugar planter's" boots.

Making his way west along Dauphine Street, he noticed a morning frost had left the cobblestones damp and slick, and once again he found himself surprised at how much early winter seemed to affect this supposedly tropical corner of the world. He had let Will sleep at the foot of his bed, giving him his coat for a blanket, and in the morning found that he had gone, which was unexpected, if not entirely surprising. Relieved to be rid of him, as if he no longer had a puppy following his every step, Moreau departed for the day's mission with a renewed sense of purpose.

Nevertheless, his pride still smarted from that embarrassing episode the night before, and he cursed himself for blundering so foolishly into such an avoidable and nearly disastrous situation. There was a consolation, however, as the evening had yielded not only a conversation with Mademoiselle de Beaumais's lady, but he had learned that the woman was staying at Le Mouton Plantation, and therefore Mademoiselle de Beaumais could surely be found there too. Such an important piece of information he would not have expected to glean after only two days in the city, even if it had nearly come at the cost of his life. To Moreau, however, the risk of death often came and went as little more than an unpleasant nagging or interruption of his business. He had gambled with his life—in battle or in duels—so many times that somewhere along the way he had managed to train himself to dismiss the danger fairly quickly.

Bringing his thoughts back to the present, he recalled Araza's threat that he would return in three days and, should they cross paths again, he would kill Moreau—or at least try. Moreau felt no particular fear of the man; he had faced better—and won. And yet, the corsairs Araza commanded was another consideration, and Moreau knew better than to make an enemy of them as a group. Perhaps more than anything, he knew he had yet to come across Araza's commander, Lafitte, who remained a mystery. If Lafitte commanded the obedience of Araza, and all those other bastard pirates, he was also a likely threat—one Moreau planned to avoid.

Frowning as he mulled over these thoughts, he turned onto St. Louis Street and his foot caught the edge of a slick cobblestone, almost sending him tumbling. After he'd regained his balance, he cursed his new boots, wondering if he should return to the inn and change into his own worn but trustworthy pair. He quickly dismissed the idea, knowing he could not afford to be late to Rampart Street. The woman from the banquette had said she'd considered sharing her carriage for a visit to a friend's plantation, and he'd also heard her mention the name of the plantation: Le Mouton. She did not strike him as one who would deny him a seat if he presented himself smartly and in good humor—which for Moreau was easier said than done.

Stepping onto Rampart Street, which appeared wider and better kept than the other thoroughfares, he saw a line of carriages lining the route that led out of the city. He approached the driver of the nearest coach and, in as polite a tone as he could manage, inquired about the woman he was looking for. The man dismissed him with a curt shrug, and for the next half hour or so Moreau waited, strolling back and forth among the coaches.

His attention was abruptly caught by the sight of a woman making her way along the line of carriages. She wore a wide-brimmed auburn riding hat and a white dress that ended in lace trim above black riding boots, a yellow shawl looped at her elbows. She glanced briefly in his direction before turning back to where the largest carriages were parked on the corner. Moreau watched her a moment, almost sure that it was she he'd met the day prior. She passed the last carriage and came to a stop in front of a farmer's wagon at the end of the street. With a quick look to either side, she grabbed the railing and hoisted herself up into the driver's seat. Moreau set off to follow, and a moment later, as he saw her reach down for the reins, picked up his pace and caught up to the wagon. "Good morning," he said in a voice loud enough to be heard but not to startle her. Turning in her seat, at first in the wrong direction, the woman peered back toward Moreau with a startled look. He gazed up at her, unsure if his features had softened into a smile; they had not, and after a moment, a look of recognition dawned on her features.

"Oh, it's you," she said. "I did not expect to see you again."

"I've been told I'm difficult to be rid of."

She peered sidelong at him. "I did not say I wished to be rid of you. I said I did not expect to see you again."

Moreau looked out over the carts and carriages lining the road. "I'm looking for transport. To somewhere I believe you are also going."

"And how do you know where I'm going?"

"You told me yesterday," he replied. "You said you had a mind to introduce me to a friend. You then said you would have offered a ride in your...carriage." She didn't need to turn her head for him to wager that her face blushed. He let the silence linger for a moment before speaking. "I've ridden in worse conditions, mademoiselle."

With a flustered sigh, the woman ran a hand down her lap. "I've no doubt of that—if your appearance is any indication. But please tell me, monsieur, what business you have at the plantation where I'm going." She lifted her chin and looked down her nose. "I'm not in the habit of offering rides to strange, one-armed men."

"There is a guest on the plantation—a young woman. She is known to a friend of mine back in France, and I've been recommended to make her acquaintance. So I believe it only polite to call on her."

The young woman gazed at him for a moment before clearing her throat loudly. She turned her head away and raised a gloved hand to her chin, only partly concealing her smile.

"Is something amusing, mademoiselle?"

"No," she said in between chuckles, "it's nothing. I just was having trouble imagining you...and your *friend*. She must be quite the charmer."

Moreau watched her gaiety for a moment, then sneered as he did a once-over of her wagon. "And I have trouble thinking you've ever driven a rusted hog-hauler like this."

Taking a moment to recover from her bout of giggling, she adjusted her hat with both hands, looking at him with a straight face.

Moreau looked back at her with a rueful expression and shrugged. "Would be a shame to ruin that pretty white dress driving this lug into a swamp." Turning away, he took several paces before she called out. "Wait, monsieur." She stood up, almost losing her hat to a strong gust of wind. "Please wait."

He took a few more steps and halted. Half turning to look back, his brow furrowed. "You don't know how to drive." He saw her shake her head slightly.

"I've *seen* it driven," she said, her tone sweetening—perhaps a little too much. "I may not have very much experience myself, but I do not think this journey is entirely suitable for a lady by her lonesome."

Moreau walked back to the wagon, then swung himself up and settled into the seat beside her. "I'm not sure what you'd have done without me here. But it seems we both need something from the other." He held his hand out, and she looked at him with a confused expression. With a weary sigh, he reached his hand into hers and took the reins. "I'll drive."

A tug of the reins—and a muffled shout from the lady—and the wagon set off down the road leading out of the city. For a few moments they sat in silence, the only sound the horse's hooves clopping on stone. Moreau cast a quick sidelong glance at the young woman, who sat comfortably, her head tilted slightly, the visible half of her face shadowed beneath the wide-brimmed hat, and a soft smile brightening her features. "Your parents' carriage, I'm guessing. Did they give you their leave—or did you have to steal it?"

"I didn't steal anything," she answered indignantly. "Perhaps *carriage* was an exaggeration, granted, but I have no need to explain myself to you." Moreau pursed his lips in response. She sighed, looking at him with a wry expression.

"Well, anyway," she said airily, "if we are to be traveling together, we ought to become acquainted." She offered a gloved hand to him. "Antonia Milroy."

Moreau looked at her hand for a moment before taking it in his and giving it a brief kiss.

"And may I have the pleasure of yours?"

"I am called Lenoir."

She looked at him with a thin smile. "Well, I hope I do not come to regret this, but I am grateful for your assistance, Monsieur Lenoir."

He nodded, gazing aside at her a moment before turning his attention back to the road. They passed a cluster of leafless oak trees to the left, and a large, open square to the right, where a sizable crowd had gathered. That did not seem out of the ordinary for this city, but what did seem unusual was how almost every person in sight—man, woman, and child—had Black skin. The square seemed to be some market or communal gathering place, with people mulling about in large groups. Men walked about in simple cloth fabrics and plain white smock shirts, while some wore no shirts at all, displaying their physiques for all to see. A group of children squealed with laughter as they chased each other behind their mother's legs. Another group stood in a semicircle, their feet stomping rhythmically as they sang, their heads rising and falling to match the tempo. Beside them, others clapped their hands loudly, the children looking up at their mothers, mimicking their clapping. Two men nearby beat steadily on drums held beneath their armpits, calling out occasionally in extended, wailing voices.

"Congo Square," Antonia said. Moreau looked at her for a moment and wondered, given her own skin color, if she had any connection to the people in the square.

"What is it?"

She pulled her gaze from the square with a hint of melancholy. "It's a free space where Negroes can go without fear." She swallowed and stared ahead with a vacant look. Moreau gazed at her for a moment before snapping the reins slightly, and they departed the square, the wagon picking up speed along the road leading west out of the city.

Before long the cobblestone streets gave way to hard-packed dirt, and the two rode in silence for a while. Moreau drove the cart at an unhurried pace and at Antonia's direction brought the wagon to the edge of the Mississippi, where a wide, flat-bottomed ferry took them across the river, which, to Moreau, seemed quite vast. Antonia paid the toll, and when they reached the far side—called the "right bank"—they disembarked and turned onto a dirt road that skirted the river.

Moreau urged the horse to a trot, and soon after, they passed along a network of flat, expansive fields marked with reeds, small shrubs, and an occasional grove of orange trees. Each of these plots was overlooked by plantation houses of varying sizes, some little more than cottages, others lavish mansions with classical facades— high pediments and arched porticos lined with tall marble columns and ornate wrought-iron balcony railings. Behind the houses, each property held a small network of outbuildings: cottages, barns, and cabins nestled on the reedy ground abutting the cypress swamps beyond. Delineating the properties were long, symmetrical irrigation canals filled with knee-high muddy water.

As the sun rose higher, the air grew warmer, for which Moreau was grateful. He cast a look aside, noticing the bent and twisted trees that seemed to inch closer to the road with each mile they traveled. He tightened the reins, slowing the horse to a walk as they passed into a dense patch of trees and shrubbery. A nuthatch chirped nearby, and in a patch of open ground a large egret flapped its gangly, elongated wings as it took flight among the reeds.

With a sigh, Moreau looked at the young woman. "I have told you my reason for making this journey. Now I would like to know yours."

Antonia considered his words for a moment. "I am traveling to retrieve something that is mine."

"And what is yours that you must come all the way here to retrieve?"

Antonia looked askance at him, twisting her lips to one side. She exhaled and adjusted the brim of her hat before answering. "If you must know, one of my father's slaves...has gone missing." Moreau blinked several times but said nothing. Antonia cleared her throat before continuing, her words coming out faster now. "Edward was always a bit of a jokester, but he never neglected his duties. At least not when given clear and proper commands and treated with a fair but firm hand. Why he would run off is...a mystery to my family."

Moreau cocked his head slightly, but the young woman didn't notice, seemingly lost in her own thoughts. Flexing a fatigued hand several times, Moreau tightened his hold on the reins, and the horse slowed to a plodding gait.

"I did not imagine," he said, breaking the silence, "someone of your complexion would own a slave."

Antonia looked at him and her lips curled. "My family owns three, if you must know."

Moreau snorted.

"It is the legal right of any property-owning man to own slaves," she continued, her voice catching just slightly. "My father was born a free man—God willing, he will die one—and cannot manage his affairs alone. Edward and the others are treated well—which is more than some masters can say."

Moreau kept his silence for a few seconds before turning to look at her. "We're being followed." He frowned when she jerked her head to look behind them, nodding for her to turn back to the front. "It's not highwaymen," he muttered, "they only appear after they've obstructed the road. And I doubt it's a solitary soldier; he would have confronted us by now."

Antonia replied with a combination of fear and anger. "How long have you known we were being followed?"

Moreau pulled on the reins, guiding the cart off the road and stopping among a cluster of reeds almost higher than the wagon. He removed his hat and murmured a few soothing words to the horse before turning to look at Antonia. "Perhaps ten minutes."

"Ten minutes?"

"Quiet," he scolded in a hushed voice, peering with a somber look through the tall reeds, which offered some concealment.

"So what do we do?"

A moment passed, and he slowly turned to look at her, signaling silence with a finger in front of his mouth. Sure enough, several seconds later the soft pitter-patter of a trotting horse could be heard approaching from behind.

The sound grew louder and then stopped abruptly, the silence broken only by the a horse's whickering perhaps forty paces away. Their own horse perked up its ears and tilted its head, causing the bit to jingle slightly. Moreau exhaled. "Whoever you are," he called out in a commanding voice, "state your business plainly. My pistol is trained on your mount." His lie was spoken convincingly enough, and no response was offered.

Moreau peered through the reeds as Antonia's breaths came in short spurts. She slid closer to him. "I'm going to count to three..." Moreau bellowed, and the sound of hooves picked up again, coming closer. Moreau took a deep breath and slowly raised himself to his full height, exposed, if the approaching horseman had a weapon.

Antonia nearly reached out a hand to grab him but dropped her chin to her chest instead. For a moment Moreau watched whoever was approaching with a hard, unreadable stare. As the rider came within ten paces, he exhaled sharply and, without looking at Antonia, grunted and jumped down from the wagon.

"What in God's name do you think you're doing?"

Will Keane swallowed hard. "My apologies, monsieur. I didn't mean to catch you up unawares."

Moreau glared at him for several seconds, then called to Antonia without taking his eyes from the boy. "It's safe to come out. The *danger* has passed." He turned to see Antonia pop her head out from the reeds with a wince. "Who is it?"

"Only this idiot," Moreau growled. He lowered his eyes and, with a shake of his head, muttered something about his own foolishness. "We've been run off the road by an adolescent pirate." He fixed the boy with a hard stare. "I hope he has a good reason for skulking about on our heels."

When Moreau had heard enough of the boy's apologies and explanations, the journey resumed, and Will reined his horse alongside the wagon as it rolled back onto the road. Moreau gave him another hard look but said nothing for a while. For her part, Antonia had recovered her nerves rather quickly; nonetheless, she scolded Will for not announcing himself sooner, offering him a reproving expression that held the hint of a wry smile. "I don't care if you thought he would forbid you from accompanying us," she lectured, "it is never proper to sneak up on someone on the road. Especially in these times, with soldiers about and corsairs travelling to and fro." She shivered, pulling her shawl tighter.

Moreau exhaled loudly. Antonia peered aside at him with a raised eyebrow. "Are you disappointed, monsieur? Were you hoping for a more...worthy pursuer?"

Moreau's features hardened, but he said nothing.

Antonia chuckled to herself, looking at Moreau with a quizzical expression. "You may feel cause to be sour, but your tracking skills at least prevented us from being caught *entirely* unaware. Had our prowler been more dangerous…" She left the thought unfinished.

Moreau adjusted his grip on the reins and shrugged. "I'm not sour. I'm simply reflecting on the oddities of fate that have found me escorting an excommunicated pirate and a woman traveling to return one of her kinsmen to his chains." He returned his attention to the road without noticing Antonia's jaw drop.

"You escort *me*?" she blurted. "You sought me out for a ride in *my* wagon. Don't speak to me of…" she trailed off. Will kept his eyes on the road, from time to time patting his horse on the neck or looking out over the fields, having the good sense not to look at either of the two riding in the wagon.

Moreau's mood softened, slightly, as the minutes passed, but he did not release his scowl. A subtle glance at Antonia was enough to momentarily alter his thoughts from a bitter curiosity of the woman's purpose for travel to a reluctant admission that her passionate mood gave her a rather charming aspect. But she caught his look, and it elicited from her a loud sigh. "Edward is *not* my kinsman," she said, visibly restraining her temper. "He was purchased by my father nine years ago. If you knew anything of our laws, you would know that the *law* respects the property rights of free men in good standing—even if you don't."

"Pardon," Moreau said wryly, "I am escorting a woman who wishes to return her *property* to chains."

"Well," she answered irritably, "had he not run away, he would not *be* in chains, he would be working. Work is service, and service is of God."

Moreau considered her statement. "He serves you," he said at last, "so you are God?"

Antonia crossed her arms and stared ahead. "You have the charm of an alligator."

Moreau shrugged. "And you have the common sense of a kitten."

A moment later they cleared a squat copse of trees and passed along a wooden split-rail fence lining the road to their left. Moreau looked out over the field and exhaled quietly. "I did not mean to insult, mademoiselle. I simply find the prospect of a colored woman in haste to retrieve a man—the idea is strange. And it brings up memories from my own country."

Antonia kept her eyes ahead. "Edward is our property, but I've never had anything but good feelings towards him. Yes, I suppose, once, he did try and kiss me—but only on one occasion. He never went beyond that with his...masculine indiscretions." She smoothed a hand over her lap as Moreau smirked to himself. "Although uncouth and mischievous, I believe him to be good. Perhaps a lesson or two in manners and he could be led to a fine maturity and decent disposition."

Moreau yawned into a closed fist, muttering something about a man or a horse.

"I believe he was coaxed," she continued, ignoring his remark. "By the other folk, those of the swamp, Le Marais. By all accounts, they are wild; killers who show no mercy, and they practice black arts."

Noticing the tremor in her voice, Moreau looked at Antonia and saw that her disposition had changed rather suddenly. Her eyes seemed focused on some invisible point ahead, and the hands resting on her lap trembled slightly. He held his silence.

To their left, the trees gave way to another parcel of open ground, which appeared to indicate the site of another plantation. The horse's ears perked up as they entered the field, and it turned its head aside to scan the ground.

"We've arrived," said Antonia.

CHAPTER 6

Le Mouton Plantation, Outside New Orleans
December 1, 1814

Spanish moss drooped from outstretched tree limbs that sprawled like long arms over the wagon as it passed beneath several massive live oaks on either side of the lane. There was less jostling and bouncing on the seashell-paved surface than on the rutted, half-frozen river road, for which Moreau felt grateful. He adjusted his bicorne hat and glanced at his pocket watch, noting that it was just before noon. The sun had cleared the thick cloud cover and now shone brightly at its zenith, bringing warmth to the travelers.

Squinting as he glanced to either side, Moreau noticed the vast tracks of flat, open terrain beyond the trees, presumably the much-lauded sugarcane fields that he claimed to be here to visit. According to what he'd heard while aboard *La Panthère*, indigo had been the dominant plant in Louisiana until a plague of caterpillars wiped out the crop. A little later, a new sugar-refining technique was developed that allowed the cane to be processed into granulated sugar and not just the gummy syrup that made rum. This discovery had brought an explosion of sugarcane development from the region's plantations, and this enterprise seemed to be no exception.

Moreau forced himself to affect an air of eagerness and enthusiasm, as one would expect from a visiting planter in search of his own lucrative plot. He shared a few words for Antonia to do the same, to which she nodded halfheartedly as she took in the expansive grounds around them. He looked back at Will, who had eased his horse back so that he rode behind the wagon, like a loyal servant should. Moreau halted beside a pile of burlap sacks, presumably loaded with sugar, that appeared close to bursting.

"Here we are," Antonia said cheerfully, favoring Moreau with a smile. She tilted her head slightly, perhaps to emphasize the sarcasm. Her hat shaded half of her face, but her cheeks gleamed with a rosy tint, and her lips spread wide over white teeth. Moreau's gaze lingered a few seconds before he pulled his attention away.

To their left was the large manor house built in the French colonial style. It appeared every bit the seat of a plantation: white pillars framed a balconied second-floor porch that was accessed by two angled staircases rising from the ground and meeting near the middle. Two dormer windows with blue shutters on the third floor divided the grey-shingled roof, and a narrow redbrick chimney released a soft, smoky coil. Moreau could not deny that it appeared to be among the finest houses he'd seen so far in America. It possessed a patrician dignity that he recognized from the manor houses in France, but lacked the heavy-handed ostentation typical of such estates, which, before *La Revolution*, had belonged to the same families for centuries.

A large white goose honked as it waddled along a path that led behind the house through a cluster of ferns and dwarf palmettos, beyond which stood an abundance of tall trees—sugar maples, live oaks, crepe myrtles, Southern magnolias, and the ever-present cypress. A sound of steady hammering came from one of the wooden structures behind the house, which were among at least a half-dozen outbuildings that Moreau assumed to be workshops, storage sheds, pantries, or perhaps servants' quarters. Beyond these was a cluster of smaller wooden shacks in well-ordered rows that extended back to a thick growth of vegetation that obscured anything farther. Past the fields to the right, Moreau noticed a glistening of sunlight from what appeared to be a stream or pond nestled among the trees, supporting his notion that the property came to a hard—or, in this case, wet—end where the fields met the cypress swamps.

Will Keane led his horse to a long hitching post on the opposite side of the lane and tied the reins off. Moreau climbed down from the wagon and turned to offer his hand to Antonia—but she only adjusted her dress and pulled her shawl close before stepping down without taking it. He sneered, turning back to take another look at the property. As Moreau looked for signs of anyone about, he noticed a man leaning on the balcony, looking down at them. With a low whistle at Antonia, Moreau removed his hat and indicated the fellow standing on the veranda. He wore a straw hat and a simple shirt of white linen beneath a tan vest. A long stalk of grass protruded from his mouth, and a beard that showed traces of red matched the shaggy crop of hair protruding from beneath the hat. He watched the visitors approach for a moment before he leaned back from the railing and walked to the nearest stairway.

"How do you do?" he asked in English, stepping slowly down the staircase. He reached the bottom and offered the three guests a polite nod. His eyes passed over Antonia, then he took a step past her to offer Moreau a firm handshake.

"How may I help you?"

If being ignored irritated her, Antonia didn't show it. She greeted the man with a smile. "My companion speaks little English," she declared. "My name is Antonia Milroy. I come from just outside the city. My traveling companions here are Will Keane, a sailor by trade, and Monsieur Lenoir, who is visiting from France."

The man gave Antonia a close examination but said nothing. Moreau took a quick last glance around the grounds before clearing his throat. "You are owner of zis estate?"

The man turned to him, seeming to notice for the first time Moreau's missing appendage. "The proprietor of this estate is not at home. I am Lionel Benton, overseer of the plantation."

Antonia smiled as if he had said something remarkably interesting. "Well," she said, "we do not wish to pull you from your duties. We came to pay a brief call on Monsieur Giroux, if he is at home, might you…"

"That's fine." Benton turned his eyes back to Antonia and for a moment said nothing. At length he turned back to Moreau with a nod. "He'll be home presently. Please follow me."

Moreau followed him up the stairs, motioning for his two companions to follow. Antonia's smile faded as she walked, while Will seemed to wish to avoid eye contact with anyone. They followed Benton across the porch through a pair of open doors into the house. Stepping into what appeared to be the sitting room, Benton turned to Moreau and offered a stiff nod before excusing himself, leaving the three guests alone to take in their surroundings, which were, in truth, rather charming.

A high vaulted ceiling enclosed an expansive drawing room, in the middle of which was a round table and four ladder-backed chairs, with silverware and a place setting for one. In one corner a medium-sized piano with a polished oak finish sat beneath a framed portrait of an older woman dressed in black in a domestic setting not unlike that which they currently occupied. Against the wall to Moreau's right was a large escritoire, its bookcase reaching halfway to the ceiling, while the wall opposite bore a marble mantelpiece, on top of which sat an ornate clock between two tall vases holding plants with long, pointy leaves. Moreau took in the room with a respectful, if indifferent, air, while Antonia looked around with wide eyes and a barely concealed grin. She stopped to smell a pair of magnolia blossoms in a vase on the table, while Will edged into the corner with the piano, holding out a hand and brushing it over its smooth, finely polished top before pulling it back uncertainly.

Moreau took in a breath, absorbing the pleasant smells of flowers, perfumes, finished wood, and the vaguely distant smell of food being prepared. He strolled across the carpeted floor and halted in front of a window on the far side of the room, tucking his hat beneath his arm. As he looked out over the sprawling grounds behind the house, his thoughts drifted to his friend Andre Valière, and Moreau compared this lavish estate with that of his friend's in Normandy. That property extended behind gardens and fields to a steep hill leading down into the ancient Silveison Forest, while this one seemed to stretch out in a long, flat plain as far as the cypress swamps. In fact, as Moreau considered his brief time in Louisiana thus far, he could not recall seeing a single rise or hillock. He had rarely, if ever, seen terrain so flat in all his years campaigning across Europe. If the English landed in a place like this, they would be hard pressed to disguise their movements, as they had done to such great effect in Spain and Portugal.

Moreau pursed his lips and turned to Antonia. "You believe your property has fled here?"

Antonia bobbed her head and almost spilled the cup of tea in her hand. "Would you keep your voice down?" Shushing him with a finger raised to her lips, she placed her cup in its saucer and spoke in a softer voice. "His name is Edward. And yes, I have reason to believe he stopped here."

"Edward," Moreau said sardonically. He glanced around the room, nodding to himself. "So, he stopped here, on his way to somewhere else?"

Antonia slowly set her saucer on the table. "Yes, I believe he may have stopped here. Where he might be now, I think…I don't know. Not for certain." Her explanation was cut off by the sound of voices outside, which drew the attention of the three visitors. The sound of hoofbeats in the lane came to a halt, followed by the shuffling of feet and opening of doors, and eventually boots climbing the wooden stairs. Moreau and Antonia exchanged a brief glance, and a moment later Lionel Benton stepped into the room, nodding politely at Moreau. "Monsieur Giroux has just returned from Mass. He will be with you shortly." He turned and left, the distant drumming of his boots echoing softly through the sitting room.

Antonia took a sip of tea and looked at Moreau with an air of satisfaction. Moreau ignored her and looked back out over the grounds behind the house, holding his hand over his eyes to shield them from the sun. As he scrutinized the various shacks and outbuildings, he muttered to himself. "I suppose Sunday is their day of rest as well. So much acreage must require scores of field hands."

"One hundred and thirteen to be exact," a new voice stated, "as of this morning." Moreau and his two companions turned to see a man standing in the doorway. He was taller than Moreau, at least six feet, dressed in a fine black suit with a turned-down collar and white neckcloth. He lowered his lean frame in a formal bow, then stepped toward Moreau with an offered hand. "How do you do, monsieur?" His soft-spoken French was marked by a hint of a Creole. "I am Cyril Tremblay, solicitor to Monsieur Giroux."

"How do you do." " Moreau motioned to Antonia, who rose and glided over to greet the newcomer with her customary glowing smile.

"A pleasure to meet you, monsieur," she said demurely as he kissed her gloved hand.

Tremblay looked at Will and nodded politely. Stepping back and tucking a small notebook into his breast pocket, he gestured out the window. "Le Mouton Plantation." His astute brown eyes reminded Moreau of a young officer or diplomat, as the fellow could not have been past his early twenties. "I see you have been offered refreshments," he said. "Monsieur Giroux will be with you momentarily."

As if on cue, another man appeared in the doorway and peered at the waiting visitors. He stood several inches shorter than Tremblay and wore a claret-colored vest, a white long-sleeved shirt with lace cuffs, and a pair of loose-fitting white breeches. "Monsieur Giroux is here now," he pronounced in raspy English. With an inviting smile at the three guests, he strolled into the room and bowed courteously. Will reached for a hat he wasn't wearing, Moreau's hard face was tempered with a subtle nod, and Antonia curtsied low and graciously.

Giroux's leathery skin looked parched by years spent under the sun, and the bronze of his face seemed on the verge of turning red. His aquiline nose was narrow, and his penetrating green eyes seemed either to squint or widen, depending on the conversation, animating his disposition with an unmistakable vigor. A crop of curly brown hair with flecks of grey covered his square head.

"Forgive me if you've been waiting long," he said, his English also accented with a Creole twang. "You've caught me between worship and dinner, and I can't seem to decide which I should be dressed for, so I hope you will forgive me for appearing a hungry heathen."

"It is for us to demand forgiveness, monsieur," Moreau stumbled in English, "for arrive upon your Sunday without announcement."

Giroux looked at him, examining his appearance with an open smile. "Pardon, monsieur," he said, taking a step closer, "but I don't believe we've had the pleasure of an introduction."

"No, monsieur, we have not. I am René Lenoir, newly arrive to Louisiana from France."

Giroux's eyes widened, and he looked at each of the guests before turning to young Monsieur Tremblay. "You didn't tell me we had visitors from the empire." He turned back to Moreau, more intent now. "A pleasant surprise indeed. Tell me, what do you think of our parish and our city, Monsieur Lenoir?"

Moreau nodded courteously. "I feel as I am in France, monsieur."

Giroux once again took in Moreau's appearance, as if seeing him for the first time. He then switched to French. "Well, forgive me if I seem overeager, but I have known several men come from Napoleon's Grande Armée, and I'll be damned if each doesn't have a story or a scar to outshine the former." He craned his neck slightly and gestured at Moreau's missing left arm. "I take it that was lost in service to the emperor?"

Moreau hesitated before looking down at his arm with a sheepish bob of his head. "If only I could tell the ladies of this city as much. Alas, I spent most of my youth on Saint-Domingue, and this was simply the result of an unfortunate accident on our sugar plantation."

Giroux listened with a creased brow, his attention rapt, and quickly flashed a fraternal smile. "Monsieur," he said genially, "it is not for a humble planter such as myself to minimize the rigors of cane planting in the Caribbean. Nor the dangers and…horrors… your people suffered."

Moreau nodded soberly and gazed at Antonia, whose face seemed to have gone ghostly white. She ran a hand across her belly before catching his stare, flashing her eyes rapidly before turning back to the host with a gracious gleam.

"And surely," Giroux said, noticing the smile, "this is your lovely lady?" He took a few slow steps closer to Antonia, who lowered her head bashfully.

Moreau suppressed a smirk. "No, monsieur."

Giroux swung his head to look at Moreau, exaggerated horror on his features. "No? You mean to tell me this young lady is not yours for the quadroon ball next week?"

Antonia's eyes bulged slightly at Moreau, and he shot a look of frustration at her. Before he could reply, she turned back to Giroux with a playful grin. "I've only come to know Lenoir over the past twenty-four hours, Monsieur. We are newly acquainted friends, to be sure, but I'm afraid the friendship goes no further than that."

Moreau forced an agreeable smile and attempted to steer the conversation back to their visit. "Monsieur, I confess that I've come here today as one seeking both information and advice."

"Oh?" Giroux motioned for them to join him as he positioned himself behind a chair at the table. He then waved a hand at two of the servants—more accurately, slaves—who proceeded to set places in front of the three guests. Tremblay remained standing a few paces away while the guests and their host seated themselves. "Will you take wine, monsieur?"

Moreau waved away the offer. "Tea will be enough, thank you."

Giroux looked at Antonia and winked, pouring a tall glass of dark red for her without asking. He poured himself a large glass and set the carafe down. "So, what in the way of information and advice may I offer you, Monsieur Lenoir?"

Moreau felt a wave of relief, both at the possibility of coming to the point and also at the sight and smell of freshly toasted bread and scones being set before them. Another large teapot was set down beside a silver tray of jellies, jams, and cookies, and each of their plates was set with bread, cheese, and some roasted local fowl over a bed of greens. "My family's holdings in Saint-Domingue—Haiti, rather—were lost in that damnable uprising," he lied. "We escaped to France with our lives, but circumstances there since Napoleon abdicated are...*unsettling*...as you've surely heard. For a Frenchman that tires of war, and has tasted the fruits of life in the New World, I see no better land of opportunity than Louisiana."

Giroux finished a bite of snipe and washed it down with a sip of red wine. He looked at Moreau with a somber expression. "I sympathize with your troubles, monsieur. We know of many who have endured such hardships, but I assure you we will not tolerate such wanton destruction on these shores. What assistance we may offer, we shall."

Moreau nodded and then glanced at his companions, who seemed as eager as he to enjoy the midday meal. Will had already finished his first cup of wine, with a second being refilled, while Antonia sat with a firm posture, taking small, slow bites, but her eyes lit up with an unmistakable thrill as each tray of food was set down. Giroux did not refrain from enjoying the feast, either. For a while the two men spoke of the plantation and its enterprise in recent years, Cyril Tremblay occasionally joining in to add a detail or confirm a date. Moreau then asked about the recent growth in the cotton trade, of which he'd heard on his voyage, asking whether the plantation cultivated any of its own. Giroux laughed humorlessly. "Associates of mine from nearby plantations are always trying to convince me to buy some of their cotton at low prices, or to get us to change from sugarcane to cotton."

"Or asking for one of our acolytes," Tremblay added.

Giroux turned to Moreau with a frown. "I'm sure on Saint-Domingue you saw what one jealous planter will do to try and chase off a rival." He said the last words with a grim smirk.

Antonia gazed at him and craned her head thoughtfully. "And acolytes—they are...?"

Giroux pointed to the two young men standing against the wall and motioned to the jar of water, then at Moreau and Antonia. "Slaves," he answered flatly. The men quickly refilled the guests' empty glasses. "Here we call them acolytes. In fact, what I believe has my colleagues most jealous is our system of merit and hierarchy."

"Some of the planters along the German Coast," Tremblay explained, "are jealous of what we've built here, so they resort to slander and calumny. Some try to poach our best acolytes. Still others, more nefarious, encourage them to run away into the cypress swamps. But any who try and threaten what we've built will find us ready with swift litigation, make no mistake."

Moreau's brow creased. "And this system of hierarchy and merit?"

Giroux reclined in his seat, pursing his lips and raising his eyebrows. "Well, we've observed that our acolytes are more productive if they feel...*valued* in their work. So we've established a system where each man, woman, and child is grouped according to seniority, merit, performance—things of that nature. Our white workers are our overseers, our older Negroes on good behavior are *prefects*, adult males who've been with us for more than five years we call *knights*, women and children over fifteen years old are our *faithful*, and the list goes on. Those who have shown wicked behavior are our *debtors*—luckily for their sake we have but few of those." He looked at Moreau, then at Antonia, his smile fading into a hard expression. He took a sip of wine and his features softened a little.

"I'm sorry we can't go out and see them working now," he went on, "but it's the Sabbath and we would not have them working. Members of society would not take kindly to *that*." His lips flattened into a grin. Moreau peered aside at the two men standing across the room like statues, towels hung over their right arms. They seemed perfectly oblivious to the conversation at the table.

"It is a busy operation," Giroux mused, "but every acolyte here knows they are a part of something special, and we are proud of that fact." He looked at Moreau with an earnest expression. Moreau nodded as he chewed a bit of bread, Antonia and Will seemingly content to enjoy their meal in polite silence. A moment later Giroux let out a quiet sigh. "Once this *embargo* is lifted, we're likely to see an enormous resumption of trade. I could use an experienced man like you by my side. This industry is not for the soft; it takes a man of backbone to lead such an operation—and you seem cut from the proper cloth."

Moreau cleared his throat. "I thank you for your confidence, monsieur. I can see you are an…enterprising shepherd to your flock."

"We try our very best. But there are always those who wish to take what another man has built. Envy, perhaps. Greed. Whatever the reason, we are rarely without our challengers. To say nothing of the troubles within."

Moreau looked at Antonia, who made a quizzical face at the last comment. "Troubles within?" she inquired.

Giroux sighed again as he looked out over the sprawling yard. He turned back with a rueful expression and spoke quietly. "Some of our acolytes have been known to *misbehave* from time to time. Oh, it isn't cause to worry, mademoiselle, just small acts like injuring livestock, spoiling meat, 'losing' work equipment. Small acts of rebellion; but we know how to deal with troublemakers. And worst of all, the runaways—well, they do not often try a second time." He looked at her, then back at Moreau, his smile long since faded. "Anyhow, you haven't come all this way to hear about my troubles."

A moment later a dessert tray was brought out—more rolls with honey and jam and a batch of candies called "pralines"— pecans smothered in creamed sugar and rich caramel—which Moreau nibbled but found too sweet to be enjoyable. Between sips of wine, Antonia raised the question of whether there was a lady of the house who might join their meal. Giroux dabbed the sides of his mouth with a napkin, then let out a quiet sigh. He shifted his gaze to Antonia with a smile that did not touch his eyes.

"Madame Giroux," he said in a strained voice, "is no longer with us." Tears welled in his eyes. "You must excuse an old man his weakness, it often overwhelms me."

Antonia reached out and rested a hand on his arm. She offered a few quiet words, which mercifully broke the silence, and looked at Moreau as if for support. For his part, Moreau glanced at his watch, then at Will, whose lips were stained purple from wine. Will did not seem affected by their host's moment of sadness, and he glanced at Moreau with a broad smile before looking away.

Moreau frowned at the boy, eager to tell him off for becoming drunk so soon. He shifted in his seat, suddenly remembering the amount of water and tea he had consumed. Giroux dabbed his eyes and mouthed a quiet thanks to Antonia, who looked genuinely distressed by his state. Excusing himself to go to the toilet, Moreau slid from his seat and walked toward the stairway at the back of the house.

―⚘―

Moreau tended to his business in a small shack nestled among a growth of ferns perhaps a hundred paces behind the manor house. He stepped back out into the brisk afternoon air feeling rejuvenated by the tea and warm meal, but looking up, he noticed that the sun had slipped behind a swelling mass of large, dark clouds that looked to be rolling east with no end in sight. He considered their long journey back to the city and reminded himself of the need to inquire after Celeste de Beaumais.

As he turned back toward the house, he heard a strange noise—a *thump*—coming from a cluster of hackberry trees several paces away. Halting abruptly, he squinted as he scanned for any sign of movement. For a moment nothing happened, then he heard another thump, followed quickly by a low, groaning sound. He took several steps closer to the grove where the noise had originated. As he approached, he saw a flash of movement among the trees, then noticed two Black men pacing slowly in a circular motion. Glancing cautiously to either side, Moreau crept several steps closer. Abruptly the two men bent down and began stomping their feet, evidently on something on the ground. The thumps came once again in quick succession, and groans quickly followed.

Moreau shielded himself behind a tree as he snuck within a few paces of the pair and saw a third man, also Black, lying on the ground. He was shirtless, wearing pantaloons that had slid halfway down his legs, and holding his hands over his head. He looked to be shaking. Moreau flinched when he saw movement behind one of the trees and a fourth man appeared. This one was white, and with slow steps he approached the panting man on the ground. He turned his head for a split second, and Moreau caught a glimpse of his face, recognizing him as the man who had greeted them and brought them into the house: Lionel Benton. Benton walked closer to the fellow on the ground and stopped, squatting down beside him. Removing his straw hat, he waved it over the prone man several times like a fan, then tapped him with it.

"You was told to clean the Grande Kettle, ain't that so? Oh, no you weren't?"

The man on the ground mumbled something, and Moreau cocked his head to hear.

"Said by Monday—" the man's words choked off in a raspy cough, and he rolled onto his side, breathing heavily.

Benton waved a hand and placed his hat back on his head. "Don't lie to me, son—only make this worse. You was told to clean it by today." Stretching his arms over his head with a yawn, he stood and then slowly sat down—on yet another Black man crouched on all fours, with his elbows and knees on the ground and his head bowed between his shoulders. "Then why was it so fuckin' dirty, then? Huh?" Benton leaned aside and spat, and the man beneath him began to shake from supporting his weight. "No reason. You just lazy." Benton then waved a slow hand at the men standing over the one lying on the ground.

Moreau scowled as they resumed kicking the man, who was helpless to defend himself from their assault, curling his body forward, then backward, as the blows thudded against his back and abdomen. After several more seconds, the beating ceased as the unfortunate man on the ground continued to groan and struggle for breath. Moreau shook his head and turned away, not looking back as he strode briskly past the hackberry trees, down the path, and up the stairs into the house.

He walked down a short corridor and paused before the doorway to the dining room, his thoughts a muddle of the scene he had just witnessed and a renewed desire to pursue his inquiry of Mademoiselle de Beaumais—and then be gone. He took a deep breath to collect himself when the sound of footsteps behind him caused him to turn abruptly, and he saw Cyril Tremblay standing a few paces away. Moreau peered at him a moment before offering a curt nod.

Tremblay offered a dry smile, nodding in turn. "Monsieur… Lenoir, was it?"

Moreau nodded again as Tremblay folded his hands behind his back. "Did you find the outhouse alright?"

"Yes, thank you."

"Very good," Tremblay replied with another smile. "Monsieur Giroux often has guests visiting the grounds. Sometimes they get turned around—we have yet to lose any free men out in the 'shaking bogs,' but we locals have heard of strange things out among the tall reeds and cypress trees after sundown." Tremblay gave him another appraising look and nodded. "I'm pleased to see you've made it back in one piece."

Moreau glanced at the stump of his left arm and shrugged. "I'm permanently not in one piece. But I manage."

Tremblay let out a hint of a chuckle, but his eyes remained keen. "I'm sure you've heard by now, these are dangerous times. English agents have been apprehended in nearly every parish from here to Baton Rouge. We must be cautious with whom we allow to roam freely." He smiled tightly again.

Moreau met his gaze for a moment, then peered out the window, seeing little beyond the wooden shacks and hackberry trees. "You seem to have little trouble enforcing your authority here. I'm sure you'll sleep soundly." He turned and walked back into the sitting room and took his seat at the table.

The plates had been cleared and the strong aroma of coffee and liquor filled the air, momentarily disrupting Moreau's somber mood. No stranger to scenes of violence and even brutality, he nevertheless found it somewhat difficult to dispel the sight he had just witnessed. As he looked at the three figures around the table, he brought himself back to the moment, and the sight of Antonia smiling warmly at him with the hint of a glaze in her eyes brought an even stronger distraction, which he forced from his mind.

"You've returned." Giroux slid a saucer and cup of strong-smelling coffee in front of him with a smile. "I was worried we were going to have to send young Mr. Keane out to find you."

Moreau took a sip and almost spit it out, as it tasted more strongly of whiskey than coffee. Forcing himself to swallow, he grinned politely at his host. "Your hospitality has been generous, monsieur. I thank you."

Giroux, whose face was now red and his eyes shining with a jovial glimmer, waved a hand. "For a gentleman of the empire, you seem a man of few words, and you boast very little compared to the officers I've known. All the same, I tell you that for you and this beautiful young lady, my plantation is at your disposal."

Antonia smiled cheerfully and glanced across at Moreau, who swallowed hard, setting his cup down more clumsily than he would have wished, spilling a bit of coffee into the saucer.

Giroux sighed loudly, peering at the clock on the opposite wall. "Anyhow," he sighed, "now that I've wasted the afternoon blubbering and drinking, I regretfully must return to more industrious pursuits. Before I beg my excuse, is there anything else I can help you fine folks with? Mademoiselle Milroy here has informed me of her missing Negro. Regretfully, I cannot claim to have come into possession of such a fine-sounding young hand, but I assure you both I will make inquiries. He won't be gone for long." He smiled at Antonia and then at Moreau.

Moreau looked at Antonia, who, despite flushed cheeks and red lips, appeared sober enough—at least more so than Will, who was now grinning at Moreau like a fool. Forcing away thoughts of what he'd seen behind the house, Moreau mumbled a few words about appraising plots of available land for his own cane plantation.

At the end of his sputtering explanation, he slipped in a remark about a young noblewoman from Normandy, a friend of a friend, and how he'd heard rumor that she had visited this plantation. Giroux received the last comment with a scrutinizing squint, his red cheeks puffing out as he considered Moreau's statement. At last, he smiled and spread him arms to show both palms. "Monsieur, I must confess, I have indeed enjoyed the company of such a woman. At her request I have kept her presence here with discretion—some might even say secrecy—but I assure you that was only to honor her wishes. Mademoiselle Celeste de Beaumais arrived here some weeks ago under rather peculiar circumstances, the details of which I will not elaborate now. But she has indeed passed an enjoyable sojourn under our humble roof."

Moreau forced his racing mind to something resembling calm— or at least neutrality. He took a breath and offered Giroux a genuine grin. "The world seems to grow smaller by the day." He looked at his host with as much nonchalance as he could manage. "Is there any chance the lady is here now?"

Giroux dismissed a passing server with a curt wave of his hand. "Regretfully, no; the young lady has traveled to spend the Sabbath with the Ursuline nuns in the city. I understand she wishes to spend the night there."

Moreau swallowed his disappointment with a taut smile. "How noble of her."

Giroux nodded thoughtfully, then looked at his guests with an expression that turned somber. "Well, my friends, this has been a wonderful visit, but I'm afraid I must tend to my Sunday duties and begin preparing for the week ahead. And, mademoiselle," he said, looking at Antonia, "I will see to what we discussed about your hand, but I must urge you in the strongest possible terms not to go pursuing those…swamp folk. Even if you believe they've coaxed him to run away, Le Marais is no place for decent folk."

Antonia looked at him with wide eyes but nodded her understanding. Moreau cast a quick glance at her, considering her expression something akin to a babe in the woods.

"Now," their host continued, "before I send you away, I must remind you—these are dangerous times. The English have been spotted at the Rigolets, and we expect them to come upon the city within weeks, possibly days."

Moreau leaned back in his chair as he took in the news, scolding himself for nearly forgetting that he would be returning to a city in a state of war. "Furthermore, those brutes from Barataria have been seen openly walking the city streets, and that rogue Lafitte is believed to be hiding out on one of the plantations. He's not someone you wish to come across in the swamps or bayous, and his men seem bolder than ever. So, I would advise you to hasten back to the city."

Moreau nodded his understanding, more eager than ever to be off.

"Allow me to see you out."

A strong wind blew through the trees in the front yard as Moreau approached the wagon, and the looming clouds he had seen earlier now hovered directly above in a bulging, grey mass, threatening a heavy burst of rain at any moment. Antonia had to hold her hat firmly to keep it on her head, and Giroux fastened a button to keep the chill wind from his chest. Moreau, looking for signs of wobbling, watched Will mount his horse. To his surprise, the boy seemed steadier in the saddle than on his feet, as he'd nearly tumbled down the stairs.

Moreau glanced back at the house and saw several men looking down from the balcony, Lionel Benton among them. Moreau looked at him, thinking himself slightly paranoid as he searched the overseer for any sign of suspicion. He had sensed something amiss from their first introduction, and the beating he had witnessed only confirmed to Moreau that Benton was like those he had seen in armies across the Continent who saw cruelty as a game to be enjoyed, and those beneath them as objects for amusement—often violent amusement.

A moment later Will Keane rode his horse across the lane and halted beside the wagon. Moreau looked down at Giroux as thunder rumbled somewhere in the distance. "I thank you for sharing your table with us."

The planter nodded, offered another smile, then took a few steps so that he stood just below Moreau. "You are welcome at my home anytime, Monsieur Lenoir."

"Thank you, monsieur."

Giroux silenced him with a raised hand. He then gripped the wagon's railing and leaned closer, speaking in a low voice. "The English will be here soon; one never knows what ideas they might inspire among our acolytes. Uprisings have occurred on this very road, and who knows what could happen should they embrace violence again? That is why we pray General Jackson arrives with his men soon. We must protect our city. As one of Napoleon's men, I hope you will lend us your aid."

Moreau peered down with an attentive expression, though truthfully his only desire was to depart before the storm broke over their heads.

Giroux leaned aside to look at Antonia and took a step back. "In the meantime, take care of this one," he said in a louder voice, smiling wryly. "Don't let her talk you into anything foolish. She may cause more mischief than she lets on. And please, monsieur, visit us again at your earliest convenience." He stepped aside and waved them off, turning back to the house as Moreau snapped the reins. As they passed beneath the live oak trees, the three travelers sat in silence, each lost in their own thoughts.

Dearest Maman,

Having passed my fourth week at this estate—what the Americans and Creoles call a manor or plantation—I can begin to paint a description of it, which is but one of many situated along the Mississippi River north of New Orleans, called the German Coast. I don't know where such a name came from, as one quickly finds in this region a decidedly French culture. If one can look past the accent, which is humorously rustic, the locals and their Negroes all speak our language, and carry on many of our customs. Anyhow, the name of the plantation on which I am currently housed is Le Mouton, which the owner says was named after his great-grandfather, who came down from Arcadia and founded a farm on this land with just a single lamb in his possession, which has grown to one of the foremost agrarian enterprises of the territory.

The proprietor of this "manoir pastoral" is a man between fifty and sixty years called Emile Louis-Jean Giroux, whose ancestors originated from La Rochelle. A fascinating man to be sure, he has been as kindly a host as I could have ever dreamed, after his men plucked me from that ghastly cypress swamp. But more of that later—for now I wish to tell you that our host has taken me on more than one turn about his grounds, which are quite enchanting. I wish you could see this charming little Eden, Maman, and I hope someday you shall honor me with a visit. Le Mouton is but a little way back from the river road that leads east to New Orleans, which is bounded by an unfortunate levy, which spoils any view below the roof of the house. The house is a simple but charming three-story mansion in colonial style, buttressed with columns and a wrapping veranda. It is of a fine, yellow color, and inside one finds an assortment of peculiarities. The dining room is small and also rather simple compared to our own, but its charm makes up for any simplicity. We spend much of our time dining with our host, with up to seven meals served at supper (the food is fine, but very different to what we are accustomed to). A room for the ladies—of which there are few apart from me and Elyse—adjoins the billiard room, which is pleasant if one doesn't mind smoke or the sight of tobacco being spit into large bowls. The Creoles take snuff, but some of the Americans prefer setting large globs of unrefined tobacco into their cheeks—the sight makes one fairly nauseous. The bedrooms are perfectly suitable, one for me and one for Elyse. The entire ground floor is composed of kitchens, pantries, and storerooms, with one room dedicated to plating food brought in from another building, where it is cooked. Creoles often have strange habits, like putting cakes on the graves of loved ones on All Saints' Day. I suppose the Americans have their own oddities as well. The Creoles look at them with some suspicion, calling them "riverboat roughnecks" or "buckskin hill people." It's all quite odd—yet delightful.

On the grounds there are several workshops, outbuildings, and an ever-active sugar mill. The yard is full to bursting with oak trees, twisted cypress trees, indigo plants, and all manner of shrubbery. Workhouses and slave cabins take up much space, but apart from that it is a fine plot of land that I wish you could see, though a strange thing happened yesterday. As I was walking along the bank of the swamp in back of the grounds, I removed my shoes and made to dip my toes into the water, which seems foolish now given how grimy it looked; regardless, the foreman took my hand and fairly wrenched me away from the bank, mumbling in his accent about some "monster" in the water, that apparently is dangerous to people. I suppose no home is without its oddities.

Most of the labor is done by the Negro hands called "acolytes," who are always hard at work on the sugar mills, or soon planting the cane, or salting meat, gardening, cooking, and so on. Monsieur Giroux has a rather fascinating way of maintaining order among his slaves, dividing them into ranks according to seniority and experience; good behavior is rewarded with merit awards, while impudence and laziness are punished, as is proper. It is quite endearing of the old man to take such attention to their well-being. Strangely, though, I've heard talk of some going missing, running away into the swamps—if one could believe such a thing. Why would they wish to leave such a pleasant home? To what sort of place would they go? But never mind such pointless concerns.

Oh, Maman, I think you would be proud of this little adventure I'm having. I miss home, but I find the charms of this place almost irresistible. I cannot remember a time I've felt so happy. Wild and virgin, yet it retains enough of our Christian customs that I can only call it beguiling. I hope to make new friends, and perhaps chance upon my friend from Guadeloupe, if he is still here.

To conclude, please don't think that I am neglecting my business with the Balas rubies. With them as security, we shall survive whatever infidelities father scorns us with. The business will sort itself out in the end.

Do write me again soon.

Lovingly yours,
C.

CHAPTER 7

River Road, Mississippi Right Bank, Louisiana
December 1, 1814

Deep peals of thunder rolled over the flat plantation fields skirting the right bank of the Mississippi, while gusts of cold air blew from the east, gently swaying the leafless trees lining the river road. By some miracle, at least to Moreau, the inevitable deluge that the dark clouds overhead promised had been held at bay thus far. He drove the horse at a steady trot, passing homesteads and sprawling meadows that looked strangely picturesque under the prematurely dark afternoon skies. Sporadic bursts of lightning flashed in the distance, and a creeping mist began to obscure the view on either side of the road.

About a quarter of an hour after leaving the plantation, Antonia lolled her head, sighing quietly, which drew a glance from Moreau, who had been silently scolding himself for neglecting to bring a cigar for the day's journey. Perhaps it was the irritability of his craving, or a lingering disorientation from the violent scene he'd witnessed; either way, he turned aside from her without a word, refusing to engage in the conversation he suspected she desired. Sensing his reticence, Antonia sighed again. "Well, *I* think it was a charming home."

A moment passed without a reply, then Will's horse whinnied, and the horse pulling the wagon responded with a rough shake of its head. Still, Moreau said nothing. Antonia pulled her shawl tighter around her shoulders and looked away. "Well, at least *one* of us appreciated the hospitality shown by our host. I think Monsieur Giroux, though somewhat…coarse…is a fine gentleman. Clearly, he has been affected by the loss of his wife, and I think that's perfectly reasonable." She adjusted her hat as a sharp thunderclap rumbled overhead. Will's horse bucked slightly, and the boy patted its neck and whispered soothingly to calm the animal down.

"I agree, Miss Milroy," Will said at last, gently kicking the horse to get it moving again. "I haven't enjoyed a meal like that since…" His words trailed off into a mumble.

Moreau tightened the reins to slow the wagon. "Your purple lips show us how much you enjoyed it," he said irritably. "You smell like a spilled bottle of wine."

Will's shoulders drooped slightly, and he kept his eyes on the road ahead.

"There's no need to bully him," Antonia said indignantly. "Everyone seemed to enjoy themself except you. If you haven't anything polite to say, perhaps you might drive us in silence."

Moreau grunted, removing his hat and setting it on the wooden seat between them. He then peered at the boy, whose lips were moving silently while his downcast eyes followed the wheels of the wagon, unwilling to meet Moreau's. A strange sight then struck him—a dense shroud of fog had enveloped the trio, completely obscuring everything to the rear of the wagon and even the trees on either side.

Antonia muttered a few words, drawing Moreau out of his daydream. "And while I wouldn't consider our journey a *complete* loss," she said casually, "I would hate to return to the city, and my mother and father, without exhausting all options."

"What options?"

She tilted her head thoughtfully. "If I know Edward, he will not have gone far. By now he's had time to reflect on his running away and likely concluded, as I have, that it was a foolish thing to do. In fact, there is somewhere nearby I think he might have gone. It's barely out of the way. I think we ought to try." She looked down as she put her gloves back on. Moreau said nothing, only peered up at the sky as if expecting it to empty on their heads any minute. "If we find him," she went on, "I should be extremely grateful for your assistance, and I would be obliged to help you search for your woman. *If* we find him."

Thinking of Celeste and whatever liaisons she might have had, or might still have, with the corsair captain, Moreau found himself suddenly reminded of the man's warning. Three days until he returned. Moreau did not fear the prospect of confronting Araza; nevertheless, facing a corsair captain guarded by dozens of rabid cutthroats seemed unwise. The sooner he found Celeste the better. He turned to Antonia with a slight nod, turning back before he saw her grateful smile. "Thank you, monsieur."

Another sharp thunderclap sounded, closer than before, and Will urged his horse slightly closer to the wagon. Antonia groaned softly, mumbling something about Louisiana weather being worse than the Caribbean. Moreau looked over at Will. "Come closer," he said in a firm voice. The boy urged his mount forward, and Moreau peered sideways at him. "Tell me what a lad of your age could have done to become *excommunicated* by your fellows in Barataria." Will's eyes went wide and he swallowed hard, but his posture remained steady in the saddle. Besides hiding and stealing, riding seemed to be the only thing the boy did with any grace or ease. "Well?"

"I...I've..." Will stammered, drawing in a breath. "I've been... branded a coward." The last word caught in his throat, and he glanced at the two in the wagon before lowering his eyes.

Moreau scowled. "What?"

After a moment the raised boy his head slightly and continued in a quiet voice. "It's true. My captain, Juanillo, branded me a coward in front of the crew. I survived a battle—but afterward was thrown overboard by the crew."

Moreau looked ahead with a pensive squint. "You survived a battle and were thrown overboard. Why would they do that?" He turned back to the boy, who stared ahead with a dazed look.

"They plucked me from the streets a year or so ago," Will answered, his voice growing more confident. "My mother brought me from Ireland, so I was told, but she died when I was little.

My earliest memories were of the other children on the streets. When they brought me to Grande-Terre, in Barataria, I'd never done much more than fire buckshot at squirrels or hogs, but they gave me a bit of training. Cannon crew mostly. I was placed on the third starboard gun on Captain Juanillo's ship, *Saturnia*."

"Maybe a week ago," he continued quietly, "we came upon a Spanish schooner in the Gulf, near the mouth of the river. As soon as it saw us, it drove right for us, not waiting to be attacked. After our first shot, I handled the sponge well enough. But perhaps a minute or so into the fight, the noise became deafening and it became impossible to hear—the smoke made it impossible to see. My breath gave out, and my hands would not stop shaking. I thought I would be sick. A man on the second gun took a ball of round shot to his leg, and it sent him spinning. When he hit the deck, he splashed blood across my clothes, and his leg was nowhere to be seen—just a bloody mess. It took him a few seconds to realize what had happened; when he did, he began screaming and hollering like a banshee. I cupped my hands to my ears, but I could still hear him. My knees buckled, and I dropped to the deck. I laid still until the fighting was over."

Will halted his tale and blinked several times, looking at Moreau for a moment before turning away. The Frenchman glanced at Antonia, who was staring at the boy with a somber expression. "That evening," Will murmured, "I was brought before the captain, and after a few words with the first mate and the leader of my gun crew, I was taken by the collar and brought to the quarterdeck. From there I was...*jettisoned*. I kicked and swam for hours—I don't know how many—until I became exhausted. Only floating bits of wreckage from the schooner kept me alive. In the morning, your ship came."

For a while only the sounds of creaking wheels and clinking of the horse's harness broke the silence. As if aware of his shame, Will allowed his horse to drift a few paces back, and said nothing more.

"You've seen battle and lived to tell of it," Moreau said at last. "That's more than most men can claim."

"And what about you?" Antonia said, her voice half startling Moreau. She nodded at his missing arm. "You look as if you've seen fighting; did you not feel fear?"

"No one is without *some* fear when they first see battle," Moreau said matter-of-factly. "Even the brave ones. But when you've mastered it, it goes from a dragon breathing fire in your face to a growling mutt chained to a post. It has no power over you—if you don't allow it." He turned to Will with a hard look. "This one simply wasn't stuck in long enough to master himself. Your gun commander should have hauled you to your feet and struck you back to your senses. I would have. Any rate, you're still alive; handle yourself better the next time."

Will still wore a forlorn expression. "No, monsieur," he said dejectedly. "I don't think I would be allowed back in. When you're thrown over the side of your ship, it is bad luck for everyone aboard to take you back. That's why I followed you out here. If I serve you, perhaps I'll find a chance to face danger again...without succumbing to cowardice."

Moreau stared at him but didn't demand further explanation. A moment later Antonia gently tapped his shoulder and pointed a finger at the road ahead. Moreau peered through the gloom and then saw what she was indicating: a narrow track leading off to the right.

"That's our turn," she said quietly, staring ahead with a somber expression and avoiding his gaze. "It's not far. I'll be quick as I can."

With a resigned grunt, Moreau turned the wagon onto the road. Will's horse bucked several times but followed as the boy brought it under control.

By now the sun had lowered to the horizon, but the thick fog hid any sign of it and made distinguishing anything beyond a dozen paces all but impossible. Moreau kept the pace slow to keep the horses fresh, knowing they had traveled a decent way and still had some miles to go. Clutching her shawl closer, Antonia shot Moreau a quick glance. "Could we move along a bit faster?"

"Perhaps. If you ask politely."

Fidgeting in her seat, Antonia rolled her eyes. "Just go faster."

Moreau craned his neck, fixing her with a mocking expression. "In a hurry, are we?" He looked back at Will, who returned his gaze with an expression bordering on mischievous.

"Mademoiselle," Moreau said in a voice that resembled the Louisiana accent he'd heard thus far, "I haven't gotten dressed up as a sugarcane-trading dandy just to be insolently ordered about." He saw that her expression had soured; in fact, Antonia appeared on the verge of being sick. Another roll of thunder added to the gloom of her expression. "What is it?" Moreau snarked. "Not used to being out in the cypress swamps after nightfall?"

Will chuckled softly, and for once Moreau did not give him an angry look. "All right," Moreau said at last, snapping the reins to urge the horse to a trot. The fog lingered over the road, however, and he kept a cautious eye ahead. Will trotted easily up to the wagon, shoulders still slumped but his face less dour. Moreau tilted his head. "I think the rougarou has her worried."

The boy chuckled, a whistle passing through his open teeth. "Maybe it's the swamp folk," he replied.

Moreau placed his hat back on his head. "Perhaps they've some magic beans they could sell us to ward off evil spirits."

Will's torso shook in a quick fit of high-pitched laughter. Moreau avoided looking at Antonia for a few seconds, half expecting her to hit him square in the jaw. After a moment, he peered aside and noticed that she didn't appear angry at all. She bit her lower lip and stared ahead, as if she'd seen a ghost. "Pardon, mademoiselle," Moreau said. "I'm just overcome with high spirits at this lovely country we're traveling through." He glanced to either side of the road, his smile slowly dropping from his features. "Quite an unfriendly-looking place—and I've seen Poland in winter."

He pulled on the reins to slow the horse, now unable to see much beyond the animal's ears. In such conditions they would not be able to see an oncoming rider until they had all but barreled into each other. After a minute or so of silence, Antonia cleared her throat and leaned forward in the seat. "Monsieur," she said, her voice trembling slightly, "I am sorry." Moreau looked at her, his customary hard face returning.

"You're sorry for what?"

Antonia peered ahead as if looking for something. Turning to check on Will, Moreau noticed his horse's ears were angled straight up, its neck arched and rigid—sure signs of nervousness. He brought the wagon to a halt and turned slowly toward Antonia, who was staring ahead with a glazed expression. Her right hand gripped the siderail with white knuckles, and she seemed frozen in place.

Moreau looked at the road ahead with a frown. The horse pawed the ground nervously, its ears now upright as well. Sitting as still as possible, Moreau noticed the complete and utter silence around them. Not a bird, not a frog, not an insect buzzing past. Absolute stillness. He exhaled slowly. "Where have you taken us?"

～～～

Moreau saw her freeze at the faint sound off to their right. Sitting upright and licking his lips, Moreau instinctively reached down to his belt for a saber that was not there, then slid his hand across his belly for a pistol that was not there either. Cursing silently, he turned his head and strained to listen. A moment later it came again: a *snap*. Barely perceptible, perhaps a twig cracking or a disturbed leaf. Whatever it was, he knew it had come from a man. Exhaling slowly, he looked behind the wagon, but all he saw was Will on his horse and the shroud of fog beyond.

"Shit."

Will looked at him with wide eyes, then jerked his head to either side of the road. The foolish lad was at least aware enough to know when danger was approaching. Moreau shifted his weight to the balls of his feet and leaned slightly forward, ignoring Antonia's uneasy look. The nerve of the woman, to lead them here and then look expectantly at him now. He wanted to grab her by the collar and snarl until she wilted, but his instincts had been honed in far too many dangerous moments to yield to base desires now.

Moreau slowly lowered himself into a crouch. "Whoever you are," he said, careful not to raise his voice too much, "I suggest you show yourself."

Silence.

He motioned for Will to dismount and come closer to the wagon. The boy quickly complied. Moreau saw a flicker of light somewhere up ahead, but the fog made it difficult to tell how far away it was. A moment passed and then another stab of light pierced the grey gloom. A torch. It swayed slowly from side to side, and then another appeared beside it. A few seconds later a third appeared. Moreau's brow furrowed as he pointed out the torches to Will, then checked for others creeping up beside or behind them. His instinct was correct: to their right and left, flashes of light could be seen—and they were coming closer.

Once again reaching for a pistol he did not have, Moreau racked his brain for a weapon he might use. He looked in the wagon bed but saw nothing but a few pieces of decayed straw and chaff. He cursed quietly. Like a wolf caught in a trap that knows it can't escape without ruinously harming itself, Moreau knew his game was up—at least for the moment. With a woman and a youth in his care, capture was the only option. His nostrils flared as he let out a sigh, slowly dropping his weight back onto the seat. As the flaming torches came closer, and the men bearing them became distinguishable, Moreau grabbed Will's collar and, without a word, hauled him up onto the driver's seat beside him. The boy didn't struggle—nor did his wide eyes turn from the approaching figures.

The sound of pelting rain broke the eerie silence, and voices could be heard from all sides, quiet but sharp and purposeful. The torches flickered in the sharp gusts of wind, refusing to be snuffed out as their bearers came ever closer. There were several men, perhaps dozens. The prospect of giving in without a fight almost caused Moreau's head to sag, but he fought back the urge and pulled his shoulders back, staring at the nearest man with a stern expression.

"If they have firearms, don't move," he whispered. "If it's knives or clubs and they try to kill us, I'll jump the nearest one. Go in different directions; find your way out through the swamp." Moreau hoped his companions heard more conviction in his words than he felt, but he sensed they knew the reality of their situation, and didn't look for a sign that either had heard him.

The cold rain fell furiously now, soaking into their clothes and causing even the nervous horses' heads to droop. Oblivious to the downpour, Moreau removed his hat. Within seconds his hair was soaked, plastered to his scalp in curling black strands, revealing the white line of scar tissue that ran along the left side of his head. He eyed the nearest man as he approached the wagon, the torchlight revealing dark, wet skin in a glaze of deep bronze. His wide eyes looked like bright, white marbles, contrasting starkly with the darkness around him, almost seeming to glow in the flickering torchlight.

It seemed every other man held a musket or long-bladed knife of some sort. A quick count showed six muskets—that Moreau could see. As more men came into view, he observed that some were shirtless, others wore simple white smocks. Loose-fitting pantaloons covered their legs. Some walked with bare feet, but most appeared to have wrapped strips of cloth or hide around their soles. He had heard that the natives of this land painted their faces before departing for a hunt or going into battle. Although it was difficult to be sure in the darkness, these men did not appear to be natives, or "Indians," as the Americans called them, but Negroes. Necklaces with pendants or what looked like pearls dangled from several of their necks, which drew Moreau to conclude that they were not recently escaped convicts or runaways—at least not all of them. Given their number and seemingly coordinated approach, he guessed they had inhabited these environs for some time.

By now he counted twelve men encircling the wagon, with more flickers of torchlight visible at various distances behind this closer circle. He thought he heard a few words spoken in his own language, but he could not make out much. The man closest to their left passed his torch to the one beside him and took a step toward to the wagon. "What are you doing here?" he asked in a clear voice in English.

Moreau did not hold his gaze on the man for long, shifting his eyes left and right, alert for any sudden movement. The man who had spoken stood in silence as the rain soaked everything in sight. At last Moreau turned and looked down. "Per'aps we make a wrong turn."

Standing beside the one who had spoken was a stocky, well-built man of average height, with short black hair. Without a word, he stepped forward and sprang up into the driver's seat in front of Moreau, causing Antonia to cry out. Will, although shaking, moved to rise to his feet—perhaps in defense of Moreau—but the man grabbed his shoulder and shoved him forcefully back into his seat like a sack. The man then turned to Moreau, his broad, grimacing face and flaring nostrils giving him the look of an angry lion. He reached out a muscular arm and clutched Moreau's throat in a cruelly strong grip, and for a moment he thought the man had crushed his windpipe.

"Answer him true, or keep your fucking mouth shut." He snarled the words perhaps an inch from Moreau's face, his breath warm and foul. Moreau felt his cheeks flushing as he gasped for air but kept his eyes on his assailant. After what seemed an eternity, the man let out a sour breath, spraying rainwater over Moreau's face as he removed his hand from his throat. Moreau gasped, his chest heaving as he fought to regain his breath. The stocky man stared at Will for a moment before jumping down from the wagon, his feet squishing on the sodden ground.

Beside Moreau, Antonia slowly uncoiled from her curled-up position and looked at the men around them, and for a moment her pale face made it look like she would faint. A short burst of nervous laughter broke the silence, and she muttered in a quiet voice. "Oh thank God."

Moreau shot her a perplexed look, then turned to see what had caused her visible relief. Another of the men stepped forward.

Slightly taller than the one who had seized Moreau, he was also well-built, but his face held a remarkably different expression. As he stepped closer, bearing a torch in his left hand, he looked up at Antonia with a grin. He halted beside the horse and nodded. "Antonia Milroy." His smile slipped as he turned to look at his fellows and, speaking in French, said, "The girl must have lost her goddamned mind."

Behind him the others broke out in fits of loud laughter. The man holding the torch looked at Antonia and his smile returned, only to Moreau, it looked more ominous than happy. Another man, older-looking than the others and with a half-bald head, walked forward and stared at Antonia with noticeable interest, squinting appraisingly.

"This is her?" he said at last. The other man nodded.

Moreau looked at Antonia, who still wore a nervous smile and seemed to be working up the pluck to say something. Wiping water from his eyes, he looked back at the men, who seemed to find humor, perhaps curiosity, in the situation. He moved to speak but was preempted by Antonia, who called out in a faltering voice.

"Edward, I...I thought I might find..." she said, her voice catching. "I've come to tell you...that I forgive you for running away." She broke off as if she wanted to say more, but perhaps thought better of it. The man Moreau presumed to be Edward looked at her with wide eyes, his head nodding slightly forward and his mouth open. The man who had choked Moreau spat on the ground.

"Come on," he said quietly to Edward. "Let's get back. Y'all can have the boy, the man is mine for the knife."

Antonia was the first to climb down from the wagon, and a man on either side grabbed her elbows and led her past a line of men standing with torches. They glared at her with hard faces, heads turning to follow as she walked past. Moreau kept his eyes on her until she was out of sight, then he climbed down. He was immediately grabbed, more forcefully than Antonia had been, and shoved repeatedly as he walked past the line of men, torchlight flickering over their fearsome faces. Moreau turned his attention to Antonia and felt a stab of pity, a sensation he had not felt in quite some time, for both the young woman and the boy—which at least kept his thoughts from his own predicament. He would need a clear mind if he was to get them out of this mess.

For several minutes they walked silently away from the road and into a dense swamp. The high canopy of cypress trees provided little shelter from the rain, which poured down now in an unforgiving deluge. The steady pace of their march helped keep Moreau from shivering, but the cold air was made worse by the soaked clothes that stuck to his chest and back. He turned back to look for a sign of the boy, but a sharp smack to the side of his head brought his eyes back forward, where they remained for the remainder of the trek.

He wiped a hand across his dripping face and pinched his eyes, recalling the last time he had endured captivity. The memory had never fully returned, as he'd had half his arm torn off and taken six rounds of grapeshot to his leg, hip, arm, and scalp at the time. The severity of the wounds had wrenched him out of consciousness as Russian and French cavalry thundered across the field all around him—and over him. When he felt his body moving again, he wondered how his comrades had found him amid the chaos and slaughter—only to realize the voices he was hearing were Russian. He knew he must have been wounded horribly, surely fatally, but they had carried him from the field anyway. Only later did he learn that he had been recognized as the leader of more than three suicidal charges by his outnumbered dragoon squadron against nearly a division of enemy cavalry. In the ensuing three days, he would be asked countless questions by enemy officers, but rarely offered them more than a painful, fevered ramble about wishing to die. In truth, he had been wounded so many times—to the brink of death—that each episode brought a vague but undeniable disappointment that he had been denied the right to pass on. To approach the threshold of eternity willingly only to be brought back to an agonizing reality of torn flesh and terrible pain was a fate he would not wish to experience ever again. However it came, let it be quick.

But somehow he felt far from death here and now, sensing only that something...*severe*...awaited them. Torture? Perhaps. He could face the prospect—he was no stranger to suffering. Captivity? That idea did not particularly disturb him either; he could endure that while biding his time for an escape. But another instinct continued to tug at him, one he found difficult to dispel: a sharp stab of guilt at the thought of that young woman in the hands of these men. What they might do to her when they reached wherever they were going was not something he cared to think about, difficult as it was to think of much else. The boy too. Would they beat him? Kill him? Turn the tables and hold him in bondage? He could not shake that thought either. He blew water from his upper lip with a frustrated sigh, setting one booted foot after the other as they tramped silently into the darkness of the swamp.

CHAPTER 8

Le Marais (Cypress Swamp), Outside New Orleans
December 1, 1814

The first indication they were nearing their destination came when two men broke off from either side of the column and strode out of sight into a nearby thicket. A minute or so later, several voices called out indistinctly as a loud rustling of bushes could be heard over the rainfall, which had mercifully slackened a little since their capture. The cane palms swiped at Moreau's knees and legs as he passed through the vegetation, and it occurred to him how much noise each of them was making. He wondered what such a thing could have been planted for, why men hiding in a swamp would place such a conspicuous obstacle outside their dwelling—unless its very purpose was to give them warning of intruders.

As he stepped out of the leafy barrier, Moreau peered down at his legs and feet, which had been protected from the sharp palms and fronds by his gawky, almost knee-high planter's boots. Most of his body ached from the cold and the soaked clothes clinging to his goosefleshed skin, but he realized his feet were completely dry. Wiggling his toes as he marched on the half-frozen ground, he felt grateful that at least a part of his body still felt warm.

As they walked on, Moreau noticed a tall cypress tree with a plank of weathered wood nailed to its trunk. It read: *Woe betide the white man who crosses these bounds.*

A low chuckle came from one of the men walking behind Moreau.

"Yuh come to de wrong place, bwoy."

Despite the obvious peril of his situation, Moreau nevertheless walked past the sign without any feeling of dread, which would have been excusable given the circumstances. On the contrary, the sign seemed something of a challenge—not unlike the sight of an enemy banner on a battlefield. Nothing to be afraid of or quail from, just a signal that dangerous foes were present; accordingly, any other consideration quickly fell to insignificance. In fact, the reminder of danger seemed to have cleared his head and brought on a heightened focus that, on occasions beyond count, he had found almost intoxicating.

Their pace slowed as they came into an area of cleared land and what appeared to be a small village: a semicircle of low, thatched-roof huts with doors facing toward the middle of the clearing. Most appeared to be humble dwellings constructed of sticks and sod, each with a steep-angled thatched roof. Several were partially covered by sheets of cotton or canvas, with wooden buckets beneath—presumably to catch rainwater runoff. A little farther stood several other buildings, each raised perhaps a foot above the ground on vertical logs that seemed to serve as stilts, likely to protect against flooding. During their ride along the river road, Moreau and his companions had passed a handful of houses with this feature, which seemed logical in areas close to bodies of water. He would not have expected to see such an architectural feature here, but necessity often had the last word—especially among those fleeing into swamps to find freedom.

As they entered the village, he noticed several small horticulture plots abutting the houses. Long rows of topsoil flecked with small mounds indicated where crops were planted in these small gardens, belying his assumption that this was just a temporary refuge. This was a home. As if to confirm this notion, a flock of chickens ran past, clucking and pecking at the dirt and fluttering small-feathered wings in short bursts of flight. The foul, soupy smell of the swamp during their trek quickly gave way to the more familiar smells of village life: herbs, spices, manure, human sweat, and something cooking in a large pot over a nearby fire. Inside one of the makeshift pens were several large domestic pigs, which grunted as they nuzzled their snouts along the mud-spattered ground. There were also several goats and at least one white-and-black-spotted milk cow inside its own pen. Stacks of chopped wood were scattered throughout the village, and the sight of three small pirogues grounded near the distant huts confirmed that they could not be far from a water source. Surely this much domestication required a good deal of pilfering from the city or the local plantations, and Moreau guessed that those responsible for procurement did not lack for boldness.

Moreau noticed several individuals he had not seen yet approaching his captors. Groups of women in twos and threes came out of the houses or drifted in quietly from other parts of the swamp; likely there were more dwellings out of sight. He watched as the villagers came to join the men, mothers holding the hands of their children or whispering to one another. Most wore simple dresses, with shawls or scarves around their shoulders and their heads wrapped with the *tignon* covering that seemed ubiquitous among the Black women Moreau had seen in the city. The children all went barefoot, leaning out from behind their mothers to get a look at what had caused this gathering. Around Moreau the circle of onlookers had grown larger, and a subdued murmur bustled about the village.

Brought in last was Will, who was given a sharp shove to join Moreau at the front of the group. The women eyed the two with curious expressions, muttering quietly or pointing at them. The men glared at Moreau or stared ahead silently. There seemed to be a collective feeling of anticipation, as if everyone was awaiting the arrival of something or someone. Moreau had yet to see any sign of Antonia. The thought of her in imminent danger or subjected to violence brought a momentary skip to his heart, but he reminded himself that she was the reason for the detour into this cursed, fog-shrouded bayou to begin with. On the other hand, had it been just Will and him, they'd likely have been slaughtered at the wagon. Realizing his thoughts were racing unhelpfully, he willed his mind to stillness as he cast a careful glance around to get his bearings—in case escape was necessary. Or possible.

In truth, he felt little appetite for escape, at least not for the moment. Knowing that their "trespassing" had been a mistake gave Moreau a feeling of righteous indignation. He brought no threat to this village; in fact, he had absolutely no interest in these people at all. What right had they to seize him and hold him as a captive? His mind hardened as he thought of how many of these primitives he could kill if he attempted to fight his way out. They might try to intimidate him; they might even kill him—but they would not have the satisfaction of seeing him tremble. If it came to it, he would show them how a legionnaire of the empire died—taking scores of them with him, spitting defiance and blood as he breathed his last.

As if sensing his rebellious thoughts, the man who had seized his throat on the wagon walked past, muttering a few words in French: "And I'll be the one to kill you…" was all Moreau heard, but the man's ferocious stare drove home the point. Moreau made a mental note to avoid that one if he was forced to fight his way out. But if it did come to that, he would die fighting—in lieu of burning, filleting, or any other manner of horror that these people surely inflicted on the white men they captured. He glanced at Will, who stared ahead with a distant expression while his knees wobbled visibly. To the boy's credit, he seemed at least to be making an attempt to show courage—if not entirely successfully.

Tempering his more aggressive thoughts, Moreau considered Antonia and Will as subordinates relying on his rank and experience, and he resolved not to instigate anything foolish, as he had done so often, until he had expended every effort trying to convince these people to release them. Even if it meant offering himself to stay in their place. It was at that moment that he saw her. Two men brought Antonia to the front of the crowd perhaps thirty paces away. The men stood still and silent as statues, while the women scrutinized her, some muttering unfriendly words in her direction. Her chest rose and fell in smooth but slightly quickened breaths.

Clearly she was frightened, but she kept an upright bearing, her chin raised slightly in a show of subtle defiance. In that moment, Moreau thought she looked beautiful.

A hush fell over the villagers at the appearance of a woman, who drifted into the circle from somewhere behind. She walked slowly, accompanied by a slightly taller man, who wore no shirt and whose lower half was covered by a cloth just slightly larger than a loincloth. In his right hand he held a long, flat-bladed dagger that glinted as it caught a reflection of torchlight. The woman held in her left hand a large gourd, from which several small sticks, or perhaps animal bones, dangled on cords and clattered softly as they swayed in the cold breeze. The pair avoided looking at Moreau as they approached, finally halting in front of a hut on the far side of the cleared ground.

The top of the woman's head was wrapped in a tignon headdress like many of the others, though hers was a fine orange cloth with a shining jewel, perhaps a large pearl, nestled in its front folds. Two large hoop earrings dangled from her ears, while an assortment of beaded necklaces adorned her neck. Her simple white dress revealed a subtly plunging neckline, and an auburn shawl was wrapped around her shoulders. She was of average height, but her very presence seemed to command attention—and obedience. Her eyes drifted unhurriedly over the group before finally settling on Moreau, whom she scrutinized with an unreadable expression. Ignoring his youthful companion altogether, she eventually gave a barely perceptible nod, and one of the men waiting nearby spread a small blanket on the muddy ground. She collected her dress in front of her and sat down, crossing her legs.

Behind her stood the shirtless man, who was gazing down at the long blade in his hand. If the woman gave an impression of stately serenity, he seemed like a snake, coiled but alert, his sinewy body hinting at the capacity for rapid, violent movement. From somewhere behind him, he produced a black top hat, which he placed on a lush head of braided hair that fell almost to his waist. A cross and several necklaces made of small bones dangling from thin pieces of twine now draped his neck. After the woman had settled herself, the fellow shot a fierce glare at the group, and the muttering turned to dead silence. He smiled then, revealing a mouth of brown and yellow teeth, some perhaps wooden; in the darkness it was difficult to tell. He paced several steps in a slow circle, looking out over the crowd as he did so. Ending up beside the seated woman, he mumbled a few words in a strange tongue before backing up to the hut, letting out a loud breath, and sliding down to the muddy ground. His head, still bearing the incongruous top hat, drooped between his shoulders, and he did not move again.

At length the woman raised her head slightly. "Few who come here uninvited," she said in French, "ever go out again." She spoke softly, but her voice carried a deep resonance that belied her youthful appearance. She seemed to Moreau to be just short of forty years of age, but from a distance it was difficult to tell. Turning to look at Antonia, she held the young woman's gaze for a moment before her lips thinned in a faint smile. The men guarding Antonia pushed her forward, and she took several steps into the circle of open ground.

"Traitor!" someone yelled.

"Mulatto whore!" another cackled, drawing several hoots of laughter.

"Death tuh di masters!"

"An fi dem ooman dem!"

The insults flew freely now, most in French or a heavily accented Caribbean dialect. A general surge of bodies accompanied the invectives, both men and women stomping their feet and waving their fists at Antonia. One of the men pointed his torch at her while shouting for her to burn. The woman sitting on the ground watched the scene unfold, her reaction calm to the point of stillness. A woman took a step toward Antonia and twisted her face angrily, hacking up and sending a gob of spittle that landed on her dress. Moreau knew there was little he could do that would result in anything short of him being beaten or killed, so he restrained himself and watched the outbursts in frustrated silence. Eventually the seated woman raised a hand, and the commotion ceased abruptly. In spite of her small frame, she spoke in a commanding voice: "You come on the *Ashé* of rain and thunder. What is your name?"

Antonia, who at first did not seem to notice that the question had been directed at her, cleared her throat. "My name is Antonia Milroy." Her voice was somewhat hoarse, but she spoke clearly. "I come from New Orleans, and I am a free woman—" She flinched as she was interrupted by an outburst from the others.

"Eh, gyal," one of the men cried out, "did she aks yuh weh yuh come from?"

The man who had grabbed Moreau's throat took several steps forward. "If you speak out of turn again, we gon' strip them clothes off you and put you in our underground *barracoon*. Don't nobody hear screams that come from down there." He fixed Antonia with a forceful but calm expression that made it plain he was not threatening her, simply stating what would happen next. Antonia swallowed hard.

"Antonia Milroy," the seated woman stated flatly, "of New Orleans. You are free?"

"I am," Antonia replied, somewhat defensively. Her lips moved as if she had more to say, but she wisely held back. To Moreau it looked as if most of the onlookers were now leaning forward, willing her to say more than necessary. The woman on the ground squinted slightly as she examined Antonia, and Moreau thought he saw her cheek twitch slightly. The man by the hut still sat unmoving, his head drooped on his chest. A goat bleated noisily behind one of the huts, drawing an echoing bleat from another pen.

Moreau pulled his eyes from the crowd and saw the woman was staring at him now. Taken aback, his features hardened as he held her gaze. The men beside him seemed to notice, and they turned their heads to glare at him, several inching closer in a wordless challenge. Moreau held back a derisive sneer.

"And who are you?" the woman asked finally, her eyes hard and unblinking. Her expression demanded a quick answer, but Moreau, hardened by years on the battlefield—and a time in captivity—felt in no particular rush to answer. He felt a palm smack the back of his head, but it had been expected and felt no worse than the cold breeze biting at his skin. In fact, it felt oddly refreshing, as fatigue had also begun to creep in since they had stopped moving. His wounds, which he often forgot whenever they didn't force him to limp, made his legs feel achy and stiff.

"My name is Marcel Moreau. I am from France."

"Eh?" a man a few paces from Moreau snapped. "Wha meek dem tink wi kya weh dem a fram?" A loud burst of laughter followed, and Moreau noticed even the woman on the ground had allowed her features to soften into a grin. He ignored the mocking comments but noticed Antonia giving him a sharp look, and then realized he had called himself by a different name since first meeting her.

"How do you know this woman?"

The men beside him looked at Moreau with eyes that seemed ready to kill. Eager, even. He knew the look, silently admitting that he probably returned their stares with one of equal hatred. The thought brought a vague but perceptible change in his thinking; perhaps he could use that to his advantage. "I met this woman yesterday in the city. She was traveling somewhere I had need to go, and offered me a ride in her wagon."

The group turned back to the woman, but she kept her eyes on Moreau. "And where did you need to go?"

No longer able to hold back a shiver, Moreau exhaled a frosty mist to keep his teeth from chattering. "We visited Le Mouton Plantation this afternoon..." At this the entire assembly let out a loud groan. The men beside Moreau muttered angrily to one another, while the women laid hands on their foreheads or pulled their children tighter to them. One of the men cursed angrily into Moreau's ear, and looking aside, he saw the stocky man from the wagon staring at him with a look that could only be described as murderous. In spite of his otherwise ambivalent attitude toward this entire proceeding, Moreau felt a perceptible chill run down his spine. Until now the mood of the group had been one of palpable hostility tinged with mockery, but something had changed at the mention of Le Mouton. The people seemed...disturbed.

Raising a hand for calm, the woman waited for the murmuring to die down. The man slumped against the hut lolled his head up and down several times, then let it fall to his chest once again. Moreau had noticed that as the crowd reacted with dismay, even the woman in apparent command had clutched her shawl around her shoulders. But her stoic demeanor quickly returned, which seemed to calm the assembly somewhat.

"What need have you to visit that place?"

Sensing the discomfort of his captors, and the momentary advantage it might bring, Moreau casually looked down at his boots, appreciating their warmth and relative comfort. "I am searching for a woman, also from France. I believe she is staying at the plantation." Another audible exclamation, less severe than before, emanated from the villagers at the mention of the plantation. "She was thought to have traveled in the company of the Baratarians. I think she may be in possession of a ruby taken from one of Lafitte's captains."

He noticed the confusion caused by this last statement and sneered, wondering if the talk of riches would be enough to throw off the line of questioning and steer it toward their greed. Perhaps he could convince them to hold him hostage in lieu of an immediate execution. If they kept him alive long enough, he might be able to plan an escape. Just then, the man from the wagon stalked over and planted himself inches from Moreau's chin. Although a few inches shorter, he stared up with open hostility, his eyes as cold as any Moreau had ever seen. "You share the blood of the oppressor. The evil of the oppressor. You are one with those who murder and steal from us." He turned his fiery eyes back to the woman, speaking in a pleading tone. "Gran Ibo, I beg permission to fight this man. Fists or blades, let me fight him to the death."

"Peace, Ogun," the woman replied coolly. "You have spoken out of turn enou—"

"What if those devils sent this one," he interrupted, "to lead them to us? If we let him go, they will learn from him how to find us. I know what white men do to learn what they want to know." His body shook slightly. "Let me kill him!"

She held her gaze on the man and a tense silence followed, until he finally let out a vicious snarl at Moreau and pushed his way through the crowd without saying any more. The woman watched him go before turning to Moreau with piercing dark eyes.

"You say you've come here by accident. I say you've come uninvited." A murmur of agreement came from the others, who seemed spurred on by the hot-blooded man's outburst. "It is true, few white men come here that ever leave again. But this is the first time we've ever been harried by a slave catcher of our own blood." She swiveled her head to look at Antonia, and every eye followed. With a mortified look, Antonia turned to meet the stares of the group, then pleadingly back at Moreau. He returned her gaze with a vacant expression, sensing that her fate—more likely condemnation—would be decided regardless of anything he said or did. He doubted it would be lenient.

To Antonia's left, a group of women pointed at her, some with angry expressions, others laughing at her obvious distress. The men glared coldly, several hurling angry curses in her direction. "This woman is no threat to you," Moreau declared. "She has made a mistake in demanding this man called Edward return with her, but she is young and knows only the ways she has been shown. Let her go and you can have me."

"We *already* have you," one of the men cried out, "and now we fixin' to kill you!" A loud burst of laughter followed. Perhaps sensing the approach of violence, some of the women began carrying their younger children toward their huts. Moreau saw the woman called Gran Ibo lean toward the shirtless man beside her and exchange a few words. When their discreet conversation was finished, she turned to Moreau, pulled her shawl tightly about herself, and stood up slowly. The reclining man sprang to his feet with surprising agility, his top hat remaining firmly in place, and stood next to her, staring ahead at nothing in particular. Eventually he reached out a hand to take something the woman had pulled from a fold in her dress. Bobbing his head as he cradled the item in his hand, he looked around at the others as if noticing them for the first time.

"Ruby, you say." His eyes grew wide, and he gazed at Moreau with a cunning smile. "Do you mean *this*?" Raising his hand, he opened it to reveal a rough, angular crystal the size of a small teacup, its surface a deep red that glowed pink as it caught the flickering torchlight. At the sight of the large gemstone, the group fell silent.

"It is the white man's greed that has brought this one here," the man declared, turning to the crowd with a theatrical gesture. The onlookers responded with cries of agreement, the men waving their torches and the women raising their voices in high-pitched shouts.

"I'm not here for your ruby," Moreau exclaimed. "I'm seeking the woman who-" A shove from behind cut him off, and he gave up trying to say anything more. Across from him one of the men set a firm hand on Antonia's shoulder and dragged her before the woman called Gran Ibo and the shirtless man, forcing her to her knees. A moment later two hands grabbed Moreau's shoulders, and he too was brought before the leaders and forced to kneel. The cries and shouts behind him seemed to recede as he looked at Antonia, panic writ plainly on her features, which until now had reflected a measure of stoic courage. Even in terror she looked beautiful. In that moment Moreau felt no fear for himself, but the thought of watching her die tore at his insides. He stole a look back at Will, who for some reason had not been addressed or threatened since they'd arrived. He saw the youngster was flanked by two men who, strangely, had made no move to restrain him.

"Let the boy go. He's guilty of nothing."

The woman looked at Antonia, then turned her eyes to Moreau. She gestured with an arm at Will. "The boy is free to go as he wishes." A hush fell over the group, broken only by one or two confused mutters. The top-hatted man bobbed his head in laughter but said nothing. "He bears the mark of the Baratarians. He is no enemy." The woman called Gran Ibo said the words with no additional explanation, but as her eyes drifted slowly toward Antonia, her face darkened. "But *you*," she said solemnly, "you have come to return one of ours to his chains." Her eyes widened fiercely, and her upper lip twisted angrily. "This is a sin beyond betrayal. You will *not* go free."

Moreau stirred and shifted his weight. "Madame, she does not know what she—"

"Be quiet," the woman snapped. Her eyes narrowed as she studied him, then she moved closer, her mouth flattening into a wry smile. "You come here unbidden, from a place of curses and evil. You demand this woman be set free." She snorted derisively, turning to the man behind her, who smiled wolfishly. She then looked out over the crowd.

"Draw the *vévé* of blood!"

At this came a deafening roar, as if a reservoir of pent-up rage had been released all at once. Angry shouts and violent gesticulations were directed at Antonia, some at Moreau as well. One man spit at his feet, while another shoved his angrily contorted face in close and growled a fearsome challenge. All around Moreau and Antonia the villagers danced and shouted in wild elation.

Rough hands dragged Moreau through the impromptu celebration back to where he had been standing previously. Antonia was placed beside him, and for a moment the two exchanged a knowing look. Antonia's eyes welled up with tears, and she rushed over to Will and embraced him tightly. Looking ruefully at the two of them, Moreau turned away so they wouldn't see his expression. For the moment, he felt no fear, his heart beat no quicker than normal, but his failure to save the young woman weighed heavily on him. His only consolation was knowing that no matter what happened to them, at least the boy would go free.

Among the crowd he noticed two women, dressed in white shirts and stoles, scattering what looked like a red-colored powder on the ground. For several minutes they worked slowly and carefully, inscribing some sort of design in the mud while the others danced around them. When they finished, they moved to either side of the clearing. Once again there was a call for quiet, and the people shuffled back to clear the space. Standing next to the shirtless man in the top hat, the woman called Gran Ibo looked out over the crowd. "May we seek blessings and guidance from Papa Lebat. May he open this vévé to cleanse this ground with the blood of the unrighteous, and purge away sin to make way for peace and justice."

Moreau snorted indignantly, drawing several angry looks. With the clarity of one who knows he has little time left, and thus no cares to speak of, he glared back at them with a savage smile. He would show them how a soldier died.

The woman turned to him, her eyebrows raised expectantly. "You wish her to go free?"

Moreau exhaled slowly, wary of a trap but nonetheless sensing a faint glimmer of hope. "Yes."

For a moment she stared back at him, her expression cold and unreadable. At length she smacked her lips and looked out over the villagers with a shrug. "She may go free..." The crowd emitted a sharp gasp. The woman held up a hand, and a tense silence hung in the air for several moments. For the first time that night, Moreau's pulse quickened. "But you must fight for her freedom."

Excited whispers passed between the onlookers, and the shirtless man beside the *mambo* chuckled, twisting the blade in his hand like one would turn a key. "You say," the woman said in a clear voice, "she knows little of what she does. Very well, since you've come as her guardian, it falls upon you to free her. If you can defeat this man," she lifted a hand toward the man called Edward, "the girl is yours, and you both may go free."

Moreau grunted as he cast an appraising look at Edward, then turned back to the mambo. "You may have noticed," he said, jerking his left shoulder, "I find myself at a slight disadvantage."

The shirtless man licked his lips and bared his dirty teeth in a combination of smile and snarl. "That is why we give you this." He reached down and picked up something from the ground: a long stick of black wood with a large, bulbous knot at one end. Raising it so the knot was beside his head, the man smiled cheekily at Moreau. Seeing Moreau's confused expression, he threw his head back and let out a burst of high-pitched laughter. As he slowly recovered in fits of diminishing chuckles, he tossed the weapon so it splashed in the mud at Moreau's feet. He then picked up a similar cudgel and motioned for Edward to come and take it, which he did. Two men seized Antonia and pulled her back to where the villagers had moved to form a semicircle around the two combatants. To a person they stared expectantly at Moreau and Edward, who stood side by side in the open ground.

The shirtless man pointed to the red powder on the ground beneath Moreau's feet, and his eyes widened. "Now we will see which of you Baron Samedi wishes to take tonight."

The mambo raised her chin and looked at both men with a sober expression. "Do you agree to this?"

Moreau considered the proposition. "If I lose...I am killed?"

The man in the top hat frowned irritably. "If you *lose*, then your troubles are over."

Moreau looked down at his club. Until now the proposition of fighting the other man had seemed unlikely to go in his favor, but with this weapon in his hand, he not only had a chance—the other man was doomed. He looked up with a shrug. "I agree."

The woman called Gran Ibo motioned to Edward. "The girl came here to return you to bondage. This man offers to take her place. If he defeats *you*, she may go free. Do you consent to this?"

Edward looked toward Moreau, and their eyes held for several seconds, neither willing to blink. Eventually he smiled and let out a chuckle. "Yea, I'll fight this cripple."

Edward stalked away several paces, tapping the club against his palm before kicking off his moccasins. He did not look worried. Moreau reached down and unlaced his boots, removing them and, finally, his socks, giving silent thanks for the warmth they'd provided his feet while he had them on. He cast a regretful look at Edward. "I'd hate to kill you."

Edward stared back at him with a grin. "I can't say the same to you."

Several of the villagers seated themselves on the ground at the edge of the semicircle; a moment later drums were set on their laps. At a signal from the top-hatted man, they began to beat time in a steady rhythm. *BOOM-boom-boom-boom, BOOM-boom-boom-boom.*

Edward held Moreau's gaze with a calm expression, but his eyes glared fiercely. "I'll make it quick."

All but unnoticed a few paces away stood Antonia, whose head swiveled from one man to the other, her expression fearful. She muttered incomprehensibly to herself as she rubbed her hands together. At length she cleared her throat. "Be careful, he's dangerous." Moreau held his eyes on the other man for a moment, then turned toward her—only to see that she was looking at Edward. Although he knew to keep his mind on his opponent and the task at hand, Moreau couldn't deny the strangely deflated feeling in his chest. Letting out a muffled curse, he dismissed the very thought of her. Turning back to his opponent, he allowed his lips to twist in a malicious sneer.

The drums beat slightly faster now. *BOOM-boom-boom-boom, BOOM-boom-boom-boom.*

Moreau closed his eyes and rolled his shoulders. His heart thumped as his breath came in slow, deep pulls, and he felt the exuberant flood of combat rage begin to course through his veins. But his mind was calm, peaceful even. Hoots and whistles arose from the crowd—but he heard none of them. If the woman had eyes for the other man, she could now watch what he was about to do to the poor bastard. *Dangerous?* She didn't know the half of it.

The mambo and *houngan*, as one woman had referred to the shirtless man, stepped slowly into the center of the semicircle. They motioned for Edward and Moreau to come closer, which both did.

The houngan raised his hand, and the assembly hushed into a silence that rippled with nerves and excitement.

The mambo took a step closer and looked at Edward. "You see the vévé beneath your feet. May the *Orisha* give you strength and courage; may you protect this *hounfour* of your people." She turned to Moreau with a cold expression. "May you fight well." The two combatants took up position beside the nearby hut. The houngan dropped into a low crouch.

The drummers beat their steady, rhythmic cadence. *BOOM-boom-boom-boom*, *BOOM-boom-boom-boom*. The villagers standing behind Edward on either side huddled in groups of twos and threes, pointing at Moreau and bantering to each other.

"Boy look like a redbone, Eddie—bash him up!"

"He prolly think this a quadrille dandy."

"This ain't no *bamboula* in Congo Square, white boy; you in a real dance now."

"You *fucked* now." A burst of laughter followed, but a few shushes and it quickly returned to quiet as the two men stepped forward. Both dropped into a fighting stance and braced their bare feet in the cold, muddy ground. At a signal from the houngan, they charged at each other.

CHAPTER 9

Le Marais (Cypress Swamp), Outside New Orleans
December 2, 1814

Moreau took two quick steps forward in a hard feint but quickly stopped, keeping his balance steady. With a grimace, Edward charged ahead, sprinting forward at breakneck speed, slowing only slightly as Moreau sprang aside. This swerve caused Edward's momentum to set him slightly off balance, and then Moreau viciously swung his club. Its thick end missed Edward's face by perhaps an inch or two, but the surprise of it caused him to wrench his weight backwards, and his feet slipped out from under him, sending him crashing down into the mud. Slightly unbalanced by the force of his swing and the muddy ground, Moreau did not press his advantage, but took a half step back to gather himself. Although he had continued to train with a sword since losing his weaker arm years before, his body had never truly adapted to the substantial weight difference between his right and left sides. Frustrated that his his potentially devastating blow had missed, he let out a curse.

Meanwhile, Edward spun away from Moreau and in less than a second regained his feet. Sucking in a deep breath, he smiled as he brushed a lump of mud off the side of his face. "Quick swing. But if you miss again, imma rip off your other arm."

Moreau swung the club at his side as he watched the other man's feet. He knew better than to fall for the bait and respond in kind, but his time away from fighting seemed to get the better of him. "If that's your best—this won't take long."

Edward smiled as he shuffled his feet laterally, regaining his composure. He stepped forward and lunged at Moreau—but it was a feint. He stopped just before coming within striking range, to test Moreau's readiness, but the latter hardly flinched. Moreau moved in a slow circle, his club held low, ready for an upswing if attacked. Wild shouts poured from the onlookers, and Moreau felt a brief temptation to look at them—and at Antonia and Will—but he forced himself to stay focused on his opponent. In a burst of quickness, he darted forward, raised his club, and slammed it into Edward's with a loud *clack*—but Moreau had not meant to land the blow, merely to attract his foe's attention. When Edward moved to defend himself from the downward swing, Moreau jerked his knee up and, in a swift sweeping motion, slammed his bare foot into the man's abdomen, which was firm, but not firm enough to keep him from grunting loudly.

Moreau then sprang back a few paces, not wishing to test the strength of his opponent's two arms against his one. With a grimace, Edward allowed his torso to sag for a moment, wheezing to catch his breath, but he recovered quickly and raised himself to his full height. For a moment he stood still, sucking in air as he looked at Moreau with a sardonic smile. He exhaled loudly and lifted his club, pointing it at Moreau. "You landed one," he said, seeming fully recovered. "I hope you ready for a fight now."

Moreau bent his knees as he attempted to conceal his disappointment that his hardest strike had barely seemed to faze the other man. He wiggled his toes and took a deep breath.

Edward stepped back and turned to look at the villagers. "If this pale beanstalk thinks I'm afraid of him—he doesn't know who we are!" A raucous cheer came from the assembly, who resumed their shouts and taunts with renewed fervor.

As Edward urged the crowd on, Moreau seized the moment and dashed forward as his feet, still warm from the boots, found good purchase in the half-frozen mud. He took several steps to his left and raised his club to strike, then dug his toes in and quickly leapt to the man's left—ducking under Edward's violent swing that tore just over his head. Pivoting and putting the full force of his legs, hips, and back into his return stroke, Moreau felt a deep *thud* as his club connected with a force even stronger than his kick into the other man's back. Moreau somersaulted, rolling away and looking back as he regained his feet. To his shock, he saw Edward on his knees, unmoving as a statue. For a moment, unsure of the blow's effect on the other man, he watched him in silence.

When he was sure Edward was not feigning hurt to lure him into a trap, Moreau took a deep breath and allowed himself a quick glance at the villagers. Several of them stared back at him in stunned silence, but most were looking with nervous expressions at Edward, who still had not risen from his knees—or even moved. For a moment, Moreau wondered if he had killed the man, or perhaps just broken his will to fight. To his dismay, however, Edward began to rock slowly forward and back; then, groaning at the effort, he climbed to his feet. Twisting his neck, which made loud cracking sounds, Edward reached down for his club and turned slowly to face Moreau. When their eyes met, it was Moreau who blinked first, as Edward took several slow steps toward him, his expression no longer smiling but set in a grim, determined glower that he had not yet shown. When Edward spoke, his words came in a low, pained rasp, but his words were clear enough. "You think I'm afraid of you?" He continued his slow walk forward. "You think *we're* afraid of you? You beat us...whip us...torture us. You hate my people...'cause *you* scared of us. *You should be.*"

Edward paused, staring at Moreau with a startling ferocity. "I'm gonna fucking kill you."

Moreau shuffled his feet, relieved that they still felt steady beneath him. Though hardened to hand-to-hand fighting from experience, his reliance on one arm was taking its toll—and it now ached. His lungs burned with each labored breath. "There was a time..." he muttered, "when I might have thought...fighting swamp-dwelling savages...beneath me. But now...I'm going to enjoy killing you." He raised his club in a challenge, and Edward raised his own.

"I'm the last savage you'll ever see." Edward bolted nimbly at Moreau, not bothering to raise his club to defend himself. Moreau swung with as much strength as he could still muster, but Edward moved inside his guard too quickly, and the club glanced off Edward's left shoulder as the man drove his head into Moreau's chest. Both combatants slammed to the ground in a violent heap, splashing mud and brown water onto the feet of the nearest onlookers, who leapt back to avoid being caught up in the deadly brawl. They tumbled over one another in a clumsy, haphazard wrestling mêlée, until Edward found himself on top of Moreau, who jabbed a fist upward into his opponent's chin. The force from the punch jerked Edward's head back, but he managed to get a grip on Moreau's wrist with his right hand while he balled his left into a fist and smashed it into the side of Moreau's face.

Stunned into a stupor that briefly blurred his vision and fogged his senses, Moreau did the only thing left to him: plant his feet on the ground and push up with all his might. The impact threw Edward forward a few inches, and for a moment Moreau felt that he might be able to wriggle out from under him, but Edward's grip on his wrist allowed the man to steady himself and pin Moreau back down with a knee. Now in a worse position than before, Moreau pushed off from his elbow and feet and even yanked his shoulders back—but nothing he did could throw the larger man off.

Another fist smashed into his face, thumping his head back down into the mud. His vision a blurring whirl of images and white light, Moreau dug his heels into the mud and again attempted to slide away. The effort wasn't successful, as Edward still held his wrist, but he did manage to move a few inches and bought himself a second or two to regain his senses. Before he could try again, he felt the man's fingers reach for his neck and start to clasp, but at the last second, he jerked aside. Seeing Edward's face lowering toward his again, Moreau did the only thing he could think of—and jerked his head up as hard as he could. He felt his forehead smash into something before falling back into the mud, spent. He heard Edward mutter an angry curse, but his hearing as well as his vision was now little more than a throbbing, agonizing blur, and it was difficult to tell if the other man was one foot away or ten.

As he lay prostrate, gasping for air, Moreau felt a hand seize his neck and was unable to shake it away. The fearsome grip closed on his windpipe, fingertips digging into the sides of his neck. With a last, desperate effort, he struggled to push Edward off him, but heels slipped as they attempted to plant in the mud, and all he could do was writhe and gasp vainly for air as the man squeezed his throat with both hands. Moreau's vision began to grow dark, and sounds became distant. He felt his body go limp, and he gave up all struggling. His vision receded and he lost consciousness.

―⁂―

What felt like a timeless, black, fever dream lasted perhaps three or four seconds in real time, and Moreau's desperate gasps for air came at the same moment his eyes opened in several frantic blinks. He was lying on his side now, and he could make out only mud and shuffling feet in his narrow, hazy field of vision. An awful burning sensation scorched through his lungs, and his neck felt as if it had been broken. Unable to lift his head more than an inch or two off the ground, he laid still for several moments, allowing his breath to come in forced, desperate gasps. His hearing returned to normal first; he began to notice the stunned mutterings of the villagers around him, reminding him that he had been in a life-and-death struggle. He thought it might be wise to defend himself, but it was no use as he could barely manage to raise his head enough to look up. When he did, he noticed the strange ethereal canopy of cypress trees framing a sky that looked as black as any he'd ever seen. He took a wheezing breath and exhaled until a fit of coughing forced him onto his side. He heard shuffling feet only a few paces away, and wondered why a killing blow had not come from Edward's cudgel.

He once again looked at the trees and sky above, and then noticed something strange. Silence. Silence all around him. Letting out a ragged breath, he rolled onto his right side and rested his elbow in the mud, looking aside. His vision seemed to have recovered, if still a bit hazy, and he noticed another oddity. All of the villagers seemed to have turned their attention away from him. With a grimace, he hauled himself upright and caught a clear view of what had drawn their attention.

Standing between a small gap in the crowd of villagers was a man; at first glance he appeared to be a white man. His dress contrasted starkly with the simple threads of the men and women inhabiting this village. His pantaloons were pale grey, tucked into knee-high black boots, and his coat was a dark-blue frock that went down past his knees. Beneath his coat he wore a brown vest fastened with several shiny bronze buttons, and on his head was a black fedora that left half of his face in shadow. Was he French?

Moreau shook his head to be sure he hadn't imagined the man's appearance, quickly regretting the intense throbbing that ensued. Wincing harshly, he took a breath as he examined the fellow who had drawn everyone's attention. After a brief glance about him, the stranger spoke in an amused tone. "Hell is empty, and all the devils are here."

His lips thinned slightly, and he turned his attention to the mambo and houngan, who stood unmoving beside one of the huts. Feeling a sudden wave of unease, Moreau cast his head to either side, wary of Edward pouncing on him again. To his relief—and surprise—he saw Edward sitting in the mud several paces way, his knees raised almost to his chest. Dark blood dripped from his nose onto his lips, and he looked nearly as stunned as Moreau felt. Turning to look at the mysterious visitor, Moreau wiped his face with his sleeve, not noticing the smear of blood left on the cuff.

"I seem to have interrupted your sport," the man said understatedly.

The heavy silence was finally broken by the soft voice of the mambo. "Once again, your arrival comes at an auspicious time." She stared at the newcomer with a hard expression. "What is it this time, Phantom? Have you come for gold? Women?"

The man called Phantom returned her stare with a subtle grin. "Neither. I come with one whom you might find of interest." He turned, motioning at someone behind him. "Come forward, boy."

A few seconds later a boy of fifteen or sixteen years stepped out of the shadows. His skin was dark, and he wore the simple white smock and cotton trousers Moreau had seen worn by the slaves on Giroux's plantation. Sunken shoulders and a slightly curved neck indicated his status as one such.

"His name is Philippe," the visitor declared. "I found him this afternoon as I traveled north along the bayou. I thought he'd prefer coming here—to returning to his former plantation."

A murmur arose from the villagers, and they whispered among themselves for a moment. Since the arrival of this stranger, Moreau seemed to have been completely forgotten—at least for the moment. His head throbbed and his legs and back ached, but he had regained a sense of equilibrium after a minute of normal breaths and rested muscles. Looking over at Edward, he saw the man was staring back at him with an intense expression. Moreau sat upright and returned the stare with equal intensity.

"You have nothing to fear, Philippe," the mambo said, motioning for the boy to come forward. Lifting his head with a nervous look around, the boy shuffled forward and approached the mambo and houngan, who gave him a brief examination. "He appears unharmed," the mambo said at last, turning back to the visitor, "from what I can see. But we will take a closer look at him. You have our thanks." The man replied with a somber nod. "Will you stay with us for the night?" she asked, while one of the women in white robes ushered the boy out of sight through the door one of the nearby huts.

"My affairs press me," he answered. "I have business in the city, and the governor's 'wise men' will wish to hear the latest news I bring. A terrible storm is coming their way." He then cast a look at Edward and Moreau in turn. His expression showed mild curiosity as he held Moreau's gaze before finally turning back to the woman. "But I would have a word with you, Diantha, before I depart."

The mambo, Diantha, squinted slightly before replying with a gentle nod. With a final glance at Moreau, the man moved toward the hut she had indicated, which seemed the biggest in the village. He crossed the mud-splashed fighting ground with long, athletic strides that hinted at something of a swagger, disappearing inside without another word. Another murmur followed his departure, and slowly the crowd began to disperse. After a minute or so only a dozen or so remained, each staring intently at Moreau and Edward as though hoping for more entertainment.

At the entrance of the hut, Diantha turned back to look at the two battered men, neither of whom had moved more than a few inches since their brutal combat had concluded. Shaking his head and groaning, Edward pressed his palms into the mud and pushed himself to his feet. Diantha took a step forward. "You men have honored the hounfour with your courage and fighting prowess." She looked at Edward, nodded briefly, then turned to Moreau. She observed him thoughtfully for a while, as if contemplating what to do with him. She certainly didn't seem unused to passing weighty judgments. "You may set yourself at ease, monsieur. No one here will lay a hand to harm you."

Moreau almost laughed, wondering how much more harm could be added to what he'd already sustained. Not five minutes prior, he had prepared himself to welcome death; now he was being complimented for his fighting prowess and told to set himself at ease. "And what of the girl?" he asked hoarsely, a rush of emotions swirling through him. Did this woman mean what she said—or was she just lulling him into a false sense of ease only to order his throat slit while he slept?

"You have earned a night of peace," she said finally. "In the morning you and the boy may go—the girl stays here." With that, she turned and disappeared into the hut.

Moreau sighed, settling on a feeling of wary relief, glad that at least he would suffer no more violence. His thoughts were interrupted by the approaching footsteps of his erstwhile enemy. Seeming fully recovered now, Edward strode over the chalk design called vévé—now nearly obliterated—until he stood directly over Moreau. For several seconds he said nothing. At length he reached out a hand. "You gon' get up, or you enjoying yourself down there?" Moreau stared up at him, eventually letting out a chuckle. As he allowed himself to be pulled to his feet—with a good deal of aches and stiffness—he noticed a wry smile on the man's features. Edward shook his head. "You're a wily son of a bitch."

Moreau rolled his neck and wiped a hand over his face, surprised to see caked blood staining his mud-soaked fingers. "And you're a tough bastard to bring down." He took a step and wobbled, nearly dropping to his knees, and decided to stand still until his legs had gathered fully beneath him. A little way off a small gaggle of younger women were staring at him, their expressions ranging from bewildered to mildly flirtatious.

A tall, thin young man with short hair and a thin mustache approached, his eyes bulging as he took in the two men. "Goddamn Eddie, I ain't know you could fight like that." He grinned as he slapped Edward's back, though his smile wasn't reciprocated. "I thought you was a joker like me—turns out you a hard one." His laugh showed genuine delight.

"Boy get out the way," Edward grunted as he shoved the man in the shoulder and walked past. "I need me some damn rum."

The thin man watched Edward stalk off with a beaming grin. "And you," he exclaimed, turning to Moreau, "you scared some folks tonight. Ain't no cripples come in here and do damage like that." The man laughed again, reaching behind his back and producing a small flask carved from wood. With a nod, he took a pull, then handed the flask to Moreau. Moreau looked at him as he took a long pull from the flask; whatever was inside tasted terrible, but it was liquid down his throat. "My name's Antoine. I been here 'bout two years; before that I was at Bienvenu Plantation. Alive and dead at the same time. Anyway, who the fuck are you?"

Moreau said nothing as he cradled the flask.

"Alright, don't answer," Antoine chided. "But I would like to know where a one-arm man learns to fight like that."

Moreau exhaled and licked his lips. "I wasn't born with one arm. I lost it, serving in the army."

Another man drifted over from a group standing nearby, staring at Moreau as he approached. He was short, with very dark skin and a shiny bald head. He halted a few paces away. "Wah hi say bout di army?" The man spoke so fast that Moreau cocked his head and looked at Antoine expectantly.

"He seh he did inna French army?"

Once again, Moreau could make out only a few words, and Antoine translated. Moreau nodded slowly. "Some years ago, yes."

"Ah," the short man cried out. He wobbled his head several times, appearing to smile, before looking at Moreau. His features took on a grim, fearsome appearance, then he let out a stream of invective that Moreau couldn't understand—but comprehended the meaning of completely.

Antoine sighed loudly. "Ehh, he say, they used to hunt Napoleon's men. Nail the captured ones to trees, then cut them open until they told them what they wanted to know. Would, uh, cut their ears and hang them from their own necks before they cut off…" Antoine looked down below his waist and shrugged.

Moreau let out a sharp breath as he glared at the other man.

"Would you like me to translate any more?" Antoine asked with raised eyebrows. Moreau frowned at him. Sighing, Antoine explained. "He arrived after the uprisings in Port-Au-Prince. Been here a long time. He said he was captured by the French after two years living free in the jungle, thrown back in chains, and brought here. Escaped again. Swore a blood oath that all Frenchmen were his enemy for life."

Moreau squinted as he considered what deeds this one might have done to his countrymen. For a split second, memories flooded into his mind of brutal civil wars back home, and he suppressed a shiver. "Tell him," Moreau said drily, "it is nice to meet him, too. Perhaps someday I'll return the favor."

Antoine pursed his lips. "I won't be telling him *that*. But I'll pass along your happy greetings. Ha-ha."

The short man frowned as he took another long look at Moreau. At last he threw up both hands. "Buh di bwoy can fight! He almost sen Eddie tuh Baron Samedi." With a shrug, he turned and walked back to join another group milling about nearby. Moreau shook his head, not sure if the people staring at him wanted to kill him or congratulate him.

"That's Jean-Pierre," Antoine explained. "We got several come from Saint-Domingue—before it was Haiti. The young-looking one in the middle is Francois, and the tall one with the muscles is Papa Louis. Jean-Pierre, he probably one of the more friendly ones."

Moreau nodded. "And the angry one? Who seemed *eager* to kill me? The woman called him Ogun."

Antoine gazed at him a moment before recognition dawned on his features, and his lips spread nervously. "Ah, yes. Ogun her war name for him. That's Nehemiah, probably one of the *less* friendly you likely meet. For the time being, you might want to avoid him. He don't like you."

Moreau took another pull from the flask and handed it back to Antoine. "You don't say." He let out a breath and pinched his eyes with his hand, feeling fatigue finally beginning to catch up with him. "So, what—you've all had your fun and now you'll have a *fête*?" The sudden realization hit him: he'd lost track of both Will and Antonia and hadn't seen them since the fight. "What of my companions?" he demanded with an angry frown. "What will you do to the woman?"

Antoine set a firm hand on Moreau's shoulder and smiled again. "Eh, Frenchman," he said, "calm down. Ain't nobody gonna hurt the woman, and the boy probably just out here somewhere trying to get his hands on our rum. We just had to…see what you was made of. But we not animals. Not like how they do over on the plantation you just come from. Diantha said the boy a Baratarian; that means he alright with us."

Moreau looked at him suspiciously. "Why does that make him alright? What do you all have to do with pirates?"

"Nothing," a voice declared behind him. "Because there *are* no pirates in Barataria."

Moreau turned around to see the well-dressed white man standing a few paces away, one hand resting on a sword hilt. Beside him stood the diminutive mambo, Diantha. She eyed Moreau impassively, her eyes less wary than before. "Your young companion may go as he wishes," she said as if passing sentence, "but he is not to return to Barataria." She glanced briefly at the man beside her before continuing. "As I've also said, Antonia Milroy will remain here, as our guest." Moreau licked his lower lip and was about to attempt another negotiation before the mambo raised her hand, forcing his silence. "You say she is young and knows only what she has been told. We will keep her here, to see if she can *unlearn* the virtues of bondage from those who've known its evil." She looked intently into Moreau's eyes, her expression pensive. "But some changes can't be forced from without; they must come from within."

At the soft squish of footsteps, all turned to see Nehemiah approaching. He halted beside Diantha, his broad, muscular shoulders square and erect, but his expression was one of respect. He conspicuously avoided looking at Moreau or the as-yet-unnamed visitor. Leaning closer to the woman, he muttered a few words that Moreau could not make out, and a moment later the mambo turned to her two visitors, gently clasping her hands.

"Monsieur le Phantom," she said to the visitor, "I am grateful for your rescue of Philippe. We shall speak again at your next visit." She turned to Moreau, her expression tightening somewhat. "Monsieur Moreau, in the morning one of our scouts can show you the paths that will lead you to the river road. I regret the loss of your horse and wagon, but it is a small debt to pay to come here and depart with your life. May you travel safely and find no cause to trouble us again." With a sharp look, she walked away with Nehemiah, and the two struck up a conversation that brought vocal exclamations from the young man and mostly silence from the mambo. Moreau found himself breathing a sigh of relief that not everyone in this village seemed to feel the way that man did.

Turning his eyes back to the visitor, he was somewhat startled to find the man staring thoughtfully back at him. His dark-brown eyes were keen and intelligent, and his shadowed features appeared younger up close. He was perhaps a few years younger than Moreau, yet he carried himself with the tranquil self-assurance of a soldier hardened by years of battle. Moreau knew one of his countrymen when he saw one, and admitted that the fellow might be a younger version of himself—before scars and distress had taken their toll. When he'd spoken earlier, his accent sounded strangely familiar, yet difficult to place. "Basque?" Moreau finally asked with a curious squint.

"I've not come here to answer questions from you," the man replied evenly, "at least not until you've answered mine." Moreau almost laughed at his impertinence, but shrugged his agreement. The younger man reached up and slowly removed his wide-brimmed felt hat and wiped a hand over his face. "Who are you?" he asked at last. "Diantha tells me you know of a Baratarian captain searching for a ruby. I'm curious as to how you came to be involved in such business. Are you a deserter from Napoleon? A spy for Washington?" He held up a finger and leaned in closer. "Before you speak, monsieur, know that I am courteous, but I do not suffer liars or malcontents. If you wish to keep your other arm, you will not lie to me."

His patience for threats all but used up, Moreau breathed a heavy sigh to ease a momentary swell of anger. He stared at the mysterious figure, and despite the pull of exhaustion and ill temper, he could not hold back a flood of relief at finally putting the puzzle together. He had sensed from the first that there was something different about this one, and now he finally understood why. "I am Marcel Moreau, formerly major of the Imperial Army of France. I am neither deserter nor a spy, and I don't give a damn about rubies or greedy ship captains. I've come to these shores to settle a personal matter. And you," he declared with a knowing look, "you're the blacksmith of Bourbon Street. Jean Lafitte."

The man eyed him with an impassive expression. "I have been called many things. To some I am the devil incarnate, to others a mythical hero. But to those who know me best…I am simply Jean. As you say." He spread his arms in a half bow. "But as I've told you, my courtesy extends only to those who are friendly to me and my men. In recent days that number has dwindled. So, monsieur, please state your business so I may not have cause to treat you as an enemy."

Moreau spit on the ground and looked out over the huts. What had previously been a setting of rage and violence seemed to have settled into the quiet evening scene of any small village. The cold bit at his limbs and fingers, and at last he cleared his throat, wincing from the stiffness caused by the fight. "I'm in debt to a wealthy man for no small sum of money. Retrieving this woman and returning her to her parents in Normandy will earn me a reward that would all but cover the cost—saving my life. And my honor."

Lafitte watched him with his customarily pensive expression. "A desperate man indeed," he said at last, "to find yourself brawling in the mud of a cypress swamp." Moreau smirked, not offering any disagreement. "And how long do you have to fulfill this debt?"

"Until the end of the year."

Lafitte tilted his head. "Truly?"

Moreau's face grew dark. "If time was at my leisure—do you think I would be brawling in a cypress swamp?"

Lafitte offered a tight smile. "If I have her onboard a ship," Moreau continued, his brow furrowed, "before the year is out, I believe I might return safely to my creditor and make good on what I owe. If I am still on these shores come January, 'unfriendly' men will come for me—and they'll find me. I've travelled under a false name to cover my tracks a little, but it is no mystery that I've come to New Orleans."

Lafitte chuckled quietly. "Well, you seem a man more than capable of handling sword and pistol, evidently with courage to match. What could you have done to incur so severe a debt?"

At that question, Moreau's eyes lowered to the ground and his shoulders slumped slightly. When he finally looked up, his eyes looked glazed, as if in some far-off contemplation. "After my discharge from the army," he said quietly, "I worked as a farmer on the estate of my former commanding officer. It was a pleasant life, for a little while, but my restlessness got the better of me. I felt bored after so many years campaigning at the peril of life and limb. As a man of the seas, surely you understand the call to the horizon as a soldier feels the call to march: somewhere, anywhere."

Lafitte eyed him with a somber expression and nodded slowly. Moreau took a breath and continued. "Eventually I found myself in Spain, not as a uniformed soldier but private security to a wealthy businessman from Toulouse. Very wealthy. In the spring of last year, when the army began its evacuation from the country, he set out on his return from Valencia. I was in charge of the convoy carrying his personal possessions: three years of plundered art, wares, and furniture, as well as his personal correspondence. At first, all went well...until we were set upon by guerillas in the mountains outside Zaragoza. On my orders we left most of what was in the baggage train and made a hasty run for the safety of the city. All were saved, but we had lost in excess of a hundred thousand francs of my patron's property and possessions. Nearly three years of plunder—and I was responsible. When we were safely across the Pyrenees, he informed me that I would repay him the fortune before the end of the following year...or there would be 'no corner of heaven or hell' that he would not find me and make me regret ever betraying him."

The sound of peepers from the nearby swamp punctuated the heavy silence, and Moreau wiped his mouth. The guilt of his failure ate at him, yet he felt like a weight had been lifted, as he had not yet recounted this story to another soul apart from his friend André Valière. He yearned for sleep.

Hushed voices came from somewhere nearby, and Moreau looked between a pair of huts to see several men clustered in a group. They were speaking in hushed voices, and Moreau noticed they all carried weapons of some sort. One by one they reached into a bucket and dabbed some concoction on their arms and legs, inspecting each other as they did so. Moreau turned to Lafitte with a quizzical expression. "Night patrol," the privateer commander explained. "They dab lard and grease on themselves to create an unmistakable smell."

Moreau watched the group, raising a fist to his mouth cover a yawn. "And the smell is to...draw enemies?"

"They'll go far out in various directions, like foxes, to draw off the hounds. Then, when they've muddled any coherent direction from their tracks, they'll wash it off and return here. It seems to have worked so far."

"Hounds," Moreau muttered, "from—ah, yes. I see." He nodded, remembering that these people were all runaways, hunted by slave catchers from the surrounding estates. "So, you've come all this way just to bring one runaway slave to a temporary shelter?"

Lafitte sniffed, casting a quick glance back toward the water source behind him. "I do not know you well enough to take you wholly into my confidence, but as you seem a good fellow, I shall at least tell you this: the English are this very night probing the passes into Lake Borgne, as well as several other passes leading to the city."

Lafitte gave Moreau a sly grin, and Moreau recognized the hawkish look of one animated by the prospect of coming battle. "In recent months I've received three offers—*generous* offers—from the English in exchange for my acquainting them with the various passageways leading to the city. Conversely, my treatment from Governor Claiborne, Commodore Perry, and General Jackson has been rather...impolite. Add to that the fact that nearly half my men have been arrested, my ships destroyed or seized by the American navy, and my colony in Barataria utterly destroyed. The time for my patience and their coming to their senses is running out."

Moreau stared at the privateer, astonished at how much the man was revealing to him. For his part, Lafitte eyed Moreau with a speculative gaze, as if sizing him up anew, then shook his head with a smile. "But there is still time, and I still have options available to me. I travel to New Orleans to ensure that the good governor and his allies in the legislature understand just what I have to offer them. It is a good deal more than anything they have yet offered me."

"But why continue pursuing their favor?" Moreau asked quietly. "If they continue to scorn you while the English court you…"

Lafitte looked at him with an expression that seemed both amiable and somewhat dangerous. "Rumor has it that General Jackson is to arrive in New Orleans within days. But I've never been a man to rely on rumor—there's neither sloop nor pirogue that passes along the sixty miles of bayous around the city but my men know of it. If he's not already in the city, he will be there by tomorrow at the latest. From what I've heard, he is a serious man; he will take a survey of the city, its arms and its defenses, and come to the same conclusion I have."

"Which is…?"

"In its current state, New Orleans is utterly indefensible, and the meager forces sent to defend it will be swept aside with the slightest effort from the English. And I know one more thing that the general and governor do not: a great fleet carrying fifteen thousand elite British soldiers departed the Irish coast in September with the Mississippi River as their destination. I will not tell you how I know of this, just trust that I do. So even if Jackson were to summon the genius of Napoleon, he would still lack the powder, guns, flints, and crews to offer a proper defense. And if the Creoles don't fight for Jackson and the Americans, the city is doomed. But, with my help, those scales may be tipped."

As Moreau considered this, something stirred within him that momentarily held his fatigue at bay. "So, you will take your offer to the governor and hope he sees good sense. I take it you two do not get on particularly well?"

Lafitte grinned. "A dog chasing his tail shows more guile than the governor when he comes after me. Last year his agents were unable to find our storehouses—which they will never find—so out of frustration, he posted a reward for five hundred dollars for my arrest. So what was I to do? Well, I decided to counter his offer—and post a reward of five *thousand* dollars for *his* arrest.

Needless to say, he did not take kindly to my remonstrance." He let out an exaggerated sigh, and Moreau could not help but chuckle at the story. If only a fraction of what the man said was true, not only were circumstances more dire than Moreau had thought, they were infinitely stranger than he could have imagined.

"But in spite of his forays, my prestige has only grown. Just last week I passed a lovely afternoon drinking lemonade with the good governor's wife—of course, I introduced myself under a different name—but who's to say whether she knew the blacksmith of Bourbon Street by sight?" With a grin, Lafitte gathered himself upright. "I believe the time is approaching when the governor will have no choice but to accede to my offers of cooperation. And if his maliciousness cannot be surmounted, then I will have to take my case to General Jackson. It is a rare thing, a man who lives up to his reputation—but time will tell."

Moreau nodded thoughtfully, not bothering to fight a yawn. Lafitte exhaled, then eagerly rubbed his hands together, seemingly suffering from no such fatigue. "In earlier days I would have solicited you to join our ranks. You would have been but one of many of Napoleon's former men. Your experience would have been a boon. But, alas, you best hurry back if you wish to find the girl in time. The English will arrive soon, and the folk of New Orleans are about to test their fury."

Moreau exhaled, nodding his understanding. Lafitte looked at him a moment, then tipped his hat. "Safe travels, monsieur. I wish you well on your mission. Until next time." At that the famous privateer turned on his heels and stalked back toward the bayou.

No longer concerned with thoughts of escape or self-preservation, Moreau felt a simple desire to find some safe, secluded place to sleep. A short distance away, a woman walked past with a small child asleep on her shoulder; she avoided looking at Moreau. Crouched beside a hut were two men nibbling on pieces of meat spitted on long sticks—Moreau did not care to think where the meat had come from. As he turned away, he noticed an old man sat beside the entrance of one of the stilted huts. A younger woman was feeding him with a wooden spoon, gently dabbing at his chin as he sloppily mouthed the food in slow, gummy bites. A strange feeling passed over Moreau, as if he were a hostile intruder, or at least uninvited guest—but he no longer felt any semblance of danger in this sleepy village. If anything, he wished only to avoid disturbing its tranquility.

Outside the village at the water's edge, Jean Lafitte stepped into the small pirogue that would take him through misty bayous and secret passageways to the suburbs of New Orleans.

No one saw the large balas ruby he cradled gently in his hand.

CHAPTER 10

Le Marais (Cypress Swamp), Outside New Orleans
December 2, 1814

The damp pile of straw that served as a bed was comfortable enough for Moreau to snatch a few hours' sleep, and he felt grateful for the warmth of the long-sleeve linen smock Antoine had given him. Although he woke with a splitting headache and bone-deep pains from his neck to his toes, he nevertheless felt restored enough to make his departure before the village was up and stirring. One farewell he did not manage to evade was with Diantha, who had woken before he had roused Will and led the half-awake boy through the village. The mambo did not show signs of fatigue despite the early hour, and she gave them two pieces of cornbread for their journey. Moreau then inquired about Antonia, asking whether she would be set free eventually. Diantha gave no definite response, saying only that the girl had a lesson to learn, and what might happen beyond that only time could tell. His final question concerned the sizable ruby shown off the night before, and whether they knew where it had come from. Diantha informed him that the shirtless houngan had swindled it from Tadeo Araza, providing him with a false one in exchange. That at least gave Moreau some inclination to believe her, though he doubted she was telling the whole story. With an air of indifference, Diantha claimed it would be blessed and put to use in aiding and protecting the hounfour—whatever that meant.

As he placed his bicorne hat on his head, Moreau recalled his reason for being there: Celeste de Beaumais. The previous day, which to him felt more like a week, may have thrown his search off course, but it was now time to resume. Bidding farewell to the mambo, Moreau and Will departed Le Marais while the sun still lingered among the tree stumps. Pointed in the direction of the road by one of the armed men at the edge of the village, the two then plunged into the wet leaves and fronds, squishing through mud-soaked ground for what seemed like half a day at least. As the sun rose higher, they finally reached the firmer dirt track that led to the river road a few miles west.

As they passed the site of their capture, Moreau's thoughts turned to Antonia. He had not seen her since the evening prior, standing in the flickering torchlight as the crowd seethed all around her, calling for her blood. But she had kept her dignity. With a slightly embarrassed feeling, he recalled just how beautiful she looked. Most women he knew—and men, for that matter—would have shrunk in such a position. Diantha and the others had given little indication of what might now happen to her, other than she must "unlearn the virtues of bondage" that had been instilled in her—likely by her family. The very fact that a woman could be both inherently innocent and yet guilty of such a betrayal, in the eyes of the people of Le Marais at least, seemed a strange thing to Moreau. He considered this nation he had journeyed across a sea to reach; was this really a land of liberty? An infant republic of hope and opportunity, as many of his countrymen liked to proclaim? So far, he had seen divisions between master and slave to rival the most brutal, despotic legacies of his own country's past. Worse, even. Surely these were not questions he needed to concern himself with—he had his own task to see to—but a part of him wondered if these people would not have been better off remaining under the rule of the British crown.

As they continued down the bare dirt track and approached the river road, it occurred to Moreau how much of a failure his pursuit of the de Beaumais girl had been thus far—more accurately, one failure after another. He realized he could not continue as he had, flailing about blindly in hopes that he would stumble upon her. To make matters worse, not only had he spoken of his plan to the woman in the tavern, but surely by now Celeste had learned that a man had visited Le Mouton Plantation asking after her. With her suspicions aroused, she would only make herself more difficult to find. So what was he to do? The only known connections to her were Giroux and Araza: one she trusted enough to share a roof with, and the other she now despised—or so it seemed. How to use them to bring her in? He had to set a trap.

After another hour or so of walking, their luck improved with the arrival of a horse-drawn cart loaded with timber. The driver agreed to take them as far as the ferry across from the city. From there they could cross the river and reach New Orleans on foot.

Moreau appreciated the respite that riding in the cart gave his stiff joints. As the sun reached its zenith, they came within sight of the vast Mississippi. An easterly wind stirred up small, white-capped swells along the water, and Moreau noticed an increase in traffic traveling in both directions on the river road. He observed that most of the people departing the city appeared to be families, mostly just women and children, while the lone travelers and small parties of horsemen heading toward the city were nearly all men. In his experience when families fled and men gathered, fighting was rarely far behind.

As waves lapped at the flat-bottomed ferryboat crossing the Mississippi, Moreau's thoughts began to harden into a tangible plan. He would go to Maspero's, challenge Araza to a duel, and as a condition of his victory, the Baratarian would bring Celeste de Beaumais into the city, where Moreau would apprehend her and return her to France. So, as he and Will disembarked onto the soggy soil of the left bank, he decided he would go to Maspero's that very night—and challenge of Araza. Thus far there had been no shortage of corsair bastards at the tavern; surely there would be at least one man to pass on his challenge.

The two walked in silence as they passed the first houses of the suburbs, and a few minutes later they passed onto St. Philip Street, heading toward the French Quarter. On the corner of one street, Moreau saw a large wooden panel nailed to a shop wall that declared in hastily scrawled words: *Cotton Sale, 10 cents per lb.* Another such sign read, *Negro dances and plays forbidden until further notice.* He wondered what might cause plays, of all things, to be banned by the authorities, but the sight of several armed men in tattered clothes crossing the street suggested one reason. As he looked around this "Anglo-American" quarter of the city, he felt a distinct uneasiness. It was now mid-afternoon, but the streets were strangely quiet, the handful of shops and offices either empty or boarded-up. They had not been away from the city two days, but from what Moreau could see, a heavy quiet seemed to have descended.

He looked down at the boy, who seemed to be in a gloomy mood. "What's wrong with you?" Moreau asked, looking down the street to get his bearings. Will sighed quietly but said nothing, causing Moreau to stare at him with a frown. "Did you not hear me?" Will flinched slightly, as if expecting a blow, and Moreau, not understanding the boy's mood nor inclined to pry into his feelings with a soft touch, gripped his shoulder tightly. "If you've taken a vow of silence, fine. But we're back in your city—so I suppose you can make your way from here."

To Moreau's shock and dismay, the boy began to cry. Quietly at first, but as Moreau's frown deepened, Will lowered his head and sobbed, tears falling down his face. After a few halfhearted attempts at soothing the boy's nerves, Moreau sighed and leaned down to try a different tack. "Listen to me, whatever happened on the ship, your 'cowardice,' it wasn't your fault; it was your leaders'. They were either piss-poor trainers or scared shitless themselves, so forget them, there's nothing to be done about it." He glowered at the boy. "Your moping about like a milksop will bring you nothing but more misery."

Will looked away without responding. Once again, Moreau leaned over until the boy could not avoid seeing his frown. "The world is a cold, ruthless place. I would have thought an orphaned pirate would've come to accept that." He paused a moment, resuming in a quieter voice: "Trusting to the charity and mercy of others just brings coldness and disappointment."

Moreau sighed again. Without moving his head, he shifted his eyes to look at Will, who had stopped crying but whose head and shoulders drooped forlornly. "You're the only friend I have," the boy whispered.

Moreau turned and peered down Royal Street for several seconds before he eventually spoke in a quiet voice. "I'm sorry you were left by your mother. And I'm sorry your pirate captain dumped you from his ship. But this is not my city, and the sooner you learn to take care of yourself, the better off you'll be."

Will looked more pitiful than ever. He turned away from Moreau, but this time the man made no effort to get his attention. "You know these streets," Moreau told him. "You'll be alright." He started to say more, but no words came. With a last look at the boy, he turned and made his way into the French Quarter.

~~~

As he entered the tavern, Moreau felt a momentary sense of relief. The drunken, boisterous crowds he had seen on his two previous visits were absent, and the common room was largely empty, with only a few men sitting in two separate groups and one man alone at another table. With a neutral expression he approached the counter, recognizing the innkeeper named Maspero. Turning from one of the barrels with two large mugs, the man set them down, wiping his apron. "How can I serve you, monsieur?"

"Quiet night," Moreau said. "Everything is well?"

"Nothing amiss, monsieur," Maspero replied. "Just a quiet evening." He gazed across the counter with one eyebrow slowly rising, and Moreau ordered a cup of wine to placate him. Taking a sip, he asked if the regulars were late to their evening engagements, to which the innkeeper waved a hand, claiming they likely would not be around that night.

"And their leader? The one who owns this establishment? Araza, I believe he was called."

At the mention of the privateer captain, Maspero paused briefly. "Araza doesn't own this establishment."

"He told me this was his tavern," Moreau said. "Perhaps he was just boasting."

The innkeeper finished hanging a wineglass between two beams over his head and looked back at Moreau. "I own it—with my wife, of course. On occasion he does conduct some of his business here. One might say it's his office."

"I see. And what might cause his absence on this particular night?"

"Oh, just politics."

Moreau gave him a curious look, and eventually the man sighed. "Talk is that General Jackson is within a day's ride of the city. Said to come riding in with reinforcements any time now. Think most of the boys here wish to make themselves scarce, so as not to stir up any trouble." He pursed his lips as he glanced over the empty room, then muttered something about checking the stew and excused himself back to the kitchen.

Moreau took a sip as he gazed around the room, the look of the men at the tables confirming his suspicion that they weren't Baratarians. He cursed his luck; after the chaos of the past few days, now when he'd finally wished for a confrontation, none was forthcoming. He peered around once again until his eyes landed on the stairway in the corner, and a sudden idea occurred to him. Without allowing himself time to overthink it, he stalked over to the stairs and began walking up, careful not to let his boots stomp as he ascended. At the top of the stairway he halted, listening for pursuit. A subtle glance behind showed that no one had followed, so he crept cautiously down the dark, narrow corridor.

Stopping at the first door on his right, he reached for the doorknob and twisted. Locked. With a frustrated sigh, he tried the next door, then a third on the opposite side of the hall. All locked. The sound of footsteps coming up the stairs stopped him dead in his tracks. Without bothering to see who might be approaching, he darted down the hallway and crouched down into a corner almost completely hidden in the shadows.

The footsteps grew louder as they gained the top of the stairs, and Moreau watched as a hooded figure holding a single candle emerged onto the second floor. The light hardly reached beyond its source, but it was enough to force Moreau to crouch even further into the corner. The individual's profile was hidden by the hood, and for a moment they stood perfectly still as if listening for something. Eventually, satisfied there were no observers, the stranger dug into a belt pouch, pulled out a key, and inserted it into the lock of the second door, which swung open with a slow, creaky noise that seemed to strain the door's hinges.

With hardly a sound, Moreau rose from his crouch and stole down the hall to follow the individual inside the room, relieved to see the door left ajar. Cursing his lack of a weapon—or at least something solid, should he need to defend himself—he peered slowly around the half-open door and was able to get a fairly clear look inside the room, thanks to the taper in its pewter candleholder set on a rectangular table in the middle of the space. The hooded figure stood on the far side, bent over and facing away from Moreau, who crept cautiously into the room, wary of creaking floorboards and keeping his eyes focused on the stranger. As he inched slowly forward, he could make out a small cupboard stacked with papers in the far-left corner, and a ladder-back chair beside a table set with silverware and several bottles to his right. It certainly had the look of a pirate's bureau; any space not taken up by scrolls or parchments was strewn with bottles, pitchers, and various trinkets—spoils of thievery, no doubt. Breathing as slowly and quietly as he could, Moreau crept within striking distance of the hooded figure, who seemed to be rifling through a bundle of documents in the soft light emanating from a small square dormer window. Drawing himself up, Moreau took a deep breath and stepped forward.

"Turn around. Slowly."

The figure in front of him froze, and for a split-second Moreau's heart seemed to skip a beat. The silence felt overwhelming. He shifted his weight to his front foot, ready to spring back if the stranger produced a blade. Another moment of silence—and then the hooded figure spun around to reveal cold eyes that caught the glimmering candlelight as they stared at Moreau. For a moment neither moved, and a quick glance showed that neither was armed. All Moreau could tell was that the stranger was fairly lean and several inches shorter than he. The stranger then let out a sudden, high-pitched shriek. Leaping as fast as he could, Moreau cupped his hand over their mouth, momentarily stifling the scream, but his lack of a second arm prevented him from securing a firm grip. The stranger wriggled out of his grasp and tried to make for the door, but with his one hand Moreau managed to grab the individual's cloak and drag both of them to the floor with a loud *thud*.

Careless of the noise, Moreau pounced, again placing his hand over the person's mouth to stifle a scream—and saw that the hooded figure was, in fact, a woman. For the moment, she did not resist, but her eyes glared up at him with unmistakable fury. She panted heavily, matching Moreau's own quick breaths. With a hint of recognition dawning in his eyes, Moreau smirked.

"Well now, this is a surprise," he muttered icily. "We meet again, mademoiselle."

CHAPTER 11

French Quarter, New Orleans
December 2, 1814

Moreau waited several seconds for the woman to calm down, her breaths coming in rapid huffs and her light-blue eyes darting from side to side like a cornered animal. She gave him an enraged look, and Moreau felt relieved that she had not bitten his fingers. He leaned close and spoke in a hushed voice. "I will withdraw my hand, if you agree not to scream."

Her expression did not change, and he pressed his hand tighter. "Yes?"

She held her breath, glaring up fiercely, until finally she exhaled with a single curt nod. Raising his eyebrows in warning, Moreau lifted his hand an inch or two, waiting for the scream he was sure would come. When she made no noise, he slowly lifted it higher until he could see her face clearly. It was indeed the woman from the tavern two nights prior—before Araza had sauntered in with his toughs and held a knife to Moreau's throat.

Moreau's features eased into a snide grin but quickly turned into a grimace as the woman drove herself up from the floor and shoved him off with surprising strength. Taken aback by her quickness, Moreau shifted his weight to regain his balance, crossing his arm over the woman's chest and forcing her back onto the floor, where he laid on top of her. She struggled for several seconds, gripping and poking with her fingers, but Moreau's frustration gave him renewed energy, and his strength advantage allowed him to hold her in place. She did not scream or cry out, but it took all of his effort to keep her pinned, and he began to worry what impression the sounds from the scuffle would make on the people downstairs. With a quick glance behind to make sure no one had entered the room, he turned back at her with a glare, his flaring nostrils inches from her face. "I do not wish to harm you," he growled, placing a knee on her abdomen, "but if you continue to struggle, I may have to."

They glared at each other for several seconds, and eventually he felt her arms go limp as the resistance went out of her. Wary of another trick, he eased his grip a little but did not release her. Eventually the woman whispered in a husky voice, "If you're not going to get off me, I may have to rethink my word not to scream." Moreau finally eased his hold and rose up to his feet. With a shake of his head, he reached his arm down to help her up.

Rolling onto her side, she pushed herself upright with a quiet groan. When she looked back at him, her hair was disheveled and her features had relaxed into a smile, but her eyes still smoldered. She blew a strand of hair from her face and looked around the room. "Not only have you forced yourself into *my* business, but you've surely made a grave mistake skulking about in here. When Araza finds out you've barged into his office..." She looked at him and shrugged.

Moreau straightened his jacket and walked to the door, peering out to make sure no one was within earshot. He closed it, wincing slightly as it creaked and groaned on old, rusty hinges, then turned around and took a few slow steps forward. His disappointment at finding Araza's corsairs absent from the tavern was quickly fading, and his thoughts now turned to exploiting this chance meeting. With a grunt, he gestured for the woman to have a seat in the chair beside the table. She responded with a roll of her eyes and a derisive chuckle. "For an alleged stranger to this city, you've managed to make quite a first impression."

Moreau watched her warily but said nothing.

"If the pirates don't kill you," she continued, "I wonder what those boys playing soldier outside will think of you. One can't walk two blocks here without talk of...*spies* and *troublemakers*." Her lips curled and her eyes lowered. "You could be both."

Walking over to the table, he picked up the candleholder. "I've been called worse." Keeping his eyes on her, he stepped slowly toward the pile of documents she had been rummaging through when he entered. "What exactly are you doing here?"

The woman let out an exasperated sigh. "What am *I* doing here? What on earth are *you* doing here?"

"I'm here regarding Celeste de Beaumais."

"This is the second time you've brought up that name in front of me. What do you want with her?"

Had he still possessed both his hands, Moreau would have rubbed them together. Instead, he settled for an idle roll of the fingers on his right hand. The smile he'd heard referred to as "wicked" appeared on his face. "I presume you know Monsieur and Madame de Beaumais?"

She turned aside with a scornful mutter. "Of course I know them. What I wish to know is how you know them."

Moreau met her protective glare with a look of equal intensity.

"Who are you?"

"My name is Marcel Moreau," he said quietly. "I've come to collect Mademoiselle de Beaumais and return her to France. To her parents."

"Moreau. I've heard Araza, perhaps one of his men, refer to a prowling Frenchman called 'Lenoir.'"

Moreau's expression hardened. "I gave a false name to keep anyone who might be searching for the girl from identifying me. My connection to the de Beaumais family comes from a nobleman outside Rouen. Valière. He does not wish to scandalize the family."

"I've heard the name," she replied, peering at the candle. The flame had melted away half of the candlestick, and white wax pooled in milky rivulets in the hollow of the candleholder. "But if you're so determined to find her, could you not have found a safer place to conduct your search than the office of her lover?"

"I found you, didn't I?'

She scoffed. "Lucky for you. If Araza had been here, you may have had to *fight* your way out."

"I was counting on it."

She pursed her lips, and her quick glance at his missing left arm left little doubt as to who she thought would get the better of such an encounter. "Well then, what do you want from me?"

"As I said, I need to find Mademoiselle de Beaumais. You can help me."

She folded her hands. "Trusting a man like you does not seem like the foolproof proposition you make it sound. And even if I decided to help you…it is not so simple."

Moreau looked at her thoughtfully. After a few moments of consideration, he took a step closer. "You say she loves Araza, but the feeling is not reciprocated." He watched for any sign of argument; when he saw none, he continued. "What he does want, however, may still be within his reach: the balas ruby."

"How do you know about that?"

"Never mind. The only thing I care about is finding the girl. However, I know where *he* can find the ruby. I could tell him where to find it—if he were to…draw her into the city."

For a moment the only sound was a faint wind gust rattling the windowpane. At length the woman sighed. "Even if you managed to convince Araza to meet you, and that is quite an *if*…what kind of servant would I be if I allowed you two to lure her into a trap?"

"I said nothing of a trap. Simply a rendezvous with a family friend from France." He waited a moment to let her consider the idea. "If you truly thought my intentions malicious, you would not have told me as much as you have. I'm beginning to think you might share my aims, if not my urgency."

She rolled her eyes but did not offer a rebuttal.

"I'm also guessing you have your own reasons for wishing to remove her from that plantation. No need to look at me like that, it is none of my business."

"The first sensible thing you've said all night."

"I would not ask you to put your lady in a dangerous position; but if, as you say, she still loves this man, then perhaps he can... *induce* her to come here. On some pretense. All that would be needed is his summons, and her agreement. You seem the person most likely to facilitate both." Satisfied with his impromptu plan, he looked at her with as friendly an expression as he could manage; in the past he had not always been successful.

Pulling a strand of hair from her face, she said, "I'm not sure why I'm even considering trusting the likes of you, monsieur. If my lady ever got word of this..." Her nervous look finished the thought for her. With a sidelong glance, she spoke slowly, as if thinking aloud. "Araza wants the ruby more than anything—why I'm not sure; all men have their peculiarities. And she wants to make him sick with envy, because she wants *him* back."

"All women have their peculiarities."

Her expression told him not to interrupt. "So, if Araza could be convinced of your claim, that you know where the ruby can be found, perhaps he could convince her to meet him."

"I do know where it can be found. Can you pry her from that plantation and get her here?"

The woman considered it, her features taking on an anxious aspect. "She bores easily. And though she spends half her waking hours railing against that 'pirate rogue,' she still pines for him. She'll have my hide if she learns of it before the fact...but I think I can manage it."

"Good." Moreau nodded. "A peaceful solution. I had come here to challenge the idiot to a duel."

The woman shook her head, but her expression showed little surprise. "I'm not sure who the 'idiot' is. Had he been here, he would have accepted, if he didn't have his men slit your throat. Either way, you would have been in trouble."

Moreau grinned humorlessly. "There's still time to test that notion."

With another shake of her head, she raised her eyebrows. "Well, now that we are conspiring together—are you going to ask for my name?"

Moreau looked at her and shrugged.

"Ugh," she hissed, giving him a cold frown. "You're no better than he is."

Moreau took her hand, lifted it to his lips and kissed it gently. "It would be my greatest pleasure to have your name, mademoiselle."

She pulled her hand away and reached to pick up the candleholder. "It's a bit too late for charm, monsieur. You've already showed yourself to be a...dangerous intriguer."

Moreau spread his arm and bowed his head.

"But," she went on, "as I myself have had little success thus far in uprooting the girl from her new life at Le Mouton Plantation, I suppose I might tolerate you for a little while. My name is Elyse Pasteur."

"Charmed, mademoiselle," Moreau answered as politely as he could, noting that she did not correct "mademoiselle" to "madame." "I am staying at the inn with green shutters on Dauphine Street. You may leave a note or call on me there."

With a look that revealed her surprise at having just agreed to a secret plan hatched with a prowling stranger, she gave him a furtive nod—to which he replied with a forced smile. "And then," she uttered, tightening her cloak around her, "I'll never have to see you again."

Moreau ignored her comment as he picked up the candle, motioning for her to lead the way out of the room. "And I'd assumed *you* were sleeping with him."

One foot outside the doorway she stopped, rounding on him with an indignant look. "Ugh, no! I would never come between my mistress and her...former lover."

Moreau shrugged. "Stranger things have come between friends."

"Mademoiselle de Beaumais is not my friend; she is my superior and I am her attendant. And if I am kept much longer, she will be most unhappy." Moreau grunted. With an effort she regained her calm and let out a breath. "That man left me and my lady for dead in an alligator-infested swamp; I could never be with him. But, *she's* still in love with him, and refuses to think of leaving. So I am here to try and—"

The sound of boots thumping up the stairs forced them to halt. Reaching a hand out, Moreau grabbed her arm and pulled her behind the desk, then dashed into the shadow-darkened corner behind the door. A few seconds later the faint light of a candle appeared in the hallway, quickly followed by the sound of a man's voice. Moreau peered from behind the door and saw Elyse standing nervously behind the desk, rummaging through a small stack of papers.

"Who's there?" A deep voice called out, not ten paces away.

Elyse looked up and swallowed. "Is that you, Tadeo?" she called. Silence.

A few seconds later the sound of boots tramping into the room caused her to take a half step back, and the light from the man's candelabra blended with that of the candle to illuminate nearly all of the room. Moreau slid tighter behind the door, cursing his lack of urgency while speaking with her.

"As I live and breathe," the deep voice broke the silence. "Mademoiselle from France."

"Burning the midnight oil, are we?" another man's voice sounded. Moreau cursed silently. Of course there had to be two.

Elyse smirked, looking briefly down at the papers in her hands then back up at the men standing across from her. Moreau inched his head out from behind the door. The nearest man wore a dirty, dark-green coat and had a black kerchief wrapped around his head. His hands rested on his hips, and to Moreau's frustration, a sword hilt was visible protruding from his coat. Elyse cleared her throat. "I've come with a message for your captain, but I found him away."

"Uh-huh. And is there anything else you'd like to share with us, mademoiselle?"

Elyse squinted, evidently regaining her equilibrium after being caught so off-guard. "Such as?"

The man in the black bandana folded his arms, his head turning to look around the room. "We heard voices, mademoiselle. Yours...and a man's."

Moreau winced, his heart beginning to beat slightly faster at the prospect of what he knew was coming. Once again cursing his lack of a sword, he ran a hand along his belt. Compared to the cumbersome boots in which he'd trudged to Le Marais and back, the pair he wore currently felt nimble, and he wiggled his toes.

"I don't know what you think you heard," Elyse droned. "I often speak aloud when I'm deep in thought. For those of us who *read*, it is sometimes helpful—"

"We know you're up here," one of the men cut her off in a loud voice. "If you come out now, perhaps we won't—"

Without further thought, Moreau shoved the door with all his might, and for a split second held his breath. A loud *thump* came as the door crashed into the man in the black bandana, and Moreau sprang out from behind it, landing in a crouch, ready to dive to the floor. His instinct had been correct, as the bald man beside the fellow in the bandana held a knife in his hand. Both stumbled as they moved to separate, and Moreau bounced to his toes and rammed his shoulder into the bald man, smashing his back into the nearby cupboard. With a curse, the man in the bandana dropped the candelabra, but by some miracle the candles snuffed themselves out before they hit the floor.

Pulling himself upright, Moreau turned rapidly and saw the other man reaching for his sword. Without thinking, Moreau closed his fist and slammed it into the man's face, sending him to the floor, his sword several inches out of its scabbard. Elyse, who had stood in stunned silence up to this point, edged toward the window, but as she did so, her arm struck her own candle off the table, sending it to the floor—where it set a scrap of parchment on fire. Staring first at Moreau and then back at the man slumped against the cupboard, Elyse screamed when she saw the paper burning. As the man Moreau had punched began to rise, dazed and his nose dripping blood, Moreau swung his fist again and caught the fellow in the temple, dropping him like a sack of potatoes, his head thumping hard against the floor.

The bald man bellowed angrily behind him, and Moreau braced himself for the inevitable knife attack. Moving with speed and fluidity honed by years of combat, Moreau leaned down toward the unconscious fellow and reached for his half-drawn sword, grabbing it by the hilt and ripping it from its scabbard. Not wishing to accidentally hit Elyse, he did not swing the saber as widely as he might have, but the act was sufficient to force the bald man, now fully recovered, to a quick halt. Squaring his feet beneath him, Moreau stared at the fellow, who looked familiar; surely they had met before. Dismissing the thought, Moreau lowered the sword and pointed the tip at the man's belly, causing him to jump back hurriedly, banging into the cupboard. Moreau snarled as the man in the bandana rose from the floor, and then turned and dashed out the door.

As he gained the top of the stairs, Moreau heard a loud, angry scream, followed by the bald man's heavy footsteps thundering on the floorboards of the hallway. With a careless leap, Moreau jumped down perhaps eight or nine steps in a single bound, landing hard close to the bottom of the stairway. His hip took most of the force of the painful landing, and he bounced down the remaining two or three steps without losing momentum. As he paused briefly at the bottom of the stairs, a whirling shape flashed past a few inches from his face, followed a split-second later by a *ka-chunk* as a dagger thudded into the nearby wall, its handle wobbling back and forth.

Without looking back, Moreau ran through the room, vaguely aware of several faces staring at him as he flew past. Still holding the sword in his hand, he ignored the sound of another blade being unsheathed and burst through the door into the street, where a welcome darkness flooded his senses, contrasting sharply with the light from the tavern. Unsure which way to go, he turned left and sprinted down the street, straining his ears for any sign of pursuit. His racing heart seemed to add speed to his legs, and for a block or two he ran at a dead sprint, not bothering to look at the street signs to get his bearings.

Finally rounding onto Bourbon Street, he slackened his pace a little, until an obstruction in front of him brought him to an abrupt halt. Panting heavily and holding the sword at the low ready, he cursed aloud when he realized what he had stumbled into. Standing not twenty feet in front of him were perhaps a dozen uniformed soldiers, all well-armed and most with their muskets or pistols pointing at him. Alarmed by the sudden appearance of an armed man, they stared at him with wide eyes, which Moreau knew to be dangerous when weapons were involved. From their uniforms they looked to be army soldiers, not militia, but he knew that any abrupt move would mean his death, so he slowly set the sword on the ground and raised his hand above his head.

CHAPTER 12

French Quarter, New Orleans
December 3, 1814

The first impression Moreau had of his cell—besides the darkness—was the moldy, putrid odor that seemed impossible to ignore. Once his eyes had adjusted to the dark, Moreau knew his first task would be to settle his mind into a calm acceptance of his new surroundings, lest his thoughts become overwhelmed at the prospect of an indefinite captivity. Confinement in tight spaces was not high on his list of personal fears, but no man so abruptly stripped of his liberty without formal charges or expectation of legal assistance could be expected to view such prospects favorably.

The sergeant that detained him had demanded his "city pass," the document permitting him to enter and leave New Orleans, as well as traverse its streets after sundown. In his best English, Moreau had offered his name and identified himself as a foreigner possessing no such pass. The sergeant asked what had brought him onto the streets after nightfall, what need had he for a sword, and why he was running wild like a madman. Moreau had glanced at the sword on the ground beside him, for the first time appreciating the feel of a well-cast iron blade in his hands, and silently cursed himself for running about with it so recklessly. Foreigner in a strange city or not, he knew better than to act that way, especially when soldiers were about. He had muttered something about being attacked by men who looked like pirates or vagrants, even offering a description of the men with whom he'd just clashed, but the vagaries of his "memory" were enough to convince the sergeant, who spoke no French and showed no inclination to call for an interpreter, to consider him a potential threat. Moreau's hands had been bound, and he was led several blocks to the Cabildo, the city prison, which abutted a large government building overlooking the open ground of La Place d'Armes.

The small window on the door of his cell had three vertical iron bars and looked out onto a passageway that led to a courtyard. The conversations of the guards echoed off the white plaster walls in tantalizingly quiet voices, which Moreau was unable to make out distinctly. He sat in a brooding silence for several hours until a faint natural light began to appear in the hall whenever a door was opened, indicating the approach of dawn. Eventually the sound of boots traipsing down the hallway grew louder until they could be heard outside the door. The sound of keys jangling was followed by a slow creaking as the door opened inward. Without a word, Moreau was hauled to his feet by two soldiers in makeshift uniforms of homespun cloth. Not wishing to interfere with this direction of events, Moreau said nothing as they brought him out of the cell and down the hallway. They turned and led him up a wide flight of stairs bathed in the stark early morning sunlight, which felt blinding compared to the darkness of the cell.

The soldiers led him down a narrow corridor, at last bringing him into a large office and with a hand on each of his shoulders, pushed him down roughly into a sturdy wooden chair. Opposite him was a large oak desk strewn with papers, maps, half-empty inkwells, and other paraphernalia of a military office. Moreau turned his eyes about the room, frowning at the officer that followed him in and seated himself at the desk across from him. The man had a round head topped by a thick crop of brown hair that mostly concealed his ears, broad nose, and hard blue-grey eyes, giving him a distinctly American look—to Moreau at least. He took his seat and reached for a quill and scribbled a few notes.

"I am told you are Creole. If I speak in English, will you understand me?"

Moreau nodded, not bothering to correct the label of Creole.

"Very good," the officer said. "Now, sir, you are aware that this country currently finds itself in a state of war?"

Moreau nodded again.

"General Jackson," the officer continued, "has recently issued orders that no one enters the city without a pass of citizenship or patronage of a known citizen. I'm told you lack such a pass."

"When I arrive this city," Moreau answered, "I am not made aware of necessity for having this 'pass.'"

"Regardless," the officer retorted, "we are at war, and all citizens must carry such a pass."

When Moreau said nothing, the officer picked up a quill and began writing in a small ledger, looking up when he'd finished.

"Why you are 'olding me?" Moreau demanded. "I show your gaoler proof I am from France; what more I can give you?"

The officer set his quill down and stared with a hard expression. "You've answered your own question. Any foreigner in this city without express leave of the governor, militia commanders, or General Jackson is to be detained and interrogated."

He raised a hand to silence Moreau's response. "Agents from multiple countries, namely Spain and England, have been offered massive contracts to travel among the Indian tribes, Spanish villages, and Negro communities with the express purpose of stirring up rebellion." With a spread of his hands for emphasis, he fixed Moreau with another look that said it was obvious that he should understand the concern.

"Sir," Moreau said in slow English, "I am no spy—"

"Then tell us what business brings you here."

"I already tell you that my business is private. I 'ave no concern for your little war."

"Our war," the officer growled back, "is threatened by *neutral*, ungrateful Creoles like you, who have no allegiance to—"

His words cut off mid-sentence as his attention swung toward the doorway, and he rose quickly to his feet, leaving Moreau to turn aside in his chair with an angry expression. In the doorway stood two men. The first was a tall, well-dressed man with a briefcase under his arm. He gazed at Moreau with an inquisitive expression that was emphasized by his high brow and large, thoughtful eyes. His civilian clothes and somewhat ungainly bearing gave him the look of a lawyer. Standing beside him was a wiry man of perhaps forty or fifty years of age, who stared at the officer behind the desk with a level expression. He wore a military uniform—a dark-blue coat with a high collar and bullet buttons lining the front, grey trousers, and tall, weatherworn boots. As the older man turned to look down at Moreau, the officer behind the desk raised his hand to his forehead in a salute, which was returned unhurriedly by the senior officer.

"Major," the older officer said, causing Moreau to sit up instinctively, "I have with me a man who speaks French. Perhaps I might have a word with your detainee?"

The major lowered his hand and nodded tautly, seeming to have forgotten about Moreau. "Of course, General," he said, clearing his throat. "The prisoner is yours." With that, he stepped out from behind the desk and scuttled out of the room.

The general's eyes followed the man as he departed, and he finally took his seat with a muffled sigh. He turned to look at Moreau, who noticed for the first time the intense scrutiny with which he was being observed. He did not know who this general was, nor did he particularly care, but years of soldiering had taught him to recognize when he was in the presence of a forceful man. This was one.

The general spoke a few words to the man still standing in the doorway, who took a few steps and stood beside the general's chair. Once again finding himself being silently scrutinized, Moreau used the opportunity to take a closer look at the general's features: his face was lean and pale, his cheeks sallow, and his short tuft of reddish-brown hair was turning grey. Although he looked to be suffering from an illness of some sort, his sea-grey eyes bore into Moreau with an unsettling keenness, showing no sign of the exhaustion the rest of his features exhibited. At length, he leaned back and spoke in a low but firm voice. "If you understand English, please make it known."

Moreau cleared his throat. "I speak a little."

The general eyed him for a moment before peering up at the man beside him. "Mr. Livingston here will translate for me." He sniffed and visibly fought back a painful wince before continuing, his words translated by the man called Livingston. "You have one minute to convince me you are not an enemy agent; if you fail to do so, I will have my men take you back down to the calaboose in chains, where you will remain for the duration of this campaign. What do you say to that, monsieur?"

Moreau cast a quick glance at Livingston before replying in his own tongue. "I cannot confess to a crime I have not committed."

The general listened as the man translated, then leaned slightly forward, speaking in a louder voice. "My officers believe I should place the French speakers of this city under martial law."

Moreau considered this and answered in French. "I am not from this city, monsieur. I come from France."

"And how did you come by your injury?"

Moreau glanced down at his missing arm. "A gift from Russian artillery."

The general's body seemed to stiffen slightly, and he stared intently at Moreau. "You served under Napoleon?"

Moreau nodded.

The general, seeming to take Moreau's word as truth, nodded as well. "And what kind of man was he?"

Moreau frowned. "Pardon?"

"Emperor Napoleon," the general replied, his voice level but impatient. "You served under him; what impression did you take?"

Moreau puffed out his cheeks as he considered the question. After a brief pause, he gave a subtle grin, his mind settling on an image of the emperor nearly slipping from his carriage and collapsing on an icy street in Vienna. Moreau had been a hundred paces away and barely witnessed the near-tumble, but his comrades who had seen it spoke about it for days. "The emperor is a man of flesh and blood. I rarely came close to him, but his generalship in the field was often…miraculous. A man of genius."

The general listened intently, setting his elbows on the desk and lacing his long, spindly fingers together. Exhaling, he rubbed a hand across his brow as his shoulders slumped slightly. For several seconds he kept his eyes closed and said nothing, leaving Moreau to wonder if he had said something to anger or upset the man. Eventually the general's eyes opened again, and he looked at Moreau with a slightly less severe expression.

"What is your name?"

"Marcel Moreau."

"And what rank did you hold in your army?"

"Major, monsieur."

The general leaned back in his chair, his gaze sweeping across the room and out the window as he seemed lost in thought. "Well, Major," he said eventually, his voice taking on a livelier tone, "I've heard rumors of this city, of its people. Of a festering...*rottenness* among the citizens. Smuggling, gambling, whoring, piracy. To say nothing of dubious allegiances to our Constitution among the French-speaking Creoles." He sighed as he looked at the papers in front of him. For a moment his face tightened in a slight grimace, once again looking as though he was fighting a painful spasm of some sort. "Unfriendly Creeks threaten the lands to the north, depraved pirates control the swamp passages to the south—and in between, a vast population of slaves who have just recently grown a taste for revolt."

Moreau listened attentively, but as the list of the general's concerns grew, so did his confusion. "General, with respect, I'm not sure—"

The older man's eyes pierced Moreau with an expression that quickly silenced him. A moment passed and the general let out a sigh. Keeping his eyes shut, he spoke in a different voice. "It is not my wish, sir, to drag you into a fight that is not your own. But the threat we face from a foe as mighty on land as he is on sea is, by now, beyond refutation. If they take this city, they will control access to the Mississippi River, thereby dominating the passages for trade and transport to the entire western half of our growing nation. They will stir up further Indian revolts, and ensure the

Spanish navy continue to harass our trade ships in the gulf. New Orleans will be the bottleneck with which they strangle our infant republic in its cradle." He opened his eyes and looked at Moreau with an earnest expression. "Besides, one look at you and it is plain you have seen the worst of it. War."

Moreau looked away for a moment, examining the man in civilian clothes serving as translator, to avoid returning the general's expectant stare. The fellow was now staring at him as well, his eyes almost as keen as the general's. Admittedly he did speak French rather well, and seemed to use pauses and certain phrases for emphasis when translating. At last Moreau turned back to the officer with a rueful frown. "With respect, General, I have not come here to be involved in your war."

The general stared back, his expression severe. "Major, I intend to put every man within two hundred miles of this city to arms, as such dire circumstances necessitate. I've called upon free Negroes to fight, Choctaws, notaries, clerks, and lawyers—perhaps even privateers. It remains to be seen how some of these men will fare when they're finally put to it. Your talents would be of immeasurable assistance to these untrained, *gentle* men of society."

Moreau's thoughts raced, but he said nothing.

"You are a soldier," the older man went on, "and a Frenchman. Therefore a natural enemy to the English. As I recently told my wife, I owe the redcoats a debt of retaliatory vengeance." His keen, energetic eyes belied the sickly pall that plastered the rest of his features. "And I mean to pay that debt."

The steady ticking of the clock in the cupboard was the only sound to break the silence for several moments, as Moreau's thoughts drifted among a cascade of memories from many years ago. Battles won and lost in far-off lands. Honors bestowed. Women and children of his own nation killed in cold blood. Duels fought—and won. Dead men's faces. He tried to fight back a shiver, but an involuntary twist of his shoulders betrayed his discomfort. Perhaps the two men scrutinizing him thought him a coward, or a shirker. Let them.

"Unfortunately, sir," the man called Livingston said quietly, "the commander has other pressing duties he must attend to."

Moreau glared up at him with a hard expression, reminded of the prison cell in which he'd been forced to spend the night. "And if I refuse?"

"If you refuse," the lawyer said with a glower, "then you will spend the duration of this conflict behind bars."

Moreau snorted. "I've already been detained, though I've committed no crime. What guarantee do I have that I will not be thrown back inside once this conflict is over?"

"Sir," the general said, rising slowly to his feet so that he towered over Moreau. His face was as hard as it had been when he'd entered, only now his eyes held a ferocity to match. "I mean to fight until the last redcoat is chased from these shores and driven into the sea. If you provide worthy assistance to that cause, in any capacity, you will be granted your freedom without conditions. If, however, you show ill faith to our cause or attempt to shirk your duties, you will be arrested and confined."

"So," Moreau said with a sneer, "my only way of avoiding a prison cell is…faithful service."

The general spread his hands in a display of understanding. Moreau nodded, his mind drifting to Celeste de Beaumais, then to Araza and his plan to use the latter to seize the former, allowing him to repay his debt and leave these shores for good. With a lick of his lips, he nodded. "Very well. I will serve."

With that, the general motioned to Livingston, who favored Moreau with a keen stare before departing the room. Within moments a flutter of footsteps could be heard traveling down the halls, as soldiers prepared for the departure of the general, who took several steps before pausing in the doorway. "It is my belief," he said, looking back at Moreau, "that the men I am now charged to lead possess courage. But you can introduce them to the one thing with which a soldier must truly become acquainted if he hopes to triumph."

Moreau looked at him expectantly. "What is it?"

The general showed something of a smile, though it could not quite be described as warm. "The killer within."

Moreau stood and squared his shoulders. "I shall give my best, Monsieur le General."

"I know you will."

"And what should I call you, monsieur?"

"You may call me General." With that, Andrew Jackson turned and left the room.

~~~

Dearest Maman,

I've just returned from the Ursuline convent in the city, and I think you would be overjoyed to meet the wonderful sisters I've just made my friends. They seemed interested in meeting a woman from the "homeland," and were eager to answer my questions, even offering advice as to how I may help, with the war coming on. I'm so happy at the prospect of working with them. The thought of violence seems only to elicit an urge to preparation. I do admire them so. If I'm often in the city, I wonder if I might happen upon a chance run-in with the gentleman from Guadeloupe; what he would make of my work with these sisters is anyone's guess.

Among the city folk there seems to be no small to-do about the approaching English fleet, but hardly two people one meets share a view on anything, so it hardly seems worth bothering about.

Maman, in your previous letter you told me to forget all about Papa's dreadful treatment of us, asking to hear more of my dark friend from the islands. Well, I think less of that one lately, as I have found another man, and while he may not be "mine," he is the one in whose company I have been with much of late and who I described briefly in my last letter. I wish to paint a portrait of Monsieur Giroux for you—as I find him singularly fascinating, even puzzling at times.

His accent is rough and coarse, but his manners are well suited to his station—if in a provincial sort of way. He is short and rather stocky, and has the look of a butcher or baker, as the little fellow carries a slight excess of weight. But when he turns his attentions on you, you find yourself pulled into a gaze which alternates from gentle to passionate in a mere moment, as intelligent as it is fervent. Not nearly educated to the standards of French Noblesse, he nonetheless displays a quiet curiosity and broad-mindedness that is refreshing as it is innocent. An avid listener as well as speaker, Monsieur nods and squints when another speaks, inclining his head with the same fervent keenness I've previously mentioned. In some ways he is like Papa, though I think his way is more somber and rougher on the outside, with a warm center, while Papa is warmer on the outside, with a rotten inside. Do forgive me, Maman, but you know as well as I how true it is.

After a few nights under his roof recovering from our travels, Monsieur quickly adjusted to our presence, offering us an indefinite shelter. At first hesitant, I quickly came to appreciate his generosity, and as my health improved, I ventured out among the grounds, and quickly became enamored with this peculiar homestead. Answering my questions eagerly, Monsieur happily appraised me of its history and lineage. The master has also shared his food and finest wines, often returning home from daily ventures into the city with gifts; he bought me a suitable pair of gloves, two bonnets, and has pledged to take me to the finest dressmaker in New Orleans—where I may choose whichever cloth I wish. Perhaps it's not the Chatelet or Palais Royal in Paris, but the offer is kind.

From what I've seen of the neighbors, this man Giroux is fairly worshiped by the other plantation owners, who seem to defer to his experience and success, while hanging on every word when he holds his court at supper. Papa would be distressed to learn that the planters along this coast adhere to Napoleon's Code. One can hardly escape gleeful praise or nagging questions of that stupid little man when locals hear that one is from France, but, thankfully, other Bourbon traditions are held, and it is not all Jacobin drivel.

Anyhow, I've told you of the other planters, but there are other folk here of a different sort. Black slaves are to be seen practically everywhere—perhaps a vestige of the way things were on Guadeloupe or Saint-Domingue. I don't care for the institution, but happily I've learned to become accustomed to the ways of the Creole folk, who rely on Negroes for an astonishing array of activities and labor.

The slave trade was outlawed six or seven years past, but the practice on these shores is still very much en vogue. The Negro men smile warmly, and the women, some of whom are unexpectedly pretty, often do the same. They seem to be a happy lot, and while my observations of slavery during the revolution fairly unsettled me, I think I may have been unduly harsh towards the institution. Surely, any cruelty or violence is to be condemned by any good Christian, but the industry with which these fellows work and their seemingly unending smiles give me an indication that perhaps things are not as bad as

I'd originally supposed. Some of them are quite hearty in build. On Sundays the women are allowed to wear headcovers called tignons, some ostentatiously adorned with jewels, and these hens do carry on with chatter and laughter so loud one can hardly think or speak in their presence. One rather rude Negresse called Hélène seems to always wear a scowl around me—perhaps jealous that I have found the master's favor. But there's a fool in every flock. If all the plantations were managed by Monsieur Giroux and his overseers, I have no doubt any talk of abolition would be wholly unnecessary. Still, I am your daughter and I am sure to encourage the house Negroes to be decent and bring water, lemonade, and cakes to those working out in the fields whenever I can slip such charity; but I am a guest and thus discreet.

The white laborers on site are supervised by several men, chiefly Monsieur Giroux's trusted steward, Cyril Tremblay. He seems to me a prodigious young man. Not shy about his ambitions, and industrious to the utmost, I often overhear him and the master discussing their vision for expanding and reforming the plantation and those nearby. I think they wish to establish a coalition of planters who can organize into a strong enough cabal to influence the state legislature and challenge those "urban lackeys." Oh, but I now recall something rather interesting that Monsieur Tremblay once told me.

He said that before I arrived, Giroux was a markedly different man. Evidently his loneliness had taken on a deep melancholy, and though his enterprise thrived, he suffered from pounding headaches. The property overseer, a hard man named Benton, thinks them due to grief from the loss of his wife, who died five years ago of a tropical fever. It seems her passing had a damning effect on the poor man, who, I'm told, has not been the same since. Tremblay claims Giroux worshipped his wife, who had worked to instill in him a benevolence when dealing with the slaves. But when she died something came over the poor old man, and a part of his... less benevolent side reemerged. Apparently, he would wander the house at night, whispering to his deceased wife, bemoaning that he could not save her; apparently on occasion he would even curse her for leaving him. The man said the master's lamentations seemed "something out of a tale of old." The poor man. It seems all of the care and devotion he proffered his late wife he now lavishes upon Le Mouton Plantation, his "glorious enterprise." As his land fares, he fares.

Another point of grief for the master seems to come for his pool of labor. His care for his "acolytes," as the slaves are called, is so strong that each time one runs away it seems as if a part of him goes with them. At least that's what I take from it. He cannot bear it, and so his punishments become harsher with each desertion. I've heard he and Tremblay discussing the poaching of his "acolytes," something about folk hiding in the swamps, but I hardly know what to make of such talk.

But no more of such gloomy subjects—it is my joy and pleasure that my arrival has seemed to have parted those clouds of the past, and I am as dutiful not to trouble him with bygones. The master reminds us daily that there is a plantation to manage, and a war to be survived—we must marshal our energies to the good.

I wish to hear more of home. Of you. Do please try and write more.

With affection,
C.

CHAPTER 13

French Quarter, New Orleans
December 4, 1814

The following dawn brought gloomy, overcast skies that threatened to add rain to the gentle mist that coated the city streets and sidewalks in filmy sheets. Moreau set out to present himself at La Place d'Armes at the appointed hour, dressed in his best pair of black trousers, dark-blue frock coat, and bicorne hat, which, for once, he found suitable for the occasion. On his left hip hung the sword taken from the Baratarian at Maspero's, having been returned to him upon his release from the Cabildo. He had also been informed that a pistol, powder horn, and cartridge pouch would be issued to him once he signed his name in the roster of the Militia of the State of Louisiana as a major; a formality he was to perform presently.

He traveled along Decatur Street toward La Place d'Armes and noticed that there was a strange mood in the air. The eerie, melancholy quiet that had hung over the city like a cloud upon his return from Le Marais seemed to have evaporated, and a bubbling sense of anticipation had taken its place. Though confused at first, Moreau quickly concluded that General Jackson's arrival had injected a renewed self-assurance into the citizens of the city. Though the general had spoken with a sober determination about the city's prospects for defense, Moreau doubted that he, alone at least, could wring a true fighting force out of the city's citizens. Bluster before a battle was one thing; standing fast against thousands of battle-hardened troops was another.

Stepping from the pavement onto the grass, he peered over at the formation mustering on the other side of the open ground and felt a sudden and unexpected dread. It had been years since he'd led men under such circumstances, and though he blocked out the specifics of why he felt this way, the thought of such responsibility falling to him was enough to put a knot in his stomach.

Perpendicular to the formation of soldiers was a long table set off to the side where four men in militia uniforms were seated at intervals, writing in ledgers. Nearby stood a cluster of half a dozen men in uniforms of various styles and colors, none looking as though he belonged to the regular army companies Moreau had seen. The swords and pistols tucked into their belts indicated that they were officers, but it was difficult to be sure in such uniforms—not ragged or unkempt, exactly, but irregular compared to any army Moreau had ever seen. He approached the group with a curt nod. "Good morning." They turned to look at him with curious expressions. One sported a mustache fashioned in the French imperial army style; the others were clean-shaven and possessed a reasonable military bearing. Their ages varied, the youngest hardly out of his teens, the oldest no more than forty. They muttered their greetings or nodded before one of them rested a hand on his sword pommel and addressed Moreau with the twang of a Creole accent. "Welcome, monsieur. How might we serve you?"

"My name is Moreau. I am to serve as attaché to Major General Villeré, commander of the Louisiana Militia." As Moreau spoke, he made a quick survey of the soldiers across La Place. Perhaps three hundred men stood at parade rest, their muskets grounded and gripped in an outstretched right hand.

The man who had spoken grinned slightly. "The general is out at Fort St. John, but you may report to me, Major Plauché." Nodding at the formation, the major offered his hand to Moreau. "I command the battalion you see here." He presented himself well enough in a blue frock coat and black trousers, a red sash wrapped around his waist. Moreau thought he looked a bit young to be commanding, though admittedly he had seen countless baby-faced officers during the revolution in France.

"Fishing accident?" one of the other officers asked, gesturing to Moreau's arm. The man wore a brown coat over a green vest and sported a bicorne hat.

Moreau glanced down at his folded sleeve without turning his head. "Just the fashion in my home country."

The laughter that followed nearly startled him, as he had not intended the remark as a joke—not entirely. One of the group wagged a finger at the others before turning to Moreau, speaking in English with a distinct brogue. "Aye, ye must be a real Frenchman, then. Not like these impostors." His brown-blonde hair and fair face marked him as something other than a Creole or French émigré—maybe Irish. He wore blue leggings and a matching coat made from some sort of hide and trimmed with fringe, which Moreau would later learn was called "buckskin". On his head was a hat with a dome-shaped crown and narrow brim called a "bowler." In features and dress, he looked to be the most American of the group, though he seemed to understand French and got along well enough with the Creole officers.

Major Plauché then proceeded to introduce the officers in the group: Captain Maunsel White, indeed an Irishman; Captain Dubuclet, commander of a mounted troop of dragoons from west of the Mississippi; Captain Pierre Roche, a native of France and artillery veteran of several battles; and Captain Jean-Claude Hudry, another French émigré and commander of the "French Company" composed of French army veterans and Creoles. Lastly, Major Arsène Latour introduced himself, a tall, haughty, studious-looking man in a finely cut white shirt and long brown coat. Plauché added that he was newly appointed by General Jackson to command the army's engineers.

"The rest you will meet in time," Major Plauché concluded, guiding Moreau over to the table to present his commissioning papers. After the brief formality of presenting his documents to the sergeant in charge of the roll, Moreau was given a small scroll with orders and a pass signed by Governor Claiborne and General Villeré for passage between the lines and the city. Moreau's transformation from civilian visitor to armed combatant serving in the United States Army under President James Madison was completed in less than five minutes. It seemed somewhat anticlimactic, given his recent detention and the stakes of the coming conflict, but Moreau nevertheless felt relieved when he tucked his pass into a breast pocket and the sergeant cosigned his commission papers. With that done, Plauché invited Moreau to join his inspection of the troops, who stood assembled in company formation.

Moreau peered out over the group, noticing the patchwork uniforms: a smattering of homespun cloth and buckskin jackets and all manner of hats, ranging from tricorns and top hats to hunting hats made from animal hide. A glance at the men's arms proved even more alarming; perhaps half held muskets over their shoulders, but a similar number seemed to possess crude fowling pieces, shotguns, or long-barreled rifles. A handful held sharp, pointed lances in lieu of firearms. Moreau's eyes settled on the company farthest down the formation, closest to Decatur Street. To a man, their coats appeared colorful, even festive, some a patchwork of checkered hues: blue and white, blue and black, red and white. Several wore hats decorated with feathers or cockades, and from what Moreau saw of their shoes, he did not suppose many had marched far to get there. Unsure whether the sight made him want to laugh or squirm, with a shake of his head Moreau brought his attention back to the officers in front of him.

Taking a deep breath, Major Plauché nodded to his officers. Without waiting for a command, they walked to the front of their respective companies and did the same. Moreau, needing no instruction, aligned himself behind and slightly to the right of the colonel, straightening to attention.

"Battalion, attention!" barked a sergeant from the side of the formation. A flag was raised to its full height by the *guidon* bearer at the front of the formation, and the militiamen fell in to attention.

A flurry of commands followed, and the men turned their eyes toward the colonel, who addressed them in a firm but calm voice.

"Soldiers of New Orleans, you assemble here today in sight of your homes, your fellow citizens, and as your families. Though none of us could have foreseen the crisis which has befallen our city and state, it falls to each one of us to see measures through to victory. The task before us will not be easy, but if we maintain our readiness and discipline, there is no reason to fear, for we know what must be done. Commanding General Jackson has arrived with men who have fought the ferocious Creek—and more will come! Thousands have answered the call, from Natchez and Baton Rouge to Tennessee and Kentucky—but it is *you* who must be counted upon to be this city's first line of defense. You, sons of this soil and inheritors of its culture. Have faith in your officers, who share your language and who have shed blood alongside Napoleon and his marshals, but above all, have faith in yourselves. Your training will be arduous, but that will be what allows you to triumph over your enemy when the time comes."

Major Plauché then brought himself back to attention with a crisp movement. As orders to march were cried out and echoed down the line, the major watched as the formation turned and departed from the square. The men marched in a fairly well-ordered formation, for militia, Moreau mused as he remained beside the colonel and a handful of officers who had not departed with the troops.

Even as the soldier in him relished the thought of putting these inexperienced men through the harsh forge fires of combat training, his mind returned to his primary objective: finding the wayward young woman and taking her back to France. With a slight pang of guilt, he admitted that he would do so as soon as he was able—and then he would slip away, leaving the men he had been granted rank over to make do without him. Burying his guilt, he resolved in the meantime to impose his own strong hand on their training before he collected the girl and made his escape. He would not abandon them outright, at least not before sharing some of his hard-won "lessons."

~~~

At the conclusion of Major Plauché's remarks, Moreau, now a major of the Louisiana Militia, found himself in a curious but not wholly unfamiliar position: he had nothing to do. He had been informed by Major Latour that they would remain behind on La Place, where they would wait for straggling enlistees and eventually the arrival of another battalion of troops for an afternoon review—these from the state militia and not the city itself. As well, a company from the 7th US Army, a regular line unit, was to present itself alongside the militiamen, as was a detachment from the USS *Louisiana*, a sloop anchored somewhere downriver out of sight.

Captain Dubuclet, the Mississippi dragoon commander, waited alongside Moreau beside the registration table. As a cavalryman, Dubuclet presented himself well enough in knee-high black boots, blue trousers striped with green, and a light-blue coat with piping and polished silver buttons. Though not as extravagant as the hussar uniforms of European armies, the state militia's cavalry looked passable on parade; how they would fare under enemy fire was another matter.

"Quite a mixed multitude," Moreau said absently to the captain.

"You see them riflemen dandies, the ones that was clustered on the end?" Dubuclet nodded toward the far side of La Place. "They's mostly lawyers and clerks, some judges even. What they think they gonna do when they come under fire, I don't know."

Moreau did not argue the point.

"But you ain't seen the strangest thing yet: whole companies of Negroes passing by, armed to the teeth. I thought some of the folk who seen 'em marching was gonna lose they heads. Not sure what they plan to do with them boys, but there's a lot of 'em."

"They've armed slaves?"

Dubuclet craned his neck back. "Jackson is bold, but he ain't that bold. They free men from the city. Free Black men. A regiment of 'em marched out last night to guard the Chef Menteur Road."

Moreau nodded, as surprised to hear of such a thing as the captain sounded.

"Not just them," the captain went on. "They sayin' Choctaws comin' down from Mississippi, and 'course the corsairs come up from Barataria." He grinned, whistling through his teeth. "This fancy old ball is fixin' to turn into a damned *Mardi Gras* masquerade. Will it stop the redcoats?" He shrugged and laughed, a misty fog of breath passing between purple lips.

As Moreau considered what it would take to mold such a diverse bunch into a single cohesive fighting force—if that were even possible—Major Latour approached with a parchment in his left hand and another longer, rolled-up scroll tucked underneath his other arm. His expression was that of a man on the verge of drowning but still fighting to stay above water. After pinching his nose and rubbing his eyes, he looked at the two men with a weary smile. "I must take my leave of you gentlemen. The commander wishes me to escort him downriver to inspect Fort St. Leon."

He sighed as he produced a pocket watch and checked the time, his brow furrowing as his lips moved noiselessly. At last, he looked up at Moreau and Captain Dubuclet with a regretful smile as something to his right caught his attention, and his eyes drifted to the opposite side of La Place. Turning, Moreau and Dubuclet squinted as they raised their hands against the morning sun rising over the city's rooftops. Approaching at a slow pace were two men in the dark-blue uniforms of the US Army infantry. Moreau saw the sabers dangling from their belts and the bicorne hats that distinguished the two as officers. Their heads turned sharply to face one another as they came closer, as if in the middle of a heated conversation.

"Captain, let me remind you," Moreau heard the older officer, a colonel, say, "your orders were to send the baggage train directly to Fort St. Charles upon its arrival at your headquarters."

"Sir," the captain replied in a taut voice, "I was told by Captain Mitchell last night to inspect the flintlocks as they arrived before they were sent to Chef Menteur—"

The colonel held out a hand as he halted and turned to his subordinate. "Son," he said in a tight voice, "I will not hear excuses for a failure to carry out orders. Captain *Mitchell* has seniority in promotion, and he does not currently hold a command. If you wish to keep your company, I suggest you adhere to the chain of command and follow orders."

"Sir, I followed—"

"As you were, Captain." The colonel peered aside as if to see if anyone was eavesdropping on their conversation. After a brief pause, he spoke in a matter-of-fact tone that brooked no disagreement. "Hubbard, we will speak in my headquarters this evening. Now report to Fort St. Charles with the wagons you were supposed to pass along this morning. Dismissed."

With just a hint of hesitation, Hubbard raised his hand in salute. The colonel replied with a crisp wave before turning away and making a direct line to the table where Moreau was standing with the other officers. The captain stared at Moreau as he stalked away, and a vague familiarity dawned as the Frenchman recalled the incident, or near incident, at Maspero's the night of his arrival. Hubbard had been the unfortunate officer responsible for subduing the tavern full of drunken Baratarians.

Captain White grinned as the colonel approached. "Trouble with young officers, sir?" he asked in English.

The colonel shook his head slightly, keeping his attention on the men in front of him. As Moreau got a better look, he realized that not only did this man also look familiar, but from up close, Moreau remembered him rather distinctly.

"No trouble," the colonel declared wearily, shaking Major Latour's outstretched hand. "The boy is just a bit out of sorts. I've tried to make him aware that his duties are orders and not friendly recommendations. But he is young and hardheaded."

The nearby officers muttered to themselves or grinned at the comment, Captain Dubuclet mumbling something in French about the passions of youth. Major Plauché rose from the table and greeted the newcomer, who declared himself to be Colonel Winfield. The latter looked over the group, his smile fading somewhat when his eyes landed on Moreau. "Good morning, sir, I don't believe we've met." He looked intently at Moreau. "Or have we? You look familiar."

Moreau returned his stare. "I am new to this city."

The colonel nodded. "And what is your name?"

"Moreau. Major Mo—"

"Now I have it. You were in the shop on Chartres Street when we were searching for the runaway pirate. You were purchasing a pair of boots, I believe. Though, if memory serves, I don't recall you giving the name Moreau."

Moreau looked down at his feet. "I have purchase boots, yes." He then looked up with a squint. "And you tell shop owner you come from force march of several days. Such…tiring marches sometimes cause lapse in memory."

For a split-second Colonel Winfield's eyes went cold. "A keen memory," he replied in a friendly voice. "Surely it was but the first of many such marches. We have many long days and sleepless nights ahead of us, and much work to do, eh?" He looked around the militia officers, who nodded their agreement. "What rank was it you said you were given, Mr. Moreau?"

"Major, monsieur."

Colonel Winfield's eyes widened briefly, and he turned to his subordinates with a smile. "Major, is it? You must have gained the confidence of someone of significant rank to be given such a field commission."

Moreau gently swatted a fly buzzing around his head. "General Jackson. He speak in detail of force against him. With many countrymen in your ranks, I hold my duty to offer assistance in driving English from this shores."

Winfield wasn't the only officer present to look at Moreau with raised eyebrows. Captain Dubuclet nodded toward Moreau, and Major Latour laughed cheerfully. "Ol' Hickory himself spoke with you? Perhaps *you* should command the battalion."

Moreau smiled tightly, plainly uncomfortable at the suggestion. Meanwhile, Major Plauché, who had not ceased signing the papers in his hand, passed them to a subordinate and rested a hand on the pommel of his sword. "Speaking of General Jackson, he is recently depart for inspection of fortifications; *alors*, we must get to work."

The other officers nodded, and Moreau met Colonel Winfield's curious gaze with a flat stare of his own, sensing in the other man a curiosity that felt slightly less than friendly.

CHAPTER 14

French Quarter, New Orleans
December 7, 1814

For the better part of three days, Moreau watched the drills and maneuvers of the two battalions from the position of detached observer, intending to assess their capabilities and morale before putting them to the test. Among the French-speaking militia battalions, of which Moreau was now a member, a nervous confidence prevailed, and what he saw of their enthusiasm while marching and drilling was somewhat encouraging; they were not foot-dragging conscripts like some he had seen on the Continent. Yet neither were they crack troops with well-honed discipline and confidence—a soldier's discipline often being a prerequisite for his confidence. The army regulars, the 7th and 44th Infantry Regiments, were held to a fairly austere training regimen, which their officers saw to without much need for assistance from Moreau or the Creole officers.

For the time being, the army regulars were housed in barracks at Fort St. Charles on the edge of the city, while the various militia companies had been scattered to camps near "vulnerable points" around the bayous and waterways to guard against incursions from an enemy whose whereabouts seemed an ominous mystery. Rumors abounded of a large flotilla spotted "somewhere in the Gulf of Mexico," but that meant it could be anywhere.

Moreau had been tasked with assisting Major Plauché in drilling the militia units in the basic tasks of warfare, and the two were more or less free to conduct training as they saw fit whenever the men were not assigned to labor details like felling trees or transporting provisions. Moreau's quarters were within Fort St. Charles itself, where he shared a barracks room with two captains from the 7th Infantry, seeing them only in the predawn or evening darkness.

When his thoughts were not focused on training, gambling, or the retrieval of Mademoiselle de Beaumais, they often drifted to Antonia Milroy, whose detention in the cypress swamp still gnawed at him. He told himself it was guilt over her capture that caused her to occupy such an oversized place in his thoughts, but as he settled into the routines of a soldier and reacquainted himself with the skills and prowess he had honed over years under arms, he supposed she might be surprised to see the grumpy, one-armed menace she seemed to think he was become an officer overseeing the city's soldiers. She *had* referred to him as dangerous. Regardless, as he donned his "uniform" at the start of each day—his own frock coat, bicorne hat, and black trousers, supplemented by a white sash tied around his waist—he could not deny that he felt a subtle renewal of pride.

On his third evening in camp, Moreau requested permission to lead a day's training of the two state battalions, fully intending to bring their efforts from earnest to "severe." When he presented his request to General Villeré, commander of the state militia, the general acceded with bemused interest. He was a tall man, perhaps in his late forties, with broad shoulders and the elegant bearing of a sugarcane planter who fashioned himself a New World aristocrat. Granting Moreau permission to lead the training, he said only, "Exhort them as if your emperor is watching and does not wish to be disappointed." Moreau needed no added incentive, but the Creole general's eyes had flashed with earnest zeal, and Moreau took that as the blessing needed to press the men as only one of Napoleon's veterans knew how.

Moreau joined the battalions in the predawn darkness as they mustered for drill under General Villeré's eye on the plain to the southeast of Fort St. Charles. Chosen as the site for the day's training was a riverside plantation belonging to a Monsieur Daunois, whose permission had been secured by Villeré, whose own plantation lay a few mere miles downriver. The Daunois manor house sat perhaps two hundred paces from the river road abutting the levee, just a stone's throw from the Mississippi, while the cane fields stretched a mile back until they melted into the cypress swamp. In between lay a stretch of open ground broken by the occasional orange grove or small garden, and interspersed with cottages and outbuildings used as labor sheds and slave quarters.

General Villeré sat ahorse and was accompanied by an aide-de-camp as well as the sergeant major of the New Orleans battalion, Michel Lamaze, a lean, unassuming man with black hair and eyes nearly as dark, who rarely seemed to speak in anything other than a hoarse whisper or angry shout. Moreau watched with a deepening frown as the company commanders brought their men to a halt in a fallow sugarcane field in the center of the open ground. What had begun as tight, well-spaced formations now looked like a haphazard gaggle of several hundred half-trained men, jostling and grumbling at each other as the shouts of their sergeants and officers echoed over the fields.

Needing no prompt, Sergeant Major Lamaze bellowed a two-minute ultimatum for the troops to form up, which seemed to jolt the men and officers alike into a frenzy of movement, eventually bringing them into a semblance of a military formation. When the noncommissioned officers had completed their haranguing, the two battalions stood to attention and the field fell under a solemn quiet, broken only by the occasional clinking of a horse's harness or the squishing of hooves in the damp grass.

It was now half past seven o'clock, a full hour behind Moreau's intended schedule, and the delays and pandemonium of the march—to him a very simple march—had left him in a foul humor. With a deep breath, he settled his darkening mood and dismounted, passing the reins to the sergeant major, and approached the nearest group of soldiers.

"Best give it to them in French, monsieur." Sergeant Major Lamaze muttered. "They's Creoles, mostly."

Moreau frowned as he looked at the motley group in front of him. "I'm not sure these men will understand what I have to say in any language."

He called the company commanders and staff officers over to him and spent the next quarter of an hour explaining the tasks they were to execute, by company. When satisfied he had communicated all of his instructions, he had each captain repeat their orders back to him—which took some correcting—until he was at last satisfied they understood what to do. As they marched off to their positions, Moreau sat silent and unmoving in his saddle. A few moments later General Villeré rode up alongside him. "And what should we expect now, Major?"

"A maneuver complex enough that it should fail."

The general's lips flattened slightly, but he did not inquire further. Just then Colonel George T. Ross, commander of the 44th Infantry, trotted out from behind the manor house on a bay gelding, accompanied by two aides. Compared to the militia officers, he looked immaculate in his front-to-back bicorne hat and dark-blue coat and trousers of the regular infantry. He reined in his horse beside General Villeré with an eager grin. "Good morning, General. Major." Moreau and Villeré nodded their greetings, and Moreau then gave a brief report on the battalions' expected maneuvers, after which Colonel Ross removed his hat, revealing a half-bald head covered in sweat, which he wiped with a gloved hand.

"Well, I've been told that you served under Emperor Napoleon, so surely you know what you're about." He spoke slowly, weighing his words as he turned to look out over the slow-marching columns. "But I wonder if we ought not instruct the boys on the simple tasks of soldiering, before we plunge them into maneuvers designed to fail."

Moreau exchanged a word with General Villeré, who translated for Ross.

"Colonel," Moreau said, watching the formation off in the distance, "these men must learn in a matter of weeks, perhaps days, what a regiment of my countrymen might have learned in six months. I'm told the regulars of your regiment have been bloodied fighting the Indians. These men," he nodded out toward the marching columns, which were becoming obscured by a cloud of mist drifting in from the swamp, "have no combat experience to speak of. I would like to see how they respond to…difficulty."

Perhaps two hundred paces off, the militiamen were performing a wide wheel movement that turned them so they were now marching parallel to the cypress trees beyond, as Moreau had intended. Thus far the two battalions had executed their tasks to an adequate standard—now it was time to see how they responded when things flipped head over boots. Moreau cleared his throat, then turned to the sergeant major standing a few paces aside. "Give the signal."

Sergeant Major Lamaze called out to the three guidon bearers standing with their flags aloft. "First order, commence firing." At that the flag bearers waved their standards left and right, signaling the order to fire. Moreau checked his watch, taking a mental note of the time it had taken for the order to be relayed and displayed by the guidon bearers.

For several seconds a tense silence hung over the plantation, and Moreau forced himself not to lean forward in his saddle too visibly. A moment later an abrupt flash pierced the hazy mist near the formation marching parallel to the swamp. Three or four seconds later a thunderous *boom* shook the field, startling flocks of birds from the cypress trees and causing several of the nearby officers' horses to jump.

As the cannon's blast echoed over the field, all eyes turned to see where it had come from. As Moreau had expected, loud shouts could be heard coming from the formation. More followed, and up ahead a horse bolted from the mist without a rider, and several soldiers—hopefully officers or sergeants—ran beside the formation, shouting and waving their hands. By now it was clear that the formation had come to a halt, shaken by the unexpected cannon blast. Several moments later another *boom* tore across the field—followed by more shouting and more soldiers running as the sound echoed over the plantation.

"Major," General Villeré drawled, "I'm not sure what you think these men are capable of—"

A shrill, piercing sound interrupted him, and he swiveled his head to look toward the distant tree line, from which the sound had emanated. With a cold grin, Moreau peered toward the cypress swamp, where several men ran screaming out of the trees and through the fog.

"If your company commanders," Moreau said with smug satisfaction, "had complied with my orders, they should have set a screen of skirmishers to give warning of any threat to their flank adjacent to the swamp. If not, they have just taken the shock of an unexpected artillery barrage—from *one gun*, mind—and now they must conduct a right face and fend off enemy skirmishers hidden in the trees. Now we will see," he said almost cheerfully, "how they handle an assault of cavalry from the opposite direction." Moreau turned back to watch the field with a fierce gaze, muttering inaudibly to himself.

On cue, a low, distant rumble could be heard from the left side of the field, adding to the growing cacophony of shrieking men emerging from the woods. The primal cries had not let up as a line of trotting horsemen—more accurately a jumbled mass of horsemen—began pouring from an orange grove to the left of the panicky formation. None of the men on either side of the field had loaded their guns; nevertheless, Moreau had instructed the officers to put them through the loading procedure without ammunition, and to shout as they fired. But as he looked on, Moreau could sense they had abandoned even those firing drills and many seemed to be melting away from the formation as the riders approached.

Holding the only spyglass among the group, Colonel Ross squinted at the mayhem unfolding on the field, uttering wordless sounds as he saw the events transpire more clearly. For perhaps a half minute he observed the "combat," at last handing the spyglass to Moreau as he laughed audibly. "Well, Major, your *failure* exercise seemed to have had its intended effect."

Moreau raised the glass to his eye and leveled it, sighting across the field, where a strong breeze and the rising sun were chasing away most of the mist that had obscured the view of the mock fight. Running pell-mell, the men of the New Orleans Battalion shoved and climbed over one another to avoid the thundering horses' hooves. The "cavalry," an understrength troop of dragoons, wended in and out of the infantry formation with little organization themselves, and a handful of horses ran free, having thrown their riders. The overall effect of the charge had been to turn an already disorganized formation into a chaotic mass of men scrambling past and over each other as they sought to escape the field. Fearing that a bolting horse might run down a fleeing soldier—or worse, crash into a group of men—Moreau straightened his shoulders and turned to the two officers with a slow nod.

"Messieurs," he said, trying to inject a tone of deference he did not necessarily feel, "with your permission I will go bring the chaos into order and call a halt to the exercise."

"I think that would be wise," General Villeré intoned. Colonel Ross merely looked at him with an amused expression. With that, Moreau kicked his horse forward and galloped toward the formation of running and hollering militiamen.

That evening after the soldiers had been dressed down by General Villeré for their conduct during the drill, the men dispersed to their camps in a grumbling mass. The general then summoned the officers to his headquarters at Fort St. Charles. General Jackson was still inspecting the forts along the river to the south, so Villeré and Colonel Ross presided over the meeting to evaluate the morning's training, which had generated rumors of roaring cannons and a wild cavalry stampede. To Moreau's relief there had been no serious injuries apart from a handful of twisted ankles and bumps and bruises. However, a review of the battalion commanders had been conducted, and discipline doled out to those who had shown particularly poor leadership during the chaos.

"We've relieved one captain," Villeré sighed, "two lieutenants, and six sergeants, and a dozen men have been excused for injuries or disciplinary punishments. At this pace, the English won't have to invade; they can just wait for our numbers to thin out."

Beside the general were Colonel Ross and Major Plauché; standing behind them was a soldier from the 7th Infantry, who interpreted the general's French in a quiet voice for the American officers. Captains Roche, White, and Dubuclet stood to the left side of the small room, flanked by their first sergeants, while Moreau leaned against the timber-framed wall opposite beside Captain Hudry. Exhaling a puff of cigar smoke, Moreau returned Plauché's scrutinizing look with a flat stare, tapping his cigar ash into a small pewter tray on the table. Captain Roche spoke in a quiet but firm voice. "Better to learn who the cowards are in training than under live enemy fire."

"We are meant to be training them," Plauché rejoined, "not purging them. We have limited numbers; chasing away junior officers needed for the coming battle seems an odd way of instilling confidence in the rest."

Moreau puffed on his cigar. "In my experience," he said quietly, "meritocracy is something to be championed. Men who piss their breeches at the sound of cannon or the sight of horsemen have no business leading others into battle."

Captain White nodded but said nothing, while Captain Dubuclet pursed his lips and adjusted the saber at his belt. A moment later a door creaked on its hinges and Colonel Winfield entered the room, taking a seat at the table beside Colonel Ross. He declined a cup offered by the colonel's aide, while Ross set down his own cup on the table. Moreau thought he smelled rum.

"Meritocracy in Napoleon's Grand Armée is one thing," Ross exclaimed, "but here we do not have the luxury of an endless supply of conscripts. Nor do we have years to turn civilians into soldiers."

Moreau shrugged. "If the detachment of men from the Seventh or Forty-fourth Infantry that I requested had been sent to assist us, perhaps we might not have needed to rely on firing a cannon at point-blank range."

"Our men are not toy soldiers to be played with, Major," Ross rejoined, his words slurring slightly. "We have our own tasks to perform."

Colonel Winfield nodded. "And chasing away the few officers we *do* have seems more vanity than utility."

Moreau bit down on his cigar but said nothing.

"If only we had more damn flints and muskets," General Villeré sighed, "and, for that matter, cannons—we could at least train the men to fight properly."

Major Plauché cleared his throat. "Perhaps the Baratarians will provide the flints Lafitte has promised. Word is he has over five thousand flints hidden away in caches across the bayous."

"That rogue's promises are as good as his principles," Colonel Ross muttered. "Empty as a barrel of whiskey in the hands of Indians."

Villeré rubbed his chin, his eyes red from fatigue. "Jackson's staff say Generals Coffee and Carroll are less than a week from the city with two thousand Tennesseans. If they arrive in time, surely they will have flints and arms to spare."

"General," Major Plauché's upper lip curled, "can we rely on those upriver flatboatmen? The only Kentuckians I've ever seen are inbred, eye-gouging fools who arrive only *after* a fight to collect scalps, take the rum, and harass Catholic Creole women. I trust Jean Lafitte before I trust a man from Kentucky."

"General Jackson trusts them," Captain White chimed in. At a look from Plauché he lifted his palms diffidently in the air.

"And where is Jackson?" Captain Dubuclet demanded. "Per'aps 'e is a good fighter, but he knows nothing of this city—or how to defend it."

"Be careful with your tongue, Frenchman," Colonel Ross countered, his face red and his eyes showing the early signs of a tipsy glaze. "General Jackson is your commander."

"I am not French," Dubuclet countered angrily. "I am *Louisiane*. The state where we sit. The state you've been ordered to defend."

General Villeré lowered his head as he held out a hand. "This afternoon, Major Latour wrote that Jackson is considering suspending *habeas corpus* and declaring martial law. And Livingston claims that the legislature is in a panic, devolving into shouting matches in three different languages every time it meets. We have enough trouble from above without infighting here." He let his words sink in for a moment. Moreau took his eyes from the general as Captain Roche spoke. "If the legislators are so unnerved, why don't they take up arms themselves?"

Colonel Ross sneered. "Those Creole fops care for their political power first, their plantations second; anything beyond that is a trifle."

Several of the men looked toward Villeré, who possessed both power and a plantation. If he took any offense at Ross's remark, he showed no reaction. "They are irrelevant, now that Jackson is here. What is relevant, however, is the arrival of the boys from upriver. If they fail to arrive in time..." he trailed off, turning to Moreau with a solemn expression. "In the meantime, we will train the men we *do have* to the best of our ability, with no unnecessary risk of injury. We do them no good by eroding their confidence entirely, but if they are not tested in training, they will be ill-equipped to handle the earth-shattering chaos of battle. So, I have decided to let Major Moreau lead the training again tomorrow."

The outburst that Moreau might have expected did not materialize, as the officers simply looked between him and the general with curious gazes. If they were this fatigued already, Moreau mused, God help them when the English arrived. Ross nodded slowly, and Villeré once again cast a wary eye on Moreau.

"We will assemble first formation tomorrow at six, and depart for the training grounds immediately after." He turned his head to the left. "Major Moreau has thus far demonstrated his ability at throwing our ranks into chaos; let's see how he instructs the men in firing exercises. Dismissed."

At that Moreau watched as the officers filed one by one out of the room, doing his best to ignore the doubtful looks thrown at him as they departed.

CHAPTER 15

Gentilly Plain, Louisiana
December 8, 1814

The following morning, the battalions of the New Orleans and Louisiana Militia marched into an open plot of ground just as the sun was beginning to emerge through the surrounding live oak and bald cypress trees. Already standing in the clearing were several hundred regular troops of the 44th and 7th US Infantry Regiments in their crisp uniforms and well-ordered formations, watching with hard faces as the militia approached from the road. The meadow lay roughly three miles north of the city, having once been the site of a small Spanish fort overlooking a convent along the Gentilly Road. The road itself was little more than a narrow dirt track that passed through the clearing, but it continued to the Chef Menteur Pass, a narrow waterway connecting Lakes Pontchartrain and Borgne, and thus held an important position in the defense of the city.

The air was cold, made worse by brisk gusts of wind blowing in from Lake Ponchartrain, and the men shivered as they stood waiting, puffs of frosty mist passing between purple lips and chattering teeth. Organizing the companies was slightly less chaotic than it had been the morning prior, and before long the entire field was occupied by various army and militia units. The drills began with Sergeant Major Lamaze and the company first sergeants demonstrating the proper firing technique for the smooth-bore musket, the firearm most of the men possessed.

Moreau paced slowly, keeping a wary eye on the men waiting their turn, and as the minutes passed, he found himself frequently checking his pocket watch, anxiously awaiting the report of musket fire. Eventually, as the rising sun approached the treetops, he heard the first shots echoing over the half-frozen ground. It was now after ten o'clock, and with a frustrated mutter he crossed the field to confer with the other officers. Major Plauché and Colonel Winfield stood huddled beside a supply wagon, above which the American flag snapped in the frosty breeze. Moreau touched his brow to the two men as he approached. "We're behind schedule," he declared, coming straight to the point.

Winfield looked up from a pile of papers. "Today we are firing live rounds, Major. Necessary safety precautions take time."

"I do not wish to endanger the men with haste, but two companies have spent nearly an hour between them, their rounds being checked against the trees for accuracy."

"Your point, Major?"

Another loud report of muskets sounded nearby. "The point is that your officers are training these men with an emphasis on accuracy."

"Would you prefer they train to be inaccurate?"

"No. But we are firing live rounds—with ammunition that is already in short supply. We ought to train the proper mechanics of loading until the men can perform it in their sleep. Marksmanship comes later."

"Major," Plauché cut in, "as a veteran you must understand the value of aiming properly and actually *hitting* your mark."

"That is not the priority for these men, Major."

Winfield blinked several times and shook his head. Moreau turned, pointing to the men on the firing line. "Those muskets are inaccurate, even in training, with no smoke, blood, or pounding of hooves to unnerve one's precision. If these men aim for targets in training—and miss—they will learn of the inefficiency of their weapons, and it will only lessen their confidence. They ought to be drilled until they are experts in the process of loading, firing, and reloading—which is difficult in the *best* circumstances."

Plauché stared at him with a weary expression. "Major, marksmanship is the first task of an infantryman; it is what determines victory or defeat."

"I know some of the other officers," Winfield added, "defer to you as if one of Napoleon's marshals had sprung up out of the grass. But this is not Napoleon's Grande Armée. This is *our* army. These are *our* homes. If you cannot bring yourself to adapt to current circumstances, then you are of little use to us."

Moreau exhaled quietly, turning to the formation of militia on the firing line. Even from this distance he could see that their loading, firing, and reloading was dangerously slow. "How long before they are expected to meet the enemy?"

"Well," Winfield replied, "the enemy have decided not to include us in their private war councils—so, regrettably, we haven't the faintest idea."

Ignoring the comment, Moreau squinted as he performed a few simple calculations in his mind. "A regime of training takes time," he said eventually. "If our task is to turn townsfolk into soldiers, it is useful to know how long we have."

"We don't know, Major," Plauché said. "Our navy has yet to locate the English fleet. They could be months away—or days."

Nodding slowly, Moreau looked over the field with a frown. If they wished to scorn his recommendations, that was their decision. The English were among the most disciplined and battle-hardened soldiers in the world, conquerors of his own countrymen, who had fancied *themselves* the greatest soldiers in the world. For all Moreau cared, the enemy could waltz in and rout this poor excuse for an army and take the city as their prize. All he needed to concern himself with was retrieving Celeste de Beaumais, and then he could depart this godforsaken country forever.

To his right he noticed as a company of riflemen under command of a captain named Beale, who all carried the long-barreled Kentucky rifles, set off toward a far corner of the field to train on their own. Moreau knew these men had been selected as skirmishers and marksmen, and thusly ought to train for more specialized work—and with rifles that at least made some sense. Recruited mostly from the professional cliques of New Orleans—bankers, lawyers, even the judiciary—these men seemed to possess the resources to equip themselves better than the other soldiers, their bright coats of checkered blue and white or blue and black distinguishing them from the other units.

A few minutes later Moreau was back among the militia, shouting in the face of a young man whose musket had failed to fire and who was now carelessly pointing its muzzle at his comrades as he attempted to discern the problem. Moreau snatched the weapon from him, quickly disposed of the projectile and powder, checked the flintlock, then reloaded and fired it into the swamp.

Spotting another soldier raising his musket to fire, Moreau dashed over and seized the weapon, pulling from its barrel the ramrod that had not been removed after loading, and which would have caused the musket to explode in the hapless soldier's face. No longer able to restrain his frustration, Moreau threw the ramrod at the soldier's head. "You should go home," he growled at the quaking young militiaman. "You have no place among real soldiers."

As he stalked off to inspect another company, he noticed Major Plauché watching him with a cold look. He motioned Moreau over to where he was standing.

"Major," the Creole said in a tight voice, "I don't care how much experience you have, your conduct with these men is both improper and unhelpful."

Moreau barely concealed his sneer. "There is little I can offer men who refuse to learn."

"They do not refuse to learn. They are inexperienced militia."

"Militia who refuse to learn."

"Because you don't know how to train them!" Plauché had barely raised his voice, but his words carried a tone of warning. "Major, if you cannot bring yourself to professional conduct, I am within my bounds to relieve you from your position as adjutant."

"So, what do you wish to do with me?" Moreau smirked openly now. "Return me to my cell?"

Plauché snorted derisively and looked out over the militiamen. He eventually turned back to Moreau, speaking in a curt voice. "There's little you can offer these men. You may stay and observe, or return to your quarters; it makes no difference to me." With that, he turned and walked back to the firing line, leaving Moreau standing alone at the edge of the swamp. Looking out at the boggy ground he heard only insects and the squawking of a nearby bird. A tall mass of floating reeds swayed gently in the breeze, and he wondered why anyone would choose this place to live.

By late afternoon, over a thousand musket balls had been sent into the swamp, and the men were granted a few minutes to eat a small meal before collecting their gear to depart. The sun had fallen level with the tree trunks, and a stillness hung in the air. The breeze had lessened, but as the sun set, the evening chill came on in earnest and the soldiers pulled their coats tightly around them. A few minutes later a bugle sounded assembly, and one by one the companies formed up to march the three miles back to the city. Moreau fell in with some of the other staff officers along the road.

As they marched through the flat, thickly wooded terrain, the pines were the only trees they saw which still possessed their foliage. In the dim evening light, their bark looked more grey than brown, matching the Spanish moss that hung gloomily from the branches, no longer the vibrant green of warmer months. The lengthening shadows cast long silhouettes across the road, which was strewn with pine needles and dead leaves. Moreau held up his hand to cover a yawn as his eyelids began to droop, and an image of the young woman stranded in Le Marais worked its way into his imagination. Once again, he wondered how Antonia Milroy was faring, and whether she had thought of him since their separation. Slapping himself to ward off sleepiness, his ears soon caught a vague sound from up ahead, perhaps fifes. He kicked his horse forward and soon rounded a bend, coming to a crossroad.

He brought his horse to a halt a few paces from the intersection, and for a moment he was not sure what he was seeing. An officer from an approaching formation of soldiers had plainly seen him and raised a hand in salute. Moreau returned it absently, his brow furrowed in confusion. It was not the sight of another militia battalion that had caused him to stare dumbly, but the look of the men. At first unsure if the light was playing tricks on him, he observed that every soldier in the group had dark skin. His gaze followed their ranks back to where the road disappeared among the trees, and he concluded that this must be one of the all-Black militia regiments he had heard of. A moment later another mounted officer drew up a few paces away, and Moreau saw that he wore the same officer's gorget as his own. A major. And a Negro.

"Good evening," the man said in French, not seeming to notice Moreau's curious stare. "We are nearly through. Thank your commander for his patience."

Moreau nodded, and the Black officer turned his horse and urged it to a trot, rejoining his formation as it snaked its way down the road and out of sight.

Grey twilight deepened into pitch-black darkness, and as the New Orleans streetlamps were lit, casting regular intervals of light, the returning militia battalions tramped down Toulouse Street. The city had been under curfew for nearly a week, so there was not much traffic at this hour, but the curious faces peeking out from windows and balconies indicated the excitement stirred by the sight of so many armed men within the city. The day's training seemed to have caught up with the men, and they trudged onto the grassy turf of La Place with dragging feet and slumping shoulders, grumbling and calling out to each other freely. Still irritated by Plauché's reprimand, Moreau let the lapse in discipline slide without correction.

Awaiting them as they marched onto the large open square was the 2nd Battalion of Major D'Aquin's Free Men of Color, a state militia unit composed of free Black soldiers, who stood shoulder-to-shoulder four ranks deep. For the most part, they watched the entrance of their white comrades in silence, though several invectives directed at the newcomers received one or two sharp comments in return. Once the arriving units came to a halt, the two formations faced each other across the square, a palpable unease in the air, and the expressions visible on either side could hardly be described as friendly.

Moreau halted his horse in front of Le Presbytère, a large building completed just a year earlier, and dismounted, sneaking a curious glance at the men across La Place. He recalled the little Major Plauché had told him of D'Aquin's battalion: It had been formed a mere two weeks prior and was composed of over two hundred free Black citizens from New Orleans and the nearby parishes. Despite grumblings from some of the city's leading citizens, General Jackson had ordered the unit to be equipped, armed, and even paid to the same standards as their white comrades, though Plauché had wondered aloud about the likelihood of that actually happening. Moreau had noticed the Creole major's guarded demeanor as he described the Black battalion, seeming neither openly critical nor particularly supportive. Peacetime rivalries and prejudices often fell to insignificance in the face of a common enemy—though so did accepted norms of civility and cruelty.

Once all the men had been accounted for and orders issued for the following day, the militiamen were dismissed to quarters for the night. Moreau made his way briskly through the crowd, declining an offer from Captain Dubuclet to join some of the officers for a drink. He was in no mood to socialize, and he would not give Plauché another excuse to lecture him. Stepping onto St. Ann Street, he removed his hat and scratched his head, thinking of a quick trip to Rampart Street to throw a few coins down on a cockfight. Striking steel on flint—a difficult task for a one-armed man, but one he had long ago mastered—he lit a fresh cigar, and as he crossed Chartres Street, he nearly bumped into one of the Black soldiers. Muttering a hasty pardon, he noticed the man wasn't just another soldier but the captain he had met earlier. He exhaled a puff of smoke as he put his hat back on. "I saw you on the road."

The man gave a quick nod, removing his hat. "Major Joseph Savary, adjutant to Major Louis Daquin, commander of D'Aquin's Second Battalion."

Without the hat shadowing his face, the man's features became clearer. His hair was short, his skin brown, and his eyes dark pools that suggested a calm confidence. Something about his lean, athletic frame gave him the look of a cavalryman, and his wide mouth gave the impression of being on the verge of a smile without quite getting there.

"Major Marcel Moreau, adjutant to Major General Jacques Villeré."

Savary gave him an appraising look. When the man said nothing further, Moreau frowned. "Do you find something amiss with my uniform?"

Savary tilted his head back with a slight grin. "I could tell by your speech."

"What about my speech?"

Savary waved a hand up and down. "You're a veteran. The missing arm and overlarge hat that looks foolish on anyone but a soldier—sometimes on them too. Republican, maybe imperial. Not something many one-armed men can hide."

Moreau nodded slowly. "Yes, I served. And you—a major, but you're..."

Savary's grin wilted. "Yes, I am a major. And yes, I am Black."

Moreau shrugged, uttering a halfhearted apology. Savary's smirk quickly returned. "I was born on Saint-Domingue, raised by my mother, freed when I was still a child—sixteen years later I was fighting in the French republican army. They started me as voltigeur, and if that confused stare is you not believing me..."

It was Moreau's turn to smirk. "I believe you." He examined the major's uniform, little different from that of other militia officers, but he supposed the man could have worn the same republican blue as himself. "I started in the Vendée, enlisted fusilier. Long, winding road that brought me here, but I served with men like you. Never saw one raised to major, though."

Savary sighed. "I suppose I was something of an exception. Also a long road. But here we are now."

"Indeed."

For a moment neither spoke, each pondering the turns of fate that had brought two men from the republican army of the French Revolution to the streets of New Orleans—as combatants. After a while Major Savary shook his head and looked back toward La Place. "I hope they gave your boys more than us; half my men haven't been issued weapons." Moreau said nothing. "And half the ones we do have are junk—old hunting pieces or faulty flintlocks." He ran a hand over his face, looking fatigued. "I'm not sure this city wants us in the ranks."

Moreau considered the idea, thinking it not too far off the mark. "Have they said you would receive more arms later?"

Savary shrugged. "Major Daquin thinks we'll receive more once the enemy arrives and the legislature starts pissing itself, but it may be too late by then."

Moreau nodded, grateful for the arms and supplies his own battalions had been issued. Shaking his head, Savary offered his hand, which Moreau took, and the two men offered their farewells and took their leave. Moreau turned north and began walking toward Rampart Street. One small wager couldn't hurt.

He'd gone about fifty paces when he noticed four men standing in a group on his side of the street, huddled around something. As he approached, he saw they were not men but boys, and they were standing over a shorter figure that each held by the collar. That one also looked like a youth, but it was difficult for Moreau to see in the murky streetlight. The boy in the middle held his hands over his head, but he was clearly outmatched as the other boys shoved and slapped him.

"Look at you; you're scum!"

"You drunk bastard!"

"Stop it!" the boy in the middle piped, his feet slipping on the street as he attempted to find footing.

"Shut up, filth."

"Fight back, coward!" One of the larger boys tugged the lad free and slammed him to the ground, mud splashing as he landed hard.

"Get up, you drunk pirate!"

After lying motionless for a moment, the boy lifted his head and gasped, "Stop it!"

At this the attackers broke into raucous laughter, pointing and holding their cheeks in mock horror. Moreau, who had halted to observe the one-sided altercation, moved closer, noticing that the boy on the ground seemed dazed and woozy and very likely was drunk. As he approached, the strong smell of liquor confirmed his suspicion that the boy was drunk—but he realized, to his dismay, that the boy was Will Keane.

A swell of anger swept over him, and his fatigue dissipated. Equal to his anger, however, Moreau felt a disappointment almost akin to betrayal; the boy had gotten himself drunk and into trouble in the streets. For a pirate, the lad had an almost uncanny ability to get himself into trouble—and to pull Moreau in as well. His frustration grew as Moreau considered that his attempts to instill some confidence in the boy had only brought him to this. Was the youngster utterly useless?

As Will attempted to lift himself up on an elbow, one of the boys leaned over and threw a fist into his face, sending Will's head into the dirt. For a moment, the other three stared at him, either stunned by the roughness of the blow or enjoying the effect it had. Evidently it was the latter, as they looked at each other with ravenous grins. Just as another swung his leg back for a kick, Moreau grabbed his coat and tugged forcefully, wrenching the lad back until he slammed to the ground with a *thud*, the wind knocked audibly from his lungs. With a feral grimace, the largest of the group, who had punched Will, balled a fist and swung it with all his strength. Moreau dodged the blow, letting the boy's momentum carry him forward and off balance. He then set his boot in the small of the boy's back and shoved as hard as he could. The youngster flew perhaps six feet in the air before crashing on a muddy patch across the street. Seeing this, the remaining youths exchanged brief, wide-eyed looks before scampering off as fast as their feet would carry them.

Moreau watched them go with an angry stare. The one he had kicked groaned loudly as he gathered himself to his feet, turning back to Moreau with a look of indignant horror, as if he'd just been shot. Frantically wiping dirt off his sleeves, he called out for his comrades before bolting after them with surprising speed. As his footfalls echoed down the empty street, Moreau looked down at Will. The boy lay on his side, holding a hand to his face, rubbing the left eye that was already showing signs of bruising.

"You damned fool," Moreau growled as he reached down for Will's collar. He lifted him up with a swift tug, the boy's head lolling to one side, his eyes half closed. "You're going to be the death of me…if you don't get yourself killed first."

CHAPTER 16

Fort St. Charles, New Orleans
December 9, 1814

"Drink." Moreau set the steaming bowl of soup beside the stump Will was sitting on. Huddled beneath a cotton blanket, the boy looked terrible. "I want to see you finish it before I leave." Will looked up at him and winced at the morning sunlight gleaming into his eyes, his cheeks turning even greener. "If you have to be sick, fine. But you will finish that before I report for duty."

With a lengthy exhale, the boy slowly reached down for the bowl and lifted it with both hands, bringing it to his mouth and blowing gently into it. All the while Moreau eyed him with an impatient frown. "I don't have all day, boy. Drink." Shaking his head, he spoke in a strained voice. "It will do you good; drink it."

With a deep breath, Will moved the bowl to his lips and took a small sip, showing no reaction to the army-issued soup. Satisfied that the boy at least had accomplished that, Moreau fastened his belt around his coat, adjusting the sword's scabbard with a tug. After another small sip, Will looked up at Moreau with one eye closed. His voice was a muffled rasp that matched his appearance. "I will drink it. You may go, monsieur."

Moreau sniggered. "Don't think you can pull one on me. I'm not leaving until you finish it."

Will sighed, forcing another tiny sip.

Moreau shook his head. Casting a look over the fort's parade grounds, where men were leading horses on ropes and half-dressed soldiers were hustling out of the barracks, Moreau stifled a yawn with a gloved fist. He snatched the bowl from Will's hands and took several gulps.

"Well," he said, glancing at his pocket watch, "I must go. But before I do, I suppose I should tell you that you may spend the day here—but you stay *inside* my quarters. If you must come out, for any reason, you carry this." He pulled a small note from his breast pocket and held it out for the boy, who reached for it before Moreau pulled it away. "If anyone asks…"

Will licked a pair of parched, scabby lips. "I'm your aide-de-camp. Those are my orders."

Staring for a moment, Moreau finally handed him the note. After adjusting his hat, he scrutinized the boy with a slow shake of his head. "Just what happened to you?" The question caused him to recall their departure, when he had sent Will away on his own. He hid a pang of guilt behind a furrowed brow as he handed the bowl back watched the boy take another sip. "Well?"

Setting the empty bowl on the half-frozen ground, Will turned to face him, the effort looking more painful than it reasonably should. "I made do," he rasped, pulling the blanket tighter to his chest, "mucking out stables for a few days—until the soldiers no longer needed me. So I went to the docks and managed to haul cargo for a day, until those lot were all snatched up by the navy. Since then, I've scavenged the alleys behind the taverns and coffeehouses for scraps. Night before last I slept beneath a wagon on Rampart Street. It was cold, but nothing I've not seen before. One can make do."

The earnest resignation with which the boy spoke moved Moreau to such a degree that he was briefly at a loss for words. Will, after letting out several coughs, finally spit a gob of phlegm onto the grass. "But my hunger began to grow worse, so I made my way back to Maspero's, where I waited outside the entrance."

"*Maspero's?*" Moreau scoffed. "Why would you go back to that filthy bandits' den?"

Will looked at him with glazed eyes. "I was hoping to find you."

Moreau said nothing, just nodded absently as his eyes lowered to the ground.

After another fit of coughing, Will continued in a sickly voice. "I thought perhaps if you returned, I could convince you to let me help you find the wo—with your mission. But I realized, given Araza's threat, you were not likely to return there. So I was considering giving up—when I saw him."

Moreau removed his hand from his sword hilt. "You saw Araza?"

"Yes. Well—I saw him go inside…but not come out. As I made to leave, I saw two men who had arrived with him come out. Thinking that drunk men often have loose tongues, I followed them."

The boom of a distant cannon echoed over the camp like thunder. "Did you learn anything?"

"I was following them at a distance, their steps slow and their voices rather loud. Perhaps some good news had arrived that night, like the long-awaited pardon from the governor…"

"Get to the point, boy."

"Y-yes," Will stammered, his eyes slightly more alert than before. "As I crept closer, I saw that it was Gambio and Rimbaud. One of them mentioned that Araza didn't agree with the blacksmith, and they'd had a row of some sort. Then the other said…em…that Araza was still searching for a pair of rubies, and that the blacksmith knew where they could be found."

Moreau sighed, wincing slightly. "I know all that."

"Wait, monsieur," Will said, his voice still raspy but his spirits slowly reviving. "They parted soon after, and I thought that was the end of it, but I followed Gambio—perhaps his bald head made him an easy mark. Any rate, a block or so later he climbed into a wagon; as he climbed in, I snuck behind the rear wheel. Then, as clear as day, he said to whoever was driving, 'Araza's in a twist because he thinks Jean is hiding the rubies for himself. His old strumpet is coming to the city in two days, and he plans to get hold of her then. I suppose if she has the stones, he'll marry her then and there—or slit her throat and take them for himself, haha.'

Or something to that effect." Will went silent, lowering his head with a sheepish expression, as if expecting Moreau to rebuke him for bringing bad news.

On the contrary, Moreau felt a surge of relief that bordered on joy. After a moment, he let out an amused grunt, tapping the boy on the back. "That was well done, lad. But now I must go. Stay in my quarters, keep to yourself, and if anyone troubles you, tell them they can take up their inquiries with me."

Will nodded. "Monsieur Moreau?"

Moreau half turned to face the boy.

"What is it?"

"I wanted to say...thank you. For your assistance last night."

Moreau looked at him a moment, finally giving a slight nod before turning to depart. "Stay inside."

CHAPTER 17

Daunois Plantation, New Orleans
December 10, 1814

The morning sun shone faintly in the blue sky, silhouetting a grove of orange trees that marked the eastern boundary of Daunois Plantation. A cold front had swept in overnight, dropping temperatures to the lowest Moreau had yet felt. The militiamen marching across the cane fields looked like ants, frosty breath pluming in front of them as they trudged in long lines of blue and brown. In recent days, they had shown modest but noticeable improvement, in certain areas at least, and despite their undeniable shortcomings and the hardships of camp life, they still presented themselves with energy and enthusiasm. Perhaps they did possess something of a fighting spirit.

Earlier that morning Moreau had approached Major Plauché and General Villeré, admitting that his behavior two days prior had perhaps been a bit harsh. He confessed that his attitude had been poor since the beginning, and he offered to lead the men in more exercises, should the two Creole officers allow it. After a brief consultation, Villeré told him that he could offer instruction that afternoon, if time allowed.

Lost in his own thoughts, Moreau barely noticed Captain Savary rein in his horse alongside him. The Haitian-French veteran looked at him with an expectant expression. "A word, Major?"

Moreau nodded, and when they had ridden out of earshot, Savary gave him a glare that Moreau returned with a hard expression of his own. "What is it?"

Savary blew into a gloved fist for warmth. He moved to speak but cut himself off as Major Plauché rode up. He spoke in a hoarse voice directed at Savary. "I'm told you have something you wish to say, Captain?"

Savary hardly bothered to hide his scorn. "The men of New Orleans may have warmed to the idea of our men performing manual labor, digging ditches and felling trees, but I know they're not comfortable arming us. Not in large numbers."

"At times a soldier's duty is labor," Plauché replied. "I do not choose the tasks, nor assign the details."

Savary's eyes narrowed and he turned to Moreau. "You served in the Revolutionary Army; you've never owned other men as chattel. Do you see trouble in arming us?"

Moreau thought for a moment. "I have no trouble, but perhaps these Creoles simply...care for their property. For their homes. Perhaps they wish to avoid civil strife."

"And we *don't* care for our homes?" Savary retorted. "Yesterday the enemy were spotted at the Rigolets, yet we are to be feared more than they? If these Creoles truly cared for their homes, they would arm *every* able-bodied man, not drop a few spades in our hands and send us off to dig ditches."

Wondering why this was falling on his head, Moreau shrugged noncommittally. He looked over to where the 2nd Battalion was falling in by company. Aside from the patchwork uniforms and assorted hodgepodge of arms, he admitted that they at least had the appearance of soldiers.

"Captain," Plauché broke the silence, "you know what happened on the German Coast. You know it could happen again."

For several seconds, the men held each other's stare. Finally Moreau broke the silence. "What happened on the German Coast?"

At first neither answered, though Savary's nostrils seemed to flare slightly. It was Major Plauché who pulled his eyes away first. "It doesn't matter—it's history."

Captain Savary stared grimly, and Moreau felt ever more confounded at this silent battle of wills. At length Savary leaned back and turned to Moreau. "It is history. And it *does* matter...but it should not affect the readiness of the militia."

"On that we are in agreement, monsieur," Plauché said.

"You've agreed on something, at least," Moreau said impatiently. "And while I confess my ignorance of this subject, I do know what will happen to this army if it meets the redcoats in its current state." Both men turned to look at him. "You will fail, and the enemy will take your city."

"One might start by trusting them to properly train," Savary said, raising his chin, defiant. "The enemy may have the guns, uniforms, and training—but the men of the Second are fighting for their lives."

"As are we."

"Then act like it, dammit!"

Moreau's eyebrows shot upward, and he half expected them to start raining blows then and there, but once again they simply stared daggers at each other. Sensing the men's agitation, his horse whinnied loudly and pawed the ground several times. After a few soothing caresses, Moreau broke the silence in a low voice. "The first man I ever killed was one of my own countrymen. A royalist farmhand who had taken up arms against the revolutionary government. He could not have been more than eighteen. I've never forgotten that feeling—slaying a man of my own blood." He looked up, his eyes revealing the damage to his spirit. "A civil war is more than just war; it is the most savage and unholy pestilence that can be visited upon a people—and they do it to themselves. I've seen the horror of it: women butchered because their husbands took up arms; soft-cheeked boys turned to demons, eager to torture and rape, if only to rid themselves of the hatred that was spawned within. The hatred of brother to brother. You lot here, you still have a chance for something different. A chance to set aside petty hatreds and unite in common cause. If you squander it..."

He swallowed hard, uncaring of both men's stares. When he finally looked up, he was surprised to see both slouched in their saddles, no longer glaring at each other. Their eyes were cast down, lost in thought, the only sound breaking the silence the drums and shouts of the training militia, which sounded far off yet strangely close.

"I was raised by my uncle," he resumed quietly. "He would often sing or recite verse while he worked…" Moreau paused briefly, then spoke as if recalling a memory:

> Two bulls engaged in shocking battle,
> Both for a certain heifer's sake,
> And lordship over certain cattle,
> A frog began to groan and quake.
> "But what is this to you?"
> Inquired another of the croaking crew.
> "Why, sister, don't you see,
> The end of this will be,
> That one of these big brutes will yield,
> And then be exiled from the field?
> No more permitted on the grass to feed,
> He'll forage through our marsh, on rush and reed;
> And while he eats or chews the cud,
> Will trample on us in the mud.
> Alas! to think how frogs must suffer
> By means of this proud lady heifer!"
> This fear was not without good sense.
> One bull was beat, and much to their expense;
> For, quick retreating to their reedy bower,
> He trod on twenty of them in an hour.
> Of little folks it oft has been the fate
> To suffer for the follies of the great.

For a while neither Plauché nor Savary said anything; they simply looked at Moreau with confused expressions. Eventually Savary tilted his head forward. "What on earth was that about?"

Plauché smirked, looking as if he wished to ask the same question. Moreau frowned. "The fable tells the fate of the frog, who suffers regardless of which bull wins. Who do you think will suffer if you men do not learn to work together? Who are the frogs?"

Both men squinted at him, neither offering an answer. "Your people are the frogs, you idiots. They are watching you, hoping and praying for you to deliver them from the enemy that comes closer by the day. The time you waste fighting amongst yourselves only serves to make the enemy stronger."

With an exasperated sigh, he dropped his hand onto his lap and shrugged. "I may hate to admit it, but your men have shown more fire than I would have guessed. I don't know if they will defeat the English, but I do know...they will *fight* them. They need not like each other, but they must respect each other." Savary took in a breath and looked at Plauché, while Moreau gazed at each in turn. "And what is the only sure way for one strong man to earn the respect of another?"

Savary turned to Moreau. "Whatever you have in mind, just please never rhyme to us about frogs and bulls ever again."

Plauché's stern countenance widened into a grin, and he let out a muffled chuckle. Moreau frowned at the two of them, shaking his head. Plauché's dry reserve slowly returned, and he fixed Moreau with an earnest look. "Well, what *do* you have in mind?"

A quarter of an hour later saw the men from the three different battalions called together by Major Plauché and General Villeré. In his typically understated voice, Villeré announced that their training would be somewhat different this day—that Major Moreau had a challenge for them. He then motioned for Moreau to step forward.

"Soldiers of Louisiana," he called out, surveying the soldiers in front of him. Most of them wore civilian trousers, many tattered or sewn with patches, and their shoes were worn and riddled with holes. Perhaps half sported beards or at least a bit of stubble, though there were those in the ranks barely old enough to grow either. The youngest among them could not have looked over fourteen. The Black soldiers, clad similarly to their white comrades, gripped their meager weapons with firm hands, fingers drumming restlessly on muskets and pikes, and stared at Moreau with eager attentiveness.

"I am no master of the art of war, as some of your officers seem to think. But I am a soldier. I have seen men killed by the scores, and I have done some killing myself. Above all, I know what goes into making a soldier. I was once young and brash, masquerading as a warrior to hide how scared I really was. I was afraid to kill, afraid to die, afraid to be labeled a coward. So, I buried that fear beneath my boldness, beneath my aggression. It *did not* work. When the time for battle came, my breaths came short, my knees shook, and my insides turned to mush."

A hushed murmur arose, from the enlisted and officers alike. Moreau made no effort to silence it. "A soldier," he went on, raising his voice, "is not defined by his uniform, the epaulettes on his shoulders, or the color of his flesh. What makes a soldier is what beats beneath his ribs. His heart. His spirit. And when his cause is just—as yours is now—he boldly faces fear, deprivation, even death, because that is his service. And if any of you here wish to be called soldiers, you must face what is coming your way with courage—for that is the service you have been called to render."

Moreau finished his address by calling for the men of D'Aquin's 2nd and the two white battalions to choose their best fighter, giving them one minute to select their respective champions. When the minute had elapsed, Moreau ordered the soldiers to form a circle around the two men chosen by their comrades, and hoped the fellows were, in fact, the best from among their peers. He brought them face-to-face and explained the rules of their combat: bare-knuckle fistfight, no biting, no eye gouging, no hair pulling. They were to fight until one submitted or was otherwise incapable of continuing. Once the men had agreed to the terms, Moreau sent them to their separate "corners" to limber up.

Lamaze, the Creole sergeant major, stood in his corner, surrounded by Creoles from the city, while Dunlap, a former slave from Georgia, glared across the circle and rolled his neck in anticipation. He was the taller of the two—over six feet—with long arms and lean, muscular legs. Lamaze was at least four inches shorter, but his arms rippled with lean muscles, and he looked all too willing to try his fists against the other man's.

At Moreau's signal, the men quickly closed on each other, bobbing and circling as they searched for a weakness to exploit. Lamaze launched the first punch, and the action hardly let up from there. Lamaze sent up jab after quick jab, most of which Dunlap dodged as he waited patiently for an opening before swinging his rangy arms to connect with his shorter opponent. The soldiers watched the first few moments in an a nervous silence that very quickly escalated to whistles and shouts of encouragement. Both sides made their feelings plain, and each time a fist connected with flesh, a deafening roar burst out from the aggressor's side. Moreau had thought the fight might take a minute, perhaps two, but when five minutes had elapsed with no clear victor, and both men near exhaustion but nowhere near incapacitation, he called for a minute's rest. The intermission only served to rile the two sides further, as the soldiers swirled around their respective fighters like a flood tide while the sergeants struggled to heave them back.

A look at his fellow officers gave Moreau some relief, as none were staring at him with the suspicious frowns they had worn before. Most were either muttering among themselves or pointing out tactics the combatants ought to use.

When the bout resumed, both fighters leaped forward with renewed energy. Lamaze dropped to the grass after an uppercut to his chin, but he rose to his feet a few seconds later with nothing more than a shake of his head and nod to keep fighting. Two hard shots to Dunlap's ribs stunned the him momentarily, but he quickly caught his breath, offering a smile and raising his hands to his followers, which brought the loudest cheers thus far. Ten minutes into the contest, with Lamaze spitting out a tooth and Dunlap holding his left rib, but neither willing to yield, Moreau rode his horse into the circle, halting between them.

"Men," he cried out over whistles and shouts, "we would gain little by driving two of our best champions to beds in the infirmary." He unsheathed his sword and swung it down, burying its point in the mud. "These men have earned a night of rest—as you all may profit from a day of recovery."

A motion to his left caught his eye as Captain Savary reined his horse to a stop not ten paces away. He did not look not as jovial as the men he commanded. "What's the matter, Major?" he asked. "Saw your fighter was spitting out teeth, and you strung up the white flag?"

Moreau smirked. "Both men have shown themselves fighters, there's no doubt—"

"Oh, there is doubt, Major. There will *always* be doubt when it comes to white men and how you treat us."

Moreau's face grew dark, and his fingers twitched on the pommel. "What do you propose then, monsieur?"

Savary gripped the reins in his left hand and twisted them, then unsheathed his saber in a fluid motion, the blade making a sharp, ringing sound as it cleared the scabbard. He nodded toward the far fields of the plantation. "The cavalry drill posts Dubuclet erected. I wager you today's pay I can complete the obstacle course and get back here faster than you."

Frowning and shaking his head, Moreau was barely able to see the drill course. If he squinted, he could make out the line of eight wooden posts, each with a target of some sort painted on its surface. A cheer arose from the men of 2nd Battalion, and Moreau scoffed when he turned to see what had excited them. Several paces away, Captain Savary was cantering his horse in a circle while whirling his saber over his head. Motioning to Plauché, Savary spoke quickly. "Do you have your timepiece, Major?"

Plauché reached into his breast pocket, then held up a silver pocket watch. With a grimace and curt nod toward Moreau, Savary turned his horse.

In a flurry of hooves and churned-up dirt, Savary spurred his mount to a gallop, darting past the crush of soldiers and drawing every eye on the field as he tore off at breakneck speed. The cavalry course was perhaps a half mile away, but the captain covered the distance in what seemed mere seconds, slowing his horse only slightly to weave in between the obstacles before turning and dashing for home.

"I hope he doesn't get himself killed," Major Plauché said wearily.

Moreau stretched and gathered himself in his saddle. "I think the prospect of losing to me frightens him more."

Plauché looked at his watch. "He is fast."

The soldiers continued to stomp and holler, waving their hats above their heads. Moreau cracked the bones in his neck, squinting as Savary rapidly approached from the far side of the grounds.

"He's challenged me—he better be."

~~~

The soldiers on both sides of Moreau sped by in a colorless blur, their shouts whizzing past his ears like bees rushing to the hive. The ground before him was a mat of green and brown, and the droning *whoosh* of cold air on his face, freezing at this pace, was exhilarating as he galloped ahead. Focusing his concentration on speed and form, he lowered his torso to catch less wind.

Savary had completed the obstacle course and flown back across the plantation field in three minutes and two seconds in a whirlwind of churned-up dirt, sod, and water. Moreau had watched the man like a hawk, while also looking for features on the ground that might be helpful to him when his turn came. As the first drill post came into view, he looped the reins loosely around the pommel and unsheathed his sword, a motion that felt as natural as snapping his fingers. He then pressed his knees into his horse's sides, guiding the animal as he slashed with his one arm at the first target—a smear of red paint on a tall wooden pole about a hand's width across. Careful not to swing too hard, and to angle the blade so it wouldn't become stuck, he felt the *bump* as it cut the wood, then pressed his right knee to send the horse toward the next obstacle.

Moreau kept the horse's pace steady, the animal sensing the subtle movements of its rider's legs and responding sharply. Three more obstacles passed by in a blur as Moreau swung his sword left and right, slashing with well-honed skill that brought more enjoyment than challenge. But he was not finished yet.

Coming on the final target, a thick wooden pole the height of a man, with a large melon balanced on top, he resisted the urge to pick up the pace. Moreau cared little for the showmanship of a ferocious cut, nor for what any onlookers thought of his swordsmanship, so he slowed slightly and leaned to the left in anticipation of the final turn. Steering the horse with his knees, he watched the melon with utter concentration until it was merely an arm's length ahead, then raised his saber and sliced it in cleanly in half with a soft *shing*. Pressing the horse's right side and gripping the reins as he grasped the pommel for balance, he dipped almost perpendicular to the animal, his head missing the wooden post by inches. Moreau straightened in the saddle and kicked with all his strength, churning grass and mud as he urged the steed into a breakneck gallop.

As the militia formations came back into view, Moreau came to the last obstacle on the course and slowed just slightly. What he anticipated had come from watching Savary as he made the final leg of his run; the man had ridden with bold, even reckless pace throughout and taken the obstacles with skill and fluidity, charging back home in a blinding dash. But as he had closed the last few hundred paces, he crossed a stretch of ground that splashed water up from his horse's hooves like a fountain, startling the animal into an awkward canter for several seconds before Savary's furious kicks brought it back to a gallop to close out the run.

Moreau now saw the sun's reflection shimmering on the water, likely a small irrigation channel. If his estimate was right, Moreau planned to clear it in one bound. Holding the pace steady as he came to the edge, allowing his horse to see it, Moreau then kicked its ribs twice, causing the animal to leap forward. For a moment time stopped, and Moreau felt his feet pressing the stirrups as he braced himself for the landing. A moment later the animal crashed onto the grass, the hooves kicking up turf, and Moreau again applied the spurs.

Passing the formation in a blur of brown and blue, Moreau slapped the animal's hindquarters with the flat edge of his saber and a moment later flew past the line of mounted officers waiting on either side of the starting point. He raced through the open cane fields until he saw the manor house, then reined his horse to a calm trot, letting it recover its wind as it blew out plumes of misty breath. As he turned around and cantered back to the line of waiting officers, he heard the shouts of the militiamen beyond. His horse was still panting noisily and tossing its neck, which gleamed with perspiration. To his surprise, Captain Savary was the first to approach him, flanked by Major Plauché.

Moreau exhaled loudly, realizing for the first time how heavily he was breathing. He retrieved his hat from one of the others and looked at Plauché expectantly. The Creole major chuckled slightly as he held up his timepiece.

"Two minutes and fifty-nine seconds, Major."

Moreau forced his features to remain placid, but inwardly he felt a good deal of relief. Savary looked at him with a rueful grin. "Today was your day. Well done."

Moreau nodded his thanks, sheathing his saber. He took several more deep breaths, feeling a sense of relief that the challenge was done—and he had won. The other officers chattered eagerly among themselves, or looked at him like he had just won them a battle.

A sound to his left caused Moreau to turn and look in that direction. Squinting as he peered out toward the road that led into Faubourg Marigny, he saw a figure moving in the trees. A second later he saw another, then another. Whistling softly to Savary, he got the captain's attention and nodded in the direction of whatever it was that was moving among the trees.

"More militia companies?" Captain Roche asked.

Now clearly visible along the open stretch of ground where the dirt track met the river road were lines of men marching at a brisk pace. A handful of mounted men rode along the edges of the track, calling out or looking toward where the Louisiana Militia stood milling about in the plantation fields.

"No," Major Plauché said, his gaze intent. "Well, militia, but not ours. From Tennessee." The other officers, including Moreau, turned to him with looks of surprise. "They arrived late last night and are going to present themselves to Jackson at La Place d'Armes." He favored the others with a weary grin. "I met some of their officers this morning. They've come armed to the teeth. Nearly two thousand."

As the other officers watched the road with excited murmurs, Moreau took a few steps forward. His was still looking toward the river road, though not at the long lines of marching Tennesseans. He squinted again, his eyes focused on something closer: Half a dozen canvas-covered wagons had peeled off from the road and were now approaching the mass of Louisiana militiamen. They appeared heavily laden as they lumbered across the sallow fields. But it wasn't the wagons or their cargo that interested Moreau.

In the driver's seat of the first wagon sat two women in bright dresses, bonnets on their heads and gloves on their hands. He did not have to see their faces or hear their voices to know who they were. He recognized Elyse Pasteur's figure from his two previous engagements with her, and he undoubtedly knew the woman beside her—who sat slightly more upright and waved a hand, offering a gracious tilt of her head to the closest militiamen.

Celeste de Beaumais.

CHAPTER 18

Daunois Plantation, New Orleans
December 10, 1814

Not wishing to unsettle the young woman, Moreau resisted the urge to make straight for Celeste, instead taking a moment to watch the Tennessee militiamen as they unloaded the nearest wagons. Curious about the newcomers from far upcountry, he felt somewhat uneasy about these men in their rustic shirts and buckskin coats. In fact, as they approached, he noticed his right hand begin to tremble, and he twitched the fingers several times before clenching them into a fist. A few moments later the awareness of what had so unnerved him came to the fore: these men looked strangely similar to the *Chouan* partisans he had fought during the French Revolution. Armed with hunting pieces, scythes, spades, and sometimes just their teeth, those fighters from the farms and villages of the Vendée region had supported King Louis XVI and his wife Marie Antoinette, and had fought the republican government with a savage ferocity Moreau had rarely seen. If ever.

Reminding himself that those days were long gone and these men were here to serve alongside the Creoles, Moreau dispelled the thought and approached the closest militiaman, who was supervising a group unloading sacks from one of the wagons. The man wore a brown coat with red trim, and dark straps over a shoulder supported an ammunition pouch hanging at his waist.

"Good day," Moreau said in English.

The fellow turned his head and gave a curt nod.

"You are coming from Tennessee?"

"Last I checked, that was so."

Moreau nodded. "You bring artillery?"

The man looked at him for a moment before reaching into a tin pouch at his hip, from which he eventually produced a large brown wad of tobacco. Stuffing it into his left cheek, he looked at Moreau with a thoughtful expression. "We was told General Jackson had all the guns he needs." He cleared his throat and then spit through his teeth onto the ground. "I ain't seen many on the road in. Though I heard tell about pieces taken from pirate folk or some such."

The strangely dressed man looked out at the Creole militiamen organizing themselves across the field. "Y'all got enough powder?"

Moreau rubbed his chin, finding it somewhat difficult to understand the fellow's strange dialect. "We 'ave some. The rest coming from Barataria."

The Tennesean peered sidelong at Moreau. "Who's Barataria?"

"Corsairs, led by Jean Lafitte. Pirate folk, as you say. They are once enemies of the governor, now they assist Jackson. He believe they may be useful."

"That so?" The man spat again, dark-brown spittle that looked like molasses dribbling down his chin. Wiping it away with an elbow, he continued. "Well, I reckon we could use all the powder we can get. Them Kentucky boys may not get here for another fortnight. Could be too late by then."

"You expect more soldier?"

The Tennessean tipped his hat back and rubbed his forehead. "Half the population from Louisville to Nashville is fixin' to get on a flatboat and float they selves down the Ohio to the Mississippi and join this here turkey shoot." He spat through his teeth again. "Like I said, don't know if they'll get here in time. May just be us here now." With that, he grinned eagerly, his teeth brown from the tobacco, and strode away to pass along commands to the others.

After considering this news for a moment, Moreau made his way over to a group of Louisiana officers clustered around a wagon. He ignored their conversation, his thoughts focused on facing the woman whose whereabouts had so long been an elusive game, and who now seemed ready to flaunt her presence so openly to an army of thousands. Unable to stand idle, he set off again, parting two soldiers in front of him as he made his way toward a larger group clustered in front of one of the wagons. He recognized Colonel Ross in his dark-blue uniform and long bicorne hat, and, to his disappointment, saw Colonel Winfield standing to his left. Several of the Creoles, including General Villeré and Major Plauché, he knew, but he halted in surprise when he saw the seemingly out-of-place figure of Emile Giroux, the plantation owner he had dined with some days before. Had it been only a week? He was standing on the wagon driver's perch, higher than the rest, apparently listening to someone who was speaking to him. Surrounding the wagon were at least a dozen well-dressed civilian officials.

Moreau took a few more steps and saw Giroux clearly now, his dark-green coat and claret vest standing out among the soldiers. One hand was thrust inside his vest, and he stood with an erect posture, like a general inspecting his troops. To his side stood his foreman, whose name Moreau did not recall. He was dressed the same as when Moreau last had seen him, and where the plantation owner stared out somewhat haughtily, this man scanned the group with an active alertness.

Moreau edged closer and heard General Villeré speaking in English, directing his words at the old planter. "And we are most grateful for your generosity in providing this assistance, monsieur. We can never have enough axes nor spades, and the soldiers will need these blankets as the nights grow colder. On behalf of both our battalions, thank you most sincerely."

Giroux leaned forward in a slight bow. "General," he answered in a clear voice, "it is we, myself and my associates, and indeed our entire parish, who must give our thanks. You and your brave boys are all that stand between us and the infernal hosts who threaten all of our homes and livelihoods with chaos and disorder."

Giroux nodded as he took in a smattering of applause, finally holding up a hand as he resumed speaking. "We wish you our very best; we've no doubt General Jackson will do us proud. But it is the legislature that worries us—at least all the planters I've spoken to."

Villeré tilted his head and leaned closer, an intent look on his face.

"Their policies," Giroux went on, "have emptied the streets; all the shops are shuttered. Clerks' offices are closed, and men refuse to pay their debts. Even slave sales have been halted. Can you imagine?"

"Of course these are trying times; these men need no reminder of that," a woman's accented voice cut in, silencing the mutters of the group. Every head turned to see who had spoken, and a woman in a flowing white dress that showed a fair amount of bosom stepped out from beside the wagon. She looked at the officers with a somber expression, then climbed up onto the driver's seat beside Giroux, laying a gentle hand on his shoulder. "All the same, I believe we ought not dwell on our own troubles, when these brave lads are shouldering such a burden on our behalf." She drew out each word for emphasis, and everyone, Creole or American, fell silent as she spoke.

Moreau took a breath, instinctively taking a step closer. Celeste de Beaumais, in his sights at last, and only a few steps away. And yet, as she spoke, she seemed more distant to him than she had ever been. A moment later another woman edged up beside the wagon, and Moreau recognized the now-familiar face of Elyse Pasteur.

"Truly, you men are an example to us all," Celeste resumed in a clear, sultry voice. "Your bravery, your service—words of thanks are but a hollow expression of our gratitude." With a barely noticeable look at Giroux, she stepped down from the wagon and approached Colonel Ross, offering her arm. "Colonel, though I'd prefer to stay here chatting with these handsome officers, if you would be so kind as to show us to the manor house. I would hate to be tardy for Monsieur Daunois and his wife." With a beaming smile, she blew a kiss to the nearby soldiers before turning back to walk with Ross, chuckling as he muttered something in her ear.

Moreau looked at the men nearest him, almost scoffing aloud at the fawning smiles on their faces. Men who've gone a long spell without a woman's company often behaved strangely when the spell ended. He noticed Mademoiselle Pasteur trailing behind the lady's entourage. Without hesitating, he walked up behind her and grabbed her elbow, gently enough so as not to frighten her, but firmly enough that she couldn't pull free.

"Good day, mademoiselle," he said in hushed French. "How pleasant of you to drop in."

Jerking her head around, her eyes widened when she recognized Moreau. Mercifully she did not scream, so he eased his grip slightly. They walked on at a slow pace, until she finally muttered "I suppose I shouldn't have expected any other greeting from you. You seem to understand two languages: force and more force."

She wriggled her elbow a little but Moreau wasn't ready to release it just yet. "So here we are."

"Here we are." She shot him a sidelong glance. "Well, what do you want, then?" Moreau sneered as she smiled at a line of soldiers, who watched her with enthusiastic, longing, grins. "I hope you haven't forgotten about our agreement."

"Remind me of what that was again? You ended our last engagement by bashing a man's face with a door and nearly killing another."

Moreau cast another glance at Celeste, turning his head aside as her gaze passed over the crowd and landed on Elyse. "I just need a moment alone with her. Just enough to try and talk some sense." He turned back to Elyse, who, to his surprise, was looking back at her lady with a somewhat nervous expression. "I promise I will do my best not to frighten her."

He waited as she stared ahead, her lips moving silently as if speaking to herself. Moreau once again looked at Celeste, who was standing at the foot of the stairs leading up to the veranda of the plantation house with a bored expression, evidently ignoring the conversation of a Creole officer towering over her.

As if snapping out of a daydream, Elyse blinked several times and looked at Moreau. "Two nights ago, I spoke to our...pirate friend...and he revealed, indirectly, that he believes he knows where the last ruby is. And that he plans to seize it, and then he's likely to run off." Moreau's eyes narrowed, and he ignored the crowd surging on either side of them. "Regarding your request of my lady, I shall see what I can do. But do not interject yourself into her business. That could be...dangerous. For all of us."

Moreau's brow creased. Where did Araza think to find this last ruby? Was he being truthful or just bluffing?

"Ah, Lenoir, I thought that was you." A Creole-accented voice pulled Moreau's attention, and he cast a look around. A moment later his eyes settled on a familiar face. Dressed in a dark-blue jacket over a red vest, a pair of close-fitting black pantaloons, and a black top hat was the lawyer from Giroux's estate. Moreau could not remember his name, but he was looking at Moreau with a smile as he approached, making his way toward the house.

"I hardly recognized you at first," the man went on, stepping between Moreau and Elyse and offering his hand with a broad smile. "I see you wear the garb of a soldier." Moreau's eyes briefly met Elyse's before he turned and took the fellow's outstretched hand.

"Indeed, Monsieur Tremblay," Moreau finally answered, clasping his hand firmly. "Some habits die hard." He offered Tremblay a tight smile and looked at Elyse, who quickly glanced in the direction of Celeste before turning back to the two men. "Good afternoon, Cyril," she said, her smile quickly returning. Tremblay returned her grin before looking back at Moreau with an intent expression.

"Looks like you've exchanged your planter's boots for a soldier's," he said. "I'm sure we're lucky to have you join our ranks. But I seem to recall you mentioning you had no prior service when we last met. Where did you serve?"

"I served in many places."

"I am sure. Any we may have heard of?" Moreau listed just a few of the many battlefields on which he'd fought, finishing with a glance down at his arm and a modest shrug. Cyril listened with an attentive expression, nodding somberly as Moreau concluded. He looked at Elyse with raised eyebrows before turning back to Moreau.

"Well, we are *certainly* lucky to have you taking up arms in our cause. Though, again, I do seem to recall, if you'll forgive the impertinence, you telling Monsieur Giroux that your missing arm was the result of an unfortunate accident on your sugar plantation in Saint-Domingue. Would that have been before or after your service under Napoleon?"

Moreau blinked twice and exchanged a brief look with Elyse before answering in a low voice. "A man may hold more than one occupation in his life. If you doubt my battlefield experience, I am sorry to hear it."

Tremblay slowly leaned his head forward, and raised it with a polite smile. "I have no doubt you served your emperor bravely, monsieur. I simply meant to clarify a point of confusion."

Widening her eyes at Moreau for a split second, Elyse smiled at Tremblay. "Well, Monsieur Tremblay, *I* was just about to join my lady and Monsieur Giroux to dine with Monsieur and Madame Daunois. Will you join me?"

Tremblay offered her a slight nod. "Mademoiselle, the pleasure of dining alongside the leading citizens, generals, and ladies of New Orleans is but a preamble to the pleasure of your company. I would be delighted."

"Wonderful." Elyse bowed gracefully, then turned her eyes toward the house, where her lady stood waiting on the veranda. She was flanked by Giroux and Colonel Ross, laughing at something one of them had said, though she frequently looked behind her. Moreau turned away, forcing himself not to stare.

"And will you be joining us, Major?" Tremblay asked.

Moreau shot a knowing look at Elyse. "Regretfully, no. There is still much training and...business to tend to."

Elyse inclined her head just slightly.

"Well, we shall regret your absence," Tremblay replied ruefully, "but surely we shall offer many toasts to our brave defenders."

Moreau nodded. "Surely. Though I wouldn't drink too much; the enemy are close and one must keep their wits about them."

Tremblay spread his hands. "Wise words. Let's hope they are heeded by those under arms. And those without them." He grinned widely at Moreau, his eyes flashing momentarily. "Pardon the quip, Major. I'm just thankful we have officers like you to mind the men."

Moreau stared at him with a growing scowl.

"My apologies, gentleman," Elyse cut in. "My lady looks to be calling me, so I must attend to her. Good day to you both." At that she gathered her dress with both hands and shuffled ahead to join her lady, who was now staring at her with an impatient expression.

Tremblay's eyes followed Elyse as she made her way up the stairs, and he sighed. "I suppose my place is with them." He offered his hand once again to Moreau with a polite smile. "I shall keep an eye on Mademoiselle Pasteur in your absence." Moreau shook his hand, holding back the crushing squeeze he wished to give. Tremblay took a few steps toward the house and suddenly halted, turning slowly to face Moreau, a thoughtful crease on his brow. "Ah, I almost forgot. Monsieur Giroux asked about you the other day. Doubtless your duties keep you busy, but you ought to pay him another visit. He is an ambitious man and has some…interesting plans for the estate. As a fellow planter, I thought you might wish to hear of them."

Moreau's chin lifted slightly. "What plans?"

Tremblay grinned and tapped the brim of his hat. "I ought to let the master explain. Suffice it to say, our recent…troubles with our acolytes will soon be sorted. Then our plans will finally begin in earnest."

Once Tremblay had gone, Moreau took a few slow steps closer to the porch, hoping he might overhear some of the conversation. Standing a few paces from Celeste was Emile Giroux, flanked as usual by his broad-shouldered foreman, engaged in conversation with a well-dressed older man, presumably the plantation's owner, Monsieur Daunois. Moreau sniggered at what the old man must've thought of his sugarcane plantation being trampled upon by so many soldiers. As he inched closer, pretending to take in the protruding gables of the manor house, he caught the voice of

Celeste, who stood facing Elyse with a harsh scowl. Elyse stood an inch or two taller than her lady, but her head was slightly bowed she received the hushed scolding.

"I told you not to run off without me. You know what I said about leaving me alone with them, and this is the second time you've done it." She nodded politely to a couple passing by before turning back to Elyse. "I will not tell you again."

"Yes, my lady. I'm sorry." She raised her head and, for a moment, the two women held each other's gaze until Celeste sighed visibly. Taking a moment to put on a pair of white lace gloves that extended to her elbows, she took a deep breath and resumed with a composed expression. "We will speak further when we get home. Now, let us go enjoy our meal. Lead on." She motioned for Elyse to go into the house, turning back to Giroux and the other planters, a broad smile on her face. "Messieurs, are you going to keep us waiting *all* day? The journey here has left us *famished*."

"Mademoiselle," one of the gentlemen said with a beaming smile, "we await your invitation." Celeste accepted Giroux's arm with a gracious nod, and the pair made their way through the doorway into the house, the rest following them inside.

CHAPTER 19

Mississippi River, Louisiana
December 13, 1814

The current eased noticeably as the pirogue approached the shoreline of the Mississippi's right bank, but the lighter flow was still strong enough to force Moreau to tow his paddle in the water to steady the boat as Will attempted to turn them. With an effort, the boy managed to steer the small craft into a channel leading inland, and soon they were rowing down a narrow bayou that wended until the river was out of sight behind them. Moreau rowed one-armed with a shorter paddle, glancing to either side at the wide fronds and bald cypress trees encircled by jutting knees above their tapering roots.

As they passed deeper into the swamp, Moreau tried to put thoughts of army life out of his mind, recalling the reason he had come to these shores, the consequences of which would surely mean life or death. If he did not set sail with Celeste de Beaumais by the first day of the new year, the bounty on his head would come due. Regardless of his reasons for returning to these labyrinthian swamps, there seemed to be some link, not yet clear to him, between the plantation that housed her and the maroon colony called Le Marais—that dangerous warren of cannibals and savages where strange black arts called voodoo and hoodoo were practiced by primitives all too eager to kill any who came within its mysterious boundaries. So it was said.

To their right, two large, white egrets stepped gingerly through thick cutgrass lining the bank, intermittently poking their long beaks down into the grass, oblivious to the passing pirogue. Will dipped his oar into the water, slowing the boat to a halt, and Moreau noticed what was blocking their route: a crape myrtle tree lay across the narrow waterway. Will set his oar down and hopped out with a splash. For a few moments he scanned the shoreline until at last he squatted down, momentarily disappearing behind tall stalks of cordgrass. A moment later he lurched to his feet, holding a long line of rope that stretched out in front of him.

Moreau saw the crape myrtle's branches rustling as Will, grunting audibly, tugged on the line, digging his feet into the muddy bottom and leaning back for balance. Just as Moreau was about to jump from the boat to help him, the tree rose from the water, suspended by the rope, which was looped over an overhanging branch of a stout oak. As Will proceeded to tie off the line, Moreau saw that what had appeared to be a dead-end bayou was actually a narrow, unobstructed canal of brackish water. "This blockade was one of yours? Theirs, I mean."

Will splashed his way back to the pirogue and climbed nimbly back in. "This was one I was shown. Between here and Barataria there are canals beyond count."

Moreau nodded. "Lafitte and his men knew their business."

"They still do."

They soon came to a distinct Y-shaped fork in the channel, and Moreau turned to the boy, who hesitated a moment before motioning to their left. For more than an hour they continued deeper into the swamp, the canopy overhead growing thicker with each paddle stroke, blotting out the overcast sky and casting gloomy shadows over the thick vegetation.

A little later they came to another fork, and Will hesitated again before steering them to the right into a narrow rivulet. They continued for a few more minutes, Moreau beginning to wonder about the boy's decision, before a sharp whistle turned their heads. After a few seconds, another piercing whistle sounded, and they lifted their oars out of the water and allowed the boat to slow. For a moment they sat very still, the swamp silent now.

A figure slowly emerged from behind a tree up ahead. He was shirtless and barefoot, a pair of tattered cotton pantaloons the only cloth covering his dark skin. Aiming a musket toward the pirogue, he told them to raise their hands, which they promptly did. Another man then emerged from behind a dense thicket, also aiming a musket. The pair slowly came closer, and one ordered Moreau and Will to step onto the shore. The first fellow asked their business, and Moreau explained that they had come to speak with Diantha. He nodded for Will to show the tattoo on his wrist, which he did, revealing the heron-and-anchor marking. The men conferred and, after a tense moment, motioned for Moreau and Will to follow them deeper into the swamp.

They arrived in the village from the bayou side, and Moreau again noticed the huts raised up on stilts to avoid flooding. Alongside them were several weather-beaten pirogues, oars and ropes inside their hulls. As they continued, they passed a wide pen to their left that held a dozen or so chickens that bobbed their heads and clucked noisily. The smell of feed and dung reminded Moreau of a farm, albeit one of the stranger farms he'd ever seen.

One by one, faces began to peer out from the huts, and an older man throwing feed to the chickens halted when he saw them walk past, his expression indicating his confusion. Low mutters came from the dozen or so people that had begun emerging from their dwellings, and memories from the night of their initial arrival swirled in Moreau's mind: angry faces lit by flickering firelight, braying for their death; Edward, Antonia's runaway slave, clutching his club, taking Moreau's best thumps before nearly choking the life out of him. When they arrived at the open ground in the center of the small village—the site of his fight with Edward—the villagers gathered around, pointing and staring with curious gazes. Some whispered to each other as they edged closer, but few wore the looks of outright hostility that had abounded on the night of their arrival. A recognizable face across the clearing drew Moreau's attention, and his eyes caught those of the woman he knew as Diantha. She wore a long white dress that left one of her shoulders bare and stretched down to her ankles, and her head was covered with a matching white tignon that bore a large black pearl. She stared at Moreau with an unreadable expression. "This one always comes on the Ashé of thunder," she said quietly. Lifting her chin, she spoke in a louder voice. "Barataria has been destroyed. From where have you come? Le Temple?"

Moreau nodded at Will. "The lad here told me of a secret network of waterways leading to Barataria. I asked if any led to your homestead. He said he'd come this way once, and that it was only a matter of finding Bayou Barataria—which, apparently, we just did. So here we are."

A murmur spread through the group, but Diantha's countenance didn't soften. "So, why have you come?"

"I've come with a warning. Concerning the plantation that seems to cause you so much trouble." A heavy silence followed, and for a moment he wondered if he had just aroused the group's hostility.

"And what warning have you brought?"

"I thought I might speak to that in private. With you, madame."

Diantha considered this for a moment, then spread her arms wide. "We've just held our feast of Gran Bois, the *loa* of the forest, and we have another night of feasting remaining. There is always a reason to celebrate, when one lives free."

Moreau nodded, noticing the others beginning to disperse in different directions, some stealing looks at Moreau and Will. "Once we have performed our ceremonies, I will speak with you."

Before long the sun disappeared behind the thick vegetation, casting long shadows from the tall oak and cypress trees. This quick onset of evening brought a chill to the air, and Moreau politely declined a pair of simple wool coats offered by a young woman. When he asked what the gathering was for, she nodded toward the firepit in the middle of the clearing, where two men were lowering a large cookpot onto two forked staves on either side of the pit, evidently in preparation for a large meal. A slight growl from his belly reminded Moreau of his own hunger.

Will was the first to notice her, and he offered something of a bow to Antonia Milroy, who approached them slowly, her hands clasped together. She wore the same white and yellow dress as the day they first arrived, covered by a simple woolen overcoat. She smiled warmly at Will, and Moreau's breath caught for a moment as she turned to him with a more serious expression.

Moreau pursed his lips and nodded politely. Antonia looked at him, and for the first time since her arrival, or so it seemed, she smiled at him. The tall young man called Antoine then came up beside them, glancing at Moreau, his eyebrows as high as they could go and his mouth spread in a wide grin. He placed a hand on Moreau's shoulder, then nodded at the boy before leading him off to join the others. Antonia gestured, and a moment later she and Moreau took their seats on the ground a little way from the others.

"It is good to see you, mademoiselle."

"You as well, Monsieur *Lenoir*."

Moreau smiled. "It is Moreau, mademoiselle. Marcel Moreau."

Her eyebrows rose in mock surprise. "You always did seem somewhat mysterious. I suppose there is much we never learned of each other."

He sighed, his smile fading. "I'm glad to see you are well. And even more so to see that my fears of abuse seem to have been slightly exaggerated." He allowed the hint of a sheepish grin to pass over his features. Antonia smiled back at him. "But," he continued, "I came here, in part, to bring you back home. If that be your wish."

She met his gaze for a moment before turning slowly to look at the others gathered around the cookpot. "I will return home…" She paused, licking her lips. "When the time is right."

Moreau stared silently for a moment. When he spoke again it was in a quiet voice. "You always were naïve. I won't argue with you, but I would remind you…you were born free. These people—they came here out of necessity. Survival. You have a choice."

"And I've made my choice." Composing herself with a visible effort, she forced her eyes to meet his. "As I said, I will return home. When I am ready."

At length Moreau let out a breath and nodded his understanding. "Well," she said, "I best get back to helping prepare the meal. Good evening, monsieur." Before Moreau could say more, she turned and made her way off, leaving him alone as he watched her depart.

When the stew was ready, bowls carved from gourds or tanned leather were filled and passed to those seated around the fire. Moreau and Will were served their own bowls of what a woman next to them called *gombeaux*, a rich and savory broth containing rice, carrots, celery, a hint of strange seasonings, and bits of what tasted like sausage, though Moreau chose not to ask. After a day of rowing and no food since morning, the two ate heartily. Following the gombeaux, fruits, vegetables, and nuts were shared among the gathering, each person taking as much or as little as they wished. Large gourds filled with wine were also passed around, followed by others filled with rum. Before long Moreau was feeling a heady relaxation from the feast, which, though unconventional by his customs, certainly filled his belly.

Two men then approached the firepit and removed the large cookpot. Diantha joined them by the fire, flanked by the man Moreau recognized as the houngan. He was shirtless despite the cold, and looked the same as Moreau had last seen him: ragged cotton pantaloons, thickly braided hair, and carrying the large gourd with the bones dangling from it. A ritual then began, the houngan offering a prayer in a language foreign to Moreau. This went on for several minutes, those clustered nearby listening with rapt attention, when a movement to his left caught Moreau's eye.

Moving quietly but without any pretense of stealth, a half dozen men entered the village from behind the main group, each carrying a musket in his hands. As they stepped into the firelight closer to the circle, he saw a few he could identify. There was Edward, the former slave who'd run away from Antonia's family, and behind him looked to be the islander whose name Moreau had forgotten. Jean-Louis? Most of the others he did not recognize, but the last man to arrive he most certainly remembered. Short compared to Edward, he walked slowly, almost lazily, but his frame looked as if it had been sculpted from stone. Though he arrived last, the others seemed to look to him for permission to retire from their "formation," and as the man called Nehemiah set his musket against a tree, the others relaxed. Moreau was not looking forward to a reunion with him, but knew it would come sooner or later.

After the houngan's speech was over, and Diantha had offered her own blessings, she conferred briefly with another woman before making her way closer to where Moreau and Will sat. Beside the fire two other women had begun a sort of dance, and three men, each with a different-sized drum, sat on the ground before them. Moreau turned from watching them as Diantha approached and sat beside him. For a moment she eyed him studiously, before turning her attention back ahead.

"I'm glad to see the girl is well," Moreau said, his voice muffled by the drumming.

"I suppose I should thank you," Diantha said, her features revealing little, "for bringing her here."

"What was it you did? Moreau asked. "To see such a change come over her—when I last saw her, she was terrified. Now..."

Diantha stared vacantly at the dancers. "I gave her three days to live as we once did: enslaved. By the fourth morning, she set to her chores willingly, and soon after I had to repeatedly tell her she no longer need labor under the threat. Most in bondage don't give up hoping for freedom; they simply forget it is possible. One needs hope to dream. A clever master carves away that hope, until it's replaced by a desire to not disturb the delicate peace of utter dependence."

"Giroux."

Diantha looked aside with a sneer. "That man is a fool."

"He may be," Moreau said, "but he stands for many."

"Well," she countered, "he is as *poor* a master as a man can be. His cruelty comes from his weakness, and his weakness draws the contempt of strong Negroes. It is *that* which drives us to find our freedom."

Moreau considered it was possible, even likely, that the man's cruel behavior had driven so many to attempt to escape.

"But let us not speak of that now." She raised her eyebrows as she looked at him again. "You are privileged, monsieur. Few outsiders ever get to see the *Afonga* inside a hounfour."

Moreau watched the dancers, admitting that their movements were hypnotic. "What is Afonga?"

"A dance."

"I see that. But what does it mean?"

"To you?" a deep voice said, "nothing." Without seeing the man's face, Moreau knew who had spoken. Dipping a wooden spoon into a yellow gourd, Nehemiah stood behind Diantha and stared down at Moreau with a hard expression.

Diantha peered up at him before turning back to Moreau, who thought he saw a trace of a smile on her lips. "To *us*," she said, "it is a dance meant to convey peace and blessings." Moreau nodded slowly, doubtful how much peace the man looming over him currently wished.

Nehemiah grunted, his face as cold as any Moreau had ever seen, which said a good deal. "Last time I seen you, your face was leaking. What the fuck you doing here?"

Moreau's expression turned into a glare, and he felt no desire to answer.

Nehemiah slowly squatted down, his face inches from Moreau's. "I asked you a question. What the fuck are you doing here?"

Moreau's jaw clenched, but his heart beat no faster than normal. Meanwhile, the drums began to beat louder, and the dancers by the fire gyrated and writhed in a style that Moreau had never seen before.

BOOM-boom-boom, BOOM-boom-boom.

It had been a long time since a man had truly gotten under his skin—even Araza seemed a harlequin compared to some men Moreau had fought, and killed—but something in this one's demeanor told Moreau he was not a puffed-up fool peacocking to impress women. He knew this man wanted to kill him—and would if he could. The thought brought a primal but clear-eyed desire to return the favor. With men who preferred killing to performing, there was a certain understanding, and the business was often brought to a swift, decisive conclusion. But Moreau knew this was no tavern or army camp, and even if he managed to kill Nehemiah, which was no certainty, he would never leave with his life. All he could do was stand his ground and hope no one else desired his death as much as this one. "I've come with news that might help your people."

Nehemiah stared at him as if he hadn't spoken, eventually turning to Diantha with a confused expression. "Gran Ibo, why have you let him back here? We should have killed him then; we *must* kill him now."

He turned back to Moreau, who returned his menacing stare. With as much willpower as he could muster, Moreau remained silent. Footsteps in the dirt pulled his eyes aside, and he saw two men approaching: Edward and the islander he believed was called Jean-Pierre. Edward stood a couple inches taller than Nehemiah and was less muscular, though far from weak. He halted and looked at the two of them with a wide grin. Jean-Pierre, whose face was as dark and hard as Nehemiah's, showed a smirk of his own.

"Do you two wish to be alone?" Edward asked. "You can have my hut if you need it."

Jean-Pierre let out a breath. "Nee, yuh breddah come back. Yuh mussi happi."

Both men chuckled, and Edward put a hand on Jean-Pierre's shoulder, but Moreau could see Nehemiah's hard stare hadn't softened. Nor had he moved from Moreau's space.

"Careful, Nee," Edward said, taking a step closer. "I've seen this one swing a club."

"Nah, Nee wud tek dis one inna less den ten seconds."

Diantha cleared her throat, staring at the two men. "A yuh gwine stan yah all nite a bi usless?" The two looked down at her, their expressions serious. "Now go help Tall Johnny wid di *poteau-mitan*. Go!" She waved a hand at them, and, chuckling to themselves, the two shuffled away, leaving Moreau with just one face staring at him.

Exhaling loudly, Nehemiah rose slowly to his feet, his eyes never leaving Moreau. For a moment he stood motionless, until finally he bent down and picked up his musket. Cradling it in his hands, he looked at the Frenchman once again, his expression less murderous but still like stone. "This the second time you been lucky here. You better hope there ain't a third. We not in the master's house here."

Diantha turned to Nehemiah, and at first her expression was cold, like a scolding schoolteacher, but as she let out a long sigh, it softened, and for a moment she looked sad. "What have I told you, Ogun?" Nehemiah's eyes drifted to meet hers. She shook her head slightly, turning back to the firepit with the same sad look. "When one puts hate in his heart, he lengthens the distance between himself and the Creator."

Nehemiah's expression didn't change. "With the life God has given us, he done that his own damn self." With that, he flared his nostrils and turned, stalking away into the darkness.

Moreau chose to not watch him depart, but try as he might, he could not ease the scowl on his own face. For several minutes both he and Diantha sat in silence, staring at the dancers, who now writhed on the ground, no drumming accompanying their movements. "I will try to forget about that," Moreau finally uttered, hoping to take his thoughts somewhere else. If he were able, he would have gladly killed the man then and there. If he were able.

Diantha looked at him wearily. "He's not what I'm sure you think he is." Moreau gave her a questioning squint. When she saw it, she snickered humorlessly. "If a strong-willed boy is hounded into a jungle and forced to fight and claw to survive, can he really be blamed for coming out a snarling beast?"

Moreau frowned as he considered her words, admitting that they might contain some truth. Surely he'd felt something of that in his own life. Exactly that. All the same, he wondered how the blame had landed on his lap.

"This place has known much sorrow," Diantha sighed, folding her hands on her lap. "He and I have disagreed on certain matters recently, and I'm beginning to question whether I truly do disagree." She glanced aside at Moreau. "You said you've come with news that might help us. What news?"

Moreau fastened a button on his coat as the cold night air began to bite. "I've heard…mutterings. From the people you all are evading here. I heard, with my own ears, that 'troubles with the hands' will soon be sorted, and 'plans' will soon begin in earnest." He peered at her, and she stared back with hard, narrow eyes.

After a moment she shook her head. "Thank you for that. I don't know if I'm right to trust you, but our choices dwindle with each day. That is part of our disagreement. Each soul that escapes to us is a miracle—and each one brings Giroux's men one step closer. Nehemiah thinks we must leave immediately. I think…I'm not ready to abandon those still held in that wretched place. And now it sounds as if…" She trailed off, shaking her head.

Moreau did his best not to stare, but he caught a glimpse of her misty eyes and allowed her a moment of silence.

"That planter, Emile Giroux," she went on, her eyes vacant, "has been touched by something…evil. He wasn't always as cruel as he is now—or perhaps he just didn't show it—but for some time I've felt as if something was coming this way. Some darkness." She looked up as if coming out of a daydream. "I thank you for bringing warning. Important decisions will have to be made in the days ahead."

"And the other reason I've come." Moreau shot a glance at Diantha before his eyes eventually found Antonia seated among a group of women. She did not wear a tignon like the others, her long black hair falling from her shoulders in curly waves. When she laughed, he felt his pulse quicken.

"That troublesome young woman who dragged me here—I've blamed myself for whatever I believed she had been…enduring here." He looked at Diantha with an earnest expression. "Is she alright?"

To his surprise, he saw a soft smile on Diantha's features, and she tilted her head to either side before speaking. "If you mean, is she safe and in good health? Yes, she is fine."

Moreau felt a wave of relief pass over him, and nodded. "Good."

"But," Diantha went on, "like everyone here, she has had... burdens she must carry. What grief she held buried." Her smile faded, and Moreau stared intently, willing her to say more. "Of course, her first days here were not pleasant. She cried often. When given a task, she'd cry. When given food, she'd cry. After completing a task, she'd cry. For two days it's nearly all she did. But you see her now? A change has come over her; perhaps her time in this swamp was not so bad after all."

Moreau turned back ahead, and for the first time since the night they arrived, Moreau realized she looked comfortable. Here, in this place.

"You miss her."

Moreau nearly choked, and for several seconds he avoided answering. His eyebrows raised, and in the scramble that had entangled his thoughts, and still reeling from Nehemiah's hostility, his next words came out almost against his will. "It has been a long time since I've met a woman who...who I knew from the first sight I would fight for." He blinked, suddenly aware of what he was saying, but any embarrassment fell away, and he didn't care who heard. "A woman whose very presence made me wish to be better. A simple look into her eyes, and I'd want to be stronger.... Yes, I've missed her."

When he finally recovered his wits, he blinked and peered at Diantha. She looked at him with a smile, but it seemed sad. He rubbed his scalp and looked around as if suddenly remembering where he was. "I'm sorry. I shouldn't have said that."

Her raised hand told him to stop speaking, but her gentle smile said not because he shouldn't have spoken. Overcome by a sudden desire for rest, he let out a sigh and stifled a yawn with his hand.

"I will let her tell you herself what she endured in her younger years. The burden she carries. I must tell you she is also in love." She turned to Moreau. "But not with you."

Moreau returned her sad look with one of his own, his silence the only answer necessary. For a while they sat without speaking, and Moreau was unsure if the drumming had resumed or if the pounding was just within his chest. A part of him felt a strange feeling of release, as if a weight had been lifted. Yet another part of him felt crushed, as if a giant boulder had fallen on his chest. At last, he turned to look at Diantha, his cold expression returning. "I know. I've known since I first came here."

Diantha looked at him solemnly.

"For a brief moment I cared for her, and thought perhaps she returned the feeling—but it was all in my head." He didn't notice Diantha watching him, her expression softer than any she had yet displayed. "In the end, it's for the better. I'm a soldier; anyone who's ever loved me has run off—or died. Love is not meant for me."

~~~

Moreau woke Will, who was comfortably snuggled in a pile of blankets on the floor of the hut they shared, shaking him out of a deep slumber. After motioning for silence, he led him out into the darkness of the night and across the clearing to another hut, beside which Moreau halted and squatted down. The boy rubbed his eyes and yawned widely. "What is this about, monsieur?"

Moreau glared at him, replying in a gruff whisper. "The entire reason I brought you here. You're the practiced cutpurse." He cast a glance around, satisfied no one else was awake. He nodded toward the hut's entrance. "I saw it with my own eyes; otherwise, I wouldn't send you in. Are you ready?" Even in the faint moonlight, he could feel the boy's hesitation. Sighing impatiently, Moreau put a hand on his shoulder. "We're not stealing it, just borrowing it for a time."

"But it belongs to the houngan."

"Who stole it from a maroon woman dumped in a swamp!" Moreau almost cursed himself for raising his voice. He leaned closer. "Can you do this for me, Will?"

Will looked at the entrance to the hut, his expression more sad than nervous. He turned to Moreau and nodded. "Yes."

A minute or so later the boy emerged from the hut, his eyes wide. He swallowed hard, and for a moment Moreau's shoulders sagged as he stared at the boy. Eventually Will let out a breath, looking up with a solemn expression. After another excruciating moment, he reached a hand into his shirt. He pulled it out and turned it over, exposing a large, red balas ruby that glittered as it reflected the pale moonlight. Reaching out and grasping the gem, Moreau tucked it into his own shirt and motioned for the boy to follow him.

Dearest Maman,

I write to tell you that things move along here at the plantation, perhaps not well, but life proceeds thusly at times. Elyse has broached more than once the subject of departing for home. I must say I'm beginning to find it tiresome. I think she is just giving vent to her ennui, as she has received less attention from the gentleman of the house and his associates. I cannot be blamed if they wish to speak to one of their superiors from France—and not her servant. I do hope she comes to her senses, and soon, as events with the fighting men seem to be proceeding swiftly, and there are likely to be opportunities of dining and dancing with officers— be they English or American, perhaps both—in the coming days.

At any rate, that wretch who abandoned us in a cold cypress swamp has occupied my thoughts in recent days, and though I've been loath to cause you worry, I feel it is time to finish the telling of events that brought me to Louisiana. The gentleman from Guadeloupe also enters my thoughts from time to time, and I confess I miss him terribly. The truth is—they are one and the same man. Sometimes I find it hard to believe that I could detest and long for the same person with such strong feeling. The collision of love and hate is rarely an easy thing to manage, and so far, I can hardly say I've done so. I only wish to be loved, but love does not share the desire.

Well, after an evening of dancing with this dark-haired gentleman in a coffee house in Point-à-Pitre, we struck up a fast friendship, spending our days together, and, yes, our evenings as well. Do not be judgmental, Mother; I know you were once a woman of my same age.

To speed my telling along I'll say that the offer to join a corsair and his swashbuckling crew on a brief sea voyage to the isle of Haiti seemed all but impossible to refuse, so a few days after retrieving the stones I boarded El Mendigo with Tadeo Araza as my captain, and I should reassure you Elyse and I were given our own cabin, albeit small and close, apart from those foul-smelling brigands.

We sailed across the Caribbean Sea for four days, and Maman, I've never seen water so blue. For those brief days I felt I had found the paradise of my dreams, and I don't think I harbored an unhappy thought the entire time.

After our night's stay in Port-au-Prince, of which I have little to tell as Tadeo left us with a crewman to conduct business, I found myself in a suddenly unpleasant temper. I returned to the ship with Elyse early the next morning, as we wished to bring the dresses we'd purchased ashore to our cabin before the approaching squall opened its deluge upon us.

Tadeo had told me to stay away from the aft hold, claiming there to be dangerous cargo inside. But with my mood agitated, and, being slightly bored, once settled back on the ship I found myself below deck, watching a member of the crew as he approached the entrance to the hold; he proceeded to open the lock and slip inside, leaving the door slightly ajar. My curiosity thus piqued, I crept closer and took a look inside...

Maman, when I saw the cargo that had been brought aboard, I nearly fainted. The faces were dark in such an unlit, gloomy pen, but I'll never forget the eyes. Some looked frightened, others resigned, but all turned on me with a fervent sense of...expectation. Like a babe looking up at its mother. I've seen soldiers and prisoners, but I've never, ever before seen humans held in such an ungodly, animal state. To this day the thought disturbs my sleep.

In my disbelief I hardly noticed the crewman round on me with shouts and reprimands. I fled the hold back to my cabin, and by the time I had recovered my senses, the captain found me. His anger was plain. It seemed as if the brute lurking within had surfaced for the first time—at least in my presence. Though, curiously, his anger did not frighten me, not really. What did unsettle me was the conviction I felt in his threats. I've seen enough men throwing tantrums to usually find them theatrical—but the candor in this one's severity, matched with a peculiar coldness, seemed to turn him into another man entirely. One I had not yet seen—and did not wish for further acquaintance. After allowing a moment for his passions to settle and redirect themselves, I asked of him a small craft to be taken ashore, as I no longer held a desire to participate in his filthy "enterprise." He refused, and that evening we hoisted anchor, setting sail for an unnamed port in the Mexican Gulf. Several days brought us near the Florida coast, where the waters were blue and beautiful, and I hardly saw any signs of danger that the crewmen prattled on about. Talk of English ships and American ships—really all manner of vessels— seemed to spook them, and, perhaps emboldened by their captain's open rudeness to me and Elyse, the sailors eyed us like hungry wolves, telling me to "keep my jezebel mouth closed" if we wished to see out the voyage.

So, for several days, she and I kept to ourselves, taking in the breathtaking waters when the men were occupied but remaining below decks when they seemed idle. I knew that I had the three stones, the entire purpose of my voyage to the West Indies, so I decided not to antagonize the brutes needlessly.

As we approached the coast of Louisiana, another row with our erstwhile warden left me shaken, thinking we might not make it to our destination—a hidden harbor called Barataria—as free women. I passed a frightful night worrying about our fates, after which we finally sighted land. Gods! Unwilling to be cowed by our goalers so close to our salvation, Elyse and I rushed to the deck, and soon we were sailing into a broad swath of coastline broken by islets, rivulets, and makeshift quays. We passed what looked to be a small, fortified city, with houses raised on stilts and long warehouses, cannon batteries overlooking the water passages, and a veritable forest of ship masts, presumably the fleet belonging to these rogues. This must have been the den of their commander and notorious pirate, Lafitte.

Elyse and I were then unceremoniously set in a small craft with one man to row us and told he would take us to an open-air market run by these pirates called "Le Temple." After a half a day's journey through godforsaken water passages, Elyse and I were deposited in the middle of a vast, stinking swamp. The man who'd brought us slipped away when we were seeing to our necessaries, and while this letter is my guarantor of our survival and subsequent rescue, I confess that I've never ever passed a more harrowing night—one spent in the single most wild, gloomy, and haunted abyss I have ever laid eyes on. Thank God Monsieur Giroux's men were out in those wilds hunting runaway slaves and found us, or else I know we would not have survived.

But we have, and I must thank our generous and chivalrous host for our salvation. I only wish that Adonis from Guadeloupe had not turned into such a detestable bastard. The former occupies my waking thoughts, the latter haunts my nightmares. I love you, Maman, and will supplement this harrowing tale with more news soon.

My kisses and affection,
C.

CHAPTER 20

Royal Street, New Orleans
December 14, 1814

Moreau cursed when he saw no light coming from the tavern's front windows. "Every business in this damned city is shuttered," he growled. He peered down St. Louis Street as if the innkeeper of Maspero's might appear from around the corner, but creeping shadows and pale lamplight were all he saw in the darkness. He kicked a pebble at his feet, and a moment later reached into the cartridge pouch slung at his waist, feeling a sense of relief, satisfaction even, as he touched the balas ruby nestled inside.

"Because it was never their damned jewel to begin with," he had answered when Will asked why they had taken it. *They*. It was Moreau's doing, and if the boy caught any trouble for his erstwhile theft, Moreau wasn't sure he could forgive himself. They had rowed back to the city that morning as darkness gave way to the pale-blue light of dawn, and he returned to the fort just in time to change into his uniform and report for duty. Once the day's training was done, he made straight for the one place he knew for sure he could find someone to appraise the stone—even if it was a den of pirates and cutthroats.

It was doubtful he would come across anyone from Le Marais before he could use the ruby for what he intended, but the longer he kept it, the more likely they were to believe he had stolen the gem outright, and their rage would only worsen. They had welcomed him to their home as a guest—and he had stolen from them. It would take a grand gesture, and a great deal of humility, if he was to keep his head when he finally returned the ruby to them.

As he arrived at the corner of St. Louis and Royal, the bells from the cathedral rang out, tolling the eight o'clock hour. Moreau checked his timepiece—needlessly, given the bells—confirming that he was on time. Whether Captains Savary and Dubuclet would be as well was another matter.

For several minutes he waited, watching the tavern from across the street; a light in one of the upstairs windows leading him to suspect the place was not wholly deserted. Glancing around for a sign of his comrades, he saw only a slow-moving carriage and a solitary pedestrian. At one point he noticed a large rat scurry along the wall ahead of him and slip out of sight down an alleyway. A few seconds later a lean black cat appeared out of the shadows, casting a careful look back before it also entered the alley. As he watched the dark, narrow passage, Moreau wondered if only rats feared their hunters, or it went both ways. Rats did have long teeth.

With an impatient grumble, he was preparing to call off the business when the tavern's front door creaked open. Crouching behind a balcony post, he saw a man step outside, the door closing behind him. The man halted and took several leisurely puffs on a cigar. Without hesitating, Moreau rose and made his way across the street, stopping a few steps from the stranger. "You there."

The man froze, the cigar stiff in his mouth. When he saw Moreau held no visible weapon, his postured eased slightly and he spoke in a raspy voice. "A bit dangerous, sneaking up on a man like that."

Moreau motioned toward the entrance. "Your patron, Tadeo Araza. Is he in?"

The man shifted his weight and pulled the cigar out of his mouth. "Who wishes to know?"

"Monsieur Lenoir," Moreau replied. "If your captain is at home, tell him I wish to speak with him of urgent business."

The man stared at Moreau a moment before raising his cigar and gesturing at him several times. With a grunt, he placed it back in his mouth and turned away, opening the door and disappearing inside the tavern.

Moreau's eyebrows rose. Was his luck that good? Looking down Royal, he cursed the absence of Savary and Dubuclet, thinking that their presence might indeed be called for. Once again, he thought of the cat, wondering what the animal felt as it came upon its prey. He glanced up at the second-story window and saw that the light had gone out. He blew into his fist for warmth. The night had suddenly grown quite cold.

"I had a feeling," an accented voice said from behind him, "you were too stupid to keep your nose out of my business." Moreau turned slowly. "But after what you did? Coming here seems… suicidal."

The man must have snuck out the tavern's back door or crept out of the alley to have appeared without being seen. Half concealed by the building's shadow, Tadeo Araza stood at ease in a crimson coat and tight black breeches. Moreau had to force back a scoff. "My previous visit was for a meeting with you. You weren't at home."

"So you attacked my men. And stole from me."

"I stole nothing."

Araza gestured to the saber at Moreau's hip. "That sword…it's a souvenir?"

Without looking down, Moreau shrugged. "If you wish for the sword back, you're welcome to come take it."

Araza frowned slightly. "No. I will not fight for what is already mine. But they will."

Moreau heard the sound of feet shuffling behind him and turned to see three figures several paces away. "If they wish for the sword, they're welcome to try and take it too." When they made no further move, he turned back to Araza. "But I've not come to fight. If I may explain myself before your men come any closer…I've come with an offer I think you'll wish to hear."

Araza's expression did not soften. "You have nothing to offer me."

"Are you certain of that?" Moreau's eyes lowered to the cartridge pouch at his waist. "When we last spoke, I told you a ruby you had appraised was false." He watched Araza expectantly, the other man's subtle shift in posture betraying his curiosity. After another peek behind him, Moreau continued. "I will draw my saber, to ensure your friends don't make any unwise moves. Then I will show you what is in the pouch." He raised his eyebrows at Araza, who glowered a moment before waving a hand.

"Yes, yes. Get on with it."

Moreau unsheathed his blade. Widening his feet in a fighter's stance, he looked at the three men behind him—he'd hoped for only two—and back to Araza. Seeing none had moved, he reached down and flicked open the cartridge pouch, an awkward movement for a one-armed man gripping a sword. He reached inside, grasped the ruby with two fingers, and held it up in front of him. It sparkled as it caught the pale moonlight, and Moreau caught the fervent gleam in Araza's eyes. Moreau waggled his hand. "There. A *true* balas ruby." He smirked at Araza's reaction. Without turning his head, the corsair's eyes looked warily to either side, as if sensing a trap. Perhaps he wasn't as much a fool as Moreau thought.

"How did you come by that?"

"Never mind how. What matters is I have it now."

"Yea," one of the toughs muttered, "until the captain gives us the word and we split your fuckin' head open."

Moreau slipped the ruby back into the cartridge pouch.

"You are certainly bold to come here, Señor Lenoir." Araza turned his head aside and spit onto the ground. "But I wonder if you are also stupid. Why have you brought this to me, knowing I will happily slit your throat and take it from you?"

Moreau snickered. "I do not covet this ruby, like you, monsieur, shiny and hefty though it is. As I told you weeks ago—I am searching for a woman, Celeste de Beaumais."

Araza rolled his eyes and shook his head with a scornful chuckle. "You are still besotted by that fool woman. Have her—I have no more use for her."

"How generous of you. The only concern is, of late she has taken it upon herself to assume the…matronly duties of her new home, Le Mouton Plantation. Have you heard of it?"

Araza hesitated a moment, then nodded.

"Then you know," Moreau went on, "that she enjoys the patronage of Emile Giroux, and in return he enjoys her charms and vivacity. If that's all he enjoys."

"Your conversation begins to bore me, señor."

Moreau lowered his sword. "The woman does not leave that place without a coterie of chaperones, and evidently the doting presence of Monsieur Giroux."

"And what do I care of that?"

"You don't. But you care for this." Moreau tapped the cartridge pouch with the flat edge of his sword. "I need a private audience with the woman, and you, I've been told, are the only man in this city that has captured her interest, and, consequently, you might be able to gain a moment alone with her."

For a moment Araza studied Moreau, his chin raised and his eyes lowered. At last he swept a hand in front of him with an audible sigh. "You impress me, Lenoir," he said cheerily, crossing one booted foot over the other. Moreau's knees dipped just slightly. "I can see why Lafitte told us to keep an eye on you. Unlike most men, your words, like your threats, are not idle." Turning aside, he took a few agile steps. "It is true, the young woman fancies me. And, perhaps under different circumstances, I might have taken her for my lover once again. But I have decided against that."

Moreau glanced at the three men, whose twitching fingers gave clear evidence of their intentions. With a sharp jerk of his head, Araza motioned to them, and they exchanged looks before moving off a short distance with a few disappointed mutters. "I will not have you knifed like a thief and a blackguard," Araza said, unsheathing his sword with a drawn-out flourish. "Although you seem almost as slippery as one of us—almost—I can see that you possess the boldness of a real man. So I will kill you myself."

The blade of the Araza' curved saber was at least an inch longer than Moreau's, and it glinted as it caught the light from the nearest streetlamp. Peering aside to ensure no interference from the others, Moreau raised his blade. "Since you will soon be dead," Araza said, almost cheerfully, "I should like to ask you one last question." Moreau glared ahead, his knees bent, gently squeezing the pommel in his hand. He matched the other man's fighting stance, keeping an eye on the other three men, utterly mistrustful of Araza's seeming willingness to fight him cleanly.

"Now, tell me…who are you?"

Moreau raised his blade slightly. "I am nobody."

"Tsk, tsk," Araza said, taking a step forward. "With the trouble you've caused me, I doubt that to be true. Besides, I'm not the only one who's asked the question."

"Now you're stalling."

Araza chuckled. "Alas, it is true, señor. A man came looking after you a few days past. An American officer."

Forcing his mind to stay focused, and watching for any sudden shift of weight in his opponent, Moreau barely acknowledged the statement. "And what did he want?"

Araza grinned. "He came to recruit my men for his little war—but before he departed, he asked about a grim, one-armed Frenchman. He did not seem particularly fond of you—" Araza sprang forward, crashing his saber down on Moreau's extended blade with a loud *clang*. For a second both men grimaced, Araza bearing down with all his weight as Moreau bent his knees and pressed upward with all of his own strength, attempting to shove the other man away. Araza sprang nimbly backward, assuming a relaxed stance as if nothing out of the ordinary had happened. Not exactly taken unawares, Moreau nonetheless admitted he was impressed by the speed of the man's attack—faster than anyone he had faced in years. He rolled his wrist and felt a dull stiffness; the corsair captain was strong too. "I would say the man had," Araza said, shifting his feet again, "less than friendly designs for you, señor. He claimed you had given out false names, and warned me and my men that delinquents would be taken straight to the gallows."

At Araza's mention of the American officer, Moreau suddenly felt keenly interested in what he was hearing. Thinking of the only way to wring the truth from this bastard, he flexed his legs and prepared to launch his own attack when a loud whistle pierced the night air.

"You there!" a voice bellowed, drawing Moreau's and Araza's attention. "Lower your blade." Standing in the middle of the intersection of Royal and St. Louis were two men, both holding pistols, though in the darkness it was difficult to make out their faces. Squinting, Moreau was surprised to see Captains Dubuclet and Savary. Dubuclet had his pistol leveled at Araza's three men, while Savary had his trained on Araza.

Lowering his sword, Moreau grunted. "Well, you two are right on time." For a moment no one moved, and he glanced at Araza to make sure he didn't seize the moment to stab him in the back.

Savary took several cautious steps toward him, motioning for Dubuclet to do the same. "We were held up at the fort. While you were over here having your sport, we were preparing for a battle." He took another few steps, his pistol still aimed at Araza. "The enemy, it seems, has begun his attack." Moreau's eyes went from Savary to Araza, his mind suddenly muddled with confusion.

"What's this about, then?" Savary asked, halting alongside Moreau.

A feeling of gratitude for their arrival passed over Moreau, suddenly aware of the danger to which he had exposed himself. Araza's corsairs had dropped to their knees with their hands in the air, while their leader stood with his feet spread wide in defiance, albeit with his sword lowered. Savary kept his pistol trained on Araza, who looked between the captain and Moreau before speaking in a mocking voice. "From the concerned looks of your friends here, I take it you've decided to join their cause."

Savary lowered his pistol, eyeing Araza with an amused look. "You're a Baratarian?"

Araza met his look and, ignoring his question, turned back to Moreau. "Lenoir, you disappoint me. I always took you for a survivor, not a fool."

Moreau glared back, holding out a restraining hand when Savary raised his pistol. "What are you talking about?"

Oblivious to the pistol pointed at his head, Araza snorted as he sheathed his blade. "You've thrown in your lot with the Americans. I'd have thought you more shrewd than to throw good money after bad."

Moreau frowned and lifted the point of his blade until it was an inch or two from Araza's belly. "You don't think they can win."

"Of course they can't win. They've just lost five of the last boats they had left."

Moreau frowned and looked at Savary, who said nothing to deny it. "Oh, your friends have not told you? Well, it's true. This morning on Lake Borgne, the English finally caught up to the Americans' *navy*, and snatched up their gunboats in a matter of minutes. Now they have a clear path to every waterway leading into the city. They're probably on Pontchartrain, heading toward the Mississippi as we speak. Either way, they'll brush aside any resistance Old Hickory tries to give them."

Moreau peered aside at Savary. "That is true?"

The captain nodded. "The enemy sent their ships of the line onto Lake Borgne this morning. Rumor is they sunk or took all of Patterson's gunboats. They control the entire lake now."

Moreau's brow creased, and he frowned when he saw Araza's amused shrug. "Well, there's nothing we can do about it now," Moreau said quietly. "I'll return to the fort with you; just give me a moment." Savary nodded and took a step back, glaring threateningly at the three men on their knees. Moreau lowered his sword and looked briefly at his cartridge pouch. "You want what's in this pouch?"

"What I want," Araza said, grinning malevolently, "is to finish what we started."

It was Moreau's turn to grin. He let out a sigh before sheathing his blade. "Years ago, I promised myself I would never duel again; for a time, I held to that. But for one so deserving of a harsh lesson, I'll make an exception." Araza's eyes flashed at the challenge. "Meet me at St. Louis Cemetery at dawn, the day after tomorrow. If you are the best swordsman in the city, you'll win, and the ruby is yours."

Araza's eyebrows rose. "And if the devil smiles upon you?"

"If *I* win," Moreau replied, "you arrange a meeting with the de Beaumais girl. Alone, in the city. Either way, it will be the last you ever see of me."

Araza's grin widened. "Done."

Dearest Maman,

Elyse once again alluded to our going home, to which I can only scoff. She's just being selfish; lately she only ever cares about what she desires. Perhaps it's boredom from the privations this foolish war has forced on us, though I wonder of some of her absences lately, if she's not found the attentions of some Creole soldier. I doubt she'd have the temerity to associate with Araza, whose rumored presence in the city has reached my ears, but I do not care. No one seems to know what he's about or where he is, so I won't waste further thought on him. Fool pirate rogue.

If Elyse would take my advice about improving her appearance, she might at least draw more eyes to her—but she insists on spending overmuch time in the sun and refusing even the mere hint of powder, blush, or parfum. Maman, I don't know what's to be done about her.

Affairs on the plantation are well enough, though the war has taken much of the master's stores. Happily I think he and his men have begun to appreciate my assistance, as we've visited the fighting men at their training grounds recently. I even brought my idea to the master that this recent alliance between Creoles and Americans is tenuous at best, and perhaps

General Jackson would benefit from an intermediary to liaise between the two opposed factions. A man who commands the respect of the planters and the legislature. One who thrived in such a role might even find himself suited for eminent positioning after the war. Perhaps even governor. But I will not speak conspicuously of such things yet. Such ideas must be planted delicately, like a seed, and nurtured in fertile ground. But I do think the master could be brought along to my thinking.

At times he dotes upon me like the daughter he never had and always wished for. Other times I find him looking at me as if I were his wife—it is rather a darling thing. His endearing qualities are many, though yesterday I did find him being unusually cross with one of his acolytes; it unsettled me somewhat. But I had a quiet word with him and he was quickly brought to calm—I do not think it will happen again. Come to think of it, I've also seen Benton and the others showing signs of cruelty, but I do not wish to trouble the master with any complaining, as he has much to look after with the war approaching and so cruelly demanding an ever-larger share of his crops and supplies. I can see he tires of the war, and wishes only to return to the love of his enterprise.

Curiously, I find myself thinking more of the slaves of late. I even dream of them sometimes. The evening past I dreamt I was wandering a wide field of cotton in a bright-yellow dress, that strangely turned to green, and suddenly I was in a wood. Not a swamp as such, but a dark, ancient wood like those in the German poems. I was wandering about, searching for flowers, when I saw one of the dark-skinned men. He looked at me, watching from behind the tree—as if he were afraid. I waved to him, motioning that it was alright and that I wouldn't hurt him. Then he scowled, snarling at me with bright-white teeth before dashing off deeper into the trees. I followed, hoping to make known that I was friend and not enemy, then I came upon a large gathering of his people: dark-skinned and hardly clothed. I did not feel embarrassed—in fact, they all looked at me with warm faces, welcoming, even. They turned and walked, again seeming welcome, when they came to the edge of a vast lake, not like the swamp behind this land, and yet it seemed to be the same. As I approached the waters the Negroes dispersed, fleeing into the trees as I called after them. I was sad to see them go.

As I crept closer to the water I noticed ripples on the surface, and soon waves were rippling as a strong wind picked up. Looking down at the surface I saw a vast shadow moving beneath, coming closer, growing darker as it approached. I felt a sense of danger—of doom. As it loomed below me, I felt my feet stuck, unable to lift them, as some creature or leviathan of the waters sped up to come seize me and bring me below.

I woke before anything more showed itself. It was strange, and I cannot stop thinking of it. I wish only for the Negroes to be as kind to me in waking hours as they seemed in the dream. What cause have they to be so sullen and impudent? As if they care nothing for noble blood, or even proper, decent treatment of others. Sometimes I hate them—but I think the nuns of Ursuline would be displeased with me for saying so, so I'll not indulge such base thoughts.

I love you, Maman. Please tell me you're alright.

C.

CHAPTER 21

St. Louis Cemetery, New Orleans
December 16, 1814

Two days came and went, and the morning of their duel dawned cold and windy, with a misting rain slickening the grass of St. Louis Cemetery. Large, opulent, above-ground tombs called vaults lined the "streets" in seemingly never-ending rows. Arriving at the south entrance, Moreau walked down the central avenue accompanied by his second, Captain Pierre Roche. A printer and bookseller by trade, Roche had previously served as an artillery officer in Napoleon's Imperial Army, and thus had some exposure to dueling—albeit less than Moreau.

Roche walked in the same easy manner as Moreau, though he had voiced a quiet reservation about the danger his superior would soon find himself in. Araza was not known to the captain, but Baratarians certainly were, and although popular among the city's population, many of the Creole men assumed them to be dangerous, unscrupulous fellows who played loose with traditional codes of honor and chivalry. His eyes scanned warily, as if looking out for an ambush, but when the two of them found an open patch of ground sufficient for the task, he took Moreau's sword for safekeeping without comment, as dueling tradition demanded.

A half hour passed with no sign of Araza. Then another, and both Moreau and Roche knew they had to return to duty at Fort St. Charles before their absence became conspicuous. Moreau had informed Major Plauché that he had an important personal matter to attend to, which, though not entirely untrue, would not explain his absence for the entire morning without raising suspicion. As

Moreau conceded that the man was not coming, he shook his head regretfully.

"What did you expect, sir?" Roche asked as he returned Moreau's sword. "He's a pirate. He has no honor."

"I know," Moreau intoned as they passed a massive vault enclosed by an elaborate wrought-iron fence. "But I wasn't playing to his honor. I'd hoped to pique his avarice, or perhaps possessiveness."

"Possessiveness?"

"Yes." Moreau tried to hide the disappointment in his voice. "There was a woman involved."

"Ah." The captain smiled. "There's always a woman involved."

Several days later, still with no word from Araza, and presuming him gone from the city, Moreau gave up any intention of meeting him again—duel or no duel. What had begun as a plan to lure Celeste into the city had come to nothing, so he did the only thing he could do: he waited. But not in vain, as several days later circumstances would present another opportunity to meet the woman—at a banquet honoring the city's defenders. Presumably the last of its kind before every soldier and militiaman left New Orleans for the duration of the campaign, the soiree was to be attended by the leading citizens of the city, both military and civilian, and would have an added benefit: Monsieur Emile Giroux and "several companions" were on the guest list. That fact was gleaned by Will Keane, who had made a discreet visit to the site of the event to peek at the guest list. Grudgingly admitting the boy had been helpful thus far, Moreau decided to make him an "official" aide-de-camp, albeit temporarily, and the boy was entered into the militia rolls by Major Plauché.

Several days later Moreau arrived with Plauché at La Salle Condé Ballroom, a sprawling, three-story town house on Conti Street. Supposing he looked something of a gentleman for a change,

Moreau wore a dark-blue dinner jacket and white cravat, both borrowed from the major, with matching blue satin breeches and his new planter's boots, augmented by a shave and proper wash. The two men walked in with the other officers to curious stares and muffled comments from the ladies and gentlemen milling about the entrance and front hall. Officers from the army, the city and state militias, and the Tennessee militia entered the hall alongside them, all welcomed by either Governor Claiborne, Mayor Nicholas Girod, or such leading citizens as Edward Livingston, whom Moreau recalled from his brief interview with General Jackson. The commanding general had not arrived yet but was due to make an appearance—if he could be pulled away from his duties.

The ballroom itself was on the first floor of the expansive, elegant building fashioned in the French neoclassical style. Its back doors opened onto an enclosed courtyard lined with palm trees and palmettos, while on the far side were kitchens and a plain, two-story house that served as servant and slave quarters. A steady procession of aproned Creole and Negro men passed back and forth between the buildings with food and drink for the guests mingling in the ballroom. Moreau followed Plauché through the foyer and into the main "dancing room," a large open space lit by ensconced lamps and two large, ornate chandeliers. There were at least a hundred guests, and anyone not in a servant's coat or soldier's uniform looked to be a member of fashionable society. A warm fire glowed beneath a flowing marble mantelpiece, while several large mirrors along the walls added to the feeling of depth and grandeur. Moreau thought the scene would not have looked out of place in Paris or Vienna.

The ladies sipped punch and smiled coquettishly at the ranks of well-dressed officers who entered the ballroom in growing numbers, quickly outnumbering their civilian hosts. The fashion adopted at the French court several years earlier had found its way to New Orleans several years earlier, and most of the French-speaking wives and daughters of the Creole planters wore brightly colored dresses and headpieces in the neoclassical style once flaunted by Napoleon and Empress Josephine, his first wife. Notably, one woman wore a robe of silver brocade with long sleeves, a trailing cloak, and standing collar heavily embroidered with silk, pearls, and spangles. Moreau thought the costume to be an imitation of Josephine's dress at Napoleon's coronation; whatever it was, it contrasted sharply with the drab blues, browns, and greys of the assembled soldiers.

"I don't see Savary or any from his battalion," Moreau said to Plauché, pulling his gaze from a short woman in a tight-fitting, black and purple dress that revealed a generous amount of bosom.

The major cleared his throat. "Apart from the commander, Major Daquin, none of the others from the First or Second Battalion will be present." He gave Moreau a knowing look, and the Frenchman quickly understood. "I see."

They continued through the ballroom, seeking refreshments, Moreau catching bits of conversation as they passed slowly through the crowd. He ignored the gossip of military strategy, instead focusing on the ladies and responding to their smiles with his own—or at least an expression less grim than his customary one.

"Join us for a game, Major?"

Moreau turned and saw a group of American officers seated at a nearby table. When he noticed who had spoken, he frowned.

Colonel Winfield grinned up at him as he cut a deck of cards. "We're playing *bouillotte*, a game from your country. We can accommodate one more." He motioned to one of the younger officers, who frowned at Moreau before noticing Winfield had stopped shuffling. "Captain, the major will take your seat." Without a word, the younger man slid his chair back and rose from the table. Winfield resumed shuffling. "He is also without drink. Fetch him a glass of port. Be quick about it." Moreau took the vacated seat as Winfield began dealing the cards. "You know Major Bentley," he said, indicating an American infantry officer. "And these here are Captains Moses and Garrett." He nodded toward two Tennesseans, who both wore dark buckskin coats. Their hair was longer than the infantrymen's, and one of them sported a grizzled beard. They gave Moreau brief nods before picking up their cards. Moreau did the same, arranging his cards as the dutiful captain set down a glass of port in front of him.

"One of Napoleon's fire-eaters," Winfield declared, snatching up his own hand.

Captain Moses looked across the table with a surprised expression. "You're the major who served under Napoleon?" His cheek protruded in a small bulge, and he leaned down and spit a brown wad into a pewter bowl.

"I 'ave not serve under 'im directly," Moreau answered, flicking his first card, "but I campaign with La Grande Armée."

The two Tennesseans exchanged an amused look. "Speaking of campaigns, we've not seen you in days," Winfield said. "I hope your Creoles aren't beginning to tire of camp life."

Moreau declined a handful of tobacco from Captain Garrett, instead pulling a cigar out of his breast pocket and accepting a light from Major Bentley. "Our men," he replied, "'ave been busy felling tree and digging defensive position. Only today we return to regular drilling."

Moreau stifled a curse when saw the turned-up cards; Major Bentley held the best hand. As Bentley gathered his coins and Winfield began reshuffling, Moreau looked up to see Captain Moses eyeing him curiously. His cheeks rolled in a chewing motion before he leaned aside and spat loudly. "We seen y'all out on the plantation several days past. You were training with the cavalry from Mississippi."

"The dragoons 'ave been of some assistance to us."

"That exercise you was teaching 'em—what'd they call it now? Hiding?"

Moreau accepted his cards and began shuffling. "'iving. A maneuver of last resort."

"*Hiving*," Bentley said. "What is that?"

Moreau set his first card down. "When an infantry regiment is overcome by cavalry, they are like to break into a rout, fleeing in panic and presenting a wonderful target for their pursuer. But if they are train to form square, they may close themselves off and present four…impenetrable side of bayonet to an enemy."

"We've heard of squares, Major," Winfield said.

"These weren't no squares," Moses said, setting a card down and rubbing his bearded chin.

"Often," Moreau went on, "a regiment 'ave not been trained for this. This applies to our men. So, if they are routed by cavalry but still wish to keep their lives, they may cluster together in small group of five or six, crouched back-to-back with bayonet point out, like a small…porcupine? Individual horsemen may still attack you, but you will not be trampled."

The other officers nodded or muttered to each other at this, while Moreau took a glass of water from a passing server. The final cards were revealed, and this time Moreau cursed aloud when his hand was lower only to Winfield's. Beaming at the others, the colonel collected his winnings and took a long sip from his glass.

As the colonel dealt the next hand, a group of three pretty young ladies appeared. Their hair was done up high in the European fashion, and they covered their mouths with gloved hands as they approached the table.

"Monsieur le Capitaine," one of the women said, addressing Bentley, "my friend Adeline would like to join you. May we sit?" Her friend turned aside with a giggle.

Colonel Winfield looked at the other officers and spread his arms. "We would consider it an honor, madame."

The woman who had spoken, clearly the least shy of the three, settled her gaze on Moreau with a sly grin. "Monsieur," she said in accented English, "*Mes amis* do not speak English, but they wish to know 'ow you 'ave lost your arm." Moreau watched the cards being dealt, suddenly aware of the eyes on him.

"I lost my arm," he answered in French, "fighting the Russians. In Poland. The circumstances are boring."

Smiling to hear their own language spoken, the women nodded gravely when they heard his answer. The one who'd asked stared at him, her expression serious. She spoke again in English. "They think you must 'ave killed many men."

A noticeable hush fell over the table, and Winfield turned to Moreau with an amused look. "What about it, Major? Have you killed many men?"

Moreau set down his card. "I would sooner avoid such gruesome conversation in the presence of ladies."

"Oh come now," Winfield retorted. "I find that the bewitching women of this city remind a man what he is fighting for."

Moreau smirked. "If the city's defender need reminding of what they fight for, per'aps they are not prepared for what is coming."

Winfield's lips thinned in a tight smile. "Correct me if I'm wrong, Major, but did you not find your way to our cause by compulsion? No shame if a man's heart is not in a fight on foreign shores."

"Foreign shores or no," Moreau replied, setting another card down, "I've never run from a fight in my life."

"I've no doubt. Though it has been said that you were given the choice of serving on staff—or remaining in a cell at the calaboose for the war's duration."

Moreau's glare was undisguised now. "And 'ow does one come to hear such a thing? Per'aps snooping at local taverns?"

Winfield took a long sip and set his glass down. "Major, you've soldiered long enough to know rumor passes through an army like shit through a goose. If fools want to make false, libelous claims—like you're not who you claim to be, or that you are a mercenary who holds no loyalty to the cause you serve—why fret over it?"

Holding back an angry retort, Moreau looked around the room. His heartbeat suddenly increased when he saw a group of well-dressed gentlemen stroll into the ballroom. First to enter, and assuming an eminent position, was Emile Giroux, who wore a dark-blue frock coat and tight black breeches, almost military in appearance. He removed his tall black hat and kissed the hand of a well-wishing lady. On his arm was Celeste de Beaumais, wearing a fine blue dress that flared out at the bottom and long white gloves, who smiled at the onlookers and curtsied several times. Following a few steps behind was Elyse, who held her hands folded at her waist in an unassuming posture.

Moreau checked his cards, but when he looked up, Celeste was nowhere to be seen, though the planter was still standing there, listening intently to a man in a dark-green riding coat. Quietly cursing himself for becoming distracted, Moreau turned back to the table, oblivious to the quiet that had settled over the others. "And who makes such accusations?"

Winfield's grin widened. "As I said...surely just false, libelous claims."

Excusing himself from the group and ignoring a plea to remain from one of the young coquettes, Moreau moved into the crowd with an eye out for Celeste. The room had become even more crowded, and as he strolled among the well-dressed ladies and gentlemen, Moreau found himself directly in front of Monsieur Giroux, who was standing beside a man in a black dinner jacket and appeared to be only half listening to fellow's conversation. Moreau meant to turn away, but he had caught the old planter's attention, and the man was gesturing emphatically at him.

"Monsieur Lenoir," Giroux cried out, tapping the other man for him to follow. He rushed over to Moreau, his face flushed and slightly sweaty, and shook his hand forcefully. "Monsieur, we've been rather disappointed not to welcome you back to our home. I only learned recently that you had gone for a soldier. Tremblay told me." He turned to the man beside him, who looked to be about the same age and was dressed in a similar fashion. "This is a confidant of mine, Monsieur Laboulaye." The man took Moreau's hand, his expression one of undisguised concern. "Is it true, we've lost sight of the British off Lake Borgne?"

Moreau exhaled, then provided the same vague answer regarding military preparedness that he had given to several others who had asked similar questions in recent days. The mood throughout the city ranged from haughty defiance to outright panic, often in the same person over the course of a single conversation. Concluding his recitation, Moreau attempted a reassuring smile.

Giroux nodded, his eyes wandering to a passing couple, while Laboulaye stepped closer to Moreau. "And what make you of our city, Monsieur Lenoir?"

Moreau inched back, suddenly regretting that he'd left his cigar at the card table. "It is fine."

"Just fine?"

"I think," Moreau answered finally, "the English made a mistake attacking this city. If it were me, I would have chosen a city with less guns, blades, and brawlers."

The two men looked at him a moment, before looking at each other and letting out a burst of forced laughter. Moreau stole another look around but did not see the cursed woman. "Well, as it is a sin to lie," Giroux said, handing his empty glass to a passing servant. "I must confess that I am not overly fond of this city. It has been called, by some, a warren of vice and crime, lacking order, civility, and tethered to nothing resembling Christian morality." Beside him Laboulaye's brow furrowed as he nodded his agreement. "In fact," Giroux went on, "if it is tethered to *anything*, it is disorder, violence, and sin. Our little lives in the parishes may not be perfect, but we have not seen wholesale moral disintegration such as we've seen in the city."

Moreau exhaled, unsure what to say in response. Laboulaye cleared his throat loudly, but a commotion toward the entrance pulled his attention, and a moment later every head had turned to see what had caused the disturbance. Those standing in front of the fireplace began moving backward, making way for the figure at the head of a small group of men in a variety of military uniforms.

General Andrew Jackson stood slightly above average height, but even from across the room Moreau could see he looked somewhat frail, and his movements appeared slow and labored. Nevertheless, the general passed smoothly through the crowd, pausing to spare a few words here and there, but never lingering more than a few moments in one place. Turning back to Giroux and Laboulaye, Moreau noticed their distinctly cold expressions. Giroux leaned aside to whisper something in Laboulaye's ear, causing the latter to nod and frown. Jackson nodded at the two planters as he unhurriedly made his way through the crowd toward them. Perhaps a half dozen aides flocked to the general's side. One of them, whom Moreau had met during his earliest days in the army, Major Latour, stepped next to Jackson and spoke in English. "Messieurs Giroux and Laboulaye, General. Successful planters from the German Coast."

Giroux offered his hand to Jackson, who clasped it with a firm grip and offered a hard stare. The general's face looked gaunt and pale, perhaps more so than when Moreau had spoken with him weeks before, but his uniform and his tail of hawkeyed attendants gave him a presence that drew every eye to him. His posture was rod straight, his eyes dark embers that showed little sign of fatigue. "Mr. Giroux, good evening. Mr. Laboulaye, how do you do?"

Something in the way Giroux and Jackson held each other's stares caught Moreau's attention, and for the moment Laboulaye seemed a mere spectator. "Monsieur Jackson," Giroux said in passable English, "I am surprised to see you. I was told your duties were likely to keep you from joining us here tonight."

"Presenting myself here tonight is my duty, sir," the general replied with a tight smile.

"We've been told training has been rather rigorous," Laboulaye chimed in enthusiastically. "Dare I say the courage of our own Creole defenders has surprised us all?"

Jackson smiled warmly at a lady close by before turning back to the planters with a hard expression. "It is not the courage of our soldiers that I hope to put spur to, but the contributions of our civilian population. Which reminds me, sir," he glanced at Giroux, "of a conversation I had with members of the legislature recently. Your name was mentioned—more than once."

"Oh?" Giroux said, tilting his head. "And what did those—"

"I was informed," Jackson interrupted, "that my declaration of martial law would be met with near unanimous approval by the city's leading citizens. And in exchange for such a decision, those most fervently in *favor* of such an announcement, had offered to make certain...contributions." His voice turned cold. "Some of these contributions have yet to be made."

Laboulaye began to fidget, but Giroux held Jackson's gaze. At length he clasped his hands together. "It was my understanding, General, that you hold little fondness for the legislature."

"My personal feelings are of slight concern next to my duty, sir."

Giroux nodded. "A soldier's words, surely. But while I hold fast to the belief that extraordinary times call for extraordinary measures, I nonetheless wonder at certain...unprecedented steps taken, legal though they may seem to those unfamiliar with our Constitution."

At this General Jackson's chin jerked slightly, and he subtly shifted his weight from one leg to another. Moreau knew the signs of exhaustion all too well, and this man certainly looked no stranger to them.

"If you find any of my decrees unconstitutional," Jackson said finally, his voice strong, "I advise you to take it up with the mayor, or governor."

"Oh come off it," Laboulaye blurted, "you've demanded that all planters provide as many slaves as can be spared. Your men can see to the construction of earthworks and other defensive structures; we must maintain our own. Why, just years ago the German Coast was in flames!" Suddenly aware that he may have spoken too forcefully, he recoiled under the weighty gaze of the famous general.

Giroux took a half step forward, and spoke in a level voice. "General, your soldiers have tried to claim my people on three occasions now, and I've told them repeatedly that none can be spared. I understand there's a war on, but I cannot simply abandon my enterprise."

"No one asks you to abandon your enterprise, sir. I sympathize with your wish to protect your property, but what has been decreed—and which the legislature agreed with—is both sensible policy and a patriotic sacrifice."

Giroux nodded slowly, lowering his eyelids. "Those of us of this soil, Mr. Jackson, know best the importance of defending it. The English are our enemy come from without, but you seem to appreciate quite little the damage that might come from within. Indian attacks and slave uprisings are a scourge which we have only just come to reckon with fully. We are still binding our wounds today."

General Jackson's cold blue eyes surveyed the crowd, which had grown considerably quieter, before settling back on the two men. "Mr. Giroux, there are few present who know of Indian attacks more personally than I. If you are not satisfied with the guarantees of protection I have offered, I suggest once again that you take your petitions to the legislature. I will hear no more of it from you this evening." He gathered himself before walking further into the ballroom, a half-dozen aides at his heels.

Moreau departed while the planters were joined by a handful of men who crowded around as if to congratulate them. Passing through the ballroom's large doorway, he turned right toward the staircase and had almost reached the first step when he saw a red-headed woman in a simple grey dress standing a few paces away. Her back was to him as she spoke with one of the servant women, who, like almost all of the others, was a Negro. Something close to déjà vu played in his mind, and he hesitated briefly, looking carefully behind him before slowly making his way into her view.

Elyse Pasteur's familiar face held a tight, almost harried, expression, and it took a moment before she recognized him. When the realization finally came, her eyes narrowed and Moreau could not tell if her look was good-natured—perhaps flirtatious—or something closer to miserable. Either way, he felt relieved to see her, especially since she happened to be the person closest to Celeste. "If you've come tonight to ask for me a dance," he said in a low voice, "I'm afraid I'll have to disappoint you."

Elyse offered an apologetic expression to the serving woman, who smiled diffidently before excusing herself. Elyse's squint seemed to tighten when she turned back around. "What are you doing here?"

"It's a pleasure to see you too." Moreau said, noticing the modest cleavage revealed by her dress. "You know why I'm here."

Elyse scrutinized him a moment before issuing a sharp laugh, then covered her mouth with a hand. Moreau shifted his stance so his back was to the entrance and leaned in closer. "I've no time for games. Where is she?"

Elyse smiled at a guest heading for the stairs before turning back to Moreau with raised eyebrows. "You really are besotted with her, aren't you? You might as well write her a love sonnet for all the care you've given her. Though I must warn you, she prefers men who smile out of gaiety and not to frighten small children."

"I need to speak with her. Time is running out." He wiped a hand through his hair and let out a breath. "If she'll not listen to reason, then I'll be forced to be more persuasive."

Elyse's eyelids lowered. "And what, you'll snatch her and toss her over your shoulder and row her back to France?"

"If necessary."

Elyse let out a long sigh. "Well, I doubt you'll wring much sense from her tonight. She's come in the hopes of finding one of your comrades. The one whom *she* is still besotted with. Foolish girl."

"Don't tell me she's still in love with that goddamn pirate."

Elyse shrugged. "I cannot stand the sight of the man, but my lady? Everything she does, everywhere she goes, is ultimately with the aim of getting his attention. Of *winning* him back." She shrugged again, and Moreau rubbed his forehead, thinking this could complicate matters. "Of course, she says she hates him. But that is only because she is unwilling to admit the truth to herself."

Moreau recalled that Tadeo Araza had failed to show for their duel, feeling a pang of disquiet as he wondered if the corsair captain had simply taken his crew and sailed for more profitable waters. Moreau no longer needed him as a means to find Celeste—the point was moot—but he wondered if Araza's disappearance might cause complications if she chose to chase after him. "Stupid woman."

At this Elyse's expression darkened. "Monsieur, don't take my frustration with her for a license to insult. She is my lady; I have known her nearly all her life." Her deep frown caused Moreau to squint yet again, before his lips formed a smirk.

"How inconsiderate of me," he said. He then stepped closer. "I've known women like you all my life. Lady's attendants. To men, they are always proud, to strangers they are always wary. But to their ladies? They are always meek and subservient."

She gasped and raised a hand to slap Moreau, but he reached up and caught it in midair. She looked as if she'd been struck by a blade, then bared her teeth.

"But," he said in a soft voice, leaning closer, "I've always found them quite charming." He released her hand and kissed her on the lips, holding it for a moment, turning away before she could utter anything in response. By the time her angry growl and half-shouted insults reached his ears, Moreau was halfway up the stairs, taking two steps at a time. He reached the top without looking back and turned right, heading toward the mezzanine.

CHAPTER 22

La Salle Condé Ballroom, New Orleans
December 23, 1814

Only a dozen or so guests milled about the mezzanine, which offered a clear view of the ballroom below. Moreau walked across at a slow pace, quickly realizing the woman was not there, and halted to gaze down at the guests below. General Jackson was out of sight, but Emile Giroux remained, surrounded by several individuals who looked eager to hear or share an opinion with the outspoken planter. Nearby Governor Claiborne, surrounded by an entourage of his own, was also engaged in lively conversation with several men Moreau did not recognize. He rested an arm on the banister, wondering if those below knew what could happen to civilians in a city under siege. In just a few weeks, grandées celebrated by polite society could be made to look like filthy, starving skeletons with grime-soaked faces and eyes devoid of any spirit. Children orphaned, women forced into prostitution, men pinioned to walls by bayonets...*perhaps* it would not come to that. Jackson and most of his officers seemed to hold a proper solemnity about what they would soon face, but many of the others, namely the local politicians and businessmen not enrolled in the militia, seemed blissfully unaware of the horrors that war would bring.

A bump against his shoulder jarred Moreau from his thoughts, and he frowned as a lean man in a white coat, with shoulder-length blonde hair sidled up beside him. He was leaning on a cane and removed a round *demi-bateau* hat from his head as he murmured his pardon, turning to look out over the room. Irritated that the man had chosen to crowd him when most of the space was unoccupied, Moreau glared a moment before turning away. With a mutter he turned to resume his search for Celeste when the man spoke in a low voice.

"Splendid evening."

His French was tinged with the hint of an accent. Perhaps Caribbean. Moreau examined him again, noticing the blonde beard covering his chin and the round-framed spectacles. Overall, the man gave a peculiar impression—and yet there seemed something familiar about him.

"Indeed."

The fellow turned and smiled with a look that could only be described as "simple." His eyes were glazed, and his mouth was open in a drooping smile, and Moreau assumed he was drunk, or under the influence of some narcotic.

"Makes one almost forget," Moreau muttered, "that there's an enemy army lurking nearby."

Shaking his head, he turned to leave when the man chuckled. "Oh, I'm sure the governor has it all in hand."

Moreau looked at him again: something was decidedly off. With a sigh, Moreau stepped back, and the man stepped back with him, offering his hand and a smile. Growing frustrated at the man's obtrusiveness, Moreau stepped closer. "And what is your name, monsieur?"

The fellow nodded his head in a bow and shook Moreau's hand with an iron-firm grip. "Monsieur Clements. At your service."

Moreau endured the handshake a moment before tugging his hand back. "Look here, Clements, you're interrupting my—"

"You know," the man said, gently placing a hand on Moreau's shoulder, "I recently enjoyed the privilege of dining with the governor's wife, good Creole that she is. Ah, and never did it cross Madame le Governor's wildest imaginings that she was, in fact, dining in the company of her husband's greatest nemesis." Clements slowly reached up and removed his hat—and the blonde hair came away as well, revealing a thick crop of black hair pulled back and tied in a knot behind his head.

Jean Lafitte bowed slightly.

For a moment Moreau stared dumbfounded at the Baratarian chief, quickly recognizing the man from the swamp. Finally, Moreau shook his head with a grin. "I'm beginning to understand why the governor hates you."

Lafitte smiled mischievously before placing the wig and hat back on his head.

"But why this ruse? I thought Jackson had pardoned you and your men."

"And how very gracious of him. My lads are now feted as stray sheep brought back into the fold. As for this ruse, I find the leading citizens of this city more amenable to sensitive discussions of state with a frolicsome cane planter called Clements than with a notorious *pirate chief*. Pardoned though he may be." He looked at Moreau, his eyes animated.

"I think I prefer the latter. I was ready to cuff Monsieur Clements over the head."

"The governor's wife felt rather differently."

Moreau kept his laugh low. "I can see why they don't know whether to conscript you or hang you."

"They've tried both."

Moreau shook his head again, disappointed at himself for falling for a disguise that seemed rather simple now. A clock chimed below as he cleared his throat. "Contrary to how I felt about Clements, I'm actually glad you're here. I have been wondering something—it concerns one of your sworn men."

"Araza."

Moreau nodded.

"What would you like to know?"

Moreau ran a hand through his hair. "These rubies he's searching after, I presume you've heard of them. Why does he covet them so much? A captain, with his own ship—I would think him rich enough to be above such a thing."

Lafitte looked over at the ballroom with a thoughtful expression. "It may be hard to believe, but Araza was not a greedy man. A proud one, to be sure. And vain."

Moreau kept his eyes ahead. "*Was?*"

Lafitte answered in a level voice. "He was found murdered this morning. Throat slashed ear to ear."

Moreau turned slowly and saw Lafitte's expression. It was somber enough to remove any doubt. "I don't think," the Baratarian went on, his voice serious but hardly sentimental, "it was the ruby he coveted, but the young French girl's duplicity that troubled him." He leaned forward, resting his elbows on the banister. "Some months ago, he took her as a lover, on Guadeloupe, where they met. What brought the girl to that island he never said, but as often happens with privateer trysts, relations…soured. Soon after, she rebelled against his *authority* and humiliated him in front of his crew, calling him all sorts of names. I think 'feral slave monger' struck him especially. He never really enjoyed the trade; perhaps she inflamed his guilt."

Moreau looked at him intently. "So the rubies were hers?"

Lafitte nodded. "It would seem so, though she kept them secret from him, and he only learned she had them *after* he dumped her in the swamps. Knowing Tadeo, he probably thought that by lying with her they had become his, and by allowing her to escape—with her gemstones—he'd made a terrible mistake. He was not one accustomed to making mistakes."

Moreau stared thoughtfully as the story sank in, then shook his head with a sneer. "So, his pride was wounded when he let the girl get away with *her* rubies; seems foolish enough to me." He lifted his head, frowning thoughtfully. "Though I certainly did not like the bastard…I am sorry for his suffering such an ignoble death."

Lafitte's cunning smirk reappeared. "He was too untrustworthy to have ever been called a friend. If he'd seen an advantage, he'd have been the first to stick the knife in my back. Still," his tone turned regretful, "he was a fine captain. The Americans would have benefited from a fighter like him directing their cannons."

Moreau nodded. "Likely so. But who would want him killed?"

When Lafitte finally answered, his voice was hard. "He knew as well as I that our days of freedom in Barataria were coming to an end. He never told me, but I'd learned that his plans were to sail home to Caracas with as many men as would join him. Some said he planned to take up with Simón Bolívar; whether that's true..." He shrugged. "There would certainly have been coin enough in it for him. Perhaps one of his men chose mutiny."

For a moment Moreau considered the man beside him, and his position at the head of hundreds of smugglers, corsairs, and cutthroats, each hungry for wealth and power. That very seafaring fiefdom had recently been blown to smithereens, its men scattered or impressed into serving the American cause, all after the English had offered him bribes to join their side. And still, his demeanor was calm, even cheerful—at a soiree attended by his former enemies. Chuckling to himself, Moreau wondered what it would take to unnerve the man. Likely quite a lot.

A movement below caught Moreau's eye, and he peered down at a woman in a blue dress with matching gloves reaching to her elbows. She crossed the ballroom hurriedly. Celeste de Beaumais. "Speak of the devil."

Lafitte grinned slyly before wiping a hand over his face; when he removed it, a blonde beard once again covered his chin and upper lip. "Good luck with your lady, but be quick about it. My sentries believe the English will appear within days, if not hours." Nodding his farewell, he set his cane in front of him and proceeded across the mezzanine with a slight limp, disappearing around the corner.

A minute later Moreau reached the bottom of the stairs and glanced around. Seeing Celeste nowhere in sight, he made his way through the large double doors and peered into the ballroom. A quick survey brought nothing, only the same groups he'd seen from the mezzanine. Turning to leave, Moreau halted when he noticed Colonel Winfield speaking with an older woman, who was staring at him with an absorbed expression.

"Hiving?" the woman asked.

"Well," Winfield explained, "in battle, if infantry are forced to retreat and cavalry are sent in pursuit, it often becomes a rout, and the infantry are cut to pieces."

The woman lifted a hand to her mouth. "Oh, how frightening."

"But," Winfield continued, "if their discipline holds, the best option is to split off into small groups of five or six and crouch back-to-back, with bayonets pointed out…" Moreau didn't bother hiding his snort, forcing himself not to bump Winfield's shoulder as he passed. Turning back toward the stairs, he checked the rest of the ground floor, seeing plenty of guests but no sign of Celeste. He turned back to return to the ballroom when he saw a flash of blue in his peripheral vision. A woman in a blue dress was making her way out toward the courtyard. She was average height, with dirty blonde hair and wearing long gloves. Without hesitation he followed.

Stepping into the courtyard, Moreau saw a small grove of palm fronds beside a three-tiered fountain with a cherub statue on top. A few guests mingled discreetly in a far corner, but Moreau had eyes only for the woman beside the fountain. Balancing a glass in one hand, she brought a pinch of snuff to her nose and, a moment later, sneezed. Moreau forced his breathing under control as he slowly approached her. Stopping a few paces away, he cleared his throat to get her attention. Her head bobbed at the sound, and a moment later she turned slowly. When her eyes settled on Moreau, she stared for several seconds before slipping the snuff box into a fold in her dress.

"May I help you?" Her voice was high, with a hint of haughtiness.

Moreau watched her, not sure whether to smile triumphantly or prepare to guard against unwanted intruders. He spoke in a quiet voice. "Good evening, mademoiselle."

She inclined her head slightly. "Good evening."

Moreau almost chuckled. Not at the woman's tone, which *was* impatient now, but at the fact that he had finally found the woman he had crossed an ocean to retrieve. He gave her another appraising look, noticing beneath the wide folds of her dress an ample bosom. and arms that hung neatly to her side, as if she had practiced standing in such a pose all her life. Her posture was nearly perfect, and her gaze was direct and confident, as if she had practiced standing in such a pose all her life. An aristocrat through and through. "I was wondering if I might have a word."

She exhaled sharply. "Well, you've already begun that process; why not draw it through to completion?"

Moreau nodded slowly. "Mademoiselle de Beaumais…" She started at the mention of her name, shifting her weight visibly. "I've come from France. From your home region, in fact. There's no reason to be alarmed, I wish you no harm, but…" He hesitated, worried she might turn and run. "I do bring word from your parents. They wish for me to deliver a message. They are concerned for your safety."

The young woman's eyes widened slightly, and for a moment she stared at him so intently that Moreau wondered if she would throw the contents of her glass in his face. Perhaps aware of her reaction, she cleared her throat and licked her lips before replying. "And who is it that wishes to deliver this message?"

Moreau took an unconscious step forward. "I am called Len—" he paused mid-step before settling his feet. "My name is Marcel Moreau. I have spoken with your family personally, and I come only to bring you a message from them." He hoped his voice did not harden at the lie of the last message, but it was too late for subtlety now.

"So, you've come all this way to deliver a message…" She raised the glass to her lips, sipping slowly and staring at him with a stony expression. "Moreau, was it? Well, monsieur, I should tell you that I've expected this conversation for some time now."

Moreau forced a neutral expression. "I was told," she went on, "that a 'family friend from France' had asked of me, wishing for a meeting. I supposed it to be one of my father's intimates, but you—you seem more like a…specter raised from some dark, subterranean realm." She swirled her glass with an icy smile. "No offense, to be sure."

He returned her frosty smile with one of his own. He offered no other reaction, for he had none, apart from a cold calculation forming in his mind as to whether he ought to clasp a hand over her mouth and drag her from the spot then and there. Surely any onlooker would cry out in alarm, but that seemed a small consideration when weighed against securing his quarry. At last he let out a breath, forcing a friendly tone. "You know Andre Valière? And his wife Sophie? They live on an estate called Carcourt."

She took a final sip of wine and let the glass dangle in her hand. "I am familiar with that family. What of them?"

"They have been in conversation with your parents. Before I set out for these shores, they learned—"

"Before you say any more," she interjected in a tired voice, "I should inform you that I have no intention of making any imminent return to France. Even if there were no war, I have my own affairs to tend to."

Moreau reached out to touch one of the nearby dwarf palmettos, rubbing the hard frond between his thumb and pointer finger. After a moment he let go and rested his hand on his hip. The sound of a door slamming against a wall came from behind him, and he thought he heard running feet before the sound was lost in a distant burst of laughter.

Celeste passed her eyes around the courtyard, at last settling her gaze on the dark night sky above the rooftops. "It's a shame I had to visit this city in wartime," she mused, tapping the empty glass with a finger. "Did you know," she turned to him, her expression happy, even friendly, "that the founder of this city, Monsieur Bienville, did so on Mardi Gras, Fat Tuesday itself? Oh, what a splendid time we might have had if there was no war. Masks, costumes, dancing, and feasting—in this very building! I do hope the filthy English are defeated soon."

Moreau squinted, unsure if this was some ruse to lull him into frivolous conversation before making her escape, or if she spoke genuinely. "As I said, mademoiselle, the message from your—"

She waved a hand and stepped closer, staring at him with a scrutinizing air. "You know," she said offhandedly, "you might have been handsome—before you suffered that hideous thing."

She indicated the scar half hidden beneath the hair on the left side of his head.

"And your company might have been pleasant, if you hadn't opened your mouth." He regretted the words as soon as they left his lips, but he had endured enough condescension from the woman and found himself unable to resist at least one poke. A slight curve of her lips and a flash of her eyes betrayed her irritation, but she quickly mastered herself, tilting her head back as she let out a shrill laugh. When she finally looked back down at him, her face widened in a wry smile.

"So, you are the man my father sent across the sea." She laughed again, running a finger across her left eye as if wiping a tear. "You. Some broken-looking cripple of a man. Oh, I'm sure Napoleon presented you with the *Légion d'honneur* personally. Still, I'm not surprised—Papa always was a cheap, coin-pinching buffoon with no sense of subtlety."

Moreau glared at her, a part of him relieved that her halfhearted effort of pretend friendliness was through. He started to speak, but a noise that sounded like distant thunder caused one of his ears to twitch involuntarily, and he said nothing. A moment passed and the sound was past, and he noticed the woman was staring at him with raised eyebrows.

"Tongue tied, monsieur? I'm sorry if that was a little too much. I'm sure you're a...fine fellow after all." She chuckled to herself again, and Moreau cocked his head at the sound of footsteps running through the corridor behind him.

Setting that out of his mind, he took a step closer to her. "Now listen, this can go one of two—"

Another rumble sounded in the distance, and this time he knew it was not thunder. A third rumble came, more distinct than before, and Celeste's brow furrowed as she turned in its direction. Clearly she had heard it too.

Moreau turned to face the sound as a loud clamor arose inside the ballroom, the mutters and shouts echoing clearly across the courtyard. Looking back toward the woman, he cursed when he heard the shattering of glass and saw her running past the far side of the fountain, skirt and petticoats clasped in both hands. He would have followed her as fast as he could, but the deep, rumbling sound pulled him in the other direction. Now the blasts came in quick succession, and Moreau knew these were no sentry calls or warning shots. The sound of cannons boomed, to his ears they were perhaps several miles off, but the sound was unmistakable: the English had come at last, bringing war with them.

CHAPTER 23

Condé Ballroom, New Orleans
December 23, 1814

Moreau jogged into the ballroom to find a uniformed courier standing before a solemn-looking General Jackson. Halting abruptly, Moreau ignored the angry stare of the man he'd nearly barreled into, wedging himself into the large group forming around the general. "We estimate perhaps a thousand," the courier said, "moving about Villeré Plantation. But that was an hour ago when I departed. They were pouring in from the bayou, so by now there could be at least double that."

General Jackson's expression could only be described as cold, determined fury. "Two thousand redcoats." His calm voice belied his formidable demeanor. "Less than ten miles from the city, and this is the first I hear of it?"

"Major Villeré, General Villeré's son, was in his home when they came out from Bayou Bienvenue onto the plantation grounds. He said he was taken captive—briefly. Apparently he...leapt out a window and passed word to our sentries posted along the Lacoste Canal."

Jackson let out a weary sigh. "I should like to know how they passed from Lake Borgne to be deposited right under our noses unseen."

"Treason!" someone among the crowd shouted. "A traitor in our midst!"

Jackson ignored the outburst. "Who was in command guarding the nearest bayou? Mazant, I believe."

The officers exchanged nervous looks. "I believe the major—"

"Bah, it doesn't matter now. They are here, and that is what must be dealt with." Jackson peered down at a pocket watch in his hand. "Commodore Patterson has already begun maneuvering the *Carolina*, so we have precious little time." His voice was taut, with an edge that invited no further conversation. "Alright, Generals Coffee, Carroll, Villeré and Colonel Ross will meet me at my headquarters on Royal in ten minutes. All battalions in the city or Fort St. Charles will assemble at La Place with arms and ammunition in thirty minutes. I will lead them out myself." His curt nod and hard stare were all that was needed to send the officers scurrying in all directions. "By the Eternal, they shall not sleep on our soil tonight!"

Moreau did not wait for further orders. He left the room and passed through the large double doors, and as he made his way out into the crisp evening air, he saw a familiar face. Major Plauché fell in beside him midstride. Shouts and running couriers broke through the night silence, and the city's civilians, those who had not fled for Natchez or Baton Rouge, looked out from doorways and balconies with uneasy faces. One man with a basket balanced on his head ran past, followed quickly by a wide-eyed woman, presumably a seamstress, dragging several large coats behind her. "Looks like our wait is over," Plauché said quietly.

"If they've managed to sneak themselves this close to the city," Moreau replied, "they could be here within hours."

"But I wonder," Plauché said in a low voice, "if it is wise to attack at night."

Moreau considered the question, and for a moment lacked an answer. He was no general, and Jackson's orders to assemble the troops had been given promptly, without many details. Sometimes action was simply better than inaction. "At night, their superior training will mean less. Your men may not be professionals—but they're not afraid of a few bloody noses."

Plauché looked at him. "*Our* men."

Moreau let out a misty breath, then nodded once.

A moment later they arrived at the corner of Chartres and St. Peter Streets and looked out onto La Place, then halted simultaneously. What awaited them in the square could only be described as utter mayhem. In every direction, like a massive colony of ants, soldiers of the various battalions guarding the city crashed into one another as they rushed to join their respective formations. Men tugged at bootlaces and buttoned coats, cursing and shouting as they ran. White Creoles in blue, black, or checkered uniforms raced past similarly clad Black soldiers, while Tennesseans in the brown cloth called homespun, buckskin jackets, and fur hats shouted mock welcomes to a sizeable contingent of Kentuckians, who had marched into the city only the day before. Moving somewhat more slowly, but with no less sense of urgency, were a few dozen dark-haired Indians. They seemed quieter than their white comrades—shy, even, except when speaking to their own kind—but few present mistook them for timid. Choctaws, Moreau had heard them called. They wore tight leggings wrapped with black or white strips of cloth, and buckskin jackets or coats cut from animal hide. Most wore their hair long, save for three or four of their leaders, who had shaved the sides of their heads or cut their hair so that only a thin strand ran down their back. They carried muskets in one hand held loosely at their hips, and most had sharp-bladed hatchets tucked into their belts. Though simply dressed, they nonetheless moved and spoke with an exotic air that reminded Moreau of the Mamelukes, the enigmatic Muslim warriors he had seen in La Grande Armée who had followed Napoleon home to France after his expedition in Egypt.

Forming on the far side of the open square were the soldiers of the 7th and 44th Infantry Regiments, and two small batteries of American artillerymen. The first to fall in by company, they stood in a well-dressed formation that Moreau supposed might give confidence to the less trained, and less experienced, Creole militiamen. Whether they fought as well as they marched and drilled would soon be seen.

Facing them across the square was a comparatively small group of Baratarians, who milled about in a loose formation. Wearing their customary striped smocks and dark coats, loose-fitting pantaloons, and kerchiefs of varying colors, they appeared wary in the presence of so many armed strangers, most of whom had been mortal enemies just days earlier. Several stood clustered around a massive thirty-two pounder naval cannon. Those closest to the gun stared out with taut expressions, resting an arm or a boot on its barrel, as if protecting a precious trophy from dangerous looters.

The formation situated closest to the cathedral was the 2nd Battalion of D'Aquin's Free Men of Color. Dressed like their white Creole neighbors in coats of blue, green, and brown, these men had formed into ranks rather quickly, as if aware of their uncommon status among this uncommon assembly. Armed with muskets that had just recently arrived on flatboats sent down the Mississippi, the men of the 2nd held their weapons with pride and looked more confident than Moreau had yet seen them. He saw Plauché's gaze linger over the group for a moment. His expression showed little, but Moreau thought the colonel showed a slight shake of his head. Whatever the Creole thought of arming so many Black men, Moreau hoped he knew better than to let his feelings come before his duty. One could never be sure how those beside him would perform until the fighting began, but from what Moreau had seen, these men possessed spirit enough. It would be foolish to mistrust them now.

The loud tolling of bells from St. Louis Cathedral drew both men's attention, and as Moreau crossed the square he noticed groups of well-dressed ladies, young as well as old, lining the balconies, waving handkerchiefs at the soldiers. One or two wiped away tears, but most stared out eagerly, calling out encouragement or blowing kisses.

"Well, Marcel," Plauché said, "it is time. Don't stray far; the rest of my staff will look to you if things become muddled."

"Battle is always muddled."

Plauché ignored Moreau's salute and offered his hand, which the Frenchman took with a grin, sensing the other man's nervousness. "Good luck, Major."

With that, Plauché strode off to the stables on the opposite side of La Place, leaving Moreau to once more survey the hectic scene. Troops poured in from seemingly every street leading into the square, bumping shoulders and shouting out orders. The bells continued ringing as assembly cannons thundered from Fort St. Charles, calling in any stragglers from the local bivouacs.

"Major!" A shrill voice cut through the din.

Moreau turned and saw a boy dressed in a dark-blue coat with silver piping. It was a size too large, and the grey trousers had been rolled up at the ankles, but the boy beamed with unmistakable pride. Will Keane snapped to attention with a salute. Moreau sighed, slowly returning the salute as he appraised the boy's appearance, which he found rather ridiculous. But for a change he held his tongue and laid a gentle hand on his shoulder. "Private, you look ready for war."

The boy's eyebrows rose and his lips widened.

"I have no doubt you're ready to do your duty."

"Yes sir," the boy piped.

"Listen." Moreau leaned down and looked him in the eye. "As my courier, it is your duty to assist me whenever needed. Right now, I need you at the fort." Will's smile drooped and his shoulders slumped. He opened his mouth to speak, but Moreau preempted him. "I know you want to accompany me, but now is not the time. This battle tonight will not be the last."

Too upset to argue further, the boy nodded with a vacant stare. Moreau stood back up. "Now go report to the duty officer at the fort and await any orders they give you. Go."

With a lackluster salute, Will turned and departed across La Place with a forced shuffle. Moreau watched him a moment before turning to look back across the square to where the Louisiana Militia companies stood in formation. Placing his hat on his head, he walked over to join them.

La Place had grown rather quiet now, the barking of orders from officers and sergeants the only discernable sounds. Regimental flags rippled gently in the breeze, while clouds of breath puffed out from cold-looking faces. Seeing no sign of General Jackson or his staff, Moreau paced in front of the formation, examining the men in the front ranks. At last he shook his head, letting out a harsh breath. "What's wrong? You men look like schoolboys about to shit their breeches."

A handful of those within earshot cackled, but most of the others simply stared ahead with taut expressions. For a moment the formation was silent, until someone in front spoke in a soft voice. "They say there are five thousand of them."

Moreau tilted his head back. "So what? Look around you; there are plenty of us."

"They came out of the swamp undetected," another blurted. "Who will look after our wives and daughters if they sneak into the city?"

More nervous exclamations followed as the men looked aside to each other for support. Moreau sighed.

"They defeated Napoleon!"

Another murmur of agreement followed.

"Napoleon defeated Napoleon." Moreau shook his head. "They're men, just like you." He swept his gaze across the ranks, noticing the patchwork uniforms and unwashed faces. "Well, maybe not *just* like you. But have you forgotten Washington? He did not fear men in red coats, why should you?"

He waited for a response but saw only nervous faces. They had been trained well enough to hold their ground, and Moreau did not doubt their courage, but he also knew the fear every man felt before going into combat for the first time. The tricks one's mind could play when faced with the prospect of horrific injury or death. He took a step closer, his mouth curled and his eyes staring fiercely.

"When wolves set out for the hunt," he called out in a clear voice, "they are not careless in pursuit of their prey. Prey with powerful hind legs and hooves to crush a skull. Sharp, pointed antlers to skewer ribs. The frothing breath of a beast with a savage will to live. A wolf respects the danger its prey presents—*but it does not fear it!*"

He paused, letting his words sink in. "A great army is coming this way, one that is well-trained and battle-hardened. Soldiers who defeated my countrymen. But, to hear some say, they have become overconfident. They are not accustomed to fighting war in a place like this. I know *I* am not. But this is *your* home. If you would defend it, you start by recalling that these are the violators who burned your capital city—who would burn your homes and defile your women. They are dangerous, as a stag is dangerous. Proud, fearless, with no true competition for food or mate. Only this stag has wandered into a place it does not belong. A thick, unyielding mire. A swamp where it cannot move freely. And the wolves have caught its scent. You men have trained for the last month to be soldiers, and you now have a choice: you can be the prey, or you can be the hunters."

A few minutes later General Jackson rode into La Place in full dress uniform, his large bicorne hat conspicuous in the flickering light of the streetlamps. Generals Coffee and Villeré, Colonel Ross, and their aides followed in mounted procession. Within moments the bell ringing had ceased, and the commander proceeded to issue several orders, which Moreau could not hear from his position behind the battalion. Jackson then removed his hat, signaling the order for the army to move. The first to depart were the regulars of the 7th and 44th Infantry Regiments, who turned and marched south along Decatur Street by company. With determined faces, they stepped off at a quick pace to the sound of drums and fifes, leaving a noticeable silence lingering over the square in their wake. Several minutes later the Tennesseans and Kentuckians followed.

Next to leave were the white Creole militias, Moreau riding alongside Plauché and Villeré's other staff officers. When they had departed, the last of the soldiers looking back uneasily at their wives and daughters, the free Negro battalions set off. When they passed in front of General Jackson, who had halted on the far side of Decatur Street to observe the troops' movements, he offered several salutes as the Black soldiers marched by, perhaps to encourage them or to fortify their sense of belonging. The Choctaw Indians moved out behind the Free Men of Color, walking quickly as if preferring to run, followed lastly by the Baratarians. Lafitte's corsairs hauled their few cannons and held their muskets casually over their shoulders, looking more like a mob than a proper military formation. But their easy demeanor and fierce smiles indicated their eagerness to fight.

For several miles the army marched south along the river road in silence, the only sounds the tramping of boots, clanking of kit, and occasional whickering of a horse. The evening air was crisp, and the nearly full moon bathed the plantation fields along the river in a silvery light that occasionally darkened under the rolling clouds. The wide waters of the Mississippi shimmered, though the river was mostly hidden from view behind the tall mound of the levee to the soldiers' right.

Moreau had fought in both day and night engagements, and he followed General Villeré closely as they marched, ready to lend any advice as needed. He did not expect to assume a frontline role—doubtful they would allow him to even if he'd wished—but he could not deny feeling the unmistakable tension that always set in before an engagement. Perhaps thirty minutes into their march, a courier galloped past, shouting for the formation to move to the side of the road. Not a moment after they had complied, a loud rumbling was heard and a troop of mounted dragoons thundered past in a flurry of hooves and shiny helmets. Some of the soldiers raised fists or shouted encouragement, but most simply looked on with nervous stares. As abruptly as they had appeared, the dragoons passed out of sight behind a copse of palm trees lining the road. Moreau asked a nearby sergeant where they had come from, as he did not recognize their uniforms. The sergeant said they were from the Mississippi Territory and had arrived in the city only two days earlier. As a former dragoon himself, Moreau felt better knowing that at least some horsemen were being sent ahead to seek out enemy pickets and screen for advancing patrols or, God forbid, enemy horsemen. A cavalry attack against unsuspecting infantry at night could bring chaos he was not sure the men around him were prepared for.

They marched for perhaps another quarter of an hour before the line was ordered to halt, and the men moved to crouch or sit along the side of the road, the horses swishing their tails and dropping their heads to munch on grass. Moreau allowed his mount to drink from a small puddle a moment before urging it toward Major Plauché, who was in a small clearing on the inland side of the road. When Moreau asked what had caused the halt, Plauché nodded toward the shadows ahead, from where the sound of approaching hoofbeats could be heard. A few moments later half a dozen riders emerged.

As they drew closer, Moreau recognized the broad silhouette of General Villeré, with Colonel Ross riding beside him, both men trailed by a pair of subordinates. Leaning forward, Moreau caught the tail end of a conversation between Ross and Villeré, the older Creole speaking in a tight voice. "The governor will just have to be content guarding the Gentilly Road and Chef Menteur. We have enough to worry ourselves about."

"He may miss the fighting," Ross replied, "but I avow we will not."

The small party halted when they reached Plauché and Moreau, and immediately the cause of the colonel's bravado became evident: the man's slight swaying all but confirmed that he was drunk, or at least not entirely sober. Coming straight to business, General Villeré minced no words. "Jackson has just come from a personal reconnaissance of the enemy lines. He says they are huddled snugly by their campfires." He looked around and sighed. "On the grounds of my plantation. But we will remove them soon enough."

"And their pickets?" Plauché asked.

"They've not been seen this side of Lacoste Plantation," Ross answered, his words slightly slurred. "It seems they bastards are hunkered down for the evening." A brief silence followed, and Villeré cleared his throat. "We intend to disturb their rest."

Glancing around the small group, Moreau saw determined faces, calm for the most part, though gloved hands flexing or making unnecessary adjustments to uniforms showed that even those among the higher ranks were not immune to the tension. Tapping the neck of his nervous horse, Ross spelled out the plan of action. "Coffee and his Tennesseans are to proceed north along the ditch that divides de La Ronde Plantation from Lacoste until they reach the swamp. They will then dismount and drive forward until they reach the enemy's forward positions, engage them as best they can, then wheel right by battalion and fall upon their center."

"If they don't blunder into the swamps first," one of Ross's subordinates muttered.

"Jackson is sending Pierre Lafitte with him as guide and interpreter." Villeré added. "I doubt a Baratarian captain will be turned around by a few lemon trees."

"Pierre?" Moreau blurted. "There's *two* of them?"

Villeré and Plauché both looked at him with tired stares, so Moreau simply shrugged. As Villeré continued briefing the plan, Moreau looked behind the American commander and noticed the man who had spoken a moment ago. Silas Winfield sat on his horse a few paces away, seemingly lost in thought. Was it boredom, Moreau wondered, or was the man nervous?

"As for us," General Villeré drawled, "we are to align on the left of the Seventh and Forty-fourth, advancing parallel with them. I will lead the right; Plauché, you have the center with Savary and the Second Colored. Pierre Jugeat and his Choctaws will form the left." The general looked at Plauché with a somber expression, speaking in his typically understated fashion. "Old Hickory says advance as far as you can, until the enemy or terrains stops you, but don't let your advance companies lose sight of the Seventh and Forty-fourth on your right." Plauché nodded, then looked at Moreau, perhaps to fortify himself. "Messieurs," General Villeré said in a voice throaty from fatigue, "we're to be thrown into the thick of it. Let us do our general, our families, and our country proud."

CHAPTER 24

De La Ronde Plantation, Louisiana
December 23, 1814

The Louisiana battalions waited for the Tennesseans and Kentuckians to move out first, which they did in a muted racket of stomping feet and cantering hooves, an occasional flash of light from a bayonet or flintlock breaking the darkness. Watching them as they went, Moreau felt slightly fortified by their presence, once again reminded of the devastation the Vendée rebels had wreaked upon his comrades in France. Crudely equipped farmers and hunters defending their homes were often more than a match for well-equipped, uniformed professionals—if they were well-led. Time would tell if that was the case here.

Plauché's men were next, continuing along the levee road until they reached de La Ronde Plantation, where a rider posted in the road signaled with his arms for them to turn. The Creoles complied, and for several minutes they hugged a split-rail fence that paralleled the irrigation ditch between the plantations. Running perpendicular from the river all the way back to the cypress swamps, the ditch was little more than a shallow dirt track containing a few inches of half-frozen water. They marched over flattened cane stubble, passing new, smaller ditches that demarcated individual fields. To their right the dark silhouettes of houses and outbuildings could be vaguely seen. Passing by a large barn, Moreau noticed perhaps a dozen barrels and stacks of what looked like mattresses, covered with a thin layer of dirt. As they continued their march, he saw signs of a recently harvested crop, likely sugarcane or sorghum, and all the trappings of an active plantation. Elsewhere, the grounds were flush with vegetation, small gardens of indigo, and symmetrical rows of lemon trees or orange groves. He wondered how, or if, their maneuvering would hold together with so many obstacles strewn across their path.

The troops halted beside a narrow drainage ditch as Major Plauché took a moment to confer with his company commanders. The men were quickly formed into ranks three deep and then turned south, the direction of the enemy campfires. The USS *Carolina* was to begin its cannonade of the enemy camp on Villeré's plantation any minute now, then the battalions were to advance until they made contact. Moreau rode over to join Colonel Ross, who was staring out at the grounds opposite the ditch, but there was little to be seen. Trees, shrubs, and fences threw long shadows, but nothing stirred.

In that moment, an image suddenly leapt into Moreau's mind: the young woman Antonia. Since that evening in the swamp, when he had learned she did not share his feelings, he'd felt something... foul rising within him. But now, he was overcome by a strange feeling of release. If the fool woman did not share what he'd felt, she could hang. He would go forward tonight and take as many of these English bastards to their deaths with him, and she could mourn over his bloodied corpse. The last thought came and went quickly, startling him. Shaking his head, Moreau let out a morbid chuckle, which for several seconds did not ease but grew louder—growing into a wild laughter. *I must have gone mad somewhere*, he thought to himself.

Hearing footsteps behind him, he turned to see a group of men double-timing past, behind the formation. A few seconds later another group hurried by, then another. He saw they were all Black men and concluded this must be D'Aquin's 2nd Battalion moving to take its position on the left. A rider cantered alongside each group, and as the third approached, Moreau saw him dismount and lead the animal through a gap in the units. As the man came closer, Moreau snorted when he recognized the familiar face. A moment later Plauché walked back to see who the stranger was.

Captain Joseph Savary's horse was slick with a filmy layer of sweat, and it let out a loud whinny, causing Plauché to tense visibly. Raising a gloved hand, Savary saluted, his eyes bright in the gloom. "Good evening, Majors."

Moreau nodded.

"Well, Marcel," Savary said eagerly, "what do you say? Another for old time's sake?" Moreau nodded thoughtfully. "Any sign of Dubuclet's mounted troops?" Savary reached up and removed his hat, slowly massaging his scalp. "They were at Fort St. John I heard. May be too far to get here in time."

Moreau shook his head. "They'll miss the dance."

Savary eyed him a moment, then let out a sharp laugh. "Maybe. But we won't." Moreau couldn't be sure, but he thought the captain gave Plauché a sharp look before turning back to look at his troops. "My lads have finally been given proper muskets at least. By some miracle, they've even been paid."

Moreau and Plauché watched the Negro soldiers hurrying past, the last of whom passed Savary at a trot before vanishing into the dark.

"Well," Savary said, the leather of his saddle creaking as he remounted, "I best be on my way."

Major Plauché nodded, his features revealing little. "Good luck, Captain."

Savary stared at him, his grin drooping slightly. "We need no luck, sir." He looked at Moreau and tugged the reins, wheeling his horse about. "*Vive l'empereur.*"

"*Vive la Republique!*" Moreau called as Savary rode off.

For the next few minutes, they waited in silence. Moreau took the opportunity to double-check his own equipment before recommending those in the ranks do any last-minute checks of weapons, ammunition, and water. When that was done, they waited again, impatience beginning to show on some of the men's faces.

Just then, the large, bulbous clouds ahead were lit up by a bright orange flash—followed several seconds later by the distinctive booming of cannon fire. A tense silence ensued, and every man in the line seemed to hold his breath. Once again, the skies flashed, followed by a rolling thunder that shook the nearby leaves and ferns. Moreau looked ahead for any sign of movement, but he saw only the rolling clouds, illuminated periodically by flashes of what appeared to be auburn lightning. The guns from the *Carolina* had begun their salvo, their ominous rumble arriving several seconds after the clouds had lit and dimmed again.

Plauché mounted his horse and called out in a firm voice. "It's time."

The order was repeated in tense whispers down the line, and the men fidgeted as they gripped their weapons or adjusted equipment. Their faces were no longer fearful, but eager.

Moreau mounted his own horse, "Alright, lads, let's go get shot."

Frowning at him, Plauché cried out in a confident voice, "Companies will advance!" He rode forward past Moreau, and soon the entire line stepped down into the ditch and climbed up onto the slightly softer ground of Lacoste Plantation.

The lone oak tree loomed like a lookout tower in the open meadow, and beneath its several sprawling branches Moreau and Captain Roche stood looking out at a grove of trees about a hundred paces ahead. Between it and them was a small stand of cleyera shrubs and two small sheds; the rest of the way was clear. Waiting fifty paces behind them were the advance troops of Plauché's battalion, who had taken up a position behind a rail fence. Glancing back to ensure the men were still crouched in silence as instructed, Moreau heard two cannon shots from the small American battery beside the levee road, followed by the sharp crackle of musket fire from somewhere ahead to the right. The firing continued for perhaps a minute or so, which meant the 44th and 7th Infantry Regiments had found the enemy, or at least their advance pickets.

"Well?" Captain Roche asked. "Should we advance?"

"No."

"Why not?"

"There are enemy in those trees."

Roche spat onto the slick grass. "Major, there are enemy everywhere."

Moreau squinted, cursing the fog that had settled around them. "Skirmishers," he said finally. "There are enemy skirmishers in those trees. Waiting for us." He almost smiled, thinking it a position he would have taken, with its ample cover and excellent fields of fire.

"Well, do we just sit here gaping at them?"

Moreau studied the ground between them and the grove, wondering if he ought to move up and take a closer look from behind one of the sheds. He knew he could reach them unseen, but the time it would take to get there and back might mean a missed opportunity if the enemy moved—or if any of the waiting men made a noise and gave away their position. He knew an imperfect decision now was better than a perfect decision later. "I've not fought English skirmishers," he said, shifting his weight, "but I know they carry rifles. The darkness will mitigate their range, but even so, if they spot us advancing in line across this open ground, they'll cut us to shreds before we get close."

Roche considered the situation. "So what do we do?"

Moreau looked back to where the militiamen were waiting. "Have Dubuclet's dragoons arrived yet?"

"No sign. They may have joined the Tennesseans farther up."

Moreau frowned. "Skirmishers don't like heavy infantry, but they hate horses. If we had…" He trailed off, taking a moment to think. The firing to their right had grown in intensity, though it sounded slightly more distant, meaning the battalions of American regulars were progressing. "Go bring up St. Gême's platoon, the sharpshooters. Tell Plauché not to advance yet. Go."

A minute or two later twenty men carrying long-barreled rifles trotted up to join him beneath the oak, their heavy breathing and the clanking of equipment the only sounds breaking the silence. The deep, booming blasts from the *Carolina* had ceased, but musket fire still rolled off to their right. Moreau pointed to the grove where he believed the skirmishers were waiting in ambush and explained to Lieutenant St. Gême what he intended. He motioned toward the sheds and cleyera, instructing him how to disperse his sharpshooters and when to begin firing. He sent the lieutenant on his way and told Roche to go and ready the main body of troops for action.

As the sharpshooters crept forward to take up their positions, Moreau noticed that the fog was thickening. He wondered if that would be a help or hindrance, but it was too late to worry about it now. A moment later Captain White crouched down beside him. "I've been requested, Major?" Moreau grabbed his shoulder and directed his gaze to the grove. In a hoarse whisper, he gave the Irishman his orders. For a moment, White stared at him, finally puffing out his cheeks and grinning. "Between you and me, Major," he said, "I'd like to survive this evening. I have children, and I'm a happily married man—so my wife tells me."

Moreau tapped his shoulder and nodded for him to get moving. With a shake of his head and a strained chuckle, White rose to his feet and began making his way toward the grove. As he watched the captain, Moreau ran a hand across his belt, relieved at the feeling of the pistol and saber pommel at his left hip. It was finally time. He saw White slowing as he drifted deeper into the fog ahead. Moreau could still make out the man's silhouette, but he grew fainter with each step he took.

"Who comes there?" A voice called from the darkness. Captain White froze for an instant, and Moreau nearly cursed, but the captain collected himself and took a few cautious steps forward. "Oi, lads, are you friends? I get turned around by the rebel fire."

After a brief pause, the voice called out again. "Halt!"

White halted abruptly, raising an arm. "Don't fire, you fools! I seen the rebels moving off this way."

There was a moment of silence, then a figure emerged from the fog, holding aloft what appeared to be a long-barreled weapon, but in the darkness little else could be seen. "Are you from the Eighty-fifth?"

Captain White hesitated just an instant. "What do you think, ya bloody lout? Of course I am!"

Moreau tensed a moment, and to his relief an abrupt ripple of rifle fire tore through the night. Flashes burst from where St. Geme's sharpshooters were positioned, and shortly after plumes of smoke wafted out on the breeze, obscuring Moreau's vision even more. He squinted, hoping to see White, who had dropped to the ground.

Bang! Bang! Several more muskets fired, their muzzle flashes lighting up the darkness. More shouts came from the grove. Moreau glanced behind, relieved to see the line of militiamen advancing at a brisk pace toward him.

The muskets barked furiously now, and he knew the fight was on. He heard the distinct crackle of rifle fire from the enemy's position, and hoped at least some of them had been hit, or at least startled enough to fire inaccurately. A sharp *whizz* past his ear disabused Moreau of that notion, and he quickly crouched back down with a chuckle. They were definitely returning fire now.

The militia arrived a moment later, a sergeant shouting for them to adjust their spacing. Moreau waved them on, mouthing encouragement and pointing with his saber toward the grove. Calm, steady encouragement did more to keep men's minds functioning in the face of fear than hollers or screams. That would come soon enough. "Forward, lads. Don't shoot your skirmishers. They're ahead of you." He tried to see if the skirmishers had begun falling back as instructed, but he could make out little in the rolling fog. "Don't shoot your skirmishers! They'll fall in with you."

Now that the main body of troops was in the fight, Moreau ran back to retrieve his horse, sheathing his sword so he could grip the pommel to mount the animal. He then charged forward through a gap that had been opened in the fence. As he galloped forward toward the sound of battle, he felt a boiling in his blood that bordered on ecstasy, which he tried in vain to quell, knowing the night had only just begun. When he caught up to the formation, he halted to have a look as more muzzle flashes lit up the night. Several came from the grove, and he was again relieved that it wasn't the ruinous pelting of rifle fire that could slaughter a battalion in minutes. He had seen that before.

The recommendation he had given to Plauché was for the skirmishers to harass the enemy, keeping them suppressed, or at least occupied, until the main body came forward and rushed into the grove at a dead run, screaming like devils. Perhaps the men were not ready to run, and the shouts came sporadically, but so far their nerve was holding as they advanced. Moreau struggled with his mount as it reared back, clearly unprepared for such an outburst of frightening noises and smells.

The militia continued their steady march forward, disappearing into the dense wall of smoke and fog. The firing continued a few moments before it cut off precipitously, and Moreau let out a nervous breath. Checking behind him to make sure the reserve companies had moved up to the fence, he spurred his horse forward. Reaching the edge of the grove, he saw the three ragged lines moving slowly through the trees. Captain Roche, saber held aloft, barked out orders for the rear two lines to halt, while the men in front disappeared into the fog. Moreau dismounted and found Major Plauché standing nearby.

"Three wounded," a sergeant called out, shoving a soldier aside to make his way to the major. "One missing. We've sent two back to see if he's down, wounded. Everyone else accounted for."

When Plauché saw Moreau he nodded, then turned ahead and motioned with an arm. "Major, with me."

Moreau followed as they stepped through the symmetrical rows of lemon trees. Scanning the ground for discarded weapons, kit, or blood trails, Moreau gave up when he realized he could barely see his own feet and had nearly walked into a tree. They walked in silence, finally reaching the far side, where both dropped down to a crouch. Ahead was the main field of Lacoste Plantation, a vast plot broken occasionally by trees and palmettos, ending in a cluster of tall cypress trees perhaps three hundred paces distant. More musket fire sounded off to the right, flashes illuminating the darkness, but it was too far away to concern them at the moment. The fog drifted with a strong gust of wind, partially clearing the view for a moment, and Moreau saw several rows of cottages, likely slave cabins, perhaps two hundred paces away. He squinted as he searched for signs of the enemy skirmishers they had driven off.

"They're likely regrouping among those cabins," Plauché said. "Bastards got away quick enough." His voice was calm, but his eyes were wide and his features taut.

Moreau smirked. "They know their business. Even so, I don't think they expected that."

"No." Plauché stared gravely ahead. "But they'll be back."

A moment later the rest of the men joined them, taking up positions at the edge of the tree line. Captain White walked up beside Moreau, his scowl showing what he thought of Moreau's little game of trickery. "If we survive this night, you owe me a goddamned week's worth of drink." Moreau nodded, tapping the Irishman on the back.

The men reached for ramrods and cartridges as they reloaded, some looking overjoyed to have fired their first shots in anger. Captain Jean-Claude Hudry, looking eager to get into the fight, had rushed his men forward to the right, closer to the cabins. "If the riflemen return—*when* they return," Moreau said, nodding at the cabins, "they'll likely use these as cover."

Just then a hand grasped his shoulder, and Hudry tugged him down to his knees. "What are you—" Moreau went silent as he saw what had startled the captain. About a hundred paces off to their right, two figures were approaching at a slow trot. They looked to be unarmed, and had not come from the far side of the plantation, where the enemy surely was, nor were they from Plauché's battalion. Moreau motioned to one of St. Geme's sharpshooters, who trained his weapon on the approaching men but held his fire. As the pair drew within earshot, Hudry stepped out from the grove and aimed his pistol at them. "Who are you? Rank and unit or you will be shot." The two froze, lifting their hands, and a few tense seconds passed until one finally spoke.

"Captain Mitchell, First Company, Seventh Infantry."

"Corporal Reece, Third Company, Seventh Infantry."

Hudry lowered his pistol and waved them over into the relative safety of the grove. The captain, wearing the dark-blue coat of the regular infantry, took several long sips from a canteen offered him. "We had driven their pickets off," he said finally, looking at Moreau, "and were crossing a field when we seen a group come up on our left. My major called for them to join our advance—then they fired upon us." He sighed, lowering the canteen. "We fired back, but before we could reload, we were surrounded."

"How did you escape?" Hudry asked.

The younger officer cleared his throat. "We were being taken back, when our own boys must have come forward; they fired on our captors. I struck the enemy officer, knocking him down, and we both ran as fast as we could. We thought you were the enemy." His body shook.

Moreau turned to the captain. "What did you see of the enemy?"

The man spoke in a nervous voice. "I saw no horse or artillery, lots of skirmishers. Then their grenadiers came out of the mist."

"They was like…giants," the corporal chimed.

Moreau tilted his head. "Do you hear that?"

"Hear what?" Hudry took a step forward, looking out over the field. Slowly the sound Moreau had referred to became audible to the others.

Rat-tat-tat-tat-tat, rat-tat-tat-tat-tat, rat-tat-tat-tat-tat…

The drums seemed to draw closer with each passing second, and soon the shrill cry of bagpipes pierced the night air. The two men from the 7th exchanged nervous looks as Moreau turned to Hudry. "Ready your men."

The drums rolled louder as the first main English battle lines emerged into the fields from the far side of the plantation. Moreau saw little more than shifting shapes at first, but as each line advanced it became clear that a large body of troops was pouring onto the open ground—with no pretense of stealth. Their martial music announced their intent, and their steady, rhythmic stepping displayed their well-drilled confidence. As the drums pelted the cadence, Moreau turned to the two soldiers of the 7th and spoke quickly. "You men fall back to the split-rail fence behind this position; from there you can make your way back to your regiment." Needing no further encouragement, the pair dashed back through the trees. Moreau saw Major Plauché approaching from that direction. He removed his hat and positioned himself at the front of the grove. "Here they come."

To the shrill wailing of bagpipes, the redcoats continued across the field, fanning out into a long, continuous line, broken only by gaps between battalions. Moreau sneered when he saw men in dark coats moving swiftly between the small gaps or along the flanks of the larger body. Those troops would cause severe damage if allowed to fire on Plauché's line. He said as much to the major, who ordered St. Geme's sharpshooters to open fire. Moreau felt a sinking feeling as he saw the scale of the enemy's movement. This was not an advance scouting party; this was an assault force. They moved crisply by company, like small cogs in a great machine, their limbs rising and falling in unison as they moved forward like the legs of some large insect. *Rat-tat-tat-tat-tat, rat-tat-tat-tat-tat.*

Moreau glanced at Plauché, relieved to see only steely determination.

"Prepare to fire," Plauché said to his sergeant major, and then stepped back to give his place on the line to a militiaman with a musket. Moreau did the same, moving behind the third line and mounting his horse to get a better view. The drums beat a cold, steady tattoo that sounded both blandly familiar and bloodcurdlingly stirring. For a moment he wished to return to his days as an enlisted man, a frontline combatant unhindered by concerns of tactics or responsibility. An enlisted man fought by pure instinct; an officer had to keep that same instinct in check and focus on the larger picture. As he peered down at the men in ranks, Moreau felt emotions stirring in his chest: fondness at the sight of the militiamen and yet a deep fear at the thought of his responsibility for them. He pulled the pistol from his belt—just to be ready—and noticed his heart was beating quickly. For once, he did not mind.

Rat-tat-tat-tat-tat, rat-tat-tat-tat-tat. The enemy was now less than two hundred paces away, the individual shouts of their officers becoming distinguishable. As Plauché nodded to Captain Roche, a sudden clamor arose from across the field. A deafening roar issued from the enemy, as the soldiers let out a collective primal scream. *Aaaahhhhh!* It held for several seconds, enough to fire even Moreau's blood.

"Ready!...Present!...Fire!" A volley of musket fire tore out from the militia, and Moreau's nostrils flared as his horse danced sideways and he tightened the reins to steady the animal. "Reload! Quickly now!"

Moreau watched with as much patience as he could muster, hoping the endless hours of drill had not been for nothing. Roche raised his sword. "Present!...Fire!" A thick plume of smoke followed the second volley, and Moreau waved a hand in front of his face. He could hardly see anything now. *Rat-tat-tat-tat-tat, rat-tat-tat-tat-tat.* He knew that the simple act of firing their first shots at the enemy would give them more confidence than weeks of training ever could. They were finally in it now, and fear would simply have to be discarded as the work of killing began. Tapping his heels, he guided his horse over beside Major Plauché, who was staring ahead through a spyglass. Moreau was not sure what he would be able to see in the smoke and rising fog, but he waited patiently in case the major had need of him.

Just as Moreau moved his lips to curse the infernal drumming, his horse shrieked horribly and reared. Moreau reached in vain for the pommel but felt himself sliding out of the saddle before he could grasp anything but air. He rolled off the animal's hindquarters and hit the ground with a bruising *thump*, tumbling head over heels as his hat flew off his head. For a few seconds he didn't move, relieved that the horse had not crushed him—and that he had not broken his neck. Rolling slowly onto his side, he sucked in a deep breath, feeling a burning sensation fill his chest. "Damn," he muttered, looking up at the thin trunks of the lemon trees and the fog that had lifted enough to reveal slow-moving clouds playing tag with the moon. He considered lying there for a moment when the sound of running feet nearby broke his reverie. More pounding feet, then shouting erupted all around him. "They're coming! First Company, fall back!"

Moreau lurched to his feet, no longer hearing the booming drums, only the frantic shouts and the sound of boots running past him. Steadying himself, he saw several men falling back, one halting and turning to fire his musket. Realizing he'd been in something of a daze since hitting the ground, Moreau was jolted back to full consciousness by a terrifying sight not fifty paces ahead of him: a tall redcoat soldier, made taller by a large black bearskin shako, raising a musket with a glinting bayonet as he reached the edge of the grove. He halted abruptly as a militiamen ran forward, brandishing his own musket like a club. The Creole swung furiously, but the enemy giant stepped back, lifted his musket and thrust its long iron blade into the man's belly. Screaming fiercely, he drove his legs forward, forcing the Creole backward and then pinning the poor man to the ground with a painful shriek.

Moreau watched the scene unfold, wishing he could help somehow, but as more of the redcoat grenadier's comrades swarmed into the grove, he simply turned and ran as fast as he could. He passed through the trees, one of the last to make it out, and sprinted all the way back to the split-rail fence, where a line of Creoles waved him and the other stragglers back. He hopped the fence nimbly and halted a moment to catch his breath.

"Jesus," Captain White said, looking at him with a concerned expression. "You alright Major?"

Nodding, Moreau rose back to his full height. "I lost my pistol."

White stared at him a moment before his attention jerked back ahead. Shouts from the militiamen alerted Moreau to the approaching enemy, and after a short lull, another loud voice came from the grove. "Present!...*Fire!*"

Captain White disappeared from view behind a wall of smoke, but his voice called steadily for the men to reload. They managed a second volley, a ragged one as the soldiers fired at will, before panicked cries broke out. "Here they come!"

Damning his horse for unsaddling him in the middle of a fight, Moreau unsheathed his sword, eager to redeem himself for such a clumsy equestrian display.

Another deafening roar, and a few of the Creoles turned and ran, cursed as cowards by those who remained. Captain White and most of the men closest to him held their positions. The line of redcoats, less precise and less dense than before, poured forward, their bayoneted muskets pointed menacingly at the line of Creoles. The militiamen thrust their own bayonets out, or swung their muskets like clubs as they shouted curses at the attackers. As Moreau watched the melee unfold, a short, stocky English soldier elbowed his way through the mass toward him. Moreau lifted his saber and slashed down with a vicious cut. The man ducked his head, but Moreau felt his blade strike something, hat or skull; either way, the man dropped to the ground. Not waiting to see if the man had survived, Moreau turned quickly as another enemy waded through the melee with the butt of his musket raised, his eyes wild as he swung. Moreau ducked under the weapon and thrust his sword tip into the man's torso, and he dropped back with a grunt.

The vicious hand-to-hand fighting went on for several seconds until an abrupt shift in the weight of numbers began to work against the Louisianans, and Captain White ordered them to fall back and regroup. Without sheathing his weapon, Moreau reached down and helped a wounded militiaman to his feet before joining the retreat. For several minutes he fell back with the rest, calling for sergeants and officers to rally their men once they were out of immediate danger. Reaching a row of cypress trees, he halted to catch his breath. Men ran past him, reloading and shouting as they went, some giving orders, others calling out for their company.

Standing alone under a large cypress, Moreau realized how dark the night had become. Looking back toward the enemy, he saw only open ground half-concealed by fog and smoke. It appeared the battalion had broken, and amidst the commotion and men fleeing all around him, he realized had no idea where he was.

For untold minutes he wandered through low shrubs, listing willows, and a ghostly mist that limited visibility and shrouded the moon in a hazy glow. Crackles of musket fire seemed to echo on all sides, and for the moment the fighting seemed distant—but he knew that could change. Every so often, a far-off glow would brighten the sky before it was swallowed by the darkness. As he cleared another split-rail fence, he saw what looked like a large earthen mound looming before him and extending to the left as far as he could see. This must be the "old levee" that had been built to hold the river back from fields and homes; now it was basically an elongated hill—and a useful obstacle for defense. Carefully climbing to its top, he saw only fields and a few outbuildings on the other side. Sliding down, he followed the levee for a while as he searched for Plauché's men. Passing two large oaks, he noticed a small shed a few paces to his right. Thinking it a good place for cover or to lay an ambush, he stepped quietly through a patch of ferns, his sword raised. Halting before the shed, he puffed out several misty breaths before reaching for the door handle. A muffled voice within made him freeze, and he held his sword at the ready. "Who's in there?"

Silence. Moreau peered around the far side to make sure no one had snuck up on him. "I said," he demanded in a louder voice, "who's in there?"

"We're prisoners," a faint voice replied.

Moreau frowned, gripping his saber tightly. "Prisoners of whom?" He grasped the handle and gently pulled the door open a few inches, its hinges creaking loudly.

The voice spoke again. "Are you American?"

"Maybe." Moreau then spoke in French. "Who the fuck are you?" The door opened slowly, and Moreau stepped back and pointed the tip of his sword ahead as a man in a dark-blue coat emerged from the pitch-black interior. No longer thinking of an ambush, Moreau exhaled and lowered his saber. The soldier stepped out into the pale moonlight, his face half covered in soot. There were others behind him, and Moreau called for them all to come out. Another infantryman emerged, followed by a Negro soldier in a brown coat and straw hat, and two men clothed in the brown homespun of Tennesseans. Moreau shook his head. "I hope you enjoyed a comfortable rest in there." With embarrassed looks, the last of the "prisoners" came out: two Creoles in blue-and-black-checkered coats. There were seven men in total, and Moreau sighed as he stared at the Tennesseans. "'ow did you end up all the way down here?"

The taller Tennessean, a sergeant, spat through a gap in his teeth. "We got a few shots off at their patrols, but as we moved forward, our lines scattered. Lost our commanding officer."

The other rubbed his hands on his trousers. "Our own boys started firing on us. Became a game of pull dick, pull devil. Thought we seen a friendly group, but they raised their weapons and told us to drop ours or be killed."

"They took our arms and brought us here," the other said. "That was perhaps five, ten minutes past." One of the Creoles nodded as he scratched his head. Moreau fought back the urge to laugh mockingly.

"Well, you're not prisoners anymore, so stop sulking like whipped dogs." He looked at each of them. "We must move, before your gaolers return." Motioning for them to follow, he turned and headed back to the levee.

Moreau did his best to lead them toward where he thought they'd find their own units, hoping to avoid the enemy until they could arm themselves. Before long they had found a handful of discarded weapons: one musket, a pistol, and a long pike. They weren't much, but they were better than nothing. The Tennessee sergeant took the pistol and gave his comrade the musket, while one of the Creoles grabbed the pike.

They soon came upon a cluster of small cabins surrounded by rakes, wheelbarrows, and sacks full of produce, as if the workers had fled quickly. Moreau clambered to the top of the levee with the sergeant, tugging him down when the fool tried to stand.

"We wait," Moreau growled. "I think we're near our lines, but everything is so fouled up, we're just as likely to meet the enemy."

Nodding, the sergeant raised his pistol. For perhaps a minute they waited, no one making a sound, as far-off gunfire echoed from all directions…but the immediate vicinity remained silent.

Just as he moved to slide back down, Moreau froze, raising a finger to his lips. The sergeant shifted his weight, and both turned their heads left, where the sound of voices broke the silence. Moreau waved for the others to join them atop the levee, which they quickly and quietly did. When he peered over the edge, Moreau saw a figure following along the levee as they had done. A moment later another merged, then another, until eleven men could be counted moving in their direction. Moreau whispered several quick orders to the sergeant and told him to pass them down the line to the men lying prone but ready to spring up at any moment.

Moreau watched as the men approached, their voices still unintelligible. Their dark coats could have belonged to American infantrymen or British skirmishers. He waited until the first man was directly below him and then rose to his knees, his saber ready. The sergeant aimed his pistol down at the men.

"If you move," Moreau said evenly, "we will kill you."

The men below halted mid-step, and for a moment no one spoke. The long barrels of the weapons in their hands meant they carried rifles, and as they were certainly not Kentuckians, Moreau concluded they were English. "Lay down your arms," he intoned, "and you will be spared."

A voice shouted from the enemy group, "Bollocks! You lay down yours!"

One of the enemy soldiers looked to a comrade and quickly raised his rifle, but the American sergeant was faster and fired his pistol at him. The man fell in a heap. Dead. "Now!" Moreau snarled, and with a loud roar, the other Americans scrambled down the levee without hesitation, shouting wildly. The enemy riflemen ducked or ran for cover, one raising his weapon and firing, the bullet thudding harmlessly into the side of the levee. Moreau slid down the slope, and as the man raised his weapon in defense, Moreau slashed the man across his shoulders and chest, and the fellow dropped to the ground with a cry. Another fired at the Tennessean with the musket, hitting the man in the leg. The Tennessee sergeant shot the enemy rifleman, while the Creole wielding the pike finished off the man Moreau had wounded. Within a matter of seconds, the skirmish was over, the surviving enemy riflemen running pell mell into the fog. The patchwork party of Americans stood at the bottom of the levee panting and looking around with wide eyes. Moreau picked up a discarded rifle and handed it to the sergeant, who gave his pistol to one of the Creoles. Moreau wiped his bloody blade on a dead soldier's coat as he waited for the mens' combat rage to subside. Fierce fighting could be heard up ahead, and a part of him yearned to join it. "Come on," he said, indicating the wounded Tennessean, "we'll get him back to our lines."

The sergeant did not move. "This one can take him back." He nodded at the fellow tending his comrade. "The rest of us can join the fighting. This way." He motioned in the opposite direction.

Moreau licked his lips, giving him a hard look. "You've done enough for one night."

Mutters of protest broke out, spurred on by the sergeant. Moreau stepped forward, glaring at the Creoles. "Not ten minutes ago," he growled in French, hoping the Tennesseans would understand his tone, "you were cowering in an unguarded woodshed. But since *I* found you, you've killed two of the enemy and chased off all the others. Wandering blindly into another enemy patrol and getting the rest of you killed will undo that." He waited a moment for the Creole to translate for the others, but they still looked unconvinced. For a brief moment, a part of Moreau felt a strange pride, like a father seeing his son do something brave. He looked out into the darkness with a sigh. "Alright. If you wish to wander off to play heroes, I won't stop you. But your army has given the enemy a knock in the teeth tonight, and now they'll wish to return the favor. Our advantage of surprise is gone, and they've collected themselves and are now reinforced. You lot," he pointed his saber at them, "have shown your mettle tonight, and you can hold your heads high for that. But there will be more battles in the days ahead. If you wish to live to win the larger war, come with me."

He waited for his words to be translated. The soldiers exchanged looks for a moment, then shrugging or muttering their agreement, gathered their weapons and followed him along the old levee toward the American lines.

CHAPTER 25

Rodriguez Canal, Outside New Orleans
December 25, 1814

Moreau's boots squished as he climbed up the embankment, the soil still damp from an overnight rain, which had made sleep difficult to come by. The fortification, if it could be called that, had grown by several feet in the last twenty-four hours as soldiers, militiamen, and slaves took turns digging sediment from the Rodriguez Canal and piling it onto the earthen mound now known colloquially as *Line Jackson*. The parapet stood about the height of a man and was growing with each hour. Reinforced with vertically placed boards and planks from nearby fences and barns, it stretched in a long, straight line from the river levee all the way back to the cypress swamp 800 yards inland. Spades, shovels, and mattocks had been sent from the city, and since the morning following the night battle, the earth along the canal had been churned up unceasingly, the troops digging, guarding, and sleeping in shifts.

Gaining the top of the mound, Moreau peered down at the flooded canal below, which served as a small moat. Considering the oversized role water seemed to play throughout the state of Louisiana, he wondered if they should not simply flood their enemies instead of fight them in the open field. He admitted this appeared a suitable ground for defense: flat, open terrain crisscrossed by fences, ditches, and ducts throughout Chalmette Plantation. The city's Faubourg Marigny suburb lay a safe five miles to their rear, while their flanks were protected by the river and the swamp. The sound of footsteps ascending the earthwork pulled his attention, and he lowered the spyglass with a smirk. "Not out on patrol, Captain?"

Joseph Savary raised a small tin flask to his lips. "Patrol got called off. So it's a happy Christmas indeed."

Moreau pulled a cigar from his breast pocket. "This is my gift to myself."

"I'll toast to the fact the redcoats won't have their Christmas feast in New Orleans." Savary lit Moreau's cigar, his eyebrows rising inquisitively. "Have you learned who spread the rumors yet?"

Moreau rubbed the stubble on his chin, reminded that he needed a shave. "What rumors? That I'm a drunk? Or that Plauché and I spend our nights gambling with our enlisted men instead of tending to our duties?" His mouth twisted in a sly grimace. "Let's just say I have my suspicions." He sneered as he puffed the cigar hungrily.

Savary chuckled. "If he can't call to question your tactical abilities, he can slander you in other ways."

"Let him say what he likes. A coward can hide his weaknesses in training, but war exposes a man's character eventually. A few more engagements like the other night, and he'll be exposed." The cold nipped at his ears as the flaps of his coat rose gently with the breeze. For a moment his face grew dark, and he spoke in a quiet voice. "I just pray he doesn't dare challenge my honor. If I *do* have a compulsion, it's killing men like Winfield."

Savary eyed him with a disconcerted expression, rubbing his hands together for warmth. "I just hope he doesn't get too many of his lads killed. I heard some of them grumbling about Ross's performance that night as well. They may have a few poor leaders, but the men in ranks are brave enough."

Moreau gave a reluctant nod. "I never thought to like the Americans, but they don't seem to know when to back down from a fight. Tough to defeat an army like that."

A cry from somewhere down the barricade pulled their attention, and turning back, they saw what had caused the alarm.

Perhaps three or four hundred yards in the distance, several points of light flickered, and instantly both men knew what was coming.

"Rockets!" a nearby voice cried, and after exchanging a brief look, the two men slid down from the parapet. Not ten seconds later another voice bellowed, "Rocket incoming!" All around them soldiers and laborers dropped their equipment and dove to the ground, covering their heads. A second later a loud *whoosh* sounded overhead, and Moreau looked up to see a grey smoke trail billow across the sky. Several seconds later a dull *thud* shook the ground as the Congreve rocket smashed into the muddy field somewhere to the rear. After a brief pause, another *whoosh* sounded and a second rocket soared overhead, this one twisting with a vicious jerk and careening toward the swamp, where it too crashed with a *thud*. A third rocket followed, and a fourth, whining and whistling like sparklers as they sketched grey trails that lingered overhead. The final one crashed perhaps a hundred yards away, splashing mud and dirt on several slaves huddled behind a wheelbarrow, but otherwise causing little damage.

When the danger had passed, men slowly rose back to their feet, their faces more curious than fearful, and soon they were laughing off the barrage with jests and boasts as the cleanup began, soldiers and slaves righting upturned wheelbarrows or wiping off mud-spattered tools. As the work details resumed, Moreau took leave of Savary and made his way along the embankment, trying to dispel thoughts of Colonel Winfield. Moreau was sure he had been the source of the rumors, which had begun spreading shortly after Winfield and Colonel Ross had been publicly upbraided by Jackson for their conduct during the night battle, namely losing contact with Plauché's men and nearly opening a dangerous breach in the line. Moreau had not been present for the dressing-down, but apparently Winfield left in a huff and had hardly been seen since.

Nearing one of the new artillery embrasures cut into the parapet, Moreau slowed to inspect the massive thirty-two-pounder naval cannon that had been installed that morning. Its crew, a half-dozen colorfully dressed Baratarians, scurried excitedly around its massive barrel, occasionally arguing over some small point of their toil. Two men in red bandanas and dark smocks were slathering what looked like lard or grease on the large wheels supporting the giant gun. As he came closer, Moreau saw that the piece was still mounted on what looked to be a deck carriage, which meant that it had come from one of their ships.

"And you see these large wooden carriage wheels," a clear voice announced, "they take on much friction as they roll back and forth during a battle, and begin to smolder, threatening to burn up completely…"

A moment later a man in a dark coat, tight-fitting grey breeches, and a wide-brimmed hat stepped out from among the working crewmen. A saber in a long black scabbard hung at his hip. If Jean Lafitte had reminded Moreau of a sly housecat at the Condé Ballroom, he looked every bit the corsair warlord now. Twenty or thirty of his men stood proudly behind him, while several American artillery officers stood beside the gun, listening with rapt attention. "So," Lafitte continued, "one trick to keep them from catching flame and burning the cotton bales beneath the epaulements is to simply smear the wheels with grease. Or lard. Any nonflammable coating will do. *Et voilà*, no more smoldering."

Mutters came from some of the artillery officers, but none challenged his knowledge. Moreau smirked to see the two groups, formerly deadly enemies, exchanging artillery techniques beside a Baratarian cannon placed along the American army's defensive line.

Lafitte continued down the line, the small entourage at his heels, and nearly bumped into Moreau. At first not recognizing him, the corsair commander flashed a stern look of warning, but recognition soon dawned on his features, and he offered a warm smile. "The ever-present Monsieur Moreau." He ignored Moreau's outstretched hand and pulled him in for a hug. He then laid a gentle hand on his shoulder, drawing him along as he walked. "Accompany me a moment, will you?"

Moreau smiled as he gently removed the man's hand. "Of course."

Lafitte laughed, and they put a slight distance between themselves and his small entourage.

"It seems you gave the enemy quite a greeting," Lafitte said, striding slowly. "Perhaps Jackson isn't the pompous fool I initially took him for." He took a moment to examine the parapet, nodding appreciatively. "Quite a position, for only two days of work. A good commander knows how to use the terrain to his advantage."

Moreau nodded, gazing at the large mound in turn. "We'll see how effective it is when the English artillery arrives." He didn't notice Lafitte's sly grin.

"It's a fine start," the corsair stated, "only I would have brought in even more water. By cutting the levee, one could have flooded the entire field in front of it."

Lafitte grinned at him, and Moreau's brow furrowed. "I had a similar thought." He made a mental note to take the idea to Plauché. "Anyway, to what do we owe the privilege?"

Lafitte turned slowly, his own eyebrows lowering. "I've just delivered on a promise I made to Jackson when we first met. He now knows where to find seventy-five hundred spare gunflints for his army. He might have started by searching Le Temple, but we didn't want to make things too easy for him." His sly grin returned. "I've also shared my opinion on this defensive line; in truth, it is quite good. But I've recommended extending it further into the swamp, to protect the flank. The English are not fools, nor afraid to get their feet wet."

Moreau looked down the line to where it ended near the distant cypress trees. "A fair point."

Lafitte chuckled and then shrugged. "Spend enough time among Napoleon's men, and even a ragged stray like me can learn military strategy."

As he examined the embankment again, Moreau stepped closer, glancing aside to make sure no one was within earshot. "Jean, I have a question I must ask."

The corsair commander rubbed his hands together. "Let me guess—not a question of military strategy."

"A balas ruby." Moreau cut to the point. "My time is running out, and I must persuade, or compel, the de Beaumais girl to return to France with me. Her lady told me there are three rubies in total. I've managed to retrieve one, but without all three, I fear de Beaumais will only run at the first sight of me. She already has once."

Lafitte let out a breath, resting a hand on the saber at his hip. "I am not sure I can help you. But I'll tell you something, if you swear not to tell another living soul." His eyes lowered in something of a savage scowl, and Moreau nodded. Such was the man's subtlety: he could unnerve with a frown or set you at ease with a smile; often one couldn't be sure of the difference.

"The days of Barataria's glory are over. And while it *has* been an honor to finally make common cause with the Yankees, I and my men will never be accepted by them. Not fully. So, I will do what I can to help, but Pierre and I are not long for these shores. A veteran like you surely understands." Moreau stared at him unmoving. When he said nothing, Lafitte grinned, speaking in a low voice. "I have my sights set on Galveston, and mutual friends with the Spanish governor there tell me he has an especial affinity for rubies." He snuck a hand into his breast pocket and removed it, opening his palm to reveal a balas ruby the size of a chicken egg. He let Moreau examine the stone a moment before lifting his chin with a cheerful expression.

"I had concerns that avaricious bastard Araza would try and take this from me. I never trusted him, but his fixation with you—likely from jealousy, that he'd found a man he could not intimidate—convinced me not to include him in my plans. But," he stepped closer, taking Moreau's hand and setting the ruby in his palm, closing his fingers around it, "*I* learned that you were a man not to be ignored. Take this if it will help you bring the girl in."

Moreau looked up dubiously. "You're giving this—"

"I'm *lending* it to you. Use it well, and when you've retrieved her, return it to me. But if you try to run with it," he pulled him in for another embrace, "there is no island, forest, or desert to which you can run where I will not find you." He released Moreau, his cheerful expression returning. "Use it well, Moreau, and perhaps one day you will decide to join me when I sail for new horizons."

~~~

The following morning Moreau met Major Plauché under the massive flagpole that had been erected in the center of Line Jackson. Above them the Stars and Stripes listed in the gentle breeze, standing as a direct challenge to any English claims on the land which they currently occupied, but by no means dominated. A group of soldiers crouched low as they stalked out through one of the artillery embrasures, weapons held at the ready. "Picket skirmishes" had been fought across no-man's-land ever since the night battle, and the two officers stepped aside to make room for another patrol.

"Jackson says it keeps the boys active," Plauché said wearily. "And the enemy wary. Anyhow, about your plan, it certainly is… imaginative."

The previous evening, Moreau had told the major of the plan, which he'd formulated with no small help from Will Keane, who had eagerly offered his services. The boy was to be dressed in the uniform of a captured enemy drummer boy, and was to be rowed under cover of darkness to the far side of the enemy camp, accompanied by one of Savary's men, a former slave who would be dressed as one still enslaved. The two would approach the southernmost enemy pickets, where Savary's man would explain that he was returning the lost drummer to his camp. With the guards thus distracted—hopefully, at least—six more of Savary's men, who had rowed over with Will and the other Negro soldiers, would spring out from the darkness and take the pickets captive—to ensure they surrendered; if not, knives would silence them. They would be dressed as slaves as well, to confuse the English.

"Will and one of Savary's men," Moreau concluded, "will take the sentries at gunpoint to the boats, while the others will use spades to cut the levee south of the enemy camp, flooding the entire southern edge of their lines. At least, that's the plan." He concluded with a confident nod, hoping Plauché would be a fraction as willing to go along with the scheme as Savary had been.

After a painfully long silence, Plauché let out a breath and spoke in a rueful tone. "You are an aggressive bastard, Moreau." Moreau grinned, taking the remark as a compliment. "It is certainly inventive. Though the risks to Savary's men, to say nothing of the boy, are considerable."

"The boy is ready. I wouldn't send him if I didn't think he was."

Major Plauché sighed, informing Moreau he would pass the idea up to General Villeré. "If it works," Plauché mused, "you will be considered—" He cut himself off mid-sentence and hurried forward to the look through the opening in the embankment. Pulling out a spyglass, he raised it and stood silent for several moments. Moreau peered through the and saw clearly the puffs of smoke in the distance. A few seconds later he heard a faint crackle of musket fire. Plauché handed the glass to Moreau. "Look."

Moreau peered through the scope and saw the action with much greater clarity. Posted along a split-rail fence on the far side of Chalmette Plantation were four American soldiers firing at an enemy he could not yet see. Crossing a canal a little bit closer to the line was a soldier carrying a wounded comrade who, from what Moreau could see, could barely drag his legs. The two were moving as fast as they could, and it looked like the men at the fence were covering their retreat. Abruptly, two men at the fence fell almost simultaneously, causing the two beside them to flee. Moving the spyglass slightly higher, Moreau felt a sudden twist in his stomach. Emerging from the plantation's main house were perhaps a dozen redcoats, running frantically to catch the retreating Americans.

Lowering the glass to where the wounded man was being carried, Moreau watched the two struggle for several steps until they reached the edge of a drainage ditch about halfway across the field. Seeming unsure how to cross the depression, the rescuer stood to his full height, then suddenly spasmed and slumped to the ground. The wounded man flailed his arms before sliding into the ditch.

Shoving the spyglass into Plauché's hand, Moreau moved instinctively. Swinging himself over the cannon barrel, he leapt from the epaulement, landing in the canal with a splash. He hardly felt the cold water as it quickly sogged his boots, and he cleared the far side of the ditch in several quick strides. Running across the open ground, he heard the sound of gunfire, which only compelled him to move faster.

Before long, his lungs burned and his legs felt the added weight of water-logged boots, but he kept his pace. The two surviving soldiers ran past him, frowning confusedly but without stopping. He leapt over a split-rail fence, but having just his one hand, he lost his balance and nearly fell into a small but fairly deep irrigation ditch. He looked ahead for signs of the enemy and saw two or three flashes of red, but fortunately he was almost at the ditch where the soldiers had fallen, and a few moments later he was at its edge. Sliding on his haunches to the bottom, his boots plunged into a thick layer of mud with a squish. He looked left and his heart sank, as he saw one dead body, then two. But looking to his right, he saw his target. A young soldier in dark blue was huddled on the near side of the wide trench, and as Moreau came closer, the fellow looked up with a pale, miserable face.

Crouching beside the boy and explaining who he was, Moreau inspected the wound to his thigh, which had already bled quite a bit. The lad's fearful look worried Moreau, concerned that he might become frenzied and make the bleeding worse. Moreau reached beside him and picked up a clump of dirt and placed it on wound. "That'll keep you from bleeding more," he said, reaching for his canteen and handing it to the young man. After a long sip, the fellow nodded his earnest thanks.

"Alright, let's get you out of—" A nearby musket shot forced him to duck, and he could hear harsh, excited voices—not on top of them, but too close for them to escape the ditch unseen. "Shit," he growled, looking around but seeing only the two dead bodies a few paces away. Once again without thinking, he unsheathed his sword and, with a swift, saw-like motion, cut loose the sewed-up jacket sleeve covering the stump of his left arm. Voices barked again, this time only a few paces away. Moreau lay down on top of the boy and whispered, "Play dead, lad." He dropped his saber into the mud beside the empty sleeve.

Not ten seconds later footsteps sounded at the top of the ditch. Whispers. Two, maybe three soldiers, their steps growing closer, their boots squishing in the mud. More whispers, and then a darkening over Moreau's closed eyes indicated someone was standing over him. He tried to remain completely still as the prospect of being shot filled his mind.

"Oi," a voice muttered. "Look 'ere. Proper Barney."

"Fuckin' 'ell," a second voice added. "Mad bastards."

"Brave sods, the Eighty-fifth."

"I meant the dirty shirts. Fightin' 'and-to-'and like banshees."

"At least these lot kept their scalps."

"Does me 'ead in."

"Ha ha. Right, let's get on 'fore the Indians come back."

Moreau waited for the footsteps to fade away, then rolled off the wounded soldier with a tired sigh. The young man's eyes were wide and his breathing came in forced breaths—but he would live.

Maman,

My hand trembles as I write this, and I do not know how to begin. A horrid, horrid thing has happened, and I feel as if I'll be sick.

Last night as I woke from a doze in the ladies sitting room, I heard a commotion in the adjoining billiards room. The thumping of boots and half-frenzied voices announced the arrival of several of the master's men, and I made out the familiar voice of Elijah Benton, his chief overseer. Ignorant of my presence just opposite the half-opened door, they struck up a loud, even boastful conversation that I happened to overhear. I did not mean to eavesdrop, and was even preparing to leave when I heard the name Araza—and my heart nearly stopped.

I made sure to remain hidden, and waited for the conversation to take its course, when the sound of a sword being unsheathed rang in the room. One of the men then cried out, "We didn't just run the bastard through, we got his fuckin' saber." The others erupted in laughter, one blurting out, "You did more than run him through, Desjacques, you slit his throat and cut out his lying pirate tongue!"

Maman, I don't know what to think or what to say. I snuck up to my room in a panic, and did not come out until morning, without sleeping a moment. I found Mr. Benton a little while later, and told him Elyse had overheard raised voices about some pirate named Araza, and I asked whether it was true the rogue had been slain. Benton just grinned at me, telling me to ask the man called Desjacques. I found the man in the stables. I had not seen him before, but he had a face that looked to me like a rat—his very presence made my skin crawl. Any rate, I asked him about this Araza fellow, and he grinned toothily, wiping a finger across his throat. He then asked if I wished to see the man's tongue. I ran out of the stables in tears. Oh Maman, but it gets worse. I hardly have words.

That afternoon when the master found me sobbing alone in my room, he asked me what had happened. I told him a friend, a very dear friend, had been murdered by cruel men. He seemed so earnest and so consoling—until he learned that the friend in question held the name Araza. Then his aspect took on something quite different, stern and troubled. I asked him about it, did he know the man?

After a nearly silent supper that night the master— that fucking wretch of a man—confessed quietly that Tadeo's murder had been done on his orders. The damned fool! He claims to have overheard me say to Elyse that I hated the man, and that I wished he was dead. The fool! I did not mean for the actual slitting of his throat. What right had he?

I have not been myself since this occurred, and I'm afraid to admit that I shrieked to the old man's face when I learned of such an odious mistake. The idiot. How could he have done something so cruel on a passing turn of phrase? What sort of man would take it on himself to set upon a beautiful man like Tadeo and have him slaughtered like an animal? Maman, my tears are falling on my words as I write this, and I don't know how I'll go on from this. What has he done? What have I done?

C.

CHAPTER 26

Line Jackson, Outside New Orleans
December 27, 1814

"You're sure about this?" Captain Dubuclet asked, wiping a rag over the blade of his saber. His blue dragoon uniform was soiled by mud and wear, and his eyes, though alert, were bloodshot from a lack of sleep. Beside him, Arsène Latour, Jackson's chief engineer, stood behind a survey map spread over a barrel. They were perhaps two hundred paces behind Line Jackson itself, therefore not "in danger," though from time to time careening rockets exploded randomly overhead or slammed into the dirt. Some found a target, to deadly effect, but mostly they were more of a nuisance than a true danger.

"Yes," Moreau said flatly, "Savary trusts his chosen men. Latour says it is feasible, and the boy seems more eager than any of us. It may be against my personal wishes, but he fits the drummer uniform perfectly, and his brogue will ease suspicions of enemy pickets."

Major Latour listened quietly, looking down at the map. "If," he said finally, "the levee is breached at the southernmost point of the enemy camp, even though the river is low for this time of year, it is likely to flood the entirety of Villeré Plantation. General Villeré may not relish the damage to his cane crop—but it will block the enemy's escape route downriver along the levee road. With the fields of de La Ronde Plantation already flooded, and retreat through Bayou Bienvenue their only safe route of egress, their only route forward is to attack Line Jackson directly."

Dubuclet nodded animatedly, sliding his saber into its scabbard with a *clang*. "Funneling them into a killing field. Not a bad plan—if it works."

"It will work," Moreau said confidently. Latour grinned tightly as he began folding up his map. "General Jackson has given his blessing. That is what matters."

Dubuclet looked at Moreau with a chuckle. "For weeks you've carried on about how little you care, how assuming command is a burden, and so on. Now you're planning raids and steeling minds and hearts."

Moreau stared at him levelly. "What's your point?"

Dubuclet raised his hands diffidently, chuckling again. Moreau then turned to Will Keane, who had been sitting silently on the grass. "If the boy lets us down, I'll shoot him myself...but he won't."

The party set out late that afternoon, five of Savary's militiamen dressed in the cotton smocks and woolen pantaloons of slaves, Will following them in the red and green coat of a drummer from the 85th Regiment of Foot. Moreau accompanied them to the river, where they prepared to launch two small boats once the sun had set. He nodded at Will, smirking at the boy's uniform, which did seem a proper fit. "You may no longer be a Baratarian, but you've come a long way from being cast into the sea for cowardice."

The boy swallowed hard, eagerness written on his features, though Moreau could sense his nervousness. "There's no shame in fear," he said, tapping the boy on the shoulder, "so long as you carry on anyway. Follow these men's lead, and you'll come back to a hero's welcome." Will nodded, and Moreau offered a final farewell before making his way over the levee.

That evening after the "flood party" had set off and darkness settled in, Moreau sat down to compose a letter to Elyse. Before he had written two sentences, a commotion erupted not far from his tent—really a piece of canvas draped over a stick and secured by four small stakes—caused him to set down his quill. It was the arrival of four wagons that had caused the excitement.

The drivers and workhands jumped down from the wagons and soon began unloading crates and small barrels. As Moreau walked over, he noticed that most of the laborers were Black, and from the look of their simple shirts and jackets of poor cloth—and the fact that several were barefoot—he concluded they must be slaves. Familiar faces caught his eye, but it wasn't Elijah Benton or Cyril Tremblay who pulled his attention, but the three women in the second wagon. Two alighted onto the grass, helped by Benton, while one stayed in the driver's seat, her shoulders slumped and arms crossed. Moreau thought he detected a pout on Celeste de Beaumais's face, but his gaze did not linger on her. He watched Elyse and Antonia, wondering how the mulatto woman had come to join the company of Le Mouton Plantation. He couldn't deny that she looked as pretty as ever, but before long his eyes drifted toward Elyse, who joined Tremblay, Benton, and several white workhands in front of the first wagon. He had questions for her.

As the slaves unloaded the provisions from the wagons, presumably gifts to the army from Monsieur Giroux, a group of militiamen gathered to see what had come in from the parishes. Moreau kept his distance, not wishing to draw undue attention to himself in front of Giroux's party. At one point he saw Celeste summon Elyse, and for a moment the two looked to be engaged in a heated conversation, until Celeste waved a hand and Elyse turned away to join the others. Moreau wondered what might have happened to cause friction between the two, who'd formerly seemed inseparable. Losing sight of Elyse in the growing crowd, Moreau edged closer, halting behind a group of militiamen, who gaped at the sight of the well-dressed young ladies. Flanked by Benton and Tremblay, a well-dressed man in his middle years stepped forward as if to address the crowd, and Moreau recognized the planter named Laboulaye from the evening at the Condé Ballroom.

"Brave soldiers," he called out, standing like a practiced orator, "we've come to bring what succor we can in these critical days. On behalf of all of us on whose behalf *you* all fight, we thank you and your glorious General Jackson." The soldiers beside Moreau nodded or muttered among themselves, but their attention seemed more focused on Elyse and Antonia. "What we've brought isn't much," Laboulaye went on, "but these field hands have strong arms for digging, and these smocks and blankets might provide a little warmth in these cold days. On behalf of Monsieur Emile Giroux, myself, and an ever-grateful citizenry, thank you. May God keep you safe and victorious."

He bowed his head as he concluded his remarks, and muted applause came from a handful of the assembled soldiers. Behind the crowd were perhaps a dozen slaves, their expressions hidden by bowed heads and slumped shoulders. Benton stood beside them, watching with a wary eye. Tremblay stood next to Laboulaye, who was speaking to a captain Moreau did not know, while Benton gestured at the slaves, urging them back to work.

A little way off, Antonia was speaking to two Black soldiers from the 2nd Battalion, and then, to Moreau's surprise, he noticed Elyse making her way back to where Celeste was sulking on the driver's seat. He took a few steps and halted beside the back wheel of the second wagon, hidden from Celeste but within earshot of Elyse.

"A word, my lady."

For a moment he was not sure she had heard him, but recognition flashed on her features, and she scowled openly. "This is not a good time, monsieur."

Moreau shrugged. "I may have found something that interests our mutual friend. She seems in less than cheerful spirits, but perhaps these might cheer her up." He produced a balas ruby from his breast pocket and held it out a moment, before pulling out the other. Seeing the two stones, Elyse's eyes widened and she let out a long breath. Quickly her face went from excited to something resembling melancholy, and for a moment she looked at Moreau in silence. When she finally spoke, her voice trembled slightly. "I'll tell you true, I'm surprised to see you have found that. *Those*. She's traveled a long way for those stones. They carry more significance to her than their monetary value. But I'm afraid—" she looked toward the front of the wagon, then turned back to Moreau with teary eyes. "I'm afraid those won't be enough to draw her out of her current troubles." She wiped a tear from her cheek, and for a moment Moreau stood still, unsure what to make of this unexplained drama.

"Elyse, what is going on?"

"I can explain in..." her voice trailed off as something caught her eye, and she quickly wiped away a tear. "I can't tell you now," she whispered, "but if I think of what to do next, I'll write you." Inhaling deeply, she raised her head and forced a smile. With a confused expression, Moreau turned to see what had drawn her attention, and quickly slipped the rubies back into his pocket.

"Just as I thought." Cyril Tremblay smiled as he joined them. "I was sure we'd find you at a post of distinction, Monsieur *Moreau*." Half turning to Giroux's assistant, Moreau offered a curt nod, eager to be off. As he stepped aside, however, Tremblay barred his way. Suppressing a wry smile, Moreau relaxed, taking a moment to examine the nosy little fellow. Though the young man's mouth seemed perpetually on the verge of a smile, his deep-set eyes seemed to show something approaching dismissive scorn, if not outright arrogance. Nonetheless, he seemed to emulate the good manners of his superior, taking Moreau's hand in his own.

Moreau let out a breath. "I've noticed the young Mademoiselle de Beaumais seems in low spirits. Is everything well?"

Tremblay grinned, though his eyes never seemed to change expression. "Just a small misunderstanding with the master. Certainly nothing to be troubled about. We can hardly bemoan a bit of familial disagreement while men like you bear such hazards on our behalf. My master cannot state his gratitude enough."

Moreau's lips curled slightly. "Duty is duty. Simple men like me go where we're ordered." Tremblay considered the words a moment before chuckling softly. "Monsieur, I'd hardly call you simple. But, even so, sophisticated men are hardly immune from war themselves." He gestured at the camp around them. "Within every sophisticated man lies the capacity to inflict sophisticated violence."

It was Moreau's turn to consider his words, and he turned to look at one of the slaves from Giroux's plantation; the man's head was bowed and his chest was heaving from his exertions. "Perhaps it's a man's *sophistication*, relative to another's, that allows him to enslave him."

Tremblay's expression turned rueful, and at length he spoke. "Our world is hardly void of injustice. Though, and forgive any impertinence, I wonder if it can be called *just* to conscript a foreigner against his will. To compel him to risk his neck for a cause that is not his own?"

Moreau shifted his gaze from the exhausted slave back to Tremblay. "As I said, men like me go where we're ordered." For a moment neither said anything, and Moreau noticed Elyse had wandered away out of sight. Stifling a frustrated curse, he fixed Tremblay with the most neutral expression he could muster. "Well, thank your master for the blankets. I must return—"

A slap on his back startled him.

Elijah Benton reached a hand out and clasped Moreau's. His face was a beaming smile, and he spit onto the grass with a shake of his head. "Wasn't sure if we'd see you again, Lenoir. It's good to finally inspect the front from up close." His eyebrows lifted excitedly. When Moreau said nothing in response, Benton rubbed his hands together, then blew into them for warmth. "Yes sir, this is quite a sight; all these guns make a man nervous." He looked around a moment then sniffed twice, his nose twitching. "Though I can't deny a few…foul odors. Though, 'course it ain't nothing quite as bad as a gang of hands come in from the fields." He leaned back as he laughed, and Moreau snuck a look at Tremblay, who was smiling tightly, his eyes cold and unblinking. Moreau looked at the two slaves from their plantation. They were on the edge of the group, swaying like trees in a wind as they tried to stand upright. From his time on long marches Moreau knew they would not remain on their feet much longer.

"It seems your master has been…generous enough to offer some of his hands."

Benton looked at the two haggard men. "Ah," he sighed, "them two took a bit of disciplining earlier this morning. I always tell them, it's best not to resist when our foreman starts whippin'.

Lenoir, you ain't never seen cruelty like when one coon gets to beatin' on another. Something *vicious*." He finally let out the laughter he'd been holding in, but his face grew serious again as he shook his head.

Moreau had heard enough, but one final question nagged at him. "Disciplining," he said. "What were they disciplined for?"

Glancing at Moreau, Benton chuckled grimly. "They tried to escape." His smile took on a malevolent aspect, and Moreau held his gaze for several seconds.

"More than that," Tremblay cut in. "They were caught spreading rumors of a place in the swamps. Some...*haven*. For spreading such a lie to the rest of the acolytes, corrupting them and spawning wicked notions of trying to desert themselves—that is why their punishment was so harsh. Such ideas must be squashed in the cradle, ought they not?" He titled his head as he watched Moreau, looking like some strange bird.

Turning back to Benton, Moreau noticed the man was staring at him, and for several seconds their eyes locked, hard and cold. Moreau felt an unspoken yet unmistakable sensation that was all too familiar to him: mutual hatred. He could see it in the other man, and knew Benton sensed it in him as well. All the better, he mused; at least the man had the courage to show his contempt openly.

Movement near the wagons caught Benton's eye, and he winced as the older of Giroux's slaves stumbled and fell to the ground with a *thud*. Moreau looked at the poor man, and his expression hardened. He had become inured to the sight of beatings, even killings, long ago, but something about this felt different. Violence in battle was one thing, but as he watched the man on the ground struggling to draw rattling breaths and unable to rise without assistance, Moreau wondered how in any way it could be described as necessary.

"Goddamn, Rene, you sack of shit..." Benton muttered. Collecting himself, he turned to Tremblay with raised eyebrows. "That one fixin' to be dead by planting season—if he makes it that long. Excuse me, gentlemen." With an exasperated sigh, he stalked off toward the fallen man, muttering under his breath.

The camp was nearly dark now, and Moreau left Tremblay without a word and passed in front of the wagons, searching for Elyse. What had happened to create such a strange mood in the women—and brazenly hostile attitudes in Giroux's men? Was an attempted slave escape enough to cause an open rupture between the planter and his "adopted daughter"?

He caught sight of Antonia approaching the wagon where Celeste sat. To his surprise, he saw the young woman's features brighten at Antonia's approach, and for several seconds the two women conversed with the ease of long friends. Something Antonia said even caused Celeste to giggle and cover her mouth. Moreau didn't notice Elyse until she had gone several steps past. Moving alongside her, he spoke quietly. "Is everything alright?"

After a glance aside, she pulled her shawl tighter and quickly turned away. "Yes, Moreau." He halted with a frown. After another step, she half turned back to him. "As I said, if I need you, I will write." She made her way to the wagon where the other two women sat in the driver's seat, seemingly exchanging gossip. Moreau watched the strange scene a moment before shaking his head and heading back to his "quarters." In the darkness, he didn't notice Tremblay standing off beside the first wagon with Colonel Winfield, their heads tilted forward as they conferred quietly.

CHAPTER 27

Line Jackson, Outside New Orleans
December 28, 1814

The following dawn brought a deafening rumble of artillery fire over the plain in front of Line Jackson. Overnight the English had moved several cannons into firing positions within sight of the line, and as the sun rose over Chalmette Plantation, they unleashed a salvo toward the Americans, who needed no prompting to return the favor. Moreau, overseeing a work detail felling trees near the swamp, missed the lion's share of the long-range duel, arriving back just in time to hear the last few cannonballs hissing overhead. The sound sparked a familiar feeling, like meeting an old acquaintance not seen in years. When the guns on both sides fell silent, a loud cheer arose from the Americans, their gunners having chased off a reconnaissance force that had been supported by several new batteries the English had entrenched under the cover of night. Moreau climbed the embankment to survey the damage and saw several enemy bodies scattered across the field. This had not been their main assault, but it was a reminder that the day would come soon.

Not long after the barrage, the flood party returned to camp to something of a hero's welcome. Savary's men and Will Keane had returned from their mission and were quickly surrounded by cheering soldiers. They had successfully lured two British sentries—with the help of the boy's uniform—down to the river, where they were surrounded by Savary's men and *invited* to surrender. Then, with Will and another soldier guarding the prisoners, the rest used spades and mattocks to carve two sluices in the levee near the southern border of Villeré Plantation. Within minutes, river water was gushing through the gaps, flooding the nearby fields with no sign of slowing. Before the enemy became aware of what had happened, the party returned to their boats and rowed back upriver with their prisoners in tow.

Will's face was dirt-smeared, but he was beaming as proudly as Moreau had ever seen, and the soldiers cheered him three times for his bravery. The boy's laughter as he was lifted onto someone's shoulders was enough to make even Moreau smile, dispelling some of the gloom that had infected his mood since seeing Giroux's men the day before. He brought the boy to General Villeré, who personally thanked Will for his part in the "flooding that will bring no end to our enemy's troubles," as much of the English camp now lay inundated by the brackish waters of the Mississippi. Will received the general's thanks and an award ribbon for the mission with wide eyes and a stunned silence. The ceremony made its own impression on Moreau, who watched with a stony expression that hid the pride he felt.

In the early afternoon of the twenty-ninth, a comparatively quiet day, Moreau departed for the six-mile journey to New Orleans. His horse had been shot out from under him during the night battle, so he boarded an ox-drawn wagon, accompanied by Will, who climbed into the back. Unsurprisingly, the boy seemed buoyed by the newfound respect that had followed the flooding raid, and had assumed the duties of aide-de-camp with more confidence than Moreau had yet seen.

Tucking a letter into his breast pocket, Moreau considered what its contents might mean. It had come that morning from Elyse, informing him of a rather sudden change of heart from her lady, who was now amenable to meeting to discuss a possible return to France. At first he'd hardly believed it, thinking it some trick, but then he recalled her sullen mood two days earlier, and wondered if perhaps the spoiled young aristocrat had endured enough of war's privations. Her corsair beau was no more, her dreams of fancy balls in New Orleans were on hold indefinitely, and likely the strains on the plantation were causing friction between herself and her aging host, who seemed agitated by the war's growing cost to his "enterprise." Lest he start to think his mission was on the verge of being accomplished, Moreau tempered his hopes. He had a feeling it would not be so easy.

The wagon wheels creaked as they turned onto the river road, its hard-packed surface partially shadowed by the levee to their left. Hidden behind was the Mississippi, whose slow, inexorable flows showed little sign of river traffic. The wagon's driver was known to Moreau; in fact, it was the reason Moreau had chosen him. Though Captain Hubbard's mood had been anything but cheerful when Moreau first spotted him, he now steered the wagon with a seemingly renewed spirit. When Moreau finally pulled his thoughts from Elyse's letter, he asked how an infantry captain had fallen to overseeing wagon convoys.

"My company," Hubbard responded, "was given to another captain five days ago."

Moreau considered this. "So, you fought in the night battle?"

"I did, sir," Hubbard answered. "We acquitted ourselves well enough. Even received a compliment from Old Hickory himself. But next morning Colonel Winfield came from a meeting with the general in a foul temper, gathering me and the other officers and scolding us for how we'd 'let our men down.' He personally reprimanded me for not informing him we'd lost contact with Major Plauché's militia during the battle."

Moreau snorted. "Plauché's militia lost contact with Plauché's militia that night. I can attest to that."

Hubbard nodded. "Well, my company had been in the center of the line, so I'm not even sure how it came to fall on my shoulders, but the colonel removed me from command." He fell silent, exhaling as he snapped the reins for the ox to pick up its pace. "I suppose it came down to an exchange the colonel and I had during the fight, if I'm to tell it true."

"What happened?"

"Well, sir, perhaps a half hour into the fighting I was ordered to advance on a cluster of buildings thought to be held by the enemy.

But I seen that our view had become almost totally lost in the fog, and my first sergeant told me we'd marched ahead of the other companies to our flanks, so I decided to hold until they'd caught us up before advancing by our lonesome. Just then Mr. Winfield came riding up, telling us to 'press the advance at all cost.' I told him we'd lost our sight in the fog and were waiting for our sister companies to join. He flew into a temper, repeating the order, and I repeated my objection. Eventually he...*assumed* my command and led my own men himself. I followed, not wishing to see my boys get cut down, but he became lost in the fog and smoke, and I didn't see him again the rest of the night."

Moreau reached in his pocket for a cigar. "He's an idiot."

Captain Hubbard cleared his throat. "I was just glad not too many of the boys got killed. We were able to rally most of 'em; but sending them in alone seemed foolish to me."

Moreau allowed Will to spark the flint and light his cigar. "Losing half a company needlessly. As I said, he's an idiot."

Hubbard then steered the wagon to the side of the road as a large troop of horsemen passed, headed in the opposite direction. They wore dark-blue coats and black helmets with horsehair plumes, vaguely similar to the dragoon uniform Moreau himself had once worn. Likely they were the dragoons commanded by Major Thomas Hinds, from the Mississippi Territory. He watched the last of them trot by, briefly savoring the break from the monotony of camp life.

"If I may, sir," Hubbard said, breaking the silence. "I'd like to say it's an honor to be driving you. I've, um, heard about the one-armed major from Napoleon's army. You've become something of a talisman. Sir."

Moreau leered at him. "A talisman?"

"Oh, just, well...a good-luck charm, I suppose. Some of the men seem...intimidated by you. Others like to say you're, eh, not who you say. Like you've made up stories of yourself."

Moreau took another puff. "Let them say what they like. As soon as this campaign is over, I'll be gone."

Hubbard chuckled. "They say you like a good drink, sir."

Moreau turned, unaware of the hardness of his stare. "Who's *they*?"

The captain shrugged, shrinking slightly under the Frenchman's glare. "Just rumors. But I'm sure you know rumors pass through an army like shit through a goose."

"With the same results," Moreau muttered.

For several minutes they rode in silence, the only sound the oxen's steady hoofbeats.

"Begging pardon, Captain," Will Keane chimed in from the back. "Have you seen much of the city? How are the people faring?"

"I've seen little of the city," Hubbard answered. "I've been driving or on prisoner guard, mostly."

Moreau nodded, thinking there were worse work details to be had.

"The prisoners I've seen seem to be in well-enough spirits," Hubbard went on. "Few seem despondent, besides one or two horribly wounded. There's even one major from the Ninety-fifth Rifles; some say he was the one who put torch to the White House himself. When Colonel Piatt offered him clean linen, he refused, claiming his own would be brought when they seized the city. The colonel told him he could be waiting some time." Hubbard added with a smile. "They're a confident lot—perhaps too much so. Sure, they defeated Napoleon, but we have Old Hickory. And a hundred other great officers like yourself."

For a moment Moreau puffed lazily on his cigar. When he finally removed it, he pointed it at the young captain, his expression stern. "A word of advice, lad. An officer doesn't become great by accident, nor by simply doing what he's told, but by doing what he knows to be right."

Hubbard mulled this over. "And how does one know what is right, sir?"

Moreau furrowed his brow. "Instinct, perhaps. And making your share of mistakes." He spit, then reached out, clasping

Hubbard by the back of the neck. "Now tell me, does this feel right to you?"

Hubbard chuckled, sliding his neck from Moreau's grip.

"There, you see? It felt *right* to pry yourself from my grip. Soldiering is a bit like that. If your enemy has you by the neck, you wriggle out of it; if you have him by the neck, you hang on with all your strength. Instinct—if you're not a fool—should guide your actions."

Hubbard nodded. "Did you learn that wisdom from Napoleon, sir?"

"Don't make me seize your neck again." He flexed his arm, and the captain flinched. With a wry expression, Moreau took another puff on the cigar.

"Respectfully, sir," Hubbard said, "why are you telling me this? I've been banished to driving oxcarts."

Moreau stared at the road ahead. "You arrived in this city the same day as I, you stumbled into a tavern looking about as imposing as a church mouse, and you began giving orders to a room full of Baratarians. Killers."

Hubbard turned slowly. "You remember that?"

"You looked ready to soil yourself—but when they insulted you, you pushed back. Your anger startled them; I saw it on their faces. And when they stood up to fight, outnumbering your men perhaps four to one, you didn't back down." Moreau looked him in the eyes. "You may not have your colonel's favor, but you have courage. And you will lead others again. Respect can't be ordered; it must be earned, over time. You've shown you have what it takes to earn that."

With a thoughtful gaze, the captain nodded. Moreau turned to Will Keane, who, for a change, met his gaze steadily without looking away.

They reached the city as evening shadows fell on the streets, which were eerily quiet—the only sounds the footfalls of the evening patrols making their rounds. These were old men and young boys—Creole, American, and Negro alike—who traversed the streets in small groups, calling out the hour and "All's well." The wagon halted in front of a two-story town house near the corner of Dauphine and Canal Streets. Moreau hopped down, followed by Will, and with a last look at Captain Hubbard, told him to perform his driving duties like they were the most important task in the army. That was how one made their way back from exile—one task at a time.

As the wagon departed, Moreau found himself hoping that Elyse had brought her lady, even supposing they might find passage on a ship that very night. Quickly dismissing the idea as overzealous, he approached the front entrance, ignoring a youth peddling wares on the corner. Turning back to wave Will on, he noticed something strange. Ordinarily the boy would greet others his own age in a curious but meek manner, like a cautious dog approaching a man offering food. But now Will walked with his head raised and his shoulders squared, appearing taller and older than the boy watching them from the corner. Likely it was the uniform; whatever it was, the boy was staring at Will with open curiosity.

Shaking his head, Moreau turned back to the front door: *One Seventy-Five Dauphine Street*. The town house boasted a large porte-cochère at its entrance, broad French windows on its second floor, and three arched dormers projecting through the roof. Moreau knocked three times. For several moments nothing happened, and they both looked down the street.

"So quiet," Will whispered. Moreau agreed that the streets felt strange in the absence of soldiers, plus the many families that had fled the city. As he moved to knock again, the broad, arched door swung slowly inward. An elderly woman peered out, long white hair nearly covering a dark-brown face. "What you want?"

"I am Major Marcel Moreau of the Louisiana Militia. I've come at the invitation of a friend of Monsieur Giroux."

"Monsieur who?"

"Giroux. The owner of this house."

"This house don't belong to no Monsieur Giroux."

Moreau eyed her a moment. "And who does it belong to, then?"

"That ain't none of your business."

"Well," Moreau said, "I've a meeting with a friend of his. One Seventy-Five Dau—"

"And as *I* already said," she drawled irritably, "ain't nobody named Giroux ever come by these parts."

Moreau shook his head, then produced his pass from General Jackson, reminding her of the consequences of disrupting army business. With a high-pitched laugh, the old woman finally relented, opening the door for them to enter, muttering about "fools and ghosts" as they passed through. They walked into a drawing room, where she told them to wait, then disappeared through a door on the far side of the room. The only furniture was a simple wooden table with a ladder-back chair and a high-backed armchair by the fireplace, its worn and fraying cushions displaying several visible stains. Neither took a seat. On the mantel were several stuffed animal specimens, birds mostly, and a carved figurine of a jungle cat, presumably a jaguar. Moreau took a step closer to examine it: fangs bared, front paw raised, hind legs tensed as if ready to strike. During the Atlantic crossing, the sailors had told him of jaguars' prowess and strength; thinking of that, he sighed, disappointed that he'd probably never have the opportunity to hunt one. He noticed a faint smell drifting in, stew or soup, and the aroma kindled his hunger, as he'd eaten nothing since morning. Surely a brief visit to Maspero's or one of the nearby coffee houses—if any remained open—before returning to camp could be excused.

For several minutes they waited, lost in their own thoughts. The sun had gone down, but the pale light spilling through the windows allowed Moreau to see—barely—and cast the corners into shadow. A faint glow emanated from the small fireplace, but it gave off little warmth. Moreau bent down and blew on the dying embers, hoping to revive them, but to little effect.

"Perhaps she wrote the wrong address. Should I have a look down the street, sir?"

Turning from the fire and standing, Moreau looked at Will. Perhaps he was just imagining it, but the boy really did look as if he had grown into the uniform. "Patience, lad. You've achieved one success and now you're prepared to take on the world. In due time, she'll come." Will took a moment to register what he'd been told, then dipped his head slightly, nodding sheepishly in the way he used to. Moreau shook his head with a smirk.

A dark shape flew across his vision, settling on the the nearest windowsill, and Moreau walked over to get a better look. The glass was shaking slightly as a breeze whistled through a crack in the pane. The large raven cocked its head, its eyes scanning in quick, machine-like movements, seeming to focus on nothing and everything. Moreau waved it off, and it fluttered out of sight into the night. He exhaled as he ambled back toward the fireplace. "When a city clears out, fowl and rodents grow bolder."

Will nodded, rubbing his hands for warmth. "May I ask you a question, sir?" Moreau nodded absently. "When we were returning to the city, after visiting the swamp folk, you said you'd been sent to live with your uncle when you were young. And you said your sister...had learned the first lesson of life. What lesson was that?"

For a moment Moreau said nothing. He stared down at the faintly glowing embers, casting a long shadow on the hardwood floor. "She learned that life does not distinguish the kind from the cruel. Nor does death. When the bell rings, it must be answered."

Will looked at him, and it took an effort for Moreau not to hide his expression. Eventually he met the boy's eyes and held them, neither willing to look away. The creaking sound of the front door opening broke the silence, and they both turned as a figure entered the room.

A short man in a dark coat and flat-brimmed hat passed through the doorway. As he came forward, he lifted his head, revealing a thin, angular face and bright-blue eyes, which took in the room in quick, jerky movements. He was followed by two other men, both similarly dressed. The second stood several inches taller, and removed his hat to show straw-colored hair that fell to his shoulders. The third man was slightly heavyset, wearing spectacles beneath a round-brimmed hat. The first man exchanged a brief look with the others before turning to Moreau with a smile. "Good evening," he said in Creole French.

Moreau gave a curt nod.

"Are you Mr. Moreau?"

"Who wishes to know?"

The newcomers watched Moreau, the man in front smiling, the other two with unreadable expressions. "We're friends of several planters on the German Coast. We've heard talk of your experience with sugarcane in the Caribbean. Is that true?"

Moreau held the man's gaze, his face darkening. "I ask again, who wishes to know?"

"Let's just say," the short man said, strolling toward the fire and holding out his hands to warm them, "we've a mutual friend. Emile Giroux."

"And being that we're mutual friends," the tall man added, "we'd like an answer to our questions. Around here it's considered rude not to engage in…polite conversation."

Moreau had been waiting for a sign of Elyse, thinking foolishly that perhaps this lot was her escort from the plantation. Their appearance and line of questioning quickly dispelled that notion. "If he sent you here to inquire about my expertise in cultivating cane, he wasted your time. And mine." He motioned to his dark coat, his militia uniform. "I'm a soldier, here to help the Americans. I have nothing else to say."

The first man puffed out a pair of sallow cheeks before loudly blowing out a breath, turning to Moreau with a squint. "He told us you might say as much. In which case, we were to gauge your temperament and, judging by that, to offer you a sum to return with us to the plantation. To meet with the master in person."

"I'm going nowhere."

"Oh, come now," the tall man said, "we haven't even told you the sum."

"He said he's going nowhere," Will growled, his face tightening in an angry scowl. Moreau raised his hand for calm, but seeing each of the three men take a step closer, he instead brought it to the saber at his hip. Pausing for a moment, he then quickly unsheathed the weapon, the blade clanging as it left the scabbard. He lowered the saber's tip toward the floor, allowing the gesture to speak for itself.

If he'd hoped to unsettle the three men, he was disappointed. They stared at him without moving, the short one by the fire smiling expectantly, as if he'd opened a bottle of champagne. The heavyset fellow's expression gave away little of his mood. Moreau considered him likely the most dangerous.

"We were also informed," the short man said, turning back to the fire, "that you are a man capable of great violence, and to be wary in the event you should become agitated."

The heavyset fellow made a noise, like a groaning laugh, and his lips curved in a wide grin, revealing a mouthful of crooked yellow teeth. Moreau heard the distinct sound of a pistol being cocked. Then another. In a single motion, the men in back raised their hands, the tall man leveling a pistol at Will, and the bespectacled fellow training his on Moreau. The short man's smile drooped as he stepped close to Moreau, slowly pulling a handful of papers from behind his back. "I'm so glad you received my letter, Marcel. But you never wrote back." He let out a shrill laugh before tossing the papers in the air.

Moreau's nostrils flared, and as he motioned for Will to get behind him, taking slow steps backward himself, he searched desperately for a way out. The windows were locked, with no time to open them; the stairwell at the front of the room was blocked by the two men; and in the doorway to the kitchen stood the old white-haired woman. In her hand she held a butcher knife, a wicked smile forming on her lips before she tilted her head back and let out a mad cackle.

SMOKE IN THE CYPRESS

Mother,

I write to you in a spirit of dejection I've not felt since being tossed in a cypress swamp by pirates. In fact, the general mood on this plantation has not improved since the senseless killing of Araza by that old man's henchmen. I don't know how this all could have happened. I was so happy. What am I to do?

Elyse, ever planning and scheming, claims to have made acquaintance with a Frenchman serving with the American army. I don't know his name, but this foul man practically set upon me at a dinner the night of the battle with the English. He might just as well be dead now for all I know, but either way I'm not sure I wish to accept his offer to bring me home. He said he's a friend of yours, Mother, but I do not trust him. Do you know of anyone matching this description? Perhaps one of father's pathetic schemes to ferry me home aboard a ship can account for it, though I doubt father's concern for me reaches that far. He's surely forgotten me already.

Oh Maman, the mood here is so far from the happy days of just a couple weeks ago. The war continues to deprive us of our surplus supplies, and we are called constantly to give more to the army. Giroux gives what he can, but I care nothing for their fool war. They can all die for all I care. I refuse to let the murder of my lover defeat me, though I wonder if my offers of assistance are even remembered, as I seem to receive little more than silence from the master, and cold looks from his overseers. Elyse would be more helpful if she would understand that the war means we cannot simply board a ship for France. We must make do with what we have.

*Love,
C.*

CHAPTER 28

Mississippi River, Louisiana
December 29, 1814

The sound of booted footsteps on the deck brought Moreau out of his fitful dream, and he whipped his head back only to bang it on a slab of solid wood. He muttered a curse, both from the knock and for allowing himself to fall asleep at all. The cloth covering his eyes had shifted slightly, but the narrow slit of an opening beneath his left eye showed only a faint hint of dawn's light. Turning his head aside and straining his ears, he could only make out the strange sound that had puzzled him since the boat left the city's wharves. *Whoosh—whoosh—whoosh—whoosh.* What was that?

He was standing upright, secured to a post by a strong cord of hemp that wrapped around his chest and pinned his sword arm behind his back, leaving the stump of his left arm free. He could move his head, but he could barely flex his hand and fingers enough to keep the blood circulating. He did not think wriggling free was a possibility, not without hours of work.

At the approaching sound of footsteps, he lifted his head, and a moment later the blindfold was removed, revealing the short man from the house on Dauphine Street. He stared at Moreau for several seconds before walking over to the railing farther up the deck. Turning back, his face widened into a sneer as he met Moreau's eyes. A shape off to his right pulled Moreau's attention, and he saw Will in his dark soldier's uniform. He was propped against a white-painted bulkhead, his legs straight out in front of him and his head down, hopefully only sleeping. Moreau didn't bother to hide his anger upon seeing the boy, and he grit his teeth, wondering why in God's name he had brought the lad with him to the city. He'd thought he was helping him, keeping him close to carry messages or assist with necessary tasks, but now he was a prisoner through no fault of his own. God, at least protect the boy.

"That noise you're hearing," the short man broke the silence, "is the paddle wheel churning at the stern, moving this vessel. It's powered by that there engine." He nodded toward a small cabin closer to the bow. "That paddle wheel will change river travel forever. Sadly, Mr. Moreau," his face showed exaggerated concern, "you won't be part of that future. Steam-powered boats travelling our rivers—just imagine it! Well, you had your chance to cooperate, but what was it you said? Oh yes, 'I'm going nowhere.' Well, turns out you're goin' somewhere. One last boat ride." He chuckled, his mouth widening in a slack, decayed-tooth smile. Moreau thought the man resembled a rat. Forcing himself to silence, he wriggled his wrist and flexed his leg muscles, probing for any slackness in the cord. He found none.

Stealing another look at Will, he breathed a sigh of relief when he saw the boy was awake, his wide eyes darting around. Surely he'd woken as confused as Moreau had, but the determined set to his jaw indicated that he had not yet resigned himself to captivity, despite the prospect of "interrogation," the only reply the rat-faced man had given when Moreau asked where they were being taken.

More footsteps sounded on the deck, and a moment later the heavyset man rounded the corner of the small cabin. He stopped by the railing, glancing at Moreau with a hard expression. His wore a large white apron, like a butcher. Moreau did not need further explanation to understand this fellow's role in the impending "interrogation." He stifled an irritated growl, mostly at himself for blundering into this mess.

"At the moment," Rat-face went on, "Congress has allowed for only two men to operate steamboats like this on the river. But Monsieur Giroux intends to set that to rights."

Moreau heard a raspy throat clearing.

"Where are you taking us?"

Rat-face looked at Will with an amused expression. "This *boat* is bound for Natchez." He pulled a cigar from a pocket and stuck it between his lips. "But all you need to know is…we taking you upstream for a little ride." He chuckled, eyes closing in mirth as the cigar bobbed up and down in his mouth.

The man in the apron reached down behind him, picking up a lantern and lighting a spill. He held it out for Rat-face, who puffed on the cigar until it flamed, then pointed it at Moreau with an emphatic gesture. "Do you know how ships move upstream against currents like this? Used to, anyways. The ship traveling upriver lowers its anchor down onto another ship beside it, setting the anchor onto its deck so they're 'attached.' The smaller vessel is sent out ahead, then drops its own anchor, to steady it. The larger ship then hauls in its anchor that's on the deck of the other craft, which in turn pulls it forward. So on and so forth, this gets a ship upstream. Called *warping*. Clever, to be sure, but damn time-consuming. Now, with this here steamship," he gestured along the deck, "we ain't got to warp no more. This changes everything." He nodded to the man in the apron, and the two men turned and walked around the cabin out of sight.

"Major," Will whispered, wincing as he twisted his body, "I think I can get out."

Moreau squinted at him. "What?"

Will writhed again. A moment later his eyes scanned furtively aside, as if remembering the danger they were in. He turned back to Moreau and raised a hand—which held a small but sharp-looking knife that glinted in the morning sunlight.

Moreau smirked, checking behind him. "Where did that come from?" Will's mouth spread in a wide grin and he shrugged, eyes twinkling. "I almost forgot you were once a pirate."

Will's grin held a hint of pride.

"Well, what are you waiting for? Cut yourself free, then toss—"

The sound of footsteps returning cut him off, and Will leaned back, tucking his free arm back behind him and lowering his head forlornly. The man in the apron appeared, carrying a small brown satchel, which he set on the deck a few paces from Moreau. Exhaling loudly, he crouched down and rummaged through the bag as he addressed Moreau. "Our paymasters told me a little of you. They said you're a hardheaded bastard. Not a weak cur, but stubborn, with a little iron to you. Most men like that are brittle, easy to crack once you've found their breaking point. But," he looked up, rising slowly to his feet, "they also said they want answers from you before we reach Natchez. So I've got to work quickly. No games. Just breaking a man with iron in his blood. But, as surely you know, iron only *sharpens* iron, so we must break you the only way iron can be broken." He raised a hand to reveal a long knife with a serrated edge. With a cold smile, he turned his eyes on Will. "We melt it."

"I don't know what your master wants with me, but I have nothing to hide."

The man turned back, speaking hoarsely. "Well, that's just it, sir. I'm told you've done nothing *but* hide."

With the man's attention on Moreau, Will seized the chance and began wriggling his arm that was still tied. To avoid staring, Moreau turned back to his captor. "I've hidden nothing."

The man flashed a toothy grin. "You've lied about your name, where you come from, and those you've made friends with." He leaned close enough for Moreau to grimace from his foul breath. "The Negro folk out in the swamps, you've visited them. Ah, I can see the truth in your eyes. You, sir, are going to tell me what exactly you've been up to."

Moreau mumbled a few words to buy time, and a moment later he saw Will wriggle once more before finally freeing his other arm. Moreau turned his eyes back to the man in front of him. "Alright, I've been to their swamps. What of it? I was taken against my will."

Sneaking a look at the boy, he saw Will hunched over with the blade in his hands, creeping toward the man in the apron. His eyes showed fear, but his clenched jaw showed a willingness to fight. Moreau knew stabbing a man for the first time was no easy feat; doing so at such a young age seemed nearly unthinkable. "Just what has your master so troubled? Has something gone wrong?"

The man's eyebrows rose a little, and he smiled cruelly. "Mr. Giroux tried to reason with his acolytes, but lies spread like disease, corrupting the good, loyal hands who've done nothing but honest work. Then vermin like you crept in. Now they're running off like *uuhh*—" He let out a strange-sounding gasp, his eyes bulging widely. "What was—" The man wheezed, staggering backwards and reaching an arm behind his back. He let out a quiet wheeze, then his legs buckled and he crumpled to the deck like a sack of potatoes. Behind him stood Will, staring at Moreau like a madman.

"I'm sorry," the boy said quietly. "I'm sorry. Oh God, I didn't mean—"

"Will!" Moreau barked. "Listen to me." He stared intently at the boy, hoping to shake him out of his fright. "I need you to cut my hand free." He struggled and shook his body, which seemed to get the boy's attention. Swallowing hard and flexing his fingers, Will let out a frightened groan but turned slowly toward the man on the ground, looking at him with wide eyes. The fellow was still moving, albeit slowly, sliding his legs on the deck and groaning quietly.

"Will," Moreau said evenly, "go get the knife. Cut me loose, or—look at me!—or any second the other one will be back. He'll kill us both."

With a dazed nod, Will licked his lips. Moreau twisted violently, vainly trying to free himself. "Quickly, lad!" Nodding more surely, Will stumbled over to the man and, after a moment's hesitation, gripped the knife and pulled it out of his back. The man groaned as blood poured from the wound, and Will turned away with a grimace, looking like he was about to cry. "Alright," Moreau said reassuringly, "now cut me loose and we'll get out of here."

Will slid the blade between the rope and Moreau's hand and began cutting as fast as he could. Feeling the rope slacken little by little, Moreau forced himself to remain still. He grunted as he slid his hand free and the hemp cord dropped to the deck. He reached up and put a hand on the boy's head, swiveling him so they were face-to-face. "Well done, lad."

Swallowing hard, the boy turned to look down at the dead man on the deck, but Moreau forced his head back forward. "You don't need to see that. Hey, you just saved my life." He lowered his hand to Will's shoulder and pulled him in, hugging him tightly. The boy threw his arms around Moreau and squeezed. Hard.

Letting out a deep breath and wiping away a tear, Will stepped back, looking up with a wide grin. "I saved you?"

Moreau nodded, unable to hold back a smile.

The sound of running feet jarred them back to the present danger, and a second later the rat-faced fellow rounded the corner. The tails of his black coat swung at his sides as he halted abruptly, looking on the scene in horror. His lips moved wordlessly as he stared down at his partner, who lay quivering on the deck. For a moment, his teeth gritted from side to side, then he looked at Moreau with a murderous glare before reaching a hand behind him.

Instinctively, Moreau reached for the coil of cord at his feet and threw it at the man. Thinking it was some sort of weapon, the man flinched back with a piercing cry. Seizing on this brief distraction, Moreau moved to grab Will, but the boy flinched backward, staring between him and the man in the black coat, his eyes widening in fear. As Moreau lunged to grab him by the collar, the lad charged toward him shouting, "No!" Will avoided Moreau's outstretched hand and bowled into him.

Bang! A pistol shot pierced the air as Moreau slammed into the deck, where he lay for a brief moment before realizing he wasn't hit. He hauled himself up and scrambled toward Will, stealing a quick look at Rat-face, partly hidden behind a cloud of pistol smoke, then reached and seized the boy by his coat. Placing a hand in front to steady himself, Will allowed himself to be dragged across the deck. A second later they reached the railing and Moreau shouted, "Jump!" Giving the boy a last tug, he leapt overboard—hanging in the air for a split second—before plunging into the frigid waters of the Mississippi.

He surfaced with a gasp, the shock from the cold quickly replaced by an urgent need not to drown, a task made significantly harder with his missing arm. Kicking his legs and paddling as best he could, he swiveled his head and lifted the boy above the waterline. Making for the shore, he swam with all the strength he could summon, until his feet mercifully touched the muddy bottom and he was able to drag Will to the embankment and swing him up onto the damp soil, then allowing himself to collapse in a heap beside the boy.

For a minute Moreau lay still, his chest heaving as he fought to catch his breath. Fearing the danger may not have passed, he scanned the river but saw the boat had not come about—perhaps whoever remained onboard thought he and the boy had drowned. Whatever the reason, the steamboat was a distant shape now, its long hull silhouetted against the faint-blue morning sky, while a tall pole, like a chimney, belched plumes of black smoke high into the air, tendrils coiling in the breeze until they dissipated above the treetops. With an exhausted sigh, Moreau let his head drop to the dirt.

When his wind had returned and he felt ready to move, he lifted himself up with a groan. Craning his neck and rolling his shoulders, he felt the sting of the breeze as his soaked clothes clung to his skin. Shivering audibly, he turned to Will with an amused grin. "Well, that was close." The boy didn't move, and he frowned. "Will, did you hear me?"

Finally the boy rolled onto his side. The slow movement brought a pained expression, and Moreau noticed his face was as pale as a sheet. "Will, are you alright?"

His question was answered when he looked down at the boy's stomach—which showed a dark stain spreading from a small circular hole in his shirt.

"Jesus."

Moreau swallowed hard, looking at the boy's expression. Will's eyes were open wide, staring at the sky, fearful and glazed. He slowly turned his head to Moreau. "Am I going to die?"

Moreau, moved his lips to speak, but nothing came out. He shook his head slowly, then again more emphatically. "No, boy, you're not going to…" His eyes drifted down to the wound again, and he took a deep breath. "You're going to be—let's just rest you against this tree."

Will cried out in pain as Moreau dragged him several paces before setting him upright against a thin tree. Moreau banished the thought that he'd done so only to allow the boy to die in a more dignified position, reminding himself that he'd seen men survive abdominal wounds before—hadn't he? He looked around for something, anything, to help—but all he saw was mud and waves lapping the shore. He leaned forward and pressed his hand against the wound to staunch the bleeding. "Will, there's nothing here to take care of you with. I'll do what I can to halt the bleeding, but…" His words caught in his throat. "I cannot treat this wound. I must get you to a doctor." The youngster stared back at him, his eyes low and hazy. "Nod if you understand me." Will nodded slowly. "That's a good, lad. Now I just have to find a way to move you. I've seen makeshift stretchers…" Muttering to himself, he stalked off into the nearby swamp.

His one hand made the task difficult, but after a little while Moreau had brought back several long branches, and he sat down and immediately began weaving them together. Holding the branches between his knees, and using the thinner, more elastic branches as twine to secure the larger ones, he soon made a decent makeshift stretcher, with a long branch extending from one end. Will emitted another pained groan as Moreau wrestled him onto it, then wriggled his shoulder under the branch and stood. Grasping the branch with his hand, Moreau trudged away from the river.

After a quarter of an hour, ignoring the burning fatigue in his arm and shoulder, Moreau reached the river road and checked in both directions, half expecting to see a carriage with the three men crying out as they ran him down. Turning in the direction he hoped would lead to a house or militia checkpoint, he continued on, staying close to the foliage on the side of the road to avoid unfriendly eyes. The wounded boy suffered in silence behind him. Moreau lost track of time, and as the sun passed its zenith, he admitted to himself that he did not wish to spend the night in a cane field or a cypress swamp, but he had no way of returning to the city. Even if he happened upon a cavalry patrol or a wagon convoy, it was likely he'd be considered a vagabond—or worse, a deserter. Should he make it back to camp, he could explain himself to Plauché or General Villeré, but here, on the river road, traveling with a wounded youth would raise more suspicion than sympathy, so he trudged on to the destination he had settled on, albeit reluctantly.

After what seemed an eternity, they came to a narrow dirt track that Moreau recognized—or at least hoped he did. Thankfully his exertions had kept the cold from him—as long as he was moving—though his damp undershirt still clung to his back. The sun had brought a little warmth while it hung in the sky, but as it fell among the trees, the chill returned and Moreau's labored breaths puffed out frostily in front of him. He decided to halt a moment, both to rest and to check on the boy. As he crouched down, Will's eyes opened slowly, though they showed little more than exhaustion.

"Mr. Moreau?" he asked, his eyes searching. Moreau knelt closer.

"I'm here, lad."

The boy grimaced as he swallowed, blood trickling from both sides of his mouth. Moreau lifted his hand to wipe the blood away, but Will shook his head. With an effort he breathed through his nostrils, closing his eyes as he whimpered softly.

"You're showing strength, boy. More than many soldiers I've seen."

Will nodded. "Major...you don't think...I'm a coward?"

"You were never a coward." Will nodded, smiling weakly. Moreau shook his head. "Fools who knew nothing may have said so; you just had to learn for yourself you had courage. You've found it."

He sighed quietly. Suddenly Will's eyes opened wide, and he looked around as if confused, or frightened. "Monsieur Moreau?"

"I'm right here." He gently squeezed the boy's hand.

Will nodded. "You're my friend?"

Moreau exhaled, tears welling in his eyes. "Yes. I'm your friend." Will smiled. "Good. That's all...I ever wanted.... "Thank you."

His last breath was a prolonged wheeze, a death rattle Moreau had heard before, but not from one so young. He watched as life departed the boy's body, his eyes remaining open and peaceful. When he was sure it was over, Moreau wiped his hand over Will's face to close them, then sat down beside his body.

For over half his life Moreau had been at war, and he knew better than most the random tragedies that could befall any pulled into its current. Decent, humble folk died agonizing deaths, while the lying and self-serving rose to power and asserted it over others—often disastrously. But in all his years, no death had affected him like this. An indeterminate time passed as he sat unmoving, lost in a stupor, careless of anything or anyone.

When his thoughts finally began to settle, he wiped a tear from his eye. The sight of a dead body should have had little effect on a veteran of countless battles, but the image of Will's smile swirled in Moreau's mind, refusing to depart.

In the end it was only a dutiful regard for the boy's remains that lifted Moreau from the dirt. If he could not decide the fate of Will's soul, he could at least tend to the final resting place of his body, and keep it safe from robbers, animals, or an undignified exhumation by the elements. He would dig the grave himself, and speak the final words over it—but he had no means of digging here, and he did not wish to draw suspicious passersby or be stranded in a dank swamp come nightfall. So there was only one place to go.

The shrubs and palm fronds swishing against his trousers pulled Moreau from his gloomy reverie, and he turned his head from side to side as he searched for any familiar landmark. His pace had slowed, and for some time he had felt his strength waning, but he continued on his path. Having reached the leafy barrier, he knew he had found his destination, but in his current state he could not have said if Le Marais was a hundred paces ahead or a thousand.

As he dragged the makeshift stretcher around a large cypress tree, an unexpected odor filled his nostrils. Lacking the mental energy to consider its meaning, he struggled on without slowing. A few more minutes and he noticed the trees thinning ahead, marking the clearing, and a wave of relief passed over him. He increased his pace as thoughts of water, food, and shelter displaced his gloom. Drawing closer, the odor once again assailed his nostrils. Smoke? Had they built a bonfire? The woman, what was her name, Diantha? She'd told him they never lit fires in daylight, to avoid smoke trails alerting those hunting them. Moreau wondered why they would have risked their safety. As he reached the edge of the settlement, his gaze settled on a thin tendril of smoke coming from the far huts. Or what remained of them.

Setting the stretcher down—guiltily relieved to lose its weight—he stumbled ahead to the first huts, now little more than hulks of ash and charred wood. He swallowed hard as he began to understand what this meant. Until now his thoughts had come in a slow, plodding rhythm, but seeing the wreckage of the village, a sharpness returned, and he scanned the ground ahead of him with wide eyes.

"I almost shot you," a deep voice said, and Moreau spun around. A moment later a man holding a musket emerged from behind a nearby tree. Edward wore a simple white smock and brown pantaloons, his face slightly unkempt. He came forward in slow, guarded steps, bare feet crunching on charred sticks and dead leaves. His eyes were cold.

"What happened?" Moreau asked, looking out over the charred remains of the village.

Edward took a deep breath, his chest swelling, then a noise behind Moreau drew his attention. Turning around, he saw another familiar face. Diantha stood beside the wreckage of one of the dwellings, still as a statue. She wore a simple black blouse and brown skirt, and her feet also were bare. A black tignon covered her head, though it held no pearl, and she wore no jewelry. Her head drooped slightly, and her eyes were sunken and unreadable.

Edward shuffled his feet. "Should I kill him?"

Diantha stood motionless, her eyes fixed on Moreau. After a moment, Moreau finally realized what Edward had said and turned back to him with a frown. Edward's fingers drummed along the musket's barrel. "Gran Ibo?"

Moreau looked back at Diantha, awaiting her response. In truth, he cared little for her answer, and a part of him would have welcomed death. For several moments no one moved, and finally his impatience got the better of him. "If I'm to be killed," he said tiredly, "best be about it then."

With a squint, Diantha raised a hand and motioned for him to approach, then turned and walked slowly toward the village center. Without looking back at Edward, Moreau followed.

Charred huts surrounded the clearing, a few with walls or roofs still intact, but all had been torched. Moreau coughed as he inhaled smoke, and covered his nose as he passed a slaughtered cow in one of the pens. There was no doubt the village had been sacked, its animals slaughtered, homes burned, crops destroyed—and with a sinking feeling, Moreau considered the worst of it: the almost total absence of people. Edward and Diantha remained; what had happened to the others?

Diantha halted at the village center. A turned-over cookpot lay on the ground beside the firepit, which had also been despoiled: ashes and stones strewn about the open ground. She turned slowly, and a measure of dignity returned to her features. "Do you know," she finally said, "why I didn't tell Edward to kill you?"

"I do not."

She stared at him with a hard expression. "Perhaps I should have. Or perhaps Nehemiah or one of the others will when they return." Moreau's mind stirred a little at hearing that name. "I will allow you to live," she went on, "at least a little while, so you can tell me what I wish to know."

His eyes met hers. "Which is?"

She took a step closer, glaring fiercely. "Before I have you killed, I wish to know why you betrayed my trust. *Our* trust. Why you stole our stone and ran, like a thief in the night. A coward." Her face tightened in a near snarl, and for a moment he thought she might rush him. "I will give you one chance to prove me wrong. Or else my people's suffering will pale in comparison to what we do to you."

Moreau had not retreated as she stalked toward him, but her words had the intended effect. Not because she had shouted or snarled, or even raised her voice, but he knew she meant every word. And worse, he knew he deserved them. "Madame, I don't know what happened here, but I assure you I knew nothing of this."

"I did not say you did," she growled. "I said you betrayed my trust. Like a coward and a thief."

Moreau nodded. "I am a thief. I took what was yours."

"And if you wish to keep your flesh attached to your bones, you will tell me you've brought it back."

Moreau's heart sank, recalling that the balas rubies had been on his person when he'd been abducted—and robbed. He exhaled slowly, feeling genuine remorse. From the start he had intended to return the stone, having little desire to keep it for himself, but at the thought of it in the hands of those men from the steamship, he shook his head.

"I took the ruby so I could find the woman I've traveled across a sea to find and bring home." He exhaled, running a hand through his hair. "At first, I believed her lover—*former* lover—a Baratarian captain, was searching for them. I thought if I could get them before he did, I could lure her to a meeting and convince her to return with me. The night before I first came here, he held a knife to my throat. And after I left here, he tried to duel with me. Either way, I never gave a damn about him or those cursed rubies; I just needed to find that woman so I could return to France with my head."

Diantha stared at him, her expression cold and impassive. "Why not ask me for it?"

"Why not ask the Queen of England for her crown?" He wiped a hand over his face. "I will not ask you to believe me, but I swear to you I did not intend to steal it for myself. I spoke with the woman's lady that very night, and we made a plan to lure her mistress in, claiming her pirate lover wanted a meeting. My possessing the stone was enough to get her lady's attention; her willingness to arrange the meeting got mine. That was my only thought."

Diantha shook her head slowly. "So where is it now? You must know returning to this hounfour without it is as good as a death sentence. Especially now."

"I know. But perhaps my appearance here without it gives you some small indication that I harbor your people no ill will."

"Your will be damned. Where is it?"

Moreau thought of when he'd last had the ruby, and the three evil men that had skulked into the house on Dauphine Street, throwing everything into madness. He sighed. "I had it on me, and was going to return it to you once I had the girl. But I was… waylaid. In the city." He ignored her glare, thinking of his final moments with Will. When he remembered the boy's body lay only a few paces away, a lump formed in his throat, but he forced his words out. He told Diantha how they'd gone to meet with Elyse and been held at gunpoint. He explained the strange steamship and the men's connection to Giroux and their accusations against him. At the mention of the slave owner, Diantha's eyebrows rose, but otherwise she listened in stony silence. Moreau finally got to Will being shot, and told of his death and the trek to the village.

"After what I did, I don't expect understanding, or mercy," he said quietly, "but I would ask you to allow me to dig the boy a grave and bury him, before your men do what they must. I led the boy to his—please let me say a last goodbye."

For a while neither said anything, both lost in their own unhappy thoughts. At last Moreau raised his head, ready to die as long as she allowed the burial. Diantha's eyes were lowered, and after another weighty silence, she raised her head. "We do not bury our dead here. The animals disturb the remains, and as we have no cisterns, we cannot risk our groundwater becoming putrefied. But," she sighed, looking up at him, "we can build a pyre. There's enough wood. You may collect his ashes after, if that is your people's custom."

Moreau thought about this, and deemed it appropriate—given where they were. He nodded, and for a moment her eyes bore into his. "I see you are hurt by his loss, Frenchman. And I am sorry. But look around you," her voice was quiet but hard. "Look at *my* people—what's left of them. One white boy is killed and you want tears from me? We were over fifty here—there are thousands—*more*—out there on the plantations. Think of how many of *them* have died without proper a burial. Think of what *they* have been through. My people were hounded through these swamps like wild animals, their husbands and wives beaten, children sold like cattle. We *finally* found a safe haven, only to be attacked in the night, taken back to the slave masters. Do you have any *idea* what awaits them? Do you care? Or do white men think only of their own kind?" She cut herself off abruptly, eyes fierce but full of feeling.

Moreau felt stung by the truth, shaken at what she'd revealed. If these people had been taken back to Giroux's plantation...he didn't want to think what might happen. He fought back a shudder. Diantha exhaled and turned away, pausing before speaking in a calmer voice. "Think a little on what has happened here, and your own pain might be put in perspective." Her eyes, no longer angry, met his. "Even so, I'm sorry the boy was killed. Edward will give you wood for the pyre...then we'll decide what to do with you."

Moreau watched her stride off, his thoughts a tangled knot, but no longer in a fog of despair. The sadness was present, overwhelming even, and as he looked around the burned-out carcass of the village, he felt ashamed. For stealing from people who had next to nothing—and for bringing more pain to a place that had known more than its fair share.

With a lowered head, he walked slowly back to Will's body. He would give the boy a proper farewell; beyond that, nothing mattered. To his surprise, Edward appeared and provided him with several logs, saying they were left over from the pyres they had already built for the men who died defending the village. The two then laid the boy on top of the stack of timber and kindled a fire beneath it. For a while Moreau stared at the growing flames, lost in his own thoughts.

As the fire consumed the body, he asked what had happened to the village. In sparse words, Edward explained that perhaps a dozen men had come in the dead of night, with dogs, chasing off the sentries and surrounding the village before the rest of the guards had made it back from their posts. Nehemiah, who was guarding an entrance with Antoine, had been absent, as had Edward, while Jean-Pierre and a handful of men, along with all of the women and children, had been present during the attack. Four died defending them.

"When I finally made it back," Edward muttered, staring at the fire, "all I seen were the burning cabins. I heard some screams, off that way," he nodded in the direction from which Moreau had come, "and I ran out with Nehemiah to hunt them down. But they were gone when we reached the road. When we came back here... we saw the bodies. Four of our brothers were killed, the houngan one of them." He paused again, his eyes turning watery. "And a girl named Suzette. She must've tried to fight them. Maybe too well. They put a musket ball in her head." He shook his head, turned, and walked back toward the village.

Moreau watched him go, then turned his attention back to the funeral pyre, which was lessening in intensity. For a long while he stood watch, until the fire was out completely. He recalled his first sight of Will as he was hauled aboard *La Panthère*. That seemed a lifetime ago. The boy had looked scared, almost feral. And then, as now, Moreau had harbored a secret astonishment that he had survived by clinging to a piece of flotsam in the middle of the Gulf. The lad had carried himself like a whipped dog, furtive and sneaky, but he was not the coward he'd thought himself to be. Moreau wished he had told him that long before the end. Staring with an empty look, he bent down with the small clay jar Diantha had given him and began scooping up the ashes.

"Goodbye, Will."

~~~

Maman,

I hope this letter finds you swiftly, if it finds you at all. I'm concerned about the embargo of ships in the gulf, but secretly I confess to you that, having heard nothing from you for some weeks, perhaps my letters are no longer reaching you.

I only say this because I must tell you my circumstances have changed considerably in recent days, and not for the better. Things have grown worse, Maman, much worse.

Having recovered from his silence, which I can only presume is guilt over Araza's murder, Giroux has once again begun speaking to me—but only ever to tell me this or inform me of that. We no longer speak idly of the plantation, or his lost wife, or of his plans for the future. Of late his eyes appear red and feverish, and often stare away vacantly into the distance, even when in conversation. The only time he speaks to me is to give sharp, angry outbursts about the cost of the war, or more often, his railings against the "swamp vermin" that are luring his acolytes away from him. He seems to truly believe this, and it is all the talk of the other men. They seem to have their hackles up, as if some threat is looming.

But worse, Maman—the master and his men have begun acting very strange towards me. Sometimes I'd dare call it cruel. Elyse and I are no longer permitted to travel to the city, or even depart the grounds, without permission from the master. We are to return before nightfall, and, if I'm correct, I seem to have one of his men looking at me at all times. Others seem to "check in" on me occasionally, though not in a particularly friendly manner. The strange, rat faced fellow smiled awfully at me yesterday, claiming I ought to behave or the master might send me to to the 'beast in the swamp'. I asked him what he meant, and with a feral grin, he spoke of a crocodile brought home by the master from Cuba, which had grown large and devoured the local alligators. The little villain then let out a strange laugh, and claimed it all to be in jest — but my thoughts have been unsettled ever since.

The beatings the poor slaves have to endure seem to have grown more frequent, and when I raised the matter to young Monsieur Tremblay, he grew cold and sullen, saying in a quiet voice that such things are best left to the master, and are not my concern. Oh, I don't know what to make of it all. I have no express wish to go to the city, but I cannot help a slight feeling of being trapped. Am I becoming a prisoner in this house, Maman?

Write me, please. If you wished to come here in person, I would not mind.

C.

CHAPTER 29

Le Marais, Cypress Swamp, Outside New Orleans
December 30, 1814

Moreau woke with a start, not sure if it was the cold that roused him, or the sound of rustling footsteps nearby. He shivered and leaned forward, relieved to separate from the narrow cypress tree he'd been propped against, which felt half frozen against his back. The faint warmth of a nearby fire had dried his clothes somewhat, but in the flickering light he saw the man he knew he would have to face eventually. By his expression, Nehemiah looked uninterested in conversation or even argument; his eyes carried death in their stare.

The bundle of kindling held in his arms dropped at his feet with a clatter, and for a while he simply watched Moreau. His body appeared relaxed, but his eyes, the whites bright against the darkness of the forest, bulged animatedly. Eventually his hand reached for his belt, and without a noise he slid a dagger from it, its blade thick and sharp.

Moreau looked at the blade, his expression unchanging. "Make it quick. I will not fight you."

Nehemiah's mouth twitched, his lips moving as if he were about to speak, then he shifted his feet and spoke in a quiet rumble. "I knew you would return. Even after we learned you come as a thief, I knew we ain't seen the last of you." He lifted a bare foot and moved slowly toward Moreau. "Like some...spirit. Some demon sent by the masters to torment us." He pointed the dagger at Moreau. "Will you die when I plunge this blade in? Or are you from the devil, and our weapons cannot touch you?"

At first thinking it mockery, Moreau's mood went from resigned to scornful. Not wishing to be baited into anger, and thinking his time was up, he let out a breath and looked up at the darkening sky. "If you wish to kill me, be about it. I told you I will not fight you."

He lowered his eyes to the ground. A shape moved to his left, and he knew the man was coming closer. He would not fight; let the blade be swift. He had brought Will Keane to his death. He had failed in his mission to save Celeste de Beaumais. He had done what he could for the Americans, and in return they had spread lies about him. These swamp folk had been collared and returned to a mad slave master for punishment, torture, and, if they were lucky, death. What would his own death mean? Nothing.

The footsteps came closer, and out of the corner of his eye he saw the glint of the blade. He imagined the man would slit his throat. So be it. He tilted his head back…

A rustle of leaves behind him caused his ears to twitch, and he realized his heart was beating no faster than normal. He supposed he really was ready for death. But the rustling hadn't come from Nehemiah. Curiosity caused him to turn his head. Who had come to witness his last breaths? Diantha? Did she wish to plunge her own knife in as well?

At first it was difficult to make out the figure standing a little way off, but after a moment, Edward came forward into the soft moonlight. Glancing back ahead, Moreau saw Nehemiah, still holding the blade at the ready, but he had not moved since Edward's appearance.

"I told you I would kill him."

Silent for a moment, Edward finally spoke in a weary voice. "I know, Nee. I'm not saying he don't deserve it." He took a few gradual steps closer. "But she says not yet."

An audible grunt came followed. "What the fuck do you mean, 'not yet'?"

"I mean not yet." Edward shook his head, and Moreau felt a sudden desire to let out a burst of cold, ironic laughter, and he wondered how this day could get any stranger. He doubted it could.

"Eddie," Nehemiah said, his voice almost trembling, "he's going to die. I need it to be me."

"I hear you, brother, but she says—"

"I don't give a fuck what she says!" Nehemiah roared. Stomping forward, he loomed over Moreau and grabbed his hair, pulling his head back and lifting the knife high in the air. "I'm going to kill you!"

Before Moreau knew what was happening, Edward bounded forward and shoved Nehemiah aside, positioning himself between Moreau and his would-be killer, holding up his hands. "I'm telling you, Negro, this ain't the time. Put the damn knife down." He stood with his feet apart, ready to fight, and Moreau watched the two of them impassively, feeling a small hint of regret that more conflict was occurring on his account.

Nehemiah turned his rage on Edward now, and his eyes flashed as murderously as they had for Moreau. "You gon' fight your own people now? You want to join they side, after what they done? Alright!" He turned the knife around in his hand and extended it toward Edward, handle first. "Go on and take this knife—and put it through my heart." He grabbed Edward's smock with his free hand. "Do it, Eddie. If you ain't gon' let me kill him, then do his work for him. Huh, Eddie? Do it." His chest heaved, and he blinked rapidly. "*Do it!*" His deep throaty scream rumbled through the trees. Spittle ran down his chin, and tears welled in his eyes. In seconds he had gone from unholy wrath to watery tears that spilled down his face. When he spoke, his voice was pleading. "*Do it*, Eddie. Please."

Edward swallowed, his stance still guarded but his shoulders slumped. A second later he walked over and pulled the other man to his chest. Guttural, animal-like sounds of agony, Moreau was not sure from whom, were the only sound to break the heavy silence. For a while the two men embraced, and Moreau looked away. The voice that broke the silence was a woman's, but not Diantha's.

"They're alive. He has them, but they're alive." The men pulled slowly apart, Nehemiah wiping his face, Edward finally turning to look at Antonia, who was standing beside Diantha. The young woman wore a simple blue dress beneath a grey riding cloak, and she looked at the two men, seeming oblivious that she had come upon them in such a vulnerable state. She gazed down at Moreau, hers the first face since his arrival that did not possess either hatred or disgust; in fact, she might have looked relieved to see him.

He glanced at Nehemiah, who, for the moment, seemed to have forgotten about him. Tucking the knife away, he looked at the two women. "What he gon' do with them?"

Antonia glanced at Diantha, who had walked silently up beside her, then back at Nehemiah. "I don't know, but," her head drooped, "he's gone *mad*." She cut herself off and stepped over to Edward, burying her face in his chest. As she let out muffled cries, Nehemiah turned back to Moreau, but it was Diantha whom Moreau watched. Though her eyes were sunken and her forehead was creased with worry, she held herself much like she had when Moreau first met her. Like a proud mother, perhaps a queen. "From what the girl has told me," she said, pulling her black shawl tighter, "the man's madness has taken a turn. Worse than before."

Pulling herself from Edward's embrace, Antonia wiped her eyes and composed herself with a visible effort. "I'm sorry." She cleared her throat, then let out a long sigh. "Benton has taken them and put them in their own cottages—*locked* them inside. Until the master decides what to do with them, so he says. But it gets worse. Philippe, poor Philippe, has drawn Benton's particular hatred. Maybe because he's young and rebellious, maybe the man just hates him. I don't know. But," again she took a deep breath, "I saw them put the collar on him. Benton calls it the 'dog leash.' A metal collar, lined with sharp blade points, all pointed up—toward his neck. They put it on him perhaps two days ago. If he so much as droops his head, the points…poke into his neck. Others have worn it. Some don't survive it—they cut their throats intentionally. I'm sorry…" her lips quivered, and a moment later a burst of sobs came. Diantha shared a brief look with Edward, then took Antonia by the shoulders and the two headed back toward the village.

"I say we start our revenge," Nehemiah growled, pointing at Moreau, "with that one. He's a thief, and probably spying for them sons of bitches anyways."

Edward shook his head. "He's not spying for them."

"How you know that?"

Moreau stared up at him through glazed eyes. "Giroux's men killed the boy. If any of them have returned to the plantation—I'll gladly kill them myself."

Nehemiah waved a hand. "I don't need to listen to this fucking woodpecker. He can go drown in the bayou for all I care."

Edward sighed, slowly shaking his head. Until now, Moreau had felt something like a dead man walking, but as he looked at Nehemiah, for the first time that day, he felt an ember in his chest.

"What we need is to go get our people back."

"And how do you propose to do that?" Moreau cut in. "Walk in the front door?"

Nehemiah rounded on him with a murderous look. Slowly, however, his features widened into a cruel smile. "It's Toni, ain't it?" he finally said, referring to Antonia. "She arrives, and all of a sudden you want to speak. Well, boy...she with a real man now." He chuckled cruelly as Moreau rose to his feet with a grimace.

"I've heard enough from you." He met Nehemiah's mocking stare with a hard face, his grief giving way to a slow bubbling of anger. "Provoking me will get you nothing. Look around, you selfish fool. What have you done for your people? Have *you* protected them? The same men who attacked you here just kidnapped me and killed that boy." He nodded at the ashes of Will's pyre, and his nostrils flared. "If you think I'm in league with that slave-owning bastard, you're dumber than I thought."

Scowling savagely at the last comment, Nehemiah stepped slowly toward Moreau. "I'm dumb enough to say damn the consequences if I disobey the mambo...and kill you."

Moreau stared at him, unmoving. "Your anger scares these people, but I know men like you—I *was* one once. You think anger makes you hard? It makes you undisciplined and weak." He took a step closer, and the two men were almost face-to-face. "I've put fools like you in the dirt more times than I can count. Felt their bodies go limp as my sword passed through guts and reached air beyond."

"Try it, then." Nehemiah grinned coldly.

"Having your throat slit by me would be an honor you don't deserve." Moreau smirked. "But perhaps I would do it for the pleasure—"

Just then Edward slid between them, holding an arm out as Nehemiah leaned forward. "Try it, you fucking cripple."

Just then another figure stepped into the clearing, and from the corner of his eye Moreau saw the tall profile of Antoine, who also must have escaped capture. If it had been just Edward, the fight may not have been avoided, but the other man's presence drew Nehemiah's eye, briefly disrupting the tension that had nearly boiled over. Glancing at the newcomer, Moreau's anger eased just slightly.

"Eddie, Nee," the fellow drawled, his confusion evident, "I hate to interrupt whatever game y'all playin', but the mambo wants to speak with you." He looked at Moreau and chuckled softly. "And, uh, I think she means to keep this one alive. Maybe y'all can leave that to me." He held a bowl cut from a hollowed gourd in his hand, and approached Moreau. With another look back at Eddie and Nehemiah, he sighed. "Y'all get on, I'll keep watch on him." He nodded back toward the village, and to Moreau's surprise, the two men turned, Edward gently tugging on Nehemiah's shoulder as they trudged off out of sight.

Antoine turned back to Moreau with raised eyebrows. "Oh no, you don't have to thank me. I just brought you some soup—and saved yo' fuckin' ass."

Moreau let out the breath he'd been holding in and nodded at Antoine, who shook his head as he handed Moreau the gourd. Steam was rising from it, and after a brief sniff, Moreau took several sips. Since arriving at the village, he'd forgotten how hungry he was. Ravenous.

"Yeah," Antoine muttered, leaning back against a tree, "I'm supposed to keep watch on you. Make sure you don't run off."

Moreau continued to drink, ignoring the burning on his tongue. "I have nowhere to run."

"Maybe so," Antoine said, picking up a stick and snapping it in two, then tucking it in a sack at his waist. "But if I don't watch you, Nehemiah will. I don't think you want that." Moreau said nothing. "Anyway, Diantha told me you owe us a debt. Whatever that means. She don't want you dead 'til you pay it back. That's what she say, anyhow." Moreau drained the final sip and set the gourd on the ground, slumping down against a tree. For a while he sat, contemplating all that had happened in the span of a day. "Diantha," he said finally. "I haven't seen her like this. She's shaken."

"Wouldn't you be?" Antoine said, squatting down to Moreau's level. "Hell, she got us this far. Gave us shelter, led us while those mad fools hunted us. We always knew we had to leave; maybe she waited too long. It ain't nothing she could've helped, but she blames herself."

Moreau listened, questions beginning to pile up in his mind. "And how did she avoid capture?"

Antoine exhaled loudly. "Not sharing her people's capture is why she taking it so hard, I think. She was in the city, arranging travel for us. To safety—a new refuge. Trying to, anyways. That was why her and Nehemiah was fighting before you..." he trailed off as Moreau's brow furrowed.

"Fighting about what?"

Antoine puffed out his cheeks. "Our time here been dwindling for a while now. We couldn't stay forever. Not with that mad fool hunting us. But Diantha, from what I heard, wanted to get as many from that damned plantation as she could. She thought more could be saved. Nehemiah kept sayin' we should leave as soon as possible. He got the scars to show his experience with slave masters. She gave us more time...and this happened."

A twig snapping drew their attention, and both men turned to see Edward approaching. He drew nearer, picking up several sticks, as Antoine had done, then let out a sigh as he turned to Moreau. "You're lucky to be alive, friend." He sat down on a felled tree trunk a little way off, his bare feet squishing on a bed of damp moss. The smell of a fire reached Moreau's nostrils. "Some damn mess we're in," Edward muttered, snapping one of the sticks.

Moreau cleared his throat, the itching that had irritated his throat for some days seeming to get worse by the hour. "You all were out when they came?"

Edward nodded absently. "I was out with Gael. Diantha was in Congo Square. Antoine was with Nehemiah, who's back tending the fire now." He broke another stick, then sighed. "They came with dogs and muskets. Snuck in here like they knew exactly how to find us."

Moreau lowered his eyes. "Is that why he's so...unusually angry?"

"Nehemiah?"

Moreau nodded. "Because he was gone when it happened? Perhaps he blames himself."

Moreau saw Edward exchange a look with Antoine; both men's eyebrows raised, as if secretly conferring on some matter. Eventually Edward turned back to Moreau with a somber expression. "Let me tell you something about Nehemiah. He'd probably kill me if he knew I did..." He stole a look behind, then turned back. "That boy been through a lot. I never knew him before I came here, but those that did say he wasn't always...well...like this." He shook his head, a faint smile appearing before quickly vanishing, and he looked back at Moreau. "You've heard of the German Coast uprising?"

Moreau blinked several times. "I've heard talk of it among the militia, but none wished to tell me what happened."

Edward's gaze hardened. "It was three or four years ago. A group of boys, *slaves*, from Andry Plantation, just across the river, had had enough. Maybe beaten too much, I don't know. But a group broke into the master's chamber as he slept, and took machetes to him. He managed to escape...but his son was killed, and blood had been shed. Anyway, the boys from there ran down along the river road to the next one, then the next, telling 'em how they killed one of the masters, and they wasn't fixin' to stop until they'd been set free." He paused, and Moreau pursed his lips, thinking it not an entirely shocking scenario given what he'd seen on the one plantation.

"But that wasn't it," Antoine cut in. "By morning they'd gathered up over a hundred. Boys dropped they tools, left they cabins, and joined them ones on the river road. They was marchin' to the city to demand the governor free them—or they'd kill him too."

"By the following day they had hundreds," Edward said animatedly. "Some were on horseback, some were drumming, others carrying spades, the lucky ones had muskets taken from Andry and the rest. Well, white boys in the city didn't like that—and they called out the militia. Your boys." Edward glanced at Moreau with a scolding expression. "Anyhow, they fought some skirmishes; there were battles on the roads, in the woods—but our boys were outnumbered, and had no damn training, so they fled into the swamps. Dogs on their heels."

Moreau listened intently, his expression somber. "So—Nehemiah was part of that rebellion?"

Edward let out a slow breath, lowering his head. "Nehemiah was just a young'un at the time, working at a plantation where the rebels had stopped. His big brother had run out to the fields to join the fighting, and was wounded. The survivors ran off into the cypress swamp at the edge of the property, and when the militia came down to sweep up, Nehemiah joined them, not wanting to get snatched up himself. But his brother..." Edward's voice caught, and he looked at Antoine, who picked up the tale.

"Nehemiah's brother, Jack, was shot in the leg and couldn't escape. And uh, when the slave masters leading the militia found him, they...they..."

"Killed him?" Moreau asked quietly.

"No," Edward retorted harshly, "they didn't just *kill* him. They...dragged him out within sight of the swamps, where Nee and the others were hiding, and they tortured him. For, I don't know, maybe hours. I never asked Nee myself, of course, but some say they started off by…cutting off Jack's hands. To get him to scream, and draw out those hiding in the swamps. They burned the stumps with a torch to keep him from bleeding to death. Then they cut off one of his feet…and he screamed some more. They asked him where the rest of the rebels had gone to, but Jack just screamed at them. He never gave his people up. So they cut off another foot… and he stopped screaming. All the while Nehemiah…just sat there, listening, as they cut his brother to pieces. I've heard he jumped up to go help him, but others pulled him down, not to give away their hiding place. When Jack finally died…they started cutting up more prisoners. Their screaming was heard…" Edward let out a slow breath and closed his eyes. He rubbed a hand over his face and shook his head.

Antoine nodded absently. "Eventually the militia moved on; Nehemiah and the others managed to hide out until they was gone. But not before…they…uh…cut the heads off. His brother, Jack… his head was…put on a pike on the river road. Others too. I don't know, maybe hundreds. Heads on pikes, lining the river road. Gael says when it was over, Nehemiah just stood there, for hours, looking at his brother's head…" Antoine cut himself off, and for a while neither said anything more.

Moreau stared ahead with a blank look, feeling sick. Perhaps the exhaustion of the day had finally caught up to him, or maybe it was the memories from his own past that haunted him: men, women, and children massacred, drowned, executed without mercy by his army during the Revolution in France. He had been ordered to take part, but fired over the children's heads, unable to kill them, but knowing they would drown if he did not. He exhaled loudly, shaking his head.

Antoine stared vacantly, while tears fell from Edward's eyes. "Nehemiah has cursed God's name ever since."

Maman,

It does not please me to write this—but is father at home? Could you be induced to ask him, for me, if he might come here himself? I think I am alright, but I wonder if it isn't soon time for me to depart. I am no longer allowed to leave the plantation for any reason, and I no longer think life here is suitable for me. If you or father wishes to come for me, I would not refuse. Elyse and I have begun to discuss if we should leave—in secret.

C.

CHAPTER 30

Le Marais, Cypress Swamp, Outside New Orleans
January 3, 1815

Moreau's sore throat soon worsened into a full-blown illness, making speaking or swallowing difficult, and the lice and fleas that had plagued the camp at Line Jackson must have found him, as his hair and skin itched terribly. Diantha saw to it that he was given a blanket, Antonia that he was given more broth and water, and he was allowed to rest under the roof of one of the few huts that had not burned completely. He'd lost track of the date since the new year had come and gone, and with it the time left before the bounty on his head came due. He doubted the militia had taken much notice of his absence; Plauché or Savary may have, but he doubted he would be missed. He was wrong.

For the better part of four days, Moreau lay in a fever dream, careless of anything outside the rickety walls of the small hut. From time to time, Antonia would come in to check on him, joking that Nehemiah had decided against killing him until his strength had been restored. That did not occur quickly, but on the fourth morning since his arrival, he woke with little pain in his throat and wondered what was occurring outside his small shelter. Throwing off the blanket and wrapping himself in his coat, he made his way to the fire.

Diantha and Antonia were absorbed in some sort of needlework and talking quietly. Diantha motioned for him to sit on one of the logs near the fire. He looked around at the remains of the village; one of the other huts looked to have been partially restored, while several small shelters made of branches, sticks, and leaves had been built in the immediate area. The cooking pot smelled of herbs and some bland fare, probably rice. Antonia looked up with an exaggerated smile. "Did you have a restful repose?"

Moreau took in a breath, relieved that his throat no longer felt jabbed by needles, and nodded. Diantha sniffed, setting down the scarf she'd been knitting. "That's good. There's work to be done, and you've shirked long enough."

Moreau looked at the cookpot, and a moment later Antonia got up and ladled a spoonful of its contents into a gourd bowl. "It's not much, but it's better than starving."

Moreau took the gourd and wolfed down the stew, which, while lacking flavor, went down easier than he might've thought. Setting the empty bowl down beside him, he spoke in a hoarse voice. "Thank you, madame, for not having me killed. And I would like to apologize for coming back without your stone. I intend to rectify that."

Diantha's eyebrows arched questioningly. "We ask no apology; we simply demand restitution for what you took from us. Letting you live was a sign of our good faith."

Moreau nodded. "I should also mention that I was told of, um, Nehemiah's misfortune. His brother killed in front of him and so forth.... Anyway, I did not know. I am sorry for him."

"We are too," Diantha sighed. She said no more.

Moreau wiped his mouth and looked around. He could not deny that he felt restored, and with that, motivated to begin setting things right. But with just this small group left, there was no clear way to go about that. And he knew he could not stay here forever; he still had his duties with the Americans. When he looked at Antonia, he saw her eyes watching his, and felt a pang of regret. She looked as pretty as ever, but she belonged to another man. He sighed, and she said softly, "I'm sorry about the boy." She wiped a tear from her eye. "It's all a terrible mess."

Moreau nodded his thanks, and for a while the three sat in silence.

He was about to ask Diantha what she intended to do now, when she said to Antonia, "Are you going to make me tell him?"

Antonia's eyes flashed, before she touched the top of Diantha's head soothingly. "Marcel," Antonia said, her tone serious, "the news from Le Mouton Plantation is...worse than we thought." He found that hard to believe. "We've learned, well, *I* learned, something very bad is going to happen. Soon."

Moreau squinted. "What?"

Antonia sighed, fixing him with a solemn expression. "Giroux has gone mad. Well, he's *been* mad, but recently it's gotten worse. And he's allowed that devil Tremblay to influence his thinking—even to the point of murder."

Moreau was not exactly surprised but felt unsettled all the same. "How do you know this?"

"This girl," Diantha said, looking at Antonia with a hint of pride, "is not the moonstruck lass she was when she first came here. Of her own initiative, she returned to that godforsaken plantation as a friend and neighbor, pursuing her runaway field hand. But unbeknownst to them, she was my eyes and ears within."

Moreau gazed at Antonia. "You spied?"

Diantha smirked. "Yes, and rather well."

Antonia's face showed no amusement. "Some weeks back, I returned," Antonia said, "to learn of the condition of those still in bondage. I managed to convince Celeste to let me spend a few days helping her, alongside Elyse." She looked at Moreau as she said the last name, and he felt a brief but unmistakable flutter.

"I asked Celeste, whom I treated as a friend, about the field-hands and their condition. To my surprise, she answered. Having been on the grounds for some months now, she seemed rather more awakened to their plight, having initially taken them for happily employed, productive laborers. But those *men* began to tighten the noose to a frightening degree, and even that young woman seemed alarmed. I saw her wince when Giroux shouted at a young man for dropping a serving dish on the floor. He then forced him to drop to his knees and face the wall until the meal was over. After the meal, when she mildly scolded the old planter for his cruelty, his face grew red and he stormed from the table, shouting angrily about her ingratitude.

"Any rate, I returned a few days ago, *after* our people had been taken. That's when I overheard a conversation between Giroux, Benton, and Tremblay, as they discussed ways of punishing any slaves caught talking of escape—and deterring any considering it. They claimed 'unruly hands' had been caught spoiling food, damaging equipment, and so on. So they decided on requiring all the acolytes—as they call them—to swear an oath: never to shirk, never to betray the enterprise, and never to flee without permission. But," her voice caught, and she swallowed, "it was two nights ago that Elyse told me of something she overheard: a plan for a 'more *inspired* solution' to stop the runaways. Giroux was in his study with Tremblay, and apparently they agreed on a plan to collect insurance money from...lost slave hands."

Moreau frowned. "Lost?"

"What she means," Diantha said frostily, "is that those taken from here, runaways, are *lost* property. His men came here and took our people so they could collect the insurance money from their disappearance."

"Why would they retrieve them if they wanted to collect insurance from their being lost?" Moreau asked.

"Lost doesn't mean ran away," Antonia replied. "It means *dead*. They can't collect insurance on runaway slaves that are returned—but they *can* collect it if their deaths can be proven." Moreau repressed the uneasy feeling in his gut. "How can they—"

"Fire," Diantha said in a solemn voice. "If they are killed in an accidental fire, and there are witnesses to verify it, then the loss of property already insured means the owner is entitled to compensation."

Moreau squinted. "How could a fire kill so many?"

Antonia crossed her legs and wrapped her arms around her shoulders. "That's what I wondered...until that little weasel proposed his plan. Elyse said he reminded his master that the neighboring property, Aguilar Plantation, was in disrepair, abandoned by its owner, who had moved to a home in Natchez years ago. Its grass is overgrown, no crops sewn in season, livestock sold off. He claimed that a fire originating from that property could easily spread onto the hedge of shrubs and trees bordering Le Mouton, which goes all the way to the cypress swamp. If a fire caught those trees in the dead of night, it would engulf the slave cabins nearest the border hedge, 'killing the poor souls as they slept.'"

Her voice began to quiver, and her hands shook, but she continued. "Worse than that, when Giroux muttered that no man, slave or free, would sleep through a fire blazing in their own quarters, Tremblay replied, 'If they were to be confined in their quarters for punishment—then they would not be able to escape. A terrible tragedy, but not something anyone could have foreseen.' He explained that the locks could be removed before any authorities arrived, and by that time, the harsh light of culpability would have already begun to turn onto Aguilar Plantation. Its poorly tended grounds were an accident waiting to happen. A well-respected owner of a flourishing plantation, Tremblay said, need not suffer for the carelessness of his neighbor. Insurance for lost property would be paid out with hardly any dispute, and those 'disloyal hands' could be replaced by new, loyal acolytes."

When she finished speaking, Moreau snorted. "They're fucking mad if they mean to go through with it."

"They do," Diantha said tersely. "In two nights' time."

"How do you know that?"

Antonia exhaled, shivering. "Tremblay has taken a liking to your friend, Mademoiselle Pasteur." Moreau's lips curled in disgust. "Don't worry, he has not touched her, and his affections are most assuredly not returned. But she and her lady have played a little game—pretending to be at each other's throats. Celeste mistreats and abuses her attendant, while Elyse confides of her 'misfortunate rift' to him. His one blind spot, it appears, is her kindness towards him. And she visits with him enough so as not to arouse suspicion if seen in his chambers...where she found several papers in his desk.

One was a request for 'surplus security' to be paid to several nearby plantation owners. He's taken on a half dozen outside laborers for 'security.' Their payments cease in three days' time."

Moreau listened intently, as surprised by the subterfuge of the two women as by the machinations of the little administrator. He turned to Diantha. "And you believe all this?"

The woman raised an eyebrow. "If Toni says it's true, I believe her." She shifted her gaze to Antonia. "I've made several mistakes in recent days. Putting my faith in this one was not one of them."

Moreau shook his head. "I still don't understand, why would they do this?"

Diantha snorted. "You met that man—he is a fragile child masquerading as a powerful planter. I don't claim to know what damaged him so, but isn't it clear? Every one of those who fled his sick plantation came here to be free—free of him and his ilk. To his mind, they've abandoned him. *Betrayed* him. So they must be punished."

"He's the powder," Antonia added. "Tremblay simply knew where and when to put the fuse. I don't know which is worse." She shivered.

Moreau exhaled, a hard edge to his jaw. "Those bastards killed Will. Now they plan to slaughter your people. They must be stopped." The two women signaled their agreement, but neither seemed to have a solution ready at hand. For a while they sat in a thoughtful silence, the faint warmth of the small fire growing weaker by the minute.

"We'll see nothing done," Diantha finally said, "sitting idly in our gloom. We will tend to our tasks, and the loa of the forest will provide an answer. Gran Bois and Maître Carrefour have seen us this far; they will show us the way from here."

They dispersed and the day passed with the small group tending to various chores. That evening the group of survivors gathered around the fire, which, after a day of gathering wood, had plenty of fuel, and they ate a small meal.

Somewhat surprisingly, Nehemiah had made no overt threats to him that day, so Moreau took the relative detente to restore his energy, listening to the others chatting, which seemed surprisingly lighthearted given the circumstances they found themselves in. At one point Edward, who sat beside Nehemiah, began peeling an orange. When he'd finished, he tossed one of the peels at Antoine, who sat alone, blowing into a bowl of hot soup. Antoine swatted the rind away, then began sipping his soup, until Nehemiah tossed another peel—which landed in the bowl. With a curse, Antoine dropped it, spilling the steaming contents onto the ground. Edward almost fell down laughing, and Nehemiah stared at Antoine, as if daring him to do something in response. Antonia chuckled at the young man's misfortune, and even Moreau grinned as Antoine cursed and muttered impotent threats at the two other men.

After the laughter died down, Diantha turned the conversation back to their circumstances, which were far from lighthearted. "All this time, I questioned whether we were ready. Ready to leave, to live on our own terms. The truth is, we weren't ready—but now, we might be too late. We have no choice; now we must take action."

Moreau agreed, though still wondered how he could help them. If he returned to his camp, surely he would be interrogated about his absence, and returning with help from Savary or Plauché would be as likely as bringing help from the English. As the others discussed their predicament, Moreau's thoughts drifted to the Americans. Had the final attack come yet? Were they planning their own? He thought of Captains White, Roche, and Dubuclet and wondered how the Creoles were faring. Could that strange patchwork army of men of different cultures, languages, and colors stay united in common cause?

Hearing his name spoken, Moreau stirred, looking up to see each face staring at him. "What?"

Antoine laughed aloud. "She said to tell us something about yourself. Besides a soldier for Napoleon—our *enemy*—who are you?"

Diantha stared at him with piercing eyes, not hostile but curious. "Our people," she stated, "fought your countrymen in Haiti for many years. I was told by some that you men were weak; others claimed you were bloodthirsty killers who torture for sport." Moreau's eyes drifted briefly to Nehemiah, whose face made Diantha's look downright joyful. "So tell us. What kind of man are you really?"

"I was," Moreau began quietly, "or *am*, a soldier. That is the only word I know that can be ascribed to me truthfully. From a young age I was taught to hunt, and my uncle, who sold saddles and bred horses, taught me to ride, so perhaps that is why I ended up a dragoon when Napoleon turned France into an empire." He glanced up, thinking the others would be bored, but each was watching him with rapt attention—except Nehemiah, who was looking away and did not seem to be listening.

"Any rate," he continued, "after years on campaign, and witnessing atrocities I could never explain in words, I...soured on life. I don't know when exactly it happened, but for years I seemed to wander in a fog. A bleary-eyed, vengeful state that only seemed to have meaning when I had found a worthy opponent—and killed him. I fought over nine duels in the span of four years. Perhaps I was looking for an honorable death—but it never found me. A colonel of dragoons was appointed over me in Prussia, and somehow he managed to pull me from the brink." Moreau laughed coldly. "For a time I hated André Valière, wanted to kill him, even. But he was not afraid of me, one of the few, and must have possessed both the strength to stop me and the grace to forgive me. He brought me to healing me when I was wounded, and when I was wounded again, he brought me to his home, where I stayed for a while.

"Unable to live as a farmer—the life did not suit me—I found my way to Spain, where I was taken on as household security for an aristocrat in the civil service. But by the summer of 1813, Napoleon's armies were floundering, and my patron's mission in Valencia ended, so we departed for France in August. I was in command of the convoy: thirty wagons, twenty armed guards, thirty-two civilians, and, most important of all, my patron's baggage train. Nearly four years of plunder crammed into his convoy—works of art, furniture, silverware, carpets, chests of coins, and, for good measure, his wife and children.

"Despite the overloaded wagons, for several days we made decent progress, until we reached a small town outside Zaragoza, where a guerilla leader named Espoz y Mina had been relentlessly harrying the French army. The villagers had assembled on a hacienda at the edge of the hills and were in a state of noisy agitation, so I asked what had brought about such commotion. At first reticent to speak to a Frenchman, one of them finally blurted out that Espoz y Mina's men had been seen moving through the region, and they did not want to side with his men, nor us, knowing that support for one meant reprisals from the other. I informed them that we were not a military convoy but a civilian train. We passed through the village peacefully, but a league or two beyond we spotted movement in the hills above.

Moreau fell silent, as if hesitant to continue. "Upon seeing the hills," he said finally, "occupied by the guerillas, men who had torn the emperor's troops to pieces, I took a review of those in my trust: French and Spanish soldiers, servants and valets, wives and daughters. I couldn't justify fighting a hopeless battle, only to see them overrun and slaughtered. I'd led a squadron of dragoons to near-annihilation in Poland, and the memory of that haunts me to this day. So I made the only decision that seemed right: we fled. We left the cumbersome wagons behind and made a quick escape to safety in a fortress twenty miles north, where I was confronted with the severity of my mistake. I had lost all of my patron's property and possessions. But it was there I learned of my greatest mistake. The guerillas I had been so fearful of…were simply a group of curious locals. Cowherds and shepherds traversing the heights overlooking the town. I had taken them for a dangerous enemy force—because I was afraid. Afraid to lead others to their deaths. I panicked, and tucked tail." Moreau's eyes passed over the group, landing momentarily on Nehemiah, who was now watching him with a grave expression.

"We crossed the Pyrenees in September, and when I reunited with my patron in Toulouse, I felt the cold, dispassionate wrath of a rich man who has been robbed of the greatest gift life could bestow upon him: hard-earned plunder. It wasn't the danger his wife and children had been put in that disturbed him—but the wealth gained over years, gone in a single day. He informed me that I would repay him the fortune before the end of the following year...or there was no corner of heaven or earth that he would not find me and make me regret having failed him.

"I've been afraid," Moreau concluded, "to lead others into danger ever since. One day of cowardice—for a lifetime of soldiering."

Diantha glanced pensively at him. "I don't think you a coward, Marcel Moreau. When you first came here, I thought you weak. Then I saw you fight this one...and was reminded of a cornered leopard." She sighed, rising slowly to her feet. "But violence is only ever part of the solution. It takes more courage to heal the damage within than to pay it back to a cruel world."

She wrapped her shawl tighter and gazed around the group. Nehemiah's eyes did not rise from the crackling fire. "All of you get some sleep. Tomorrow we end our mourning—then we take our next steps."

The following day Moreau woke to a heavy mist enshrouding the village. He thought it fitting given the events of recent days. "Antonia's gone to see to a few tasks," Diantha said, handing Moreau a cup of hot tea. She saw his curious look and smiled. "She'll run some errands for us. A lifelong free woman escapes suspicion."

"And she has a horse," Edward blurted, smiling at Diantha, who ignored his enthusiasm.

"Otherwise," a new voice added, "she could ride on Antoine's scrawny ass into town." Behind Edward, Nehemiah rubbed the barrel of his musket with a small rag, and noticed their attention turned on him. "The hell y'all lookin' at me for? Boy's useless as a lame mule unless he running somewhere. Usually from a fight."

Edward chuckled. "Or from Dyola after he steals her rum."

Moreau saw that Diantha was using a rock to grind a white powder in a wooden bowl. When he squinted at it, she simply said, "We don't go to a fight without preparing our vévé."

"A fight with the plantation?" he asked.

"We're not just gonna let them take our people." Edward said flatly. Nehemiah's hard stare showed where he stood on the matter.

"Well enough," Moreau said, "but Antonia said they've hired additional security on top of the overseers already there. That's at least a dozen armed men."

"At least," Edward replied.

"If you scared, you can leave," Nehemiah muttered.

"I'm not afraid," Moreau said, turning his eyes on him, "but I can count. The handful of us, with two muskets between us, against more than a dozen, is foolish, not brave."

Diantha ground away at the powder, ignoring his comment, while Edward shrugged. Approaching footsteps caused Moreau to turn, and he saw the Haitian called Gael run up. The man was average height and slightly heavyset, but he moved with agile grace. "Mambo," he said, breathing easily. "Im yah. Whah four wid 'im."

Diantha nodded, setting her bowl on the ground. "Well, let's go see what Le Phantom has to say."

> *Maman, please send father, or any help. Who was that man I met in the city? Do please send anyone you can. I am afraid.*
>
> *Your daughter Celeste*

CHAPTER 31

Le Marais, Cypress Swamp, Outside New Orleans
January 4, 1815

A small guard of four Baratarians trailed Jean Lafitte, while one walked beside him. The bald man was nearly a head shorter than his commander, who wore a dark-blue coat with gold trim and piping, not unlike one of Napoleon's marshals. As they came closer, Moreau shifted his eyes from the commander of the Baratarians to his bald companion, who wore grey trousers and a simple grey coat over a white shirt. With a start, Moreau recognized him, though he wasn't sure from where. Finally recalling his first night in the city at Maspero's, he shook his head.

"What's the matter?" Lafitte asked, nodding as he approached Diantha's group. "You look like you've seen a ghost."

The men with him halted behind him. They were dressed in red or blue coats, still sporting bandanas or hats, but they looked slightly more kempt than when Moreau had last seen them. Two carried large sacks over their shoulders, all wore curved swords at their sides, and two had pistols visible on their belts.

"Forgive my guarded appearance, madame," Lafitte said, taking Diantha's hand and gently kissing it. "I hope you understand we come as friends."

"You come and go as you like, Jean," Diantha said. "It wouldn't matter what I thought of your appearance."

He gave her a charming smile, though Moreau saw the creases on his face and the bags under his eyes. Despite his grace and ease, he was exhausted.

"Well, *Jean* comes and goes as he pleases, but *Le Phantom* knows to tread lightly on the sacred grounds of your hounfour, madame." His eyes scanned briefly to either side, and he spoke in a gentle voice. "I am truly sorry for your misfortune. I hope the small help I bring might provide some relief. It is all I could spare." He turned back and nodded. The bald man, Gambio, as Moreau remembered, whistled to the men others, and they began unloading the sacks, which looked to contain small bags of food and some weapons as well.

Lafitte met Moreau's eyes with a grin. "It is good to see you well, Major. There was worry in your camp when you failed to appear for so many successive roll calls. But I had a feeling you had your business in hand."

Moreau watched him a moment before glancing at the stump of his missing arm. "I've always disliked the puns of sailors."

"And I've always distrusted professional soldiers." His eyes flashed a moment before he laughed heartily. He stepped forward and the two men embraced. "You know," Lafitte said, leading Moreau toward the firepit, "some thought you deserted to the English. I had to threaten to hang one of my men for spreading false rumors."

Moreau smirked, patting the man's hand on his shoulder before removing it. "You're a good man, Jean, and a good friend. And I don't believe half the bullshit you say." Lafitte laughed as he motioned for the rest to take seats by the fire.

When his guards had unloaded the bags, they stood a few steps back from the rest, scanning the nearby swamp. They, in turn, were watched closely by Edward and Nehemiah, who did little to disguise their hard stares. Whatever truce Le Phantom had with Diantha and her people, it was not lost on former slaves that Lafitte's fortune had come from the slave trade.

Nevertheless, for a while Lafitte and Diantha engaged in light conversation, discussing circumstances in the city or past meetings in happier times. The group from Le Marais ate heartily of the bread and poultry Lafitte's men had brought, augmented by several bottles of wine and some fine-smelling tobacco leaves. Moreau was relieved to finally eat something more substantial than broth, and after he'd eaten a chicken leg, several rolls, and that creamy confection called a praline, he puffed on a cigar tossed to him by the Baratarian commander.

"The people of the city are bearing up well," Lafitte said, sipping a small glass of port, "and we've just returned from an inspection of Le Temple, to ensure our last stores of flints, powder, and muskets have been sent to Jackson's men." He turned to Moreau, his face serious. "Speaking of Old Hickory, I dined with him and Messieurs Livingston, Latour, and Davezac only two days ago. We agreed that the English are out of options, and that the attack will come any day now. So you ought to return to the lines before you miss the grand finale."

Moreau tapped ash from his cigar, suppressing the guilt he felt for his absence. "I will return when I can," he said finally, "but in the meantime, the militia are in good hands. Plauché is no fool."

Lafitte grinned slyly. "You there," he said, gesturing to Nehemiah, who was standing a few steps back from Diantha. "Why don't you have a seat with us, monsieur?"

Nehemiah lifted his chin. "Why don't you mind your fucking business."

Gambio, seated to Lafitte's right, produced a blade from his sleeve so fast that even Moreau was taken aback. The man's expression hardly changed, other than to assume a slight frown, but his knuckles showed white on the hilt of the dagger. Lafitte slowly pushed Gambio's hand down and shook his head. "It's alright, Vincent. These people have seen much sorrow; we know ourselves what it's like to have our homes burned, our livelihoods destroyed, and our dignity affronted." He looked at Nehemiah, then Moreau, settling on Diantha. "But, of course, gratitude is always a virtue."

Diantha smiled impassively. "Your provisions are more than generous," she said, "and the weapons cannot but be useful. As you can see, we do not lack for enemies." Lafitte nodded, his face darkening. "But we also know you are a busy man, and surely have other affairs to attend to."

Lafitte puffed on his cigar and nodded. "I'll be inspecting the forts at Petite Coquilles after this, then on to the city." Sighing, he rose slowly to his feet, his guards shifting restlessly, eager to be off. "My lady, a private word, if I may?"

Diantha nodded and the two strode off out of sight, engaged in some deep conversation.

Moreau took advantage of their absence to converse with Gambio, who informed him that he'd been sent on errands throughout the swamps of the region: from Lake Pontchartrain and the Gentilly Pass all the way south to English Turn on the Mississippi. He assured Moreau that every waterway within sixty miles of New Orleans was patrolled by Baratarians or the American navy, spitting as he said the last two words.

"From what I've seen," Gambio said, "Jackson would do well to inspect the right bank batteries across from Line Jackson."

Moreau replied with an inquisitive look.

"Well, Jean thinks if the English are stupid enough to try a frontal attack against the main lines, they'll be carved to pieces. But if they manage to cross the river and sweep the right bank, turning the batteries on Jackson's men from across the river?" He cocked his head with a knowing grin.

Moreau squinted, his mind turning the idea over. After a moment he felt a sudden urge to hug the ugly man—for a reason entirely unrelated—when footsteps caused him to turn around.

"Well," Lafitte said, resting a hand on his saber hilt, "that's enough port for me, if I wish to keep my wits." He winked at Diantha. When he spoke again, his voice was clear and sober. "I know you are all eager for revenge against the men who ravaged your homes. You will have it. But be cautious, I know a little of Giroux, and though petulant, he has accrued men and resources for himself while most of the other planters have given theirs to the war effort. Be patient, and strike only when you are ready." He looked at Moreau and nodded. "A word, Monsieur Moreau?"

Moreau followed Lafitte as he strolled slowly away from the others. When the Baratarian commander turned to face him, Moreau once again saw the face of a man driven to exhaustion. Lafitte exhaled wearily, speaking in a quiet, earnest tone that he seemed to save for private conversations. "I did not expect to see you here, Marcel."

"Me neither. But I cannot abandon them now, after all this."

Lafitte nodded. "I understand. And I wish them well, but the uncertainty of waiting robs more men of their nerves than the sound of guns, in my experience. Do not let them throw their lives away, if you can prevent it. I do believe the game is almost up, one way or another."

"Which game is that?" Moreau asked. Lafitte stared vacantly a moment, then fixed the Frenchman with an ominous stare. "Moreau, two days ago my men reported seeing two…strangers at the docks. They were not Americans, and though discreet, they visited several customs houses…asking about a man come from Le Havre."

Moreau's eyes hardened.

"They were looking for you."

Moreau let out a grim chuckle. "They were. They've come to collect a debt. And my time to pay it is gone."

"Men like that," Lafitte said, "do not arrive with a warning. They come with daggers in the night."

Moreau nodded. "Or poison. Or pistols."

Lafitte took a step closer, resting a gentle hand on Moreau's shoulder. "She told me of your theft of her stone—bah, don't trouble yourself about it. I've given her triple its value from my own stores." Moreau looked up, incredulous.

"My friend, I have treasures that would make King George blush; it is nothing." He gazed around, a thoughtful look on his features. "My time in Louisiana is drawing to a close, Marcel. I am grateful to finally show my true colors to the Americans, and I will continue to do all that I can, but our hold at Barataria is destroyed, and my men grow restless. As do I."

"Why are you telling me this?"

Lafitte smiled. "Come with me. Bah, don't look at me like that; you would be a valuable addition to our number—those that remain, anyway. I've heard the Spanish governor of Galveston covets rubies. If you can recover the one taken from you.... Anyhow, that is where I plan to go, as soon as I can depart." He eyed Moreau expectantly. "Come with me. Diantha will not begrudge your departure; she has been reimbursed for her loss. But you, my friend, are being hunted by professional killers. I can offer you protection, and those rascals will be none the wiser. Think of it: wealth and plunder enough to rid yourself of debt forever. Leave those troubles in the Old World, and your pursuers in your wake. A few years working with me, and others will soon owe *you*."

Moreau let out a long sigh as he considered what he was hearing. The new year had come and gone, and his assassins had finally arrived. Could he avoid them long enough to escape? Could Lafitte truly offer him a future filled with treasure and security? At length he rubbed his jaw, chuckling to himself.

"When I first arrived in this city," he said, "all I heard was talk of the 'Blacksmith of Bourbon Street' and Lafitte and his *ferocious pirates*. Well, I befriended one of your number, a boy not twelve. He accompanied me here—you may remember him. Anyway, I finally met the famed blacksmith, or Le Phantom, as the life was being choked out of me. By that one over there." He pointed at Edward, who was sitting beside Nehemiah. "Your arrival saved my life. Now, if I can save any of theirs, I must try. The boy was killed by the men who did all this. And if I ever rejoin the Americans, I will finish my business with them too. So, Jean, I wish you luck in Galveston, or wherever the tides carry you, but for now my place is here. My assassins will just have to wait."

Lafitte spread his hands, grinning ruefully. "I had to try, monsieur." He embraced Moreau once more, tapping his shoulders affectionately. "I wish you well, Marcel. The Americans are in good hands, and God help anyone who crosses both you *and* Diantha."

Moreau grinned, offering his thanks.

With that Lafitte bid farewell to the others, then melted into the mist with his men at his heels, true to the name given him by these people. A dreary silence settled among those remaining, until Moreau met Diantha's eyes. Each stared intensely at the other.

"Well, now that we have sufficient weapons," Moreau said, "we might as well plan."

"Plan for what?" Antoine asked over the brim of his soup bowl.

Diantha looked around the group, her gaze severe. "To go get our people back."

The following day Antonia rode back to the city to procure more provisions—blankets, flour, fresh water—and to complete one especially important errand given to her by Moreau. She returned late in the evening with her saddlebags overloaded with supplies, but it was the following morning, with the arrival of a captain in the American army, that the real purpose of her trip bore fruit.

Captain Hubbard's arrival at Le Marais was met with no particular fanfare, but after a long conversation with Moreau, the way in which he could offer assistance became clear: men and, more importantly, boats. Moreau had managed to convince Diantha and Edward to allow the young captain into their refuge not because they needed guns or powder—Lafitte had provided those—but because Moreau knew the American army had commandeered every barge, flatboat, and pirogue from the Gulf to Baton Rouge for the duration of the campaign. When Edward asked Moreau what they needed boats for, Moreau smirked, weighing his plan for how they could best infiltrate Le Mouton Plantation, with minimal casualties, and with a fighting chance to save as many of the slaves as possible.

"It's bold," Moreau explained, "but we can't just saunter up the main drive with our intentions stamped on our foreheads. Well, he added wryly, "*you* will, but only as a distraction."

He then described his plan of attack, which involved Captain Hubbard and his sergeant, McCann, escorting Edward to the main entrance, claiming he was a runaway they had captured in the swamp. Simultaneously, Moreau, Nehemiah, Gael, and Antoine would row two small pirogues, "borrowed" from Hubbard's command at the city docks, and approach the plantation from the bayou that marked its northern boundary. While Giroux, Benton, and the rest were collecting their prize at the entrance, Moreau's party would sneak ashore, neutralize any nearby guards, and unlock the slave cabins. After sending the escapees toward safety across the river road and out of sight from the plantation, Moreau and their other three would make their way to the entrance. At the appointed signal, Captain Hubbard and McCann would reveal their charade, and every one of their guns would unleash hell on the plantation owner and his guards. That done, they and the freed slaves would scape into the relative safety of the cypress swamp, and from there south toward Le Temple and what remained of the Baratarian hideouts.

Edward shook his head with a grunt. "It's not bold—it's mad." He looked at Captain Hubbard, who had joined them for Moreau's walk-through using stones and sticks to represent the features of the plantation. "I don't know this one, and I'm not in a hurry to trust him to lead me up to the lion's den without Giroux's men shooting us then and there."

Moreau eyed the young captain, whose attention was still on the mock plantation. "I trust him," Moreau said. "He's made of sterner stuff than you may think. And he's been shoved as far from the front as possible by his fool commander and is eager to prove himself."

Hubbard, who did not understand the French that Moreau and Edward spoke, looked at Moreau with a curious expression. Moreau smiled. "They debate whether or not they should kill you," he teased. "I tell them wait until after the mission. If you muck it up, I'll do it myself."

If he found the jibe humorous, Hubbard didn't show it. At length he drew himself up, his dark-blue uniform with silver piping and long officer's hat seeming out of place in this swampy warren. "It's a fine plan, Major. But...I'm not sure of the legality of me engaging in conflict with a propertied plantation owner. However unsavory his behavior may be."

Nehemiah snorted loudly, glaring at the captain with a cruel smile. "You ain't sure of the *legality*?" He shoved forward from the tree he had been leaning against and walked slowly toward Hubbard. "What about the *legality* of locking our fucking people in cabins and burning them alive? Is *that* legal?" He halted inches from Hubbard's chin, looking up at the taller officer with a hard stare. The rest waited in a tense silence. Relieved to see the captain not backing down, Moreau looked at Edward with a smirk, and Edward sighed. Stepping over to Nehemiah, he put a hand on his chest and chuckled. "Alright, Nee, you made your point. He ain't gonna help us if you get to fussing and fighting with him."

Nehemiah finally relented, grimacing at the captain before turning away with a low growl. Hubbard swallowed hard and looked relieved to see Moreau grinning at him. "I can get two boats, and maybe another soldier or two. But, sir, we're in deep waters here. I hope you know what you're about."

Moreau looked into the fire and nodded. "The best ships can *only* sail in deep waters." He pulled a flaming twig from the fire and lit a cigar, taking several puffs. "We have enough pistols, knives, and cutlasses, thanks to Monsieur Lafitte. The question is," he looked around at every man present, "do you have the stomach for a stand-up fight with these men?"

Edward grinned, looking at Antoine and then Nehemiah. Antoine, who'd been standing quietly beside Edward, bobbed his head. "I ain't been one to go looking for fights, but I seen what you and Edward got into when you first came here. If y'all unleash that mess on that planter and his boys, and Nehemiah bring his machete..." He shook his head and chuckled. "I ain't fixin' to be on the wrong side of that. Shit, I'll go."

Edward shrugged. "I'm in. Nee?"

Nehemiah squatted down and stared into the flames with an unreadable expression. He let out a breath as he looked up at Moreau. "We let one white boy into our swamp, and now we doing some stupid shit like this." Turning toward Edward, his nostrils flaring, he spoke in a low voice. "I was born for this. Of course I'll go."

CHAPTER 32

Le Mouton Plantation, Outside New Orleans
January 7, 1815

Gentle ripples spread across the water where dim moonlight pierced the cypress trees, clumps of Spanish moss drooping from their gnarled branches. The narrow, murky canal had opened into a wider bayou, which Moreau admitted made for a rather picturesque setting. Supposedly this waterway would carry them behind the fields of Le Mouton Plantation, but crossing open water under moonlight increased the risk of exposure, and he whispered to slow the pirogue. In front of him, Gael backed his paddle—wrapped in cloth to muffle noise—into the water, slowing their pace. The boat to their right, bearing Antoine and Nehemiah, pulled slowly ahead. The two men were paddling faster than Moreau would have preferred. Stealth, not speed, was key here.

Seeing no lights or structures yet, Moreau fidgeted impatiently, wiggling his toes and relishing the comfort of his planter boots. They had been retrieved, along with his dark militia coat, by Captain Hubbard, who had returned for this raid after a brief spell at his post in the city. Tucked in Moreau's belt was a pistol gifted him by Lafitte, along with a replacement saber from the city's armory, also courtesy of Hubbard. Admittedly, the young captain was taking a significant risk by returning, and for providing the two pirogues formerly used by the army to ferry weapons across the Mississippi. He claimed no one would question his few hours' absence, but still Moreau appreciated his help, especially as rumors had spread that the English were marshalling for their long-awaited assault.

Moreau checked his timepiece: almost the appointed hour. If all remained on schedule, Hubbard should be nearing the front entrance of the plantation with Sergeant McCann and their "captured runaway," Edward Milroy. Hopefully it would appear they were returning a slave to a planter who might know what to do with him. If things went according to the plan, their arrival would cause a stir among the guards at the entrance, attracting the attention of Giroux and the others and luring them to the front, allowing the boat party to unlock the slave cabins in the back of the grounds. That group would then join Hubbard, McCann, and Edward in dealing with the plantation owner and his guards.

Nevertheless, Moreau knew that no mission, however well prepared, progressed without a stick being thrust in its spokes. Soon a faint light came into view up ahead. A moment later more lights showed farther off, and as the trees along the bank loomed closer, he saw the silhouettes of the slave quarters and workshops, finally glimpsing the outline of the manor house's roof perhaps a quarter-mile away. He twitched his fingers as he watched the boat carrying Antoine and Nehemiah slide onto the muddy bank. Finding a gap in the tall swamp grass, Gael guided their pirogue to the shore and stepped nimbly from the bow. He turned and tugged the bow partially onto the embankment and pulled a long knife from his belt, then crept slowly through the trees toward the slave cabins.

Moreau swung his legs over the side and dropped softly into shallow water. His boots were thick enough that he did not feel water right away, and after stepping onto the muddy bank, he halted, tilted his head, and listened. For several moments he heard only the cypress branches swaying in the breeze, and the steady drum of his heartbeat. When he was satisfied no alarm had been sounded, he stepped forward to join Gael, who was waiting in the trees.

A forceful tug on his right foot caused him to wince, and he grunted as he lost his balance and fell forward onto the muddy ground. Turning back with a grimace, it took him a moment to register what had happened, and when he saw what had grabbed his boot—and still held it's grip—his eyes widened.

"Fuck."

In a state of near shock, he stared at the large crocodile, its serrated black hide seeming like some strange suit of armor, slick and glistening in the dim moonlight. Instinctively Moreau threw both arms out, gripping frantically for purchase on the muddy ground with his right hand. The tugging persisted, and he felt his hand slipping despite a firm grasp. The monstrous creature held his right boot in its jaws, and wrenched several times in quick succession, dragging Moreau's feet and ankles into the water. When it stopped tugging, Moreau noticed its huge reptiian eyes: two small, lifeless beads, devoid of any intelligence save a mechanical attention to its immediate task, which presently seemed to be dragging tugging Moreau into the swamp—and devouring him.

Moreau dug his left bootheel into the ground, but another tug from the beast pulled him almost knee-deep into the water. "Shit."

He swung his right foot once, twice, three times with as much strength as he could manage, but his efforts were no match for the ferocious animal. A thought of the pistol at his belt flashed through his mind, but he dared not release his grip on the bank, tenuous as it was. Sliding deeper into the muddy water, he felt the croc clamp down even harder, the terrible pressure beginning to cause serious pain. He thought if the monster bit down again, his anklebone might break, so he jerked his foot with all his might—to little effect.

A sudden pressure on his left shoulder caused Moreau to snarl, and he turned his head, expecting to see another crocodile. But it was Nehemiah's hand that gripped him, and he saw the man's grimacing face, teeth flashing, as he grunted with effort. "Pull, goddamit!" Nehemiah growl, reaching his other hand under Moreau's right armpit. "Pull!" Moreau felt as though he would be pulled apart, and he cried out as he pushed down with his free leg.

He set his hand down again and pushed, jerking his right ankle as he did. For another few seconds this tug- of- war continued until

Moreau heard a sound like paper being torn, and the boot slid off his right foot as the crocodile's head raised up in the air. Chomping with a terrifying strength, the reptile's jaws slammed together with a sound like one cannon ball being dropped on another. Moreau fell back against Nehemiah, and as both men scrambled back up into the mud. In a flash the crocodile turned and disappeared beneath the surface, sending small waves onto the bank, which soon eased into gentle ripples, belying the chaotic and primal scene that had just taken place. Moreau rolled onto his side and let his head drop onto the ground, panting loudly. Nehemiah's own heavy breaths were audible, and for a moment neither man moved a muscle.

When Moreau finally looked down, he expected to see a mangled and bloody stump—if it was still there at all. To his surprise, though very pale, his foot was uninjured. As if to make sure, he wiggled his toes and felt only a little pain—thankfully nothing seemed to be broken. Recalling who had saved him, he looked toward Nehemiah, who was now sitting up, exhausted. He stared at Moreau, no longer breathing heavily, but with eyes still wide with strain. Moreau rose to a crouch, almost laughing at the thought of his sturdy planter's boots saving his life—or at least his foot. He groaned as he stood and extended his hand to the other man.

"Thank you."

Nehemiah licked his lips and lifted himself to his feet, ignoring Moreau's outstretched hand. He reached to the cord that served as his belt and produced a pistol, cocking the hammer with a hard expression. "Let's get this over with." He stalked off into the trees as if nothing unusual had happened, leaving Moreau to catch his breath as he looked at his bare foot, smirking to himself before following Nehemiah into the tall swamp grass.

Thankfully the slave cabins were closer than the workshops, so their approach was obscured to anyone milling about the grounds. They moved cautiously nonetheless, covering one another as they crept between the dwarf palmettos and oaks. After five minutes or so, with no sign of any guards, they reached the two long rows of small shacks that extended in either direction for several hundred feet. As Moreau pushed forward, a movement to his right caught his eye. Antoine, distinguishable by his tall, lean frame, halted abruptly and dropped to the ground, followed by Nehemiah and Gael. Moreau froze, searching for whatever had startled them, then crouched behind a thin oak and waited. A few seconds later he heard soft footsteps, and a figure passed between two of the shacks before stopping. In the darkness, the man's face was impossible to make out, but the long barrel of his musket was easily seen. He stood motionless a moment, his misty breath billowing in the night air.

"Jesse, that you?" The man shifted his weight and cocked his head, listening. "The foreman wants you watching the *bousillage*."

Moreau slowly turned toward the three men on his right, but they were no longer in sight. Mouthing a curse, he prayed they weren't stupid enough to cry out or use their firearms. The man with the musket waited a moment before turning back toward the manor house. As two shapes crept quietly toward him, the man turned hastily turned around. "Who's ther—" Nehemiah and Antoine pounced on him like wolves on a deer. Moreau saw the flash of blades in the pale light, then heard a grunt as the man dropped.

Moreau winced, waiting for a shout, but it didn't come. He heard only grunts and thuds as the men's knives rose and fell, until the sounds drifted away and silence returned. Moreau let out a relieved breath, and Gael, a few paces in front of him, emitted a grim chuckle. Several moments later Nehemiah approached, Antoine a few steps behind. Nehemiah's eyes were murderous, and Antoine's, from what Moreau could see, looked wild and frenzied. He had never killed before, Moreau realized, feeling a brief pang of pity for the young man. Nehemiah broke the silence. "The distraction at the gate is late," he said in a hard voice. "You better hope that captain ain't betrayed us."

Moreau stepped forward, catching a glimpse of the dead body in the short grass. He had to admit he was impressed; their attack had been quick and lethal, preventing the man from crying out, or firing a weapon, and alerting the entire plantation. Moreau looked down at his bare foot and wiggled his toes. "You have the shears?" he asked Gael.

The short man raised a pair of sharp metallic cutters. Hopefully they were strong enough to cut the locks.

"Alright. We've made it this far; let's do what we've come to do. Gael, Antoine, work your way in from the outer cabins. Your people will be confused and frightened—be sure to keep them quiet. And send them that way," Moreau motioned to his left, "away from the house. Jean-Pierre or Tall Johnny gets the last pistol. Nehemiah and I will keep watch while you work. Go."

They scattered, Gael going to the right, Antoine to the left, each with a pair of crude shears to cut the locks, while Moreau and Nehemiah moved forward. A moment later the latter two were in position, each with a view of the workshops a hundred or so paces ahead. Both stood still as statues as they watched for movement. And then the thing Moreau feared most happened. Muffled cries arose as the prisoners began to emerge from the cabins. Moreau could hear Gael's accented voice imploring them to quiet, but every so often a cry or sob could be heard as the number of escapees grew and they made their way toward the fields on the far side of the plantation.

A loud commotion erupted from somewhere toward the front of the plantation, and the excited screeches and hollers could only mean that Edward and his "captors" had arrived. Moreau licked his lips, impatiently waiting for the rest of the cabins to be emptied. He knew they would not have much longer and hoped the distraction would buy them a few minutes more. His hopes were dashed, however, when he saw three men approaching from the manor house. Two were armed with muskets, the third was carrying what looked like a long, heavy club. Moreau swallowed hard, fingers twitching on the pistol in his hand. He turned, looking for Nehemiah, but he was not there, and Moreau muttered a curse. The three approaching men halted and huddled together as if to confer. Their voices were faint, and Moreau strained to listen.

"Don't know. You go check the *grande* kettle house; we'll check here and give you the signal." The fellow with the club turned and trotted out of sight while the other two continued forward.

Moreau's heart thumped in his chest as someone flew into his field of vision and drew up beside him. He raised his pistol, but Nehemiah swatted it down with a sneer. "Calm down, snow leopard, it's just me." He leaned forward and glanced out just long enough to see the two approaching men. His nostrils flared as he looked at Moreau. "You ready?"

Moreau shoved the pistol into his belt and slowly drew his saber, wincing at the soft *clang*. The men were still coming closer, but Moreau started when he saw a lone figure standing atop the veranda of the main house.

"What is it?" Nehemiah whispered.

"There's a man standing watch on the veranda."

"So? We kill these sons of bitches, then take him."

"Listen, you idiot..." Moreau stopped, shaking his head and fighting to keep his voice low. "Just listen. That man on the veranda, whoever he is, is still alert. He's the one to be wary of. It's likely Benton." Nehemiah still had murder in his eyes, but he did not interrupt. "Your people are not out of this yet. The closer we get to freeing them, the greater the danger. We kill these two, but keep quiet. Lower your head and follow my lead."

They emerged from behind the tree together, Nehemiah's head lowered and his knife hand behind him, Moreau gripping his collar. The two men halted abruptly, feet shuffling in the dirt. Moreau spoke with the best Creole accent he could manage. "Look here, caught me one trying to escape." He pushed Nehemiah forward, keeping his head down but stealing a quick peek at the two men, who were now less than twenty feet away. At least they had lowered their weapons.

"Jesse? That you?"

A tap on Nehemiah's shoulder was the signal, and both men leapt forward, Moreau slashing with his saber and Nehemiah thrusting with his knife. They dispatched their victims with a hushed but savage ferocity, Moreau eventually having to pull Nehemiah away from his victim's corpse. As Moreau took Nehemiah's shoulder, he saw the man's crazed eyes and allowed him a moment to pull himself together. When he was sure the young man would not cry out in rage or triumph, and somewhat surprised that he had not, Moreau led the way forward again.

When they finally reached the workshops, the main house came into view just ahead. More lights now shone in the windows, and frenzied voices could be heard. One figure, somewhat stooped and moving slowly, halted at the banister atop the veranda and looked out toward the workshops and slave cabins. For several moments he stood motionless, watching. It had to be Giroux. A moment later he was joined by a lean man with a slight bob to his step, like some curious bird. Moreau took him to be Tremblay.

Soft footsteps nearby drew Moreau's attention, and Gael came up behind him, joined by Jean-Pierre, who nodded eagerly as he conferred with the other islander, both drumming fingers on the barrels of muskets taken from the dead guards. As they looked at the manor house, they saw that the two Creoles on the veranda had been joined by a broad-shouldered man, surely Benton, and then Moreau's heart sank in his chest as all three began pointing and looking in their direction. Mercifully they didn't seem to have spotted him or any of the others, as their conversation seemed unhurried. His view of the front lawn was blocked by several large oak trees, but Moreau knew Edward would be brought to the main house soon, making their escape all the more difficult. Not to mention that the bodies of the dead guards would be found eventually.

Moreau suddenly recalled something else that made his stomach lurch. In the shock following his tussle with the crocodile, he had completely forgotten one of his primary objective of this entire endeavor: rescuing Elyse. Well, more precisely, Celeste de Beaumais, but one hardly expected to find one without the other. As Moreau watched the men on the balcony, he had another gloomy thought: what if Giroux had decided to lock the women away, to prevent them from witnessing the burning of the slave cabins?

He did not have long to worry, however, as Giroux began pointing toward the cabins again, waving his arms animatedly. Tremblay hurried back inside, and Benton let out a shrill whistle and pointed toward the cabins. More men could soon be heard hustling in their direction. Confirming with Gael that the prisoners had all been freed, Moreau readied them for a fight with the approaching guards. He whispered for Jean-Pierre and Gael to keep watch over Nehemiah, worrying about the man's bloodlust, while Moreau made his way into the house to rescue the two women. More shouts from the front lane drew their attention, and they noticed perhaps a dozen men with torches and muskets approaching the house. In front walked Captain Hubbard and Sergeant McCann, their tall shakos and buttons glinting in the torchlight. Between two others a lone figure stumbled forward, rough hands gripping his tattered shirt. Edward.

Guttural curses came from the men around Moreau, but thankfully they made no move. A moment later Antoine jogged up and was almost fired on by a wary Nehemiah, who turned back with an angry look.

"Don't shoot," Antoine said, visibly nervous.

"I ain't gonna shoot you," Nehemiah chided. "We 'bout to skin these crackers, though." Antoine chuckled nervously, though the blood dripping from his knife showed his willingness to do what was needed.

Moreau nodded at Antoine. "Your people made it to the fields?"

"Yea. Diantha and what's-her-name bringing them across the road now."

Moreau smirked. In combat sometimes one's memory recalled strange things, and forgot others that were obvious. He moved to ready them when a bloodcurdling shout came from their left.

"They gone!" a man's voice bellowed. "Boss, the cabins is empty and they all fuckin' gone!"

A heavy silence fell over the plantation, and for a moment no one moved a muscle. Moreau and Nehemiah finally exchanged a look. "We go now," Moreau said evenly. "Keep spread out, one fires while the other reloads. Don't be foolish…"

Nehemiah stepped out from cover and began walking slowly toward Edward. More shouts, and now several of Giroux's men began running toward the cabins. Nehemiah continued forward slowly, screened by the cypress trees, until the first of the approaching guards came within thirty paces. Nehemiah slowly raised his pistol…aimed…

Bang! The man dropped in a heap. Beside Moreau, Gael and Jean-Pierre raised their muskets. *Bang! Bang!*

Smoke filled the air, but Moreau did not wait to see if they had hit anything. Leaving the two islanders, who seemed to prefer fighting together, he tapped Antoine on the shoulder and motioned for him to follow as he set off for the house. More shouts came from the group around Edward, and a musket shot rang out, but Moreau stayed to the right, hugging the trees between the house and workshops. Two more shots sounded, and Moreau forced himself to resist the urge to assist in the skirmish unfolding. Reloading a pistol was extremely difficult with only one hand; he would have to make his single shot count. For now, his blade would do.

He ran in a low crouch, pausing once behind a crape myrtle before sprinting for the back stairs. Just as he was about to reach them, the loud *thud* of boots could be heard on the veranda above, and he and Antoine dove for cover behind a cluster of dwarf palmettos just as two men ran into view. As they shouted to each other, Moreau nodded at Antoine to reload his pistol, which he did with shaking fingers.

Bang! Bang! The men fired toward the cabins, whooping excitedly. Moreau watched them make their way down the steps as they reloaded. Foolish. He tapped Antoine's arm and the young man rose up and fired. *Bang!* One man fell, sputtering as he tumbled all way to the bottom of the steps and rolled onto his side. The other fellow eyed Antoine with shock, and when he saw who had fired, his eyes widened in rage. Screaming a primal challenge, he raised his musket like a club and bounded down the steps in a fury. Moreau stood, squared his feet, and raised his sword. The man swung his musket at him, but Moreau ducked and slashed upward, his saber cutting cleanly across the man's torso. The man's legs buckled and, with a painful cry, he dropped to the ground. Out of habit—or was it mercy?—Moreau plunged his blade between the man's shoulder blades, dispatching him instantly.

Keeping alert for other threats, Moreau grabbed Antoine by the shirt and half dragged him up the stairs. The young man had become a killer, and though he smiled reflexively, even laughed from shock, his eyes showed his fear and disgust. Moreau peered to either side of the veranda; seeing no one, he slid the blade into its scabbard and pulled out his pistol.

"Well done," he whispered. "Now get that pistol reloaded and cover me from here. Can you do that?" Without looking at him, Antoine nodded. "If anyone unfamiliar comes—shoot. If you see women, for God's sake hold your fire. I'll be back in a moment." Moreau then twisted the doorknob and entered the house.

Holding his pistol ready, he entered the spacious hall that wrapped around the inner rooms of the second floor. More shots and screams came from the yard. He forced away the temptation to go help as he approached the second door to his right. It was slightly ajar, showing a soft light from the room within. He crept forward and lowered his pistol to his waist. Peering inside, he saw a long billiard table, red and white balls scattered as if in mid-game. A half-finished cigar lay in an ash tray, smoke still rising from it, and the room smelled strongly of tobacco. After another glance behind he lifted his bare foot to the door and shoved it open.

Nothing. He checked the next two rooms—empty bedrooms—while shouts and screams carried on outside. At the end of the hall he found the dining room, its long table seemingly prepared for breakfast—plates, glasses, and cutlery set out for several people. A flurry of footsteps sounded in the hall, and he ducked behind the table, pistol ready, but the footsteps fell away out onto the veranda and down the stairs. Moreau stood back up, thinking it time to check the rooms upstairs. If the women were still on the grounds, they must be there. As he rounded the dinner table, he glanced down at the porcelain bowls and shiny silverware, and a strange thought suddenly occurred to him: all this delicate cutlery and silverware in a house that had so quickly become a scene of carnage—this must have been what the German Coast uprising felt like. But that was not the thought his mind settled on.

As he peered down at one of the ivory-handled knives to the right of a large plate of blue and white china, an image filled his mind's eye: Will Keane. Brows furrowing at the idea of the youth coming to mind in a moment like this, Moreau recalled that on the first night after meeting the boy at Maspero's, the lad had shared how he'd escaped from the Cabildo prison....*you tie the blade to your leg or on the flat part of your foot, and there it is, if you're ever locked in a cell.*

Moreau looked at the knife again, and smiled.

CHAPTER 33

Villeré Plantation, Outside New Orleans
January 8, 1815

On the grounds of Villeré Plantation, some twelve miles east of Le Mouton and six miles east of New Orleans, an officer descended the slope of the levee in the dead of night, followed by two aides. Below him dozens of men scurried about the banks of the Mississippi in a hushed frenzy. Observing the men and silently exhorting them to move faster, the officer finally saw what he had come for. Pulled along by a half dozen men, the first small boat emerged from a narrow canal that had been cut through the levee. The craft settled into the river and was held in place by sappers in grey smocks while twelve red-coated soldiers climbed aboard. They handed each other paddles and packed in tightly before being shoved off by the sappers. The officer checked his watch. They were nearly two hours behind schedule.

A minute later another boat cast off from the left bank, followed quickly by another. Then another. They were bound for the right bank and, God willing, no alert American sentries would notice them. Impulsively checking his watch again, the commander of the British Army, Major General Sir Edward Pakenham, gently stamped his feet against the night chill. Leaning toward the nearest aide, he spoke with the patrician air of a royal officer. "We've fallen behind. If the lads can be induced to move more quickly, please see that they do." The aide nodded obediently, his face hardening.

A moment later a tall officer descended the levy, followed by an orderly. Smoothing a hand over his uniform, he halted beside his commander, and for a few moments the two men watched the boats casting off in a meaningful silence. Finally the commander turned to his subordinate, extending his hand. "Good luck, William." Colonel Thornton took his commander's hand and the two exchanged the genuine smiles of men who had ridden into the jaws of death together countless times.

"We will do the Duke proud, sir."

"You will do us all proud," General Pakenham said quietly. "You are Britons, the bravest of the brave. God be with you." Thornton saluted, turned, and climbed aboard the nearest boat, followed by his orderly. Pakenham watched them paddle off, waving and smiling faintly. After the boat was lost to sight in the river mist, his smile faded and he turned and made his way back up the levee toward the main British camp.

In less than twelve hours, he would be dead.

The top stair groaned as Moreau reached the third floor, and he winced testily, having made no noise on the others. He waited a moment, pistol raised, finally edging forward, his bare foot feeling cold on the wood floor. Muffled shouts came from somewhere downstairs, and he began to wonder if he could jump from the roof uninjured, should he become trapped up here. Continuing down a narrow hallway lit by two wall lamps, he checked the first door: locked. He did not press the issue, thinking to circle back after checking the rest. After peering into an empty room, he saw a light at the end of the hall. Inching ahead he saw that it came from a half-opened door, and his instincts told him to go straight there. Moving slowly, he winced again as a floorboard creaked. He paused to listen a moment before continuing. As he approached, all he could see through the opening was white and maroon wallpaper. He stopped when he heard a muffled sound from within. A man's voice? He crept closer, gently raising and lowering his booted foot. When he was inches from the door, his ears twitched.

"Of course everything has changed. It's quite natural for you to feel some anger. But you should not blame yourself."

Moreau inhaled deeply, closing his eyes. Tremblay. That weasel of a man was speaking to someone.

"Once in Natchez things will be different. A new beginning. An opportunity to start anew. I know you would like that." A pause, and Moreau raised his weapon—but he froze when he heard a softer voice. A woman's voice. He had not heard what she said.

"As I said, circumstances have changed. But," Moreau heard footsteps inside, "Elyse will join you. I've arranged for her travel accommodations. She will travel with me, under my protection."

At the mention of Elyse, Moreau's nostrils flared. He had heard enough. Squaring his shoulders, he heaved back and slammed his boot into the door, which crashed loudly against the far wall. Moreau leapt through the doorway, swinging his pistol left, then right. His eyes quickly scanned the room, noticing a large canopy bed with white drapes. To his right was a large oak desk, papers flying into the air from the draft of his entry; a few smaller shelves and a velvet chair lined the far wall. In the faint lamplight Moreau saw a man on the far side of the bed.

It was indeed Cyril Tremblay. If he looked stunned, his expression was equally one of curiosity. On the bed lay Celeste. She lolled her head at Moreau as he stepped into the room, but his gaze did not linger on her. He kept the pistol aimed at Tremblay, and for a moment his index finger twitched on the trigger. The man returned his gaze, his taut expression easing slightly as he surveyed Moreau from head to toe. Setting a teacup gently down at the foot of the bed, he folded his hands in front of him, and looked up with a glib expression. "Good evening, Monsieur Moreau. I'd half expected you to be behind all this commotion."

Moreau took another step into the room. "Shut up."

Tremblay spread his hands diffidently, but a subtle smirk formed on his lips. Keeping the pistol pointed at him, Moreau glanced at Celeste. Her eyes looked bloodshot and dark smudges lined her cheeks; she'd been crying. Her long white dress had several unfastened strings over her breasts, but she looked otherwise fully clothed. Moreau did not want to think what might have happened to her. "Who are you?" she asked absently, her voice quiet and slightly slurred.

Moreau didn't answer. As he turned his attention back to Tremblay, a clatter of footsteps behind him caused him to turn, and he flinched as another figure sprang into the room. Raising the pistol, he immediately brought it back down. Elyse Pasteur halted mid-stride, hair swishing about her face before she raised her hands and shrieked at the sight of the weapon, ducking down as Moreau took an instinctive half step toward her. Thinking Elyse's scream would bring others, Moreau pushed past her and peered down the hallway before tucking the pistol into his belt and grabbing her arm. Whispering for her to be calm, Moreau held Elyse firmly as she tried to tear away from him. With a fearful shout, she balled her fist and smacked him on the head. In the heat of the moment, he hardly felt it, though he ducked to avoid another blow.

"It's me, Elyse. Look, it's me." After a moment he managed to calm her, and she grasped his elbow in a firm grip. "It's me," he said quietly, looking into her eyes. "We've come to rescue you." He nodded at Celeste on the bed. "And your lady."

Elyse's panting eased, and she stared at him in disbelief. "Edward, Nehemiah, all of the survivors have come," Moreau said. "Everything will be alright." She swallowed, her eyes darting about as she attempted to process everything amidst the chaos. Moreau gave her a moment, thinking she looked very pretty, given the circumstances. After savoring this warm feeling, so out of place in the horror of the night, he smacked his lips, reminding himself the danger he was in—they all were in. He peered into the hallway again. Nothing. "No!" he snarled, when he turned and saw the open window, its white curtains listing gently with the breeze. He pushed past Elyse and crossed the room in quick strides, shoving his head out the window.

Shouts still came from the far side of the house, and he thought he could hear the sound of steel clashing on steel. But no more gunfire. He looked right and left—no sign of Tremblay. Shaking his head at his stupidity, he felt an intense urge to pursue the man across the rooftops and to wherever he might have run. For several heartbeats he allowed this internal battle to play out, until he recalled the two women behind him. With a frustrated breath, he pulled himself back away from the window.

Elyse was now cradling her lady's head in her arms, speaking softly as Celeste's muffled sobs broke the eerie quiet. Moreau scratched the back of his neck, a swell of emotions rippling over him. Try as he might, his attempts to banish the warm swelling in his chest failed, and he felt ashamed for allowing himself a moment of weakness in the middle of such a dangerous rescue. He forced his mind back to the task at hand, and the danger they were in, but as Elyse looked across the room at him, his chest swelled again.

He walked over slowly and looked down at her. She gently set Celeste's head on the pillow, kissing her, then stood in front of Moreau. She gazed up at him, her hair disheveled and her large green eyes wide with fear yet fiercely determined. Her mouth slackened a little, as if she were about to cry. In that moment, Moreau thought he had never seen anyone more beautiful.

"You're...here to rescue us?" she asked.

Moreau nodded.

She stared at him another moment before her eyes fell to his chest. Soon tears began to fall, and she whispered without lifting her head. "Thank you." Wiping a tear away, Moreau gazed at her another moment before lifting her chin and kissing her on the lips. She gripped his arm harder and returned the kiss, finally throwing her arms around his shoulders.

The night air smelled of smoke and sulfur, and Moreau gently let go of Celeste's arm, drawing the pistol and aiming it across the veranda as the two women shuffled down the back stairs. Elyse supported most of Celeste's weight as they descended, taking one step at a time. Moreau thought of Tremblay and again had to suppress the urge to turn and pursue the coward. He'd be more likely to run into one of the guards—if any still lived. As the women reached the bottom of the stairs, he moved closer, pistol at the ready, and led them away from the house toward the oaks and dwarf palmettos, and the relative safety of the darkness.

Halting behind a large oak, he saw one body near the steps and another closer to the lane leading toward the house, but he couldn't tell who they were. Seeing no movement, he wondered whether they should make for the front entrance, to try to find Captain Hubbard or—*Bang!* A pistol shot tore through the darkness, its muzzle flash momentarily illuminating the yard to their left. A few seconds later loud cries and the sound of steel ringing on steel could clearly be heard. That made Moreau's decision rather easy, and he whispered for the women to follow as he turned and ran in a crouch toward the swamp and the waiting pirogues.

They darted from bush to bush, tree to tree, passing the work cabins and crossing the open ground to the slave cabins. It was a relief to see the doors open and swinging on their hinges, a sign of freedom for those formerly locked within. And no fire burned. As they stole through a gap in the row of cabins, Moreau felt a sudden surge of triumph, recalling how for days he had steeled himself for the possibility that all of the people of Le Marais, men and women he had come to know and care for, would soon be murdered by a vindictive planter and his underlings. Waving the women ahead of him, pistol still at the ready, he caught a glimpse of moonlight reflecting on the water ahead. They were close. Stealing a look back into the darkness, he prayed the others had found an escape, or at least still lived.

The sight of one of the pirogues in the trampled swamp grass nearly caused him to sprint ahead, but he knew Celeste was in no state to travel so quickly. God knows what the poor woman had endured. He slowed as they reached the embankment and snatched a paddle from the boat, turning to help the women into the pirogue.

A brutal force struck him in the side, forcing the air from his lungs and knocking him to the ground as a blur of motion rolled past him. In a daze, he turned his head to see what had hit him, and saw a man in brown pantaloons and a white smock quickly rising to his feet. Even in the dim moonlight Moreau could make out the sturdy figure of Elijah Benton. Recognizing him gave Moreau a sudden burst of energy, and he rolled in the opposite direction, jumping to his feet.

"No!" Elyse cried out, watching from a few paces away, still supporting Celeste on her shoulder. "Marcel, watch out!"

Moreau ignored her and turned to face his adversary—who was already lurching forward in another attack. With a stab of fear, Moreau realized his pistol had been knocked from his hands, and the split second he spent glancing aside for it was the only opening Benton needed.

Moreau had just enough time to raise his one hand before the man charged at him at full speed. Bouncing to his right, Moreau avoided a head-on collision, but Benton anticipated the move and grabbed Moreau's coat, spinning him around and slamming him to the ground. Benton then leapt over him and swung a fist at Moreau's jaw.

Moreau twisted aside, and the fist smashed into the murky soil with a *thud*. Moreau managed to throw two quick jabs that struck the man on his bearded chin. Benton's large head snapped back, but despite the pain in Moreau's knuckles, the punches seemed to have little effect, and Benton grunted as he grasped the Frenchman's collar.

Thump! A fist crashed into Moreau's forehead, blurring his vision. Mercifully it was a glancing blow, but the man was strong, and his next punch caught Moreau on the forearm as he tried to deflect it, driving hand into his face. Snarling angrily, Moreau thrust a finger into Benton's eye with all his strength. One man wasn't leaving this fight alive—and Moreau wasn't dying tonight.

Screaming as he jerked his head back, Benton rained down more blows. Moreau managed to avoid the first few, but two or three punches landed, briefly stunning him. Moreau recalled times he had been hit by larger, tougher men, and he allowed his anger to build until he finally thrust a brutal knee into the man's groin. Benton was knocked backward and, with a roar of pain, slowly regained his feet, but the brief movement back allowed Moreau to also rise to his feet. Benton exhaled loudly and spit into the water. After a moment, he looked across at Moreau with wide, crazed eyes.

"From the moment I met you, Frenchman," he said, spitting tobacco juice into the water, "I fucking hated you." His hand went down to his side—and he slowly pulled a long, wide-bladed knife from his belt. Bending his knees, he took a menacing step forward. "Your story ends tonight. In this swamp." His fingers twitched on the knife.

Moreau, strands of black hair covering half his face like a spider-web, watched the man impassively. An image of Will Keane flashed in his mind's eye, and he thought of the boy stealing a knife from the galley of La Panthère. *"While he served the captain supper, I snatched one of his knives.... Tie the blade to your leg or on the flat part of your foot, and there it is, if you're ever locked in a cell."*

Moreau wasn't in a cell, but if he ever needed the blade tucked in his boot, now was the time. Whimpering quietly, and curling into a ball as if to protect himself, he slipped the blade out of his boot, shaking his head back and forth fearfully.

Benton licked his lips, a scornful sneer forming on his lips. "I was gonna ask if you had any last words, before I gut you like an uppity negro. But you just a plain coward." He let out a deep, throaty chuckle and shook his head.

Moreau smirked. "I'll see you in hell—but you go first." As Benton plunged his knife down, Moreau swung his own blade up, parrying the thrust and then jabbing and burying the point of his knife in the overseer's barrel chest. Benton gasped in horror, and Moreau lifted his bare foot and shoved it hard into the man's midsection. With a grunt, Benton staggered backward, his hands grasping for purchase but finding only air. Time seemed to stop as he tumbled into the water with a loud splash.

A second later he surfaced, crying out as he flailed his arms and shook his head, hair sticking to his forehead like brown cloth. He wiped a hand across his face. "You son of a bitch—" His words cut off as a giant black shape rose up out of the water behind him, and a pair of enormous jaws lined with razor-sharp teeth clamped down on his shoulder, dragging him back into the water with an even bigger splash than before. Benton's legs kicked and thrashed, until they were finally dragged under and the surface grew still, save for a few ripples, and man and beast were gone.

CHAPTER 34

Le Mouton Plantation, Outside New Orleans
January 8, 1815

The sun rose a few hours after the plantation's overseer was dragged into the cypress swamp, and Moreau finally considered it safe enough to bring the two women back to the main house. He arrived to a sight that seemed both unbelievable, and wholly welcome. The grounds were quiet, no workers or slaves scurrying about their tasks. The livestock were all in their pens, apart from several chickens and honking geese, and the house looked as stately and welcoming as it had on the day Moreau first arrived, several weeks ago. It felt like years. Edward's was the first face he saw. The man was looking for any discarded weapons they could use, ever the conscientious leader, as Moreau had begun to notice. He flinched nervously when he saw Moreau, but his expression quickly eased into a smile. "It's good to see you alive."

"You too."

Soon after they were joined by Antoine, who was holding his left forearm, blood seeping through his fingers. He put on a smile when he saw them but winced every so often at the pain from the sword slash beneath his elbow. Nehemiah appeared a moment later, along with Jean-Pierre. The islander was uninjured, moving with the usual spring in his step, but Nehemiah's arm hung in a makeshift sling made from one of the slain foremens' shirts. His shoulder had taken a musket ball, and the wound looked fairly serious, but he waved away Edward's concerned look.

"He hit my shoulder, I put my knife in his ribs. I call that a good fight."

Moreau did not feel wholly at ease until he heard word, from an uninjured Captain Hubbard, that the escapees had safely made it into the swamp beyond the plantation grounds and were being tended to by Diantha and Antonia. Elyse expressed her relief when she heard this as well, voicing her desire to join the two women as soon as possible. Beside her Celeste still stared in a daze, but her whimpering had stopped with the sunrise, and Elyse promised her that the danger was passed and she wouldn't leave her side for anything.

Gael had taken two bullets to the chest early in the fight and had died instantly. Setting the man's body onto a horse-drawn cart with Edward's help, Jean-Pierre offered some quiet words in his native patois, then lifted his head to the sky and sang a song, the words to which Moreau did not understand. Nehemiah and Antoine bowed their heads in silence. Moreau, a few paces back, did the same along with the women.

As they readied to depart to join Diantha in the swamp, Celeste looked at Moreau and appeared slightly more alert. At length she raised a finger and motioned him over. As he leaned in close, she spoke in a quaking voice. "Thank you, monsieur." She paused, wiping a tear from her eye. "He was the devil. I don't know what else he would have done had you not come." Clasping her arms around him, she began sobbing softly, trembling as she gripped him. At length Celeste allowed Elyse to lead her away, her attendant speaking soothing words as they departed, leaving Moreau as befuddled as he was relieved.

He learned that Emile Giroux, architect, or at least facilitator of all this madness, upon seeing that his surviving men had thrown down their weapons, had groaned quietly, then walked calmly into his drawing room and raised a pistol to his head. Captain Hubbard had seen him walk inside, then heard the shot. Tremblay, for his part, had gotten away. At least, no one had seen a body. His fate would never be known, barring some miracle—though in Louisiana strange forces often seemed to be at work.

Before departing the plantation, Elyse approached Moreau on the veranda of the manor house and looked at him with a concerned expression. "Wherever you go, Marcel, do be careful. I would hate to hear anything happened to our savior. My savior." She smiled wryly and Moreau nodded. He watched the two women walk away down the front lane with a surge of conflicting emotions. To his surprise, he found that he did not want to see Elyse depart. Not now, nor ever.

The remaining rescuers scoured the grounds for survivors and took five men from the plantation as prisoners. These were placed in manacles personally by Captain Hubbard and put under Sergeant McCann's supervision. When the final search was completed, they gathered up their weapons and assembled around the horse-drawn cart bearing Gael's body. The wounded Nehemiah and Antoine climbed aboard and set off to find their people, who had been promised safe passage into Barataria by Lafitte, until they were ready to travel on to their next destination. As the cart rolled away, Nehemiah looked back at Moreau, giving him a barely perceptible nod, before turning back ahead with a solemn expression.

Moreau watched the cart roll out of sight, then turned to confer with Edward, Jean-Pierre, Hubbard, and McCann. The two men of Le Marais would have joined their people in the swamp, but the sound of distant cannon fire had drawn their attention, and for a moment they all stood still, listening. Ominous booms rumbled over the fields, and Moreau and Hubbard exchanged a knowing look, realizing that the battle for New Orleans had finally begun. Moreau let out a sigh, explaining to Edward and Jean-Pierre that the three soldiers would have to depart, duty calling them to the sound of the guns. The excitement and fear that had driven them the night before had gone, and they all looked as tired as Moreau felt. But Hubbard soon had his shako on his head, and McCann and Edward rounded up horses to take them east. Moreau once again thought of Elyse, as he was helped onto a horse brought from the stables by Edward. He offered a farewell to the two men but frowned when he saw them holding lead ropes of their own.

"What are those for?" Moreau asked. "Horses aren't much help in the swamps."

Edward slipped a bridle over the horse's head. "We took care of our own, and now they're safe." He climbed into the saddle.

Jean-Pierre tossed him a musket before mounting his own animal. "You risked your pale white neck for us," Edward said, grinning, "now we ought to return the favor."

Moreau squinted, thinking it another joke, but when he saw that the man was speaking in earnest, he shrugged. "Alright. If you can ride, follow me."

He spurred his horse, and the small group cantered down the lane and out onto the river road. The cannons boomed without interruption, and as they urged the horses to a full gallop, Moreau thought of his kiss with Elyse, and for the first time in many years, he rode to battle with an unmistakable desire to live.

For twenty minutes or so they rode along the river road, passing not a single soul. As the firing grew louder, they halted abruptly when they came to an armed checkpoint. A lad in militia uniform, no older than fifteen or sixteen, stepped into the road, holding a musket that looked taller than he was. He raised a hand in greeting, and offered the challenge: "Hickory." When they gave no response, he frowned and his expression grew confused as he noticed the odd appearance of their party, and he took a half step back. "Y'ain't here fer mischief, is ye?"

Captain Hubbard rode forward. "I'm returning from a mission to deliver pirogues to a friendly party. We're now returning to the lines."

The boy swallowed, shaking his head. "Yes, sir. Uh, but ye didn't give the password. I ain't s'pose to let no one through 'thout it."

Sergeant McCann brought his horse forward. "Lad, do you hear those guns? We're returning to fight, and you're hindering us. You can either let us through," he reached down and produced his pistol, "or I can make the decision for you—by shooting you in the head." Cold, blue eyes stared down at the confused youth, who squinted up at him.

"Alright, Sergeant. Go 'head." He stepped aside and waved them through.

They cantered along the road for another few minutes before they began to see signs of war, which, to Moreau, seemed less than encouraging. Personal items and discarded equipment, canteens, knapsacks, and even muskets lay strewn about the road.

Moreau exchanged a look with Hubbard, who seemed as perplexed as he. A moment later they came upon a group of soldiers trotting in their direction. As the guns boomed in the distance, Moreau's party halted along the side of the road and waited for the soldiers to approach. They shuffled by, in groups of two or three, without stopping, hardly bothering to look at the five horsemen halted by the edge of the track.

As they urged their horses forward again, Moreau saw a larger group approaching, also on foot and moving rapidly. They wore plain coats and shirts of militia, and Sergeant McCann observed that they were from the Kentucky or Tennessee regiments. As they hurried past, most avoided eye contact, or looked away quickly if they caught Moreau or any of the others watching them.

"Where are you going?" Hubbard called out. None of them answered or even stopped to look at him. If anything, their pace seemed to quicken. Moreau let out a breath, rubbing his scalp. A few seconds later another group came into view, crossing from a stretch of open ground to the right and making their way toward the road. The cannons rumbled louder now. Was the enemy getting closer?

They continued through a stretch of woods and then onto a patch of ground that had been cleared of trees. Perhaps a half mile off to their left, they could see the shimmering water of the Mississippi through gaps in the remaining trees. As they surveyed the terrain, they saw a company-sized group coming at them—at a dead run. Drums beat sporadically, and fifes played a few notes before cutting off abruptly. Off to the open ground on either side Moreau noticed single men or small groups running away from the sounds of the battle.

"Where are they going?" Hubbard asked incredulously.

Moreau shifted in his saddle, a sinking feeling in his gut. The battle was not going their way.

"They're being routed, Captain," Moreau said quietly. "There's no order to be had when men flee an enemy in that state. Only thing to do is let it run its course. Maybe try and gather up as many stragglers as you can."

A moment later the retreating company flew past in a flurry of stamping feet and trampling hooves, several tossing packs or cartridge pouches onto the road to run faster. Several yelled frantically, urging the mounted men to find safety while they could. Moreau scanned the group for an officer, finally settling his eyes on a lieutenant, who looked back at him with a frenzied expression. For a moment the man looked as if he was going to stop, moving his lips as if to speak before turning his head and doubling his pace to catch up with his men. A voice called out from within the muddled formation "They're coming…we'll have to find…another rallying point…"

Up ahead more men were coming into view—hundreds. To Moreau it looked as if a whole battalion was running pell-mell across the field. He now felt a legitimate concern at what was happening, and in that moment a *boom* tore across the field. A cannon shot—somewhere close. "Jesus," he muttered.

Several horsemen emerged from the far woods, followed by more groups of militia on foot. As they came closer, Moreau spotted two men in coats that must've belonged to the Tennesseans or Kentuckians, and one in the dark-blue coat of an American regular. Urging his horse out toward them, Moreau waited for them to get closer. When they halted a little way off, Moreau almost choked.

Colonel Winfield jerked the reins of his mount violently, seeming to struggle with the animal that pranced and pawed the earth. If the animal looked nervous, the colonel's face appeared contorted with rage or fear—perhaps both. He looked at the group by the side of the road, frowning at its strange composition, then met Moreau's gaze. For a moment it looked to Moreau like the colonel's shoulders lowered, and he averted his gaze. After a moment he turned back at Moreau with angry eyes, as if he'd caught him doing something wrong. Moreau stared back impassively, wondering what Winfield had to say for himself. Hubbard began to speak, but he closed his mouth when he saw the strange standoff taking place.

"What's happened here?" Moreau finally asked, addressing one of the militia officers.

The man cocked his head and spit onto the ground. "They come up from the south. Took our First Battery under Colonel Morgan. Then they turned the guns on us, took the Second Battery. Turn *them* guns on *us*. We gave 'em some fire, but they kep' comin.' Now they won't stop, and we can't get the boys in line." He spit again. "That's about alls I know."

Moreau nodded, considering the river's right bank to be the soft underbelly of Jackson's entire defensive line—if the English were shrewd enough to cross the river. Almost exactly what Lafitte had said he'd do if he were in their place.

Meeting Moreau's hard stare, Colonel Winfield's nostrils flared and his teeth looked to be grinding. After a moment, Moreau let out a genuine laugh, smiling toothily as he shook his head. "Go have a drink, Colonel. We'll get things in order."

Without responding, Winfield spurred his horse past Moreau's group, the other officers exchanging confused looks before making to ride after him. Moreau held up his hand, motioning for them to stay. The officer who had spoken shrugged and nodded, and held his position.

Behind Moreau a peal of laughter broke out. Turning back, he saw Jean-Pierre nodding his head with a broad smile. "He did 'fraid." Edward laughed too, nodding his agreement. "Man looks like he soiled his trousers."

Moreau watched a large body of militiamen run past, shouting or grunting as they jostled one another to reach the safety of the trees.

"What do you think, Major?" Captain Hubbard finally asked.

Moreau licked his lips, then turned to Edward. "When I first came to your people," he said, his quiet voice incongruous with the clamor around them, "and you were choking the life out of me...there was nothing I could do; you were simply stronger. My salvation, if you wish to call it that, came like a phantom from the swamp." He turned his gaze right, toward the cypress trees at the edge of the swamp. "We go into the swamp, use it to our advantage. Right now, that's the only thing that might surprise the enemy, slow their progress and force them to engage us until the rest of the army can get reorganized. Might."

Issuing a few, brief orders, Moreau directed Hubbard, McCann, and the two militia officers to fan out, facing the line of retreating men, until they managed to collect perhaps a hundred men too shamed, or too tired, to retreat past them. Most went around them in their panicked retreat, but a few dozen were enough. Moreau assembled the stragglers, a mixture of Tennesseans, Creoles, and a half dozen free Blacks, and led them to the cover of the nearest cypress trees. When they were finally settled, the men stared at Moreau with wide eyes as the cannonade abruptly stopped—meaning the enemy were on them.

Sure enough, a minute or two later the *rat-tat-tat* of drums and the shrill peal of fifes sounded up ahead, and for a moment the group waited under the trees in a nervous silence. Moreau looked at the two former slaves, who stood beside the free Black soldiers, appearing taller and stronger in their white smocks and battle-fatigued faces. They even offered them a few words to bolster their courage.

Beside Moreau, Captain Hubbard and Sergeant McCann stared at the growing mass of red-coated English soldiers marching out from the trees. The two men looked steady, undaunted by the odds their few hundred faced against the battalions marching crisply and confidently across the open ground.

Rat-tat-tat-tat-tat. The drums rolled, and a few enemy skirmishers moved past their position, unaware of the rag-tag force hidden in the trees. Moreau looked at the militiamen huddled all around. Dirty, tired faces that had not seen a razor in days stared back at him: young men, others too old to fight, a man with spectacles who looked more like a lawyer or banker than a soldier. Moreau thought back to the first day he had seen the Americans train, wondering how many would die in their defeat, which seemed to him inevitable. He thought the only thing they possessed that might provide even a glimmer of hope would be hearts willing to fight. They lacked the experience and training of their enemies, but if they had the will to resist, they had a slim chance. The men around him drummed their fingers nervously, but they looked ready. Ready to fight. Ready to die. That was all he could ask of them.

"Ready muskets," he called out. "Fire!"

EPILOGUE

Some days after the battle, when the wounded and the prisoners had been tended to, with assistance from Celeste, Elyse, and the nuns of the Ursuline Convent, Moreau made a final visit to New Orleans before his departure. A celebration to fête the defenders of the city was held, and Andrew Jackson and Jean Lafitte were to be honored, in equal measure, as the Baratarian commander at last revealed himself openly to the people of the city. He accepted their congratulations warmly, offering a few words in French and English, and General Jackson did the same. The two men, if not friendly, at least seemed appreciative of the significant strain and sacrifice offered in common cause against their mutual foe. It was at this party that Moreau finally reunited with his former comrades, Captains Roche, White, and Dubuclet. After assuring them that he was indeed alive and had not taken the form of a swamp phantom, he came across Captain Savary and Major Plauché, who, though no less relieved to see him, seemed more inclined to believe his tale of time in the swamp with the harried people of Le Marais—and their near-disaster at Le Mouton. The two men, divided by race and upbringing, mingled easily with the Creole gentlemen and ladies, who offered profuse praise and even adoration, and Moreau quickly came to understand the nature of their friendship, having undergone a similar bond with his friend Andre Valière. Two men, different in breeding and politics, who nevertheless, through the trials of military life, sword, and blood, now shared a bond as strong as brothers. Stronger. And each would give his life for the other.

When he'd made his rounds and eaten, drunk, and smoked to contentment, Moreau left the gathering for his small room on Dauphine Street. At long last he had resigned his commission—

Plauché had signed his resignation papers on the spot—and, with relief, Moreau realized he would never need to spend another night under arms as an American soldier. The thought brought relief, like a weight being lifted from his shoulders, as well as a hint of sadness that he would likely never see his comrades again. But he was a soldier and had said goodbye to more comrades than he cared to count, so he contented himself with his memories of their company, relief and melancholy combining in subtle harmony, and accepting that time would march on regardless of how he felt. It always had, and it always would.

The following morning as he packed his bags, he found a note that had been slipped under the door. It was from Jean Lafitte. It was accompanied by a small pouch that held something weighty inside.

Short and to the point, Lafitte's note gave assurances that the villagers from Le Marais were safe in a temporary home in what remained of Barataria, and would be offered free passage on his ships when he finally departed for Galveston. His price had been one of the balas rubies, which Celeste had given up claim to, as she had received a letter from her father saying that he and her mother were departing from France at once to bring her home. At the victory banquet, the young woman had told Moreau that the fortune the rubies would have brought was no longer needed—as her father would remain with her family for as long as he lived. Satisfied with just the one ruby, Lafitte assured Moreau that the people from Le Marais would find new lives of freedom in Galveston, or wherever they wished to go after that. He also noted that his first act upon reaching the open waters of the Gulf would be to scatter Will Keane's ashes overboard—in full view of his ship's crew and with full honors of a fallen Baratarian.

Moreau shed a tear as he read those final words, but felt grateful for the corsair's act of kindness. When he had packed his few belongings and paid his bill, he departed, making his way toward the docks. Awaiting him outside his inn, having offered her final services to Celeste de Beaumais, was Elyse Pasteur. She had agreed to join him on the maiden upriver voyage of the steamship *Enterprise*, to a small riverside town founded by Frenchmen, called St. Louis. When she had asked him how he planned to pay for the voyage or what came after, Moreau grinned and told her not to trouble herself. Patting his breast pocket and feeling the sturdy weight of the third balas ruby within, he turned onto St. Philip Street.

ABOUT THE AUTHOR

Owen Pataki graduated from Cornell University in 2010 with a degree in history. In 2011, Owen joined the army, and in 2014 was deployed to Afghanistan, serving with the 10th Mountain Division. Following his military service, he attended the MetFilm School in London. His first novel was *Where the Light Falls* (2017) followed by *Searchers in Winter* (2021). He now lives in New York where he is working as a screenwriter and filmmaker.